❦

"*Mayhap this is one of those fifty-seven erotic points on a woman's body you boasted of once. Just nod your head if I am right.*"

Rain shook her head vehemently. *Good Lord! Had the man memorized every dumb thing she ever said?*

Selik chuckled with glee, not believing her one bit. "Yea, for some women, the sweet spot is behind the knees, right at the crease. For others, between the thighs. Then there are the tips of the breasts. Even the arches of the feet. But I think I will start my exploration with your ears, dearling. What say you to that?"

She groaned.

"Ah, well, you do not have to say aught. I will kiss each place on your skin until I discover each and every one of your erotic weaknesses."

"Gdmfppppft."

"My thoughts exactly," Selik said as he bit her gently on the earlobe . . .

Romances by Sandra Hill

THE RELUCTANT VIKING
THE OUTLAW VIKING
THE TARNISHED LADY
THE BEWITCHED VIKING
THE BLUE VIKING
THE VIKING'S CAPTIVE (formerly My Fair Viking)
A TALE OF TWO VIKINGS
VIKING IN LOVE
THE VIKING TAKES A KNIGHT

THE LAST VIKING
TRULY, MADLY VIKING
THE VERY VIRILE VIKING
WET AND WILD
HOT AND HEAVY

FRANKLY, MY DEAR
SWEETER SAVAGE LOVE
DESPERADO
LOVE ME TENDER

SANDRA HILL

The OUTLAW VIKING

AVON
An Imprint of HarperCollins*Publishers*

AVON BOOKS
An Imprint of HarperCollins*Publishers*
10 East 53rd Street
New York, New York 10022-5299

Copyright © 1995, 2011 by Sandra Hill
ISBN 978-0-06-201909-7
www.avonromance.com

First Avon Books mass market printing: June 2011

Avon Trademark Reg. U.S. Pat. Off. and in Other Countries, Marca Registrada, Hecho en U.S.A.
HarperCollins® is a registered trademark of HarperCollins Publishers.

Printed in the U.S.A.

10 9 8 7 6 5 4 3 2 1

This book is dedicated to my four sons:
Beau, Rob, Matt, and Daniel. Any one of them
could have been the model for my Viking hero,
Selik, who is handsome, brave, strong, and sensitive.
Not surprisingly, there's a bit of the "outlaw"
spirit in each of them.
And to the god with a sense of humor depicted
in this book. He had better be saving me a
special place "up there" after giving me four
unconventional "Viking" sons.

AUTHOR'S NOTE

A Viking museum does exist in York today, as depicted in this novel. It commemorates the great Coppergate archaeological dig, which unearthed many treasures related to Viking Age England, 800–1000 A.D., shedding new light on the proud, fierce Norsemen.

However, the massive oil painting of the Battle of Brunanburh that brutally ended Viking domination in England, with my war-ravaged hero Selik in its center, is pure fiction.

Or is it?

Modern scientists are just beginning to understand genetic memory, and, truth be told, my family tree on my father's side can be traced directly back to Viking times through thirty-three generations to the great Viking Rollo (or Hrolf the Ganger).

Perhaps the scenes I describe in Viking England are mere figments of an overactive imagination based on an innate attraction to these magnificent people who are a biological part of me. Logic would certainly say so.

On the other hand, couldn't they be more than that?

Perhaps, somewhere in an ancient, moldering castle or a long-neglected museum corridor, there hangs just such a portrait of Viking history. I like to think so.

Stranger things have happened.

CHAPTER ONE

You could say it was live art . . .

"Mommy, make the big lady move. I can't see."

Thoraine Jordan felt her face flame with embarrassment at the loud whine of the small child behind her. She sensed people around them turning to look at the object of the remark and then having to crane their necks upwards.

Big! That was the key word.

Rain grimaced. After all these years, the cruel word should have stopped hurting, but it never had.

Sighing wearily, she glanced at her mother, Ruby, whose lips formed a thin white line of suppressed anger. Rain squeezed her hand reassuringly, not wanting her overly protective mother to say something that would create a scene.

Turning to face the little boy who'd made the innocently cutting comment, Rain said, "Step in front of us, honey. We're in no hurry."

"Oh, no, ma'am," the child's mother protested quickly. "He dint mean no harm. He's jist overtired from waitin' so long."

The crowd continued to gawk curiously, and Rain wished she could disappear. "That's okay. We don't mind," she told the young woman.

After the lady and child moved sheepishly ahead of them in the line that stretched in front of the Viking museum, Rain's mother whispered, "You're too kind. Children should be taught from an early age that certain remarks are inappropriate."

"Oh, Mother! He merely commented on an obvious fact. I'm six feet tall. There's no hiding that."

Her mother dismissed her words with a short jerk of her hand. "Sweetie, you're a beautiful woman. I thought you got over that height hang-up long ago. You have no reason to be embarrassed."

Rain put an arm around her mother's shoulder and gave her a quick peck on the cheek. "I'm thirty years old, and you're still worrying about my feelings being hurt. That's precious."

"Humph! To me, you're still my baby. Doesn't matter to me that you're a physician—or that you've delivered a few babies yourself. I'll always think of you as my little girl."

Rain flicked her long blond braid over her shoulder and looked down at her body meaningfully. "Little? Hardly!"

Her mother's mouth pursed indignantly. "You're just big boned, Rain, like your father. You've never been over-weight."

Trying to change the subject, an old and tiresome one, Rain teased, "Which father, Mom?" An enigmatic smile passed over her mother's still attractive face. It had been a family joke for years that her unorthodox mother claimed to have had a time-travel experience thirty years before, when she'd met Thork Haraldsson, an outsize Viking version of her husband, Jack Jordan. In fact, her mother contended that Rain was conceived in the past and born in the present. Even worse, her mother insisted that, while her Viking father, Thork, had died before Ruby had returned to the future, she'd left behind Rain's Viking half brothers, Eirik and Tykir.

Geez!

"Don't start on me, young lady," her mother chided, wagging a forefinger at her with mock sternness. "In a way, Thork and Jack were both your father. They were both very tall men and identical in appearance, except that your Viking father had more of a muscular build."

Rain rolled her eyes at that enticing mind-picture. Her father had been a good-looking man. In a more muscle-clad body, he would have been drop-dead gorgeous.

Her mother reached over and touched the antique dragon brooch on the lapel of Rain's white silk blouse. "It pleases me to see you wear the brooch Thork gave me."

"Just because I wear it doesn't mean I believe."

Her mother chucked Rain playfully under the chin. "I know that, silly." She caressed the pin lovingly, a dreamy expression clouding her face. "I wonder what happened to the matching brooch, the one Thork wore on the other shoulder of his mantle."

Rain smiled at the whimsical look on her mother's face, then hesitated before she spoke her next words. "I never believed all that nonsense of yours. I still don't, but lately I've been really confused and—well, I don't know."

Her mother raised an eyebrow in question.

"The nightmare has returned."

A soft gasp of dismay escaped her mother's lips. "Oh, honey, I'm sorry. I didn't know. I've been so preoccupied since your father's death."

Rain dismissed her mother's concern with a wave of her hand, explaining, "The dream is nothing new. I've had it intermittently since I was a child, since Eddie was killed in that Lebanese bombing." Rain had been only twelve years old when her older brother, a Marine, had died on duty in Beirut, but it had changed her life forever. "I haven't had the dream for a long time, but it's back—with a vengeance."

"The same dream?"

"Yes, but more intense . . . and graphic. Sometimes I feel like I'm caught in a vortex, being drawn toward something—or someone—in terrible need or pain. In a way, that's why I decided to become a doctor, you know. The pictures of death and despair I saw in my dreams—well, I interpreted them as a kind of calling to the medical profession."

"That and that blasted pacifism of yours."

Rain smiled, knowing her outspoken mother didn't share her views on nonviolence.

"It doesn't help that you work in that inner-city hospital, you know. Talk about a daily dose of needless violence!"

Rain decided to steer the conversation away from that volatile topic. Her mother would much prefer her surgeon daughter to practice in a nice, safe suburb, closer to home.

"Anyhow, Mom, the dreams occur almost nightly now. I hate going to sleep anymore. And I wake with the most grueling migraine headaches. I wonder if—"

Her words halted in midsentence as a group of tourists exited the underground Jorvik Viking Centre and the line in which Rain stood began to inch forward. Ever since Rain's mother had read of the Coppergate archaeological dig here years ago, she'd devoured newspaper and magazine articles detailing the thousands of artifacts taken from the site—treasures that gave new insight into the fierce, proud people who'd flourished there under a series of Viking kings from 850 to 954 A.D. She'd yearned to return to the site of her alleged time-travel journey.

After they paid their money and entered the building, the docents ushered them into "time cars" which would whisk them back one thousand years through a reconstruction of an actual street in Jorvik, Viking Age York. The museum was populated by life-sized, lifelike figures of primitive Norsemen and its sounds and smells were redolent of a teeming market town of the early medieval period.

About to remark on the wonderfully executed dioramas, Rain looked at her mother and took a quick, sharp breath of alarm at her white complexion and hands clasped to her chest.

"Mother! What's wrong?" The doctor in Rain emerged

immediately. She feared her sixty-eight-year-old mother was suffering chest pains.

"It's just like it was then," Ruby whispered shakily.

"What is?"

"This street—Coppergate. See the thatched roofs, the wattle-and-daub houses? Oh, Rain, it takes me back so vividly!"

Rain breathed a sigh of relief that her mother wasn't ill. Personally, she considered the houses pretty crude and failed to share her mother's enthusiasm, but she kept her thoughts to herself.

They moved on and watched a burly blacksmith making the much-prized Viking sword. He worked five rods of metal into tightly twisted ropes, then hammered, filed, and welded again until he'd forged the deadly weapon. He explained that the whole pattern-welding process took one hundred hours for just one sword and that the Vikings valued them so much that they gave them names, like Leg-biter or Adder.

As their car moved along slowly, haunting medieval music permeated the air, floating sweetly from a primitive carved pan pipe played by a blond-haired boy. In fact, all the figures in the exhibit had pale hair, from the lightest shades of platinum to fiery red. The huge men sported carefully groomed beards and mustaches and hair down to their shoulders. Most of the women and girls wore braids, some hanging to the waist and others tucked under neat cloth caps.

Industrious craftsmen toiled in front of the houses, carving wooden bowls, polishing amber stones, or working with brass. They gave the lie to the traditional image of Vikings as ferocious rapers and pillagers of peaceful folks.

Rain inhaled deeply, picking out the odors of fresh straw, wood shavings from the shipbuilders, smoke from the hearth fires, and faint, inland salt-water breezes—even some of the unpleasant smells that would have prevailed in a primitive city of this size.

After completing the one-hour tour of the Viking museum,

they strolled arm-in-arm around the lobby, viewing drawings and photos of the archaeological excavation.

"Oh!" her mother exclaimed sharply, coming to an abrupt halt.

They'd come to a massive oil painting depicting the Battle of Brunanburh in 937 A.D. which had ended, once and for all, Viking dominance in Northumbria, according to the small card under the picture. The Dark Age knights battled on a flat-topped volcanic hill near Solway Firth. The huge painting detailed artistically the thousands of fallen warriors, including five Viking kings and seven jarls, a son of the Scots King Constantine, and two cousins, two earls, and two bishops of the Saxon King Athelstan.

Her mother's voice trailed on, but Rain heard none of it. A chill rippled over her body, and a migraine headache slammed full-force behind her eyes. Tears streamed in a silent path down her face.

Rain's nightmare vision had come to life.

Over the years, like pieces of a crossword puzzle, she'd viewed parts of this battle scene in her dreams—the blood-soaked earth, gaping wounds, hacked-off body parts, screaming horses, and overwhelming carnage. No wonder she'd become a pacifist, opposed to all wars as senseless, after viewing this human tragedy over and over and over.

Even the man in the center of the painting was familiar. The tall blond giant stood with widespread legs encased in cross-gartered leather shoes. Many of the men around him wore leather or metal helmets with nose guards, but the handsome Viking's long platinum hair blew freely in the wind. Blood soaked his short-sleeved, calf-length mail tunic and dripped from the sword and shield that he held in arms outstretched in entreaty to the gloomy gray sky, as if calling out in anguish to Odin. His ravaged, desperate face drew Rain, almost seemed to pull her into the painting, into the midst of the horrible maelstrom.

Rain stepped back sharply to escape the magnetic pull of the scene. The painting frightened her.

Her mother's face drained bloodless, and her lips trembled as she exclaimed, "Oh, my God! It's Selik."

"Selik?" Rain croaked out, barely holding raw emotion in check. "Who's Selik?"

"Don't you remember the young man I told you about who was a Jomsviking knight, along with your father Thork?"

Oh, no! Not the time-travel stuff again!

But Rain squinted her eyes nonetheless, trying to better see the central figure in the painting. "You don't mean the handsome rake who seduced all the women, the one who always teased you and joked with the children?"

"That's the one. He was so good-looking, like a Norse god. And charming! He just smiled and the women melted."

"I don't know," Rain said skeptically. "This man looks too grim and battle-scarred to be the same person. You must be mistaken."

Her mother stared thoughtfully at the contorted face. "Maybe you're right. Selik was a lover, not a hater."

Rain shivered. "Let's go, Mom. I've had enough of Vikings for one day." Her mother laughed, and they walked back to their hotel, only a few blocks away.

That night Rain's nightmare returned, but now all the pieces of the puzzle came together in one horrid, gruesome battle to the death, complete with the sounds and smells of war. When she saw her lone Viking warrior raise his sword and shield to the sky and scream out his agony over his fallen comrades, Rain cried too, waking her mother and probably half the hotel as well. After she calmed down and sent her mother back to bed, Rain huddled in the window seat and stared blindly out at the street, knowing she'd never sleep again that night.

Soon after dawn, she dressed, left a note for her mother, and walked the empty streets of York for hours. She was the first one in line when the museum doors opened at nine.

Rain made a beeline for the lobby where the oil painting hung. Scaffolds had been erected overnight, and laborers worked noisily on repairs to the high plaster ceiling. Rain ignored the barrier put up to keep tourists away from the work area and moved as close to the picture as possible. Then she pulled a small paper bag out of the large carryall slung over her shoulder. She unwrapped the magnifying glass she'd just purchased in a tourist gift shop and examined the compelling Viking soldier—*Selik*, her mother had called him. She rolled the name softly on her tongue.

Rain had no doubts now. Selik was the specter who'd been haunting her dreams for years. She furrowed her brow in confusion. What did it mean? Did she have some kind of telepathic skill? Was the dream a message or warning of some type?

"Hey, lady, look out!"

Rain glanced apprehensively up to the shouting man on the scaffolding. At the same time, she heard a loud cracking noise. She had no time to move out of the way of the massive block of heavy plaster ceiling that fell ominously toward her.

Rain felt a sharp pain on top of her head, then nothing. The physician in her recognized instantly that she'd been dealt a fatal blow. Then, miraculously, Rain moved spirit-like over the huge pile of rubble that covered her body and viewed the scene dispassionately. Workmen tried frantically to get to her, but Rain didn't care.

A shimmering white light approached, and Rain smiled, feeling an incredible peace envelop her.

So, this is what it's like to die.

But then the beautiful white light formed a hazy, body-shaped figure, and its head moved slightly from side to side, halting her progress. Its hand pointed her in another direction.

War is definitely hell . . .

Rain recognized the sweet, sickening scent immediately. She'd been in too many hospital emergency and operating rooms awash with the wasted life force of countless victims to remain ignorant of the deathly odor of blood.

She felt wetness on her face and the suffocating weight of the fallen plaster. Apparently she hadn't died after all. She tried to lift the heavy object off her chest and face, then slowly opened her leaden eyes to see better.

"Help!" Rain screamed at the horrifying sight she saw. It wasn't plaster that pinned her to the ground, but a man—a very large man by the weight of him. She hadn't realized that another tourist had been standing next to her in the museum before the accident. Or was it a workman? And the sticky wetness that covered her face and linen jacket—was that her blood or his?

She screamed again while grief and despair tore with sharp talons at her throat. She felt as if she had been buried alive. When no help came, Rain braced her feet firmly on the ground, bending her knees, and placed her palms on the man's chest. With a mighty push, she heaved the body off her and stood up shakily.

Stunned, she reached blindly for her carryall on the ground and grabbed a handful of tissues and Wash 'n Dries to clean her face. Glancing about, Rain gasped and quickly closed her eyes to escape the overwhelming horror that surrounded her.

Slowly, reluctantly, with a dull ache of foreboding, she unshuttered them again, dreading what she would see. Some way, some crazy, convoluted, humanly impossible way, she had landed in the middle of her dream—at the Battle of Brunanburh in 937 A.D., more than one thousand years ago, just the way it looked in the museum painting.

She looked down and saw that the mail-clad man who'd covered her face and chest had his head half-severed at the neck. That accounted for all the blood. A man near her feet—a handsome youth whose body was protected only by a tightly fitted helmet and a thick leather vest over a thigh-length tunic and leggings—had a sword still stuck in his chest. His open eyes—a pale, pale blue—stared up at her.

Nausea churned Rain's stomach and rose to her throat.

Bending over, she vomited repeatedly until only bitter bile remained. She threw her bloodstained blazer to the ground and used the rest of her tissues to wipe her mouth, then turned stoically to view her surroundings.

Thousands of men lay dead and dying about her on the plain. *Weondun*, the museum card had called the flat-topped volcanic plain, or "Holy Hill." More like "Unholy Hill," Rain thought, recalling that it had once been the site of some heathen temple.

If ever Rain felt justified in her pacifist views, it was now. Everywhere she looked, she saw evidence of man's inhumanity to man. Some soldiers had succumbed instantly from quick thrusts of a sword or battle-ax; others were grotesquely mutilated and missing body parts—arms, legs, heads.

Rain retched again, then picked up her shoulder bag and moved gingerly through the fallen warriors. She slipped often in spots slick with the vast quantities of lost blood and human viscera.

Although the battle appeared to be a decided Saxon victory, judging by the disproportionate number of large, Viking-clad soldiers in their conical helmets and mail tunics who lay on the field, death had taken its toll indiscriminately among the thousands that day. Fair-haired Norsemen, English-looking Saxons, dark-eyed Welshmen, Scots in their clan plaids, and Irish in their saffron trews—all fell, side by side.

Rain wanted desperately to believe that this was all a dream . . . a nightmare, but the stark reality surrounding her told another story. Despite her resistance, Rain was beginning to believe she had traveled back in time—just as her mother had claimed all those years.

Rain's misery weighed heavily on her shoulders. Why was she sent here? What could she possibly do?

Considerable distance separated her from the savage hand-to-hand combat still taking place among hundreds of soldiers on the far side of the once verdant plain. Rain could see the

Saxon troops with their shield walls as they moved with
deadly force toward their foes. The Viking companies fought
valiantly in a defensive wedge formation, with chieftains
at the point and the lower ranks spread out fan-like behind
them.

For some reason, she wasn't frightened. Just disgusted.

A soft nicker drew Rain's attention, and she turned to see
a large horse standing at the edge of the field, its saddle
empty and its reins trailing on the ground in front. The destrier nudged the bloodied, mail-clad chest of the knight who
lay before him, then raised its soulful eyes to Rain, as if she
could help its master rise.

Rain wiped her nose and turned back to the battlefield with
a sob. So many needed her medical skills, far more than one
doctor could handle. And the wounds required more than
the basic medical items she carried in a compact emergency
kit in her carryall. She shook her head in despair.

With a deep sigh, Rain began to inch her way along the
edge of the battlefield, stopping wherever she felt she could
be of some help. She applied a tourniquet to the upper arm
of one pleading Scots knight with a deep cut at the elbow,
using a strip of leather lacing torn from his shoes. She didn't
know if it did any good. He'd lost so much blood.

Rain moved on to dozens of men, uncaring of their nation-
ality, stanching wounds, pulling out swords, holding a hand,
closing dead eyes. She stood finally, arching the kinks out
of her aching back. The hopelessness of her efforts overwhelmed her. She started to back away from the field, then
shrieked as she bumped into a hard body. She giggled, almost
hysterically, as she realized that the horse had followed her
around the battlefield. Rain put her arms around its neck and
laid her face against the warm white mane. "Oh, horse, what
should I do?"

As if in answer, a roar of loud curses and clanging metal
erupted behind her, and Rain realized that she'd moved unconsciously closer to the fighting.

Then she saw Selik.

Oh, God above! The poor, forsaken Viking stood alone and outnumbered, trying to defend himself against a dozen well-armed Saxon knights intent on killing him.

Many companies of men still fought in hand-to-hand combat around the field, wielding swords, battle-axes, and long pikes. Selik stood alone among the fallen Vikings in his troop, bellowing out his rage at the Saxon attackers. Holding his shield with his left hand, he swung a sword expertly with the other, felling one by one the Saxon soldiers who tried to overtake him. Finally, exasperated by the slowness of his efforts, he pulled the fitted helmet from his head, releasing his long blond hair. He threw his shield to the ground and picked up a long-handled lance with a pike and a battle-ax on the end.

In a fanatical rage, he took the offensive. Heedless of his own mortality, Selik pursued the remaining Saxons to their bloody end, oblivious of the carnage he reaped. A few of the soldiers backed away, eyes rolling in fear, but Selik gave no mercy. Using both hands, he leapt forward, cutting right and left as he cleared a path to the Saxon lad carrying a banner emblazoned with a golden dragon. He sliced the banner pole with one swift slash of his ax, then dispatched the youth with a stab of his pike to the neck. Blood gushed from the severed artery of the poor boy's throat.

Rain shuddered with horror at Selik's butchery. This man had haunted her dreams for years. Some link had connected them through the centuries, but how could she possibly be drawn to such a brutal beast?

Finally, only one of the enemy remained in Selik's immediate vicinity—a Saxon prince, by the looks of his highly polished mail and helmet embossed with the same insignia that decorated the banner lying at his feet.

"Say your prayers, Saxon cur. Today you meet your god," Selik snarled in a harsh, raw voice as he and the Saxon knight exchanged thrusts of their weapons. They seemed evenly matched in expertise.

One thrust went into the Saxon's leg, but he ignored the

wound. "Nay, you bloody pagan! 'Tis you who join Odin, though 'tis more likely a fiery underworld awaits your black soul." He parried Selik's next thrust and got home one slice through Selik's armor above the waist.

"Tell your god today that 'twas Selik the Outlaw who sent you on your final journey." A grim smile thinned Selik's lips cruelly, as if he enjoyed this deadly exercise.

The Saxon blanched, as if recognizing the name of the notorious Viking. Then a crafty grin split his face. "Didst thou know, whoreson, 'twas my cousin Steven who killed your wife and child?" he taunted maliciously. "And 'twas sweet meat the maid was, so Steven claimed, as he spread her thighs afore her death and—"

His words died on his lips as Selik exploded with superhuman strength fed by his fury. He thrust his lance clear through the Saxon's chest and up through the neck, heaving him high on the blade. Then he stuck the base of the pole in the ground so that the young nobleman died on spear point in plain view of his horrified comrades in the distance.

Selik staggered over to pick up his shield and sword, wiping the bloody blade on his hose. Appearing momentarily stunned, he turned pain-glazed eyes to the carnage around him, realizing for the first time that he stood alone. He scanned the field solemnly in tortured disbelief, taking in the overwhelming defeat.

Then, standing on widespread legs, he raised his sword and shield to the sky in outstretched arms, crying out his desolation in a raw and primitive manner. His pale hair blew softly in the wind while tension-coiled muscles bunched under his mail-covered tunic.

"Odin! All-Father!" he keened. "Take me to Valhalla. Do not forsake me."

Rain heard a loud noise and realized that some angry Saxons had left the skirmishes still going on at the other side of the plain and had gathered forces to come after Selik. He needed help—desperately.

Swallowing a harsh sob, Rain yelled, "Selik!" But he didn't

hear her, even though she stood only a few yards away. *"Selik!"*

Still no response.

Rain turned frantically, searching for some means of escape, and saw the faithful horse behind her. *Thank God!* She rushed back and grabbed the reins.

Rain hadn't ridden a horse in twenty years, since her days at summer camp, and this was no pony. Desperation gave her courage. "Come on, honey," she crooned to the skittish animal. "You've got to help me." After several unsuccessful tries and some choice swear words directed at the shifting horse, she climbed clumsily onto the destrier's huge back and guided him carefully over to Selik.

"Selik, come with me. Hurry!" she ordered loudly.

At first, he just lowered his shield and sword and stared at her in confusion. His burning eyes reflected the tortured dullness of his soul in the aftermath of his berserk fight.

"Hurry! We've got to escape," Rain urged, holding out her hand to him.

Suddenly alert, Selik's head swung to the fast-approaching enemy warriors and took in the peril at a glance. Swinging up behind her with lightning agility, he grabbed the reins and set the horse quickly into a gallop. They soon lost the Saxons who pursued on foot, but Rain knew others on horseback, implacable and murderous, would follow soon. They didn't have much time.

For more than an hour, they rode swiftly in silence. As they passed other escaping soldiers along the way, mostly on foot, Selik shouted out in a brusque, deep-timbred voice directions to their eventual meeting place.

The rough ride bruised Rain's bottom and chafed raw the inside of her widespread thighs within her linen slacks, but a part of her reveled in the odd comfort of being in the cradle of Selik's arms. An aura of peace came over her, transmitted by the strength of Selik's body, and her despair lessened under the indefinable feeling of rightness. Despite the horrendous cruelty she'd just seen him display, Rain sensed that this ferocious Viking held the key to her future and the reason for her journey back in time.

Rain tried to speak several times, but her voice came out garbled and breathless due to the jolting of the horse's swift movement and her inability to turn and ask Selik her questions. She had a tough enough time holding on to the horse's mane. Selik's silence erected another barrier to conversation.

So Rain leaned back against the Viking's massive chest, feeling his strong heartbeat, even through the flexible mail coils of his armor. Ripples of unexplainable pride coursed through her when she watched the corded muscles of his forearms flex as he moved the reins to direct the destrier through the seemingly impenetrable forest they were now traversing.

Selik finally stopped to rest their heaving mount. His huge body slid easily off the horse, which he drew to the edge of a secluded stream. Then he deftly removed his mail garment, under which he wore a sweat-soaked tunic. Dropping to his knees, he drank greedily of the clear water before dunking his face, then shaking his head like a shaggy dog. Then he sluiced water over his forearms up to the short-sleeved garment. Rain watched, fascinated, as muscles rippled enticingly across the back of his tightly fitted garment. Her pulse quickened when he stood and stretched his powerful body, then sank with easy grace to the ground. He leaned his head back against a wide tree trunk, closing his weary eyes.

Not once did he look at Rain or offer to help her from the horse, which grazed lazily at the water's edge. She might as well be invisible. Rain dismounted clumsily with a soft curse and knelt. The ice-cold water she carried to her mouth in cupped hands tasted like nectar. She drank her fill, washed her face and hands, and dabbed some bloodstains off the collar of her blouse with a water-dampened scarf. Then she turned to Selik.

Despite his exhaustion, Selik radiated a magnetic vitality. Her feelings for him defied reason, but Rain understood perfectly her physical attraction. He was about thirty years old, her own age, but taller—at least six-foot-four. And muscular! Criminey, he looked as if he could bench-press a bus. His long, pale hair lay sweaty and lank down to his shoulder blades, but Rain knew it would be beautiful when clean.

Pain had carved harsh lines into his face. His nose appeared to have been broken at one time. Ugly scars and purpling bruises, old and new, marred his sun-bronzed face and arms and legs, wherever flesh was exposed, including a particularly gruesome, long-healed white line that zigzagged from his right eye to his chin. Exquisite wide bracelets encased his massive upper arms, barely visible beneath the sleeve of his tunic, bespeaking some wealth or status.

He raised a hand to rake his wet hair off his face, and Rain gasped as she noticed the word *rage* carved into one forearm. The raised white scars had to have been made with a sharp knife long ago. What did it mean?

Rain looked back to his face. His arresting good looks totally captivated her, even though she recognized that many modern women would consider him too rugged and muscle-bound—not aesthetically correct.

Selik must have sensed her perusal. He opened his eyes lazily, and Rain could have easily drowned in their changeable grayish-green depths. But no emotion emanated from their coldness, just a soulless lack of interest.

"Who the hell are you?"

Some welcome!

But at least Rain could understand his language. She'd been worried that she wouldn't be able to communicate with these primitive people. Actually, Selik should be speaking some form of medieval English, Rain realized with a frown. Hell, he probably was, but God, or whoever the mastermind of this fiasco was, had given her some built-in translator. If it was a dream, the lack of a language barrier was understandable, Rain reasoned. If it was time travel, language was the least of her concerns.

She shook her head to clear it and answered his question about her name. "Rain. Rain Jordan."

"Rain? What manner of name is that?" he scoffed disdainfully as he looked her over slowly, insultingly, from head to toe and back again. "Why not snow or sleet or mud?" Then he added scornfully, "Or tree?"

Tree! Hey, it was one thing for a little boy who didn't know any better to insult her about her height, but a screwed-up, vicious Viking whose life she'd just saved? No way!

"You ungrateful bastard! I just saved your life." She blinked to stem the tears in her eyes.

Selik rose and stretched his arms wide to remove the kinks of his long ride. "'Tis no favor you did me, wench," he commented flatly. "'Twould be far better if I had died. This life holds naught for me."

Rain glared at him angrily, uncaring now if he saw her humiliating tears. "How dare you value life so little? Do you know how many men you killed today?"

"Nay. Dost thou?" he asked in a bored tone of voice as he put his mail armor back on. "Didst thou keep a death tally?"

Rain felt blood rush to her face. "No, but I'll bet it was hundreds. Don't you feel any remorse for your butchery?"

"Nay. Why should I? They deserved all they got and more."

"How can you say that, especially about the young boy with the banner you killed near the end?"

"I killed a boy?" Selik tilted his head questioningly, obviously trying to remember the incident. How could anyone kill another human being and not remember? Rain wondered sadly. Finally, Selik shook his head as if it didn't matter. "Every Saxon is my enemy, man or boy. So the runic words say on the scorn pole I erected against King Athelstan long ago." Then he looked at her suspiciously. "Are you perchance one of Athelstan's camp followers?"

"Camp follower!" Rain's cheeks burned with an unwelcome blush. "No, you jerk, I'm not a whore—or a Saxon."

Rain realized then that Selik had mounted the horse and was preparing to depart. *Without her!*

"Wait! You can't leave me here."

Selik arched one eyebrow in a haughty, just-watch-me attitude, and started to turn the horse. "Can I not?"

"That's my horse," she fabricated quickly.

"Liar," he countered with a maddening smile.

"Come back here!"

"Nay, I will not do your bidding, harpy." He grinned. "But fear not, 'tis certain other hersirs will pass by. Mayhap one of those soldiers will be more overcome than I with the blood-lust of battle and offer his protection in return for a hot cellar for his manroot."

Manroot! Rain bristled with indignation. "You insulting pig. I wouldn't be a root cellar for any man—let alone a damn barbarian like you."

Selik just laughed, flashing a dazzling display of straight, white teeth, a sharp contrast to his deeply tanned skin.

The shock of his imminent desertion held her immobile for a moment. Rain panicked then as Selik proceeded to leave the clearing. Icy fingers of despair clawed at her composure.

What would she do in this strange time and place without Selik as her lodestone, loathsome as he was just now? She racked her brain for a solution and came up with only one idea.

"Selik!" she shrieked desperately to his departing back. "What would your old friend Thork think of your abandoning his daughter like this?"

He stopped immediately.

Uh oh! Rain's heart began to hammer wildly as Selik spun in the saddle and pierced her with icy gray eyes. He walked the destrier slowly back to her, and Rain was tempted to turn and flee.

Not only had the question not brought out his protective impulses, Selik looked as if he might kill her. Muscles bunched tensely in his arms from clenched fists to massive shoulders. His full lips thinned to a compressed white line of fury. His eyes glittered with threat. Reaching for the dagger at his belt, Selik glided off the horse smoothly and walked purposefully toward her.

Rain did turn then and ran for her life.

CHAPTER TWO

✧

Being a Viking's guardian angel is hard work . . .

Cursing angrily, Selik chased the tall woman into the forest, sprinting to catch up. Frigg's *blood!* He was wasting precious time on the troublesome wench.

"Halt!"

The giant wood sprite responded by letting a branch swing back and hit him smack in the face as she laughed shrilly, a note of hysteria edging her voice. Never stopping, she continued to dart swiftly through the thickly wooded area on long legs covered with unseemly male leggings.

"You dare much to claim Thork as father," he shouted with exasperation. "'Twill be a pleasure to skin you alive, you lying bitch." When she didn't answer and eluded him still, he threatened, "I will pull your lying tongue out of your head and eat it raw."

Selik heard her gasp at his last, ridiculous words and say something incoherent that sounded like "Yeech!" A slow, secret smile twitched his lips. So, the lackwit thought he was a barbarian? Hah! Well, he would show her.

"If you stop now," he cajoled, getting closer, "'twill be a swift death for you. Mayhap a neat lop of your head. Do you persist in this useless chase, though, you force me to prolong your pain." That should paint the wench some vivid mind-pictures.

"Go to hell," the impudent vixen yelled back.

Damn her impertinence! Didn't the foolish maid know the danger she faced in rousing his temper? He had killed many a man for less.

"Perchance your golden eyes would look good without eyelashes," Selik offered smoothly, meanwhile breathing raggedly from the exertion of his pursuit and the aftermath of battle weariness.

He furrowed his brow. *Golden eyes?* Holy Thor, when had he noticed the color of her eyes? He shook his head to clear the unwelcome image and lashed out ruthlessly, "Damn your eyes! Mayhap I could remove your eyeballs, as well."

The woman snorted in disdain, or disbelief, and another branch swung back, this time hitting him in the abdomen, opening the sword wound he had received earlier.

Now he was really angry.

Blood oozed from the cút, and he hurt like hell—another reason to beat the impudence out of the dull-headed trouble-maker. *Odin's spit!* He squandered valuable minutes pursuing the silly creature when he must needs put as much distance as possible between himself and his Saxon enemy.

There was an additional threat here, as well. Selik had recognized the man he killed earlier, the noble thane hoisted on his standing pike. It had been Eadric, Athelstan's own cousin. The king had put a bounty on Selik's head before the battle; now the Saxon bastard would want him alive and kicking for the slowest torture possible.

And worse yet, Eadric had claimed to be Steven of Gravely's cousin, as well. Bloody hell! He and Steven had more than enough reason to kill each other on sight without this latest fuel added to their mutual hate. Had Steven been at the battle site? Selik wondered suddenly, and he considered returning to end their blood feud once and for all time.

But then Selik looked toward the mad wench who ran in

front of him. He could not disregard the sly wench's outrageous claim. He knew she was not Saxon. Her stature, pale honey hair, and fine features told the truth of her Nordic heritage. But neither could she be daughter to his dead friend, Thork, and she would pay dearly for missaying the truth and delaying him needlessly.

"Enough!" Selik roared finally. The witch had bedeviled him overlong. With a mighty lunge, he tackled her from behind. She hit the ground with a loud "oomph!" and he landed flat atop her.

The fall knocked the wind out of Selik. He lay still for several moments with his face buried in the burnished gold web of the maid's luxuriant hair, which had come loose from its braid. Its sweet, seductive fragrance, an odd mixture of flowers and spices, overwhelmed his senses, making him forget momentarily the brutality and emptiness of his life and remember a time when he had relished the leisure to appreciate the little things of life. Like a woman's scent. Or the feel of lush feminine curves molded perfectly in the cradle of his body.

Selik's frozen heart thawed for a second with feelings he had long disciplined himself to disdain. *Oh, Astrid,* he thought suddenly, and a pain so fierce he could not stand it swelled his heart and threatened to burst the walls of his aching chest. He missed her so much. Tears welled in his eyes in memory of the last time he had seen his wife. The bloody, gruesome mind-picture tormented him endlessly. Would it ever go away?

A gentle nudge jarred him back from his unwelcome reverie. The horse had followed him through the woods.

Thor's blood! he growled in silent self-disgust over his maudlin daydreams. It was years since he had allowed himself such extravagant self-indulgence over his long-dead spouse.

Raising himself on straightened elbows, Selik realized that the woman did not move beneath him. Had she died from the force of his hitting her with his substantial weight?

"Mumpfh!"

"What?"

The wench raised her head and grumbled, "Get off me, you big oaf. You must weigh as much as that horse—*my* horse, incidentally. Do you want to crush me to death—before you have a chance to eat my tongue?"

With a soft, reluctant chuckle, Selik allowed her to roll over on her back but kept her pinned to the ground with his lower body.

"Your shrewish tongue outruns your good sense, wench. Methinks 'twould be too tart for my taste."

Brush burns, grass and dirt covered her face and lips. Pieces of grass and twigs stuck in her disheveled hair and marred her silky shirt. She spit rudely to clear her mouth.

Selik momentarily forgot the reason for his anger, so entranced was he by the allure of the woman who lay beneath him. He brushed several loose strands of golden hair off her shoulder. Like amber silk, it was. He rubbed the threads sensuously between his calloused fingers.

Turning his eyes upward, he noticed a fearsome bruise high on her forehead, its purplish tones stark against her creamy skin. Selik couldn't stop himself from touching it gently with a forefinger, and her full lips, like crushed rose petals, parted involuntarily on an indrawn breath of pain, showing off uncommonly even white teeth.

The wench's honey-brown eyes held his, questioning, probably wondering what he would do next, and for long moments Selik could not help himself from gazing at her with longing. The vast emptiness inside him felt suddenly full and warm. When had he last felt this way? *Astrid,* he realized immediately and berated himself scornfully once again.

Suddenly, Selik saw the foolishness of his action. He was behaving like a besotted lackbrain dawdling with a maid while the Saxon hounds nipped at his heels. He pulled out the dagger at his belt and held its razor edge against her neck.

"What do you here, wench?"

"What would you have me do? I can't move," she snapped.

"Do you deliberately mistake my words? You must needs take your situation more seriously." He pressed the gleaming blade tighter and drew a thin line of blood like a drizzle of wine in new snow. "Your paltry life means naught to me."

"Oh, really! Don't you think you're being a bit dramatic?" the foolish witch said scornfully, as if she feared him not. "Besides, it would be a lot less messy if you didn't cut my jugular vein. I would suggest here at the kidney, or here through the diaphragm."

She pointed to two places on her body that Selik knew would bring instant death, as well as the large blood-pumping spot on her neck. How did a simple female know such? And what was a die-frame?

Rain saw the confusion on Selik's face.

A voice echoed in her head, *Save him.*

Surprisingly unafraid then, she stared up at the hardened warrior hovering over her. "Would you really kill me, Selik?"

"In a trice."

"I don't think you would," Rain asserted with more confidence than she felt, "and furthermore, even though you act like a bear, I'm not afraid of you."

"Then you are truly a halfwit, I warrant."

Rain shrugged, trying to ignore the words in her head that kept repeating, *Save him. Save him. Save him . . .*

Selik frowned, seeming disturbed by her brave front. Couldn't the fool hear her teeth chattering?

"How dost thou know my name? Why were you at Brunanburh?"

"I'm not sure," Rain admitted hesitantly. "I think . . . I think God sent me."

Selik snorted rudely in disbelief. "Why would God do thus?"

"To save you," Rain offered weakly.

"Me? God cares naught for such as me." He surveyed her through slitted eyes while he sheathed his knife, then asked reluctantly, as if he couldn't believe he was saying the words, "Save me from what?"

"From yourself."

Selik slapped both hands to his head in disbelief. Still kneeling atop her, he threw his head back and hooted with laughter.

Rain knew Selik didn't believe her. Who would, under the circumstances? She lowered her lashes quickly to hide the disappointment, then waited patiently for Selik to recover from his infuriating fit of laughter.

Finally, he wiped his eyes and shook his head in wonder at her arrogant claims. "'Tis too much. The maid declares herself my guardian angel. Sweet Freya! The battle today must have unhinged my mind. Mayhap the wench got hit on the head as well." He looked pointedly at the bump on her forehead. Little did he know it had happened a thousand years from now in a Viking museum. Or was it this morning? Rain wondered with a frown.

Selik continued to chuckle.

Rain clucked her tongue, chafing now under his continued ridicule. Good heavens! Her words weren't *that* funny.

But Rain wasn't really annoyed. Despite the danger of the Saxon pursuit and Selik's threats, her troubled spirits calmed, and she felt a strange peace being with the ruthless Viking, as if she'd finally found her place in life.

And, besides, she rationalized, Selik had been through absolute hell that day . . . and probably had for years. It showed in the scars and poorly healed broken bones and empty eyes. No matter how much she hated his brutality, Rain couldn't stop herself from admiring Selik, the man, almost as she would a wounded animal with a fine pedigree that had been battered but still maintained its innate beauty.

Save him.

Rain almost groaned aloud at the persistent inner voice. How would she ever be able to penetrate the utter emptiness at the bottom of his desolate eyes? Would he let her get that close?

"My mother was right about you," Rain whispered huskily, still pinned to the ground by his body.

Selik raised an eyebrow.

"You're gorgeous."

Selik snorted rudely. "'Tis of no importance. And do not dare try your paltry charms on me. 'Twill not work. Leastways, I lost whatever looks I had many years past." Then he hesitated, as if pondering something. "You mentioned your mother. Do I know her?"

"You did. Her name was Ruby . . . Ruby Jordan . . . before she married—"

"Argh!" Selik jumped up, glaring down at Rain. Then he pulled her roughly to her feet, noticing something for the first time. His eyes narrowed suspiciously as he pointed to the brooch on her lapel and asked, "Where did you pilfer *that?*"

"My mother gave it to me."

"'Tis impossible." He put a hand to his brow and rubbed, obviously troubled. "Nay, not Ruby. You cannot be her daughter. Or Thork's."

He searched her face then, looking for a resemblance, which Rain knew was there if he'd only see it. Suddenly, Selik seemed to remember something. Before she had a chance to react, he took her blouse by the lapels and tore it apart, uncaring of the rips or popping buttons.

"How dare you?" Rain sputtered and tried futilely to hold the edges of the shirt together. Selik knocked her hands aside.

He stared at her breasts incredulously, but not with lust. "For the love of Freya! You wear Ruby's strange undergarment. Lingerie, methinks she named it."

"This is not my mother's bra." Rain clamped her jaw shut defiantly, then demanded to know, "How did you ever see my mother's underwear?"

"Hah! Every man in King Sigtrygg's court saw the scandalous garment when she removed that traitorous Brass Balls *shert* of hers. She even went into business making the wispy things while she lived amongst us."

Criminey! Selik was repeating the same ridiculous story her mother had told for years. And no one had believed Ruby, herself included. Maybe this wasn't a dream, after all. Rain clasped both widespread hands to her mouth in horror.

Oh, my God! Could time-travel really be possible?

"Listen, I assure you that Ruby is my mother, and she always said Thork was my father." Rain decided not to tell him—at least, not yet—that her mother also said Jack Jordan was her father as well. "I can give you all the explanations you want, but don't you think we should get away from here first? If the Saxons capture us, it won't matter who I am."

Selik nodded reluctantly and whistled between his closed teeth. The dumb horse came ambling toward him like a lovesick swain. How did Selik do that? It was probably a female, Rain decided with disgust, wondering if he had the same effect on women in general.

Selik put his left hand on the saddle and vaulted onto the horse, then looked down at her expressionlessly while she scrambled to repair the damage to her blouse as best she could and rebraid her hair.

"I will take you with me—*for now*—but heed me well, wench," he said finally, "do you play me false, I will not hesitate to kill you." Then he reached down and grabbed her by an elbow. With one rough motion, he swept her up into his arms, weightlessly, and held her snugly across his lap.

Rain rubbed her elbow in chagrin but decided not to push her luck by complaining. *Holy cow!* Aside from the unnecessary roughness, Rain marveled that Selik could have lifted her so easily. She couldn't remember the last time anyone had picked her up. She was too big. Wasn't she?

"And do not wiggle your arse like you did afore," Selik ordered insolently as the horse began to move. "Your bawdy games will gain you naught. Even if I had the time, I would not rut with such as you."

Rain couldn't remain silent this time. "Your arrogance revolts me. I have no interest whatsoever in making love with you."

"Hah! Love has naught to do with mating. When a man feels the need to relieve himself betwixt a woman's legs, 'tis rutting, pure and simple. Ofttimes 'tis simpler to do it himself."

Rain's upper lip curled with disgust, and she turned her eyes heavenward. "I pity you if you think of lovemaking as a bodily function."

"In truth, 'tis much like pissing," he persisted.

Rain detected a hint of humor in Selik's voice and turned to look back at him as they rode. His blank face told nothing, but a slight twitch of his lips betrayed a barely suppressed grin.

"Humph! Well, you're certainly different from the man my mother described. To hear her tell it, you had a reputation as a great lover."

"What nonsense! Well, mayhap," he admitted on second thought, "I did have wordfame as a lover once, but 'twas long ago." He shrugged. "I no longer care."

In spite of herself, Rain giggled. "You have no idea what a strange conversation this is for me. With my failure rate in sexual relationships, I'm no one to criticize."

"What is your meaning? Failure rate? Do you not mate with your husband?"

"I'm not married."

"Aaah."

"What does that mean?"

"It means I understand now. You are an unwed woman who ruts with men."

"Hold it, buster. Don't make any rash judgments. I'm not promiscuous, if that's what you're implying."

"I imply naught. 'Tis you who speak of bad ruttings with men to whom you are not wed."

"I wish you'd stop using that ugly word."

"Which word?"

"Rutting. Animals rut. If you can't refer to it as making love, at least call it having sex."

Selik laughed again, deep and throaty, and the sound rippled musically in Rain's ears.

"Just how many men have you *had sex* with?" he asked with a chuckle, his arms tightening around her imperceptibly like a warm cocoon.

"That is none of your business." Rain stiffened her back indignantly.

"Methinks you have had no man, wench, with that wasp-ish tongue. No man would risk his male parts with its razor edge."

Rain lifted her chin indignantly. "Don't think that just because I'm—I'm tall, that no man has ever desired me."

The brute made a small choking sound behind her neck. "Well, now you call it to my attention, you are rather . . . *large*. In truth, some men are put off by . . . *largeness*."

Tell me about it.

"So, what of these *few* men who desired you?"

Geez! He had a one-track mind. Oh, what difference did it make, Rain decided. "When I was eighteen, I had a really bad sexual experience, an unfortunate one-night stand. In the past twelve years, I've had only two serious love affairs. They didn't work out very well."

Selik remained silent for several moments, considering her words. "So, you have seen thirty winters. I did not realize you were so long in the tooth."

"I'm no older than you," she retorted hotly.

"Well, then, we must both be long in the tooth, sweetling," he concluded with a soft laugh. He pressed her cheek against his chest, indicating an end to the conversation, and expertly put the horse into a faster pace.

Sweetling! Rain snuggled closer and put her arms around his waist for balance. Weariness overwhelmed her. This time-travel business was exhausting.

Before she dozed off, somehow confident that Selik would protect her from any danger, Rain wondered how she would ever be able to save this savage Norseman who referred to lovemaking as rutting, who killed men as easily as he'd stomp on ants, and who'd just as soon be dead himself. Rain vowed that she would help him, God willing, and somehow, in the process, she hoped to regain her own life as well. But the question was—would it be here in the past, or in the future?

Rain slept peacefully until she felt the horse climbing a sharp incline. The path it followed wended through near-impenetrable brush and vines, which Selik slashed aside when necessary with his sword. Fierce, primitive soldiers stood watch silently along the way, waving them forward when they recognized Selik, then covering their tracks immediately after. Soon they emerged onto a flat clearing atop the hill. From here they could see for miles around, obviously a good vantage point for detecting any pursuing enemy.

Rain was surprised to see that hundreds of Vikings and their allies, including the Scots and Welsh, had escaped the Saxon assault. Many of the men still wore battle raiment, while others covered themselves with wolf skins and other animal furs as the cool autumn evening approached. Only a few women were present, cooking over open fires off to the side.

Some tents had been erected, but most of the men lay on the open ground, resting or treating wounds. At least she could be of some help as a physician.

Rain turned to offer her medical skills and noticed the proud, arrogant set of Selik's shoulders. Even in a crowd, his presence was compelling, but no welcome greeted Selik from his beaten comrades. An air of isolation surrounded her lone Viking, as if he were an outcast of some sort.

Selik dismounted and helped Rain off the horse. A number of men stared at her with curiosity. Lord, by the ferocious, barbaric looks of them, she'd landed in a den of Dark Age warlords.

"Go help the women," Selik directed curtly.

"Huh? Cooking? Me?"

"Do my ears play me false? You question my orders already?" Selik hissed through gritted teeth.

"No, it's just that I thought you'd need my medical skills."

"Go to the cooking fires," he snapped in a choked voice. Some of the men snickered at her questioning his orders.

"I'm a doctor, for heaven's sake," Rain muttered petulantly as she started to stomp off.

Selik grabbed her braid and pulled hard, jerking her back sharply.

"Ouch! What'd I do now?" She yanked her braid out of his hands and squared her shoulders defiantly, despite his stormy face.

"Your flapping tongue defies reason, and I warned you about missaying the truth. First, you claim to be a guardian angel. Now, a healer. What next? The goddess Freya?"

Rain closed her eyes for a moment and sighed deeply. "I *am* a physician. I spent many years studying to be a doctor. I'm a surgeon at Holy Trinity Hospital."

Rain heard hoots of disbelief and derision around her, but Selik rubbed his chin and eyed her speculatively.

"A physician!" he grumbled with a resigned shake of his head. "Bloody hell! The gods surely showed their displeasure by dumping this feminine blight on me this day." Before she could protest, he grabbed hold of her wrist and pulled her toward the nearest tent, demanding, "Show me."

Rain soon discovered that three tents held wounded warriors in a triage system based on the severity of their injuries. Still carrying her shoulder bag containing an emergency medical kit, she entered the tent with the most grievously wounded. For hours, she worked like an automaton as best she could with her limited supplies—suturing wounds, treating shock, and trying to avoid infection wherever possible.

At first, Selik stood guard over her, watching her every move. He stopped her when she tried to give pills to several men, but let her continue when she assured him they were just aspirin and Tylenol, mild painkillers, much the same as the herbs his own healers used. She gave Darvon to some men who needed stronger medication.

When she finished with all the patients in her tent, Rain went outside and stretched her back to remove the kinks. She knew she'd treated only a few of the many victims. She heard loud moans and screams from the other tents, where God only knew what kind of primitive medical practitioners doctored the helpless victims.

Selik stood alone, propped against a tree trunk on the other side of the clearing, apart from his military comrades. Their gazes locked for a second, and Rain wondered what he had been thinking, standing in the chill night air.

He needs you, the voice said.

Hah! He needs a good shot of pacifism. That's what he needs.

Then Selik gave her a questioning glare, as if asking why she was resting when so many needed her help. *The boor!*

Rain walked huffily into the next tent and gazed in horror at a young man lying on a long table, protesting wildly the restraints of several men who held him down. Rain couldn't believe what she saw. Then, as the victim turned his face toward her, Rain screamed in horror.

It was her brother Dave on the table, and a floundering, Dark Age Dr. Greg House wielded a knife the size of the Grim Reaper's blade, preparing to amputate his leg. Worst of all, the contaminated blood of other patients covered the healer's instrument and his cleric's garb, even his tonsured head. Apparently, he'd used the knife over and over without cleaning or disinfecting it.

"Stop!" Everyone in the room turned to look at her as she rushed forward. "Don't you dare touch my brother, you bloody butcher." With a force fed by pumping adrenaline, Rain knocked the healer aside, taking in the medical problem immediately. The deep wound above the knee was bad, and he'd probably sustained some permanent muscle damage, but she thought she might be able to save his leg. Of course, he'd

lost a lot of blood, and she had no plasma, but it was worth the risk. Wasn't it?

"Don't worry, Dave, I won't let them cut off your leg."

The young man raised his eyes hopefully and clutched her hand tightly. Refusing to relax his grasp, he tried to speak, but she told him to save his strength.

Of course, it wasn't Dave. Her *real* older brother was forty-two years old and was probably playing golf right now, since it was Saturday. This man couldn't be more than twenty. He must be one of the Viking Age half brothers her mother had told her about.

"Are you Eirik or Tykir?"

"Tykir," he rasped out.

"Well, Tykir, I'm your half-sister Rain, and I won't let them take your leg."

"Do you swear?" he asked, still clutching her hand.

"I promise to do everything possible to save your leg."

Hearing a flurry of noise behind her, Rain turned to see a furious Selik, his eyes blazing hotly. He stood in the doorway of the tent, flanked by the healer and the men who'd been holding Tykir down.

"What manner of trouble do you cause now?" he snarled, moving toward her purposefully, obviously intending to remove her bodily from the tent. Rain stood her ground bravely, holding her arms outstretched protectively in front of her newfound kin.

Rain shook with anger and fear, but she knew she had to speak quickly. "They'll kill him if they amputate his leg—especially with that dirty blade. I won't let them do that to my brother."

"Brother? What nonsense do you spout now?"

"Tykir. They want to amputate—"

With a hefty swipe, Selik knocked Rain aside and to the ground. The healer snickered with satisfaction above her.

Selik leaned over the patient with concern. "Tykir? Oh, by all I hold sacred, boy, I did not know you were in the battle. I thought you safe in the Norselands with your Uncle Haakon. Damn that Ubbi for disobeying my orders."

"Do not blame Ubbi," Tykir whispered. " 'Twas my idea."

Rain stood and brushed off the seat of her pants. Fascinated, she watched the ferocious Viking caress Tykir's face with remarkable gentleness. It was the most compassion she'd seen in the cold Norseman thus far. Perhaps there was hope for him, after all.

"Let the woman heal me," Tykir pleaded, rising on his elbows. "Do not say me nay on this, Selik. Much do I prefer to gamble death with the wench than lose a limb. For the sake of my father, grant me this boon."

Selik turned stonily to Rain. "Can you truly save the leg?"

"I think so . . . if we hurry. And providing I get all the help and materials I need." She looked pointedly at the angry healer and the hostile men.

Selik paused, torn between the outrage of his comrades and Tykir's urgent exhortations. He held up a hand to halt the angry suggestions of the men. *"Quiet!"* he bellowed and turned decisively to Rain. "What dost thou need?"

Rain could have kissed the stubborn knight for his support, begrudging as it was. She banked her emotions, though, and demanded, "Boiling water, lots of it, needles, clean cloths. Put everything into the water to sterilize; then lay the cloths somewhere to dry where they won't touch anything impure."

She gave orders like a drill sergeant to the men around her, wanting the table scrubbed thoroughly and dozens of torches lit for better visibility. When the makeshift operating table was prepared, she removed all of Tykir's clothing, much to the embarrassment of Tykir and the consternation of the cleric, who proclaimed huffily, " 'Tis unseemly of the maid."

"Listen, little brother, what you have or don't have below the waist is of little consequence here. You want to save your leg, don't you?"

He nodded weakly.

Rain patted his head reassuringly. Lord, he was only a

boy. He should be enjoying life, not fighting in a useless war. She sighed with weary resignation. Whether tenth-century or modern-day life, some things never changed. One pointless war after another.

Rain decided not to remove the tourniquet above the wound until just before the surgery, but she examined the injury closer to determine the depth of the cut. The muscle damage might not be too bad, but some veins needed to be reconnected as soon as possible to get the blood supply going again before the leg atrophied. It would take hours under the best of circumstances. How would Tykir ever stand the prolonged pain?

Rain rummaged in her medical kit. Of course, she had no anesthetic. And the strongest pain killers she carried were Darvon and codeine, and only a few of those. They would be better used after the surgery. Would she have to rely on alcohol to dull Tykir's senses? Criminey! She'd kill her brother just probing around in that horrendous wound.

But there was another way, Rain realized suddenly. Did she have the courage to try it?

Dr. Chin Lee, a colleague at her hospital, had been teaching her acupuncture for the past few years as an alternative to traditional painkillers and anesthetics, but she'd never tried the procedure on her own. She inhaled deeply and made a decision.

"Selik, can you find me some long needles with very sharp points?"

He nodded.

"Bring as many as you can find, and make sure you put those in boiling water, too." He frowned at her dictatorial tone but had the grace to wait until later to reprimand her. When everything was ready, she demanded, "Everybody out of this tent."

"Nay. We stay to witness her atrocities," the healer protested.

"The boy needs to be held down," one man argued.

"Mayhap she practices sorcery," still another offered.

"Selik," Rain pleaded, "if all goes well, Tykir won't need to be restrained."

"Hah! He will be dead," the healer declared shrilly, and the others affirmed his accusation with much grumbling.

Selik considered her words, then compromised, "Father Cedric and I will remain to witness your work. The others will stay outside the tent in case they are needed."

"Well, then, you both have to scrub your hands."

"The wench demands overmuch," Father Cedric whined.

"Selik, my brother is in more danger from infection than from the wound itself. Dirt and tainted blood carry bacteria, a deadly killer in open wounds."

At first, Selik glared at her stubbornly, but then he looked to Tykir's pleading face. He told the healer with finality, "We do as the wench asks—for now."

They left the tent to scrub up, muttering curses when she added that they should wash under their fingernails as well. Rain turned to the barely conscious Tykir.

"Honey, I'm going to do some things to lessen the pain. You'll feel better right away, and you shouldn't even be able to tell when I probe in your wound to repair the damage. Do you trust me?"

"I must needs trust you," he said uncertainly.

"There's one thing, though, Tykir . . . the way I'll stop the pain involves sticking needles in your skin in at least ten spots."

His eyes widened, but then he gave a weak, pain-filled smile and chuckled. "Best you prick me afore Selik returns, lest he skin you alive. He has a fearsome aversion to needles."

Thanking God for her almost photographic memory, Rain mentally reviewed Dr. Lee's lessons on ancient Chinese medicine. She pictured the meridians that divided the human body and the three hundred and sixty-five "gate keepers" or puncture points where the meridians supposedly emerged to the surface. Even Dr. Lee, with all his expertise, hadn't been sure how acupuncture worked as a natural anesthetic, but he contended that when a sharp point was inserted in precisely the right spot it sent a message to the brain which released natural opiates, such as endorphins and enkephalins, to mask the pain.

Tykir was scared to death, but the brave boy just pressed his lips together tightly and closed his eyes as she stuck the long needles into various parts of his body, including his head. Then he looked up in wonder. "'Tis a miracle. I feel no pain."

Rain closed her eyes for a second. *Thank You, God!*

"Nay!" Selik and the healer shouted together as they entered the tent and saw what she'd done with the needles. At first, Selik swayed from side to side, his huge body threatening to fall into a dead faint at the sight of the needles. Then he picked her up bodily, softly whispering various obscene tortures he would inflict on her for hurting his injured friend, but Tykir spoke up weakly, "Nay, Selik, the needles kill the bloody pain. I gave her permission to do thus."

Selik eyed Tykir dubiously and finally told the babbling healer, "Shut your teeth, man, or depart."

The operation took hours, with a white-faced Selik holding the magnifying glass she'd purchased early that morning to examine the museum painting.

Was it really only this morning, or a lifetime ago?

Despite the acupuncture, Tykir mercifully passed out midway through the procedure. At the end, Rain's fingers shook with tension and exhaustion as she completed the final sutures, bandaged the leg, and put on the splints.

Shaking his head, Father Cedric left the tent, muttering, "Sorceress! Devil's Spawn! Black Arts!" But Selik just watched her steadily, deep in thought, as she picked up her meager supplies. He stepped outside and spoke to someone, then came back and helped her. Finally, he drew her protestingly from Tykir's side, assuring her that a guard would watch him through the night and call her if there was any change. He led her to a small tent nearby and pushed her inside.

"'Tis the best I could do," he apologized, indicating the sleeping furs on the ground and the basin of water for bathing.

A cup of water and a wooden plate with a hunk of bread and several slices of fire-blackened meat sat on a small stool.

Selik's consideration surprised her. She turned to tell him so, but he'd already left.

CHAPTER THREE

⊛

Doctor, doctor, give me the news . . .
 After gobbling the unpalatable food down hungrily and drinking all the cool water, Rain removed her outer clothing and gave herself a quick wash as best she could with the limited supplies. What she wouldn't give for an underarm deodorant!

She put her slacks back on and eyed her dirty, torn blouse distastefully. Then she saw the large—very large—reddish-brown stain on its back.

Blood! How could that be? She reached around and felt her skin. No cuts there. And it couldn't be Tykir's blood on her back. Then realization hit her as she remembered that the Saxon's blade had cut through Selik's armor. The jolting ride on the horse must have opened the wound, and the stupid Viking didn't have the good sense to complain.

Saving Selik was going to be a lot harder than she'd thought. Rain put the blouse back on and stormed out with her medical kit, stepping defiantly in front of the vigilant guards and over sleeping warriors as she made her way to Selik's tent.

He'd removed the mail shirt and his cross-gartered leather

shoes. Standing barefoot in a thigh-length tunic, he was drinking deeply from a large goblet. At Rain's choking sound, Selik turned his head to look back at her over his shoulder. His slumberous eyes held hers in a questioning caress for several long moments before he asked in an amused voice, "To what do I owe this honor? Didst thou get a heavenly message?"

Rain swallowed dryly at the sight of Selik's eyes boldly raking her. Lord, what a devastatingly handsome man he was! Even his feet were beautiful—high arched and well-formed. Although the tunic covered a good portion of his body, Rain's eyes feasted on the slim waist and hips, wide shoulders, and bunching muscles everywhere.

She made a mental note to proceed with caution. To a six-foot-tall woman, this more than six-foot-four male looked awfully appetizing. She shook her head to clear her senses, then blushed at the knowing grin on Selik's face as he turned around.

"Didst change thy mind about the rutting?" he asked with a mocking twist of a smile that didn't quite reach his eyes.

"Oh!" she gasped, his crudity taking the steam out of her simmering blood. "No, you randy goat. I came because of the blood. *Your* blood." She turned and showed him the back of her blouse. "Why didn't you tell me about your injury?"

He shrugged. "'Tis of no importance. The healer can treat my piddling wound on the morrow."

"He will not!" Rain declared vehemently. "I wouldn't let that butcher near you. Now take off your tunic."

Selik arched an eyebrow at her protectiveness but walked toward her with slow, sensuous grace, lifting his tunic over his head as he approached. He wore only a sort of loin cloth underneath.

Rain bit her lower lip to hold back an exclamation at the magnificence of his finely honed body. Then she looked at the deep, ten-inch slash across his abdomen and chastised him sharply, "Are you out of your ever-lovin' mind? A wound like this is serious. It needs cleansing, an antiseptic, and at least fifty stitches."

"The bad beddings."

"Oh, there's nothing really to tell. It's just that I can take it or leave it—sex, that is." Rain frowned. Good Lord! Why would she disclose something so intimate to a virtual stranger? Because Selik was not a stranger to her, she realized; she felt as if she'd known him all her life. Also, by talking of herself, she might take Selik's mind off his grief.

"Thor's Blood! You are blunt."

"You asked," she said defensively.

"When didst thou last have a man betwixt your thighs?"

"You're a bit blunt yourself, mister," Rain laughed, then thought for a moment. "Two years."

"'Tis true? I can hardly credit it, but then the bed sport does repulse some women. Somehow, though, methought you more hot-blooded than that. Mayhap you did not have a man with the right skills."

"Oh, please, spare me the male ego. I'm not repulsed by sex, and I can reach an orgasm as well as any woman. After all, there are fifty-seven erotic points on a woman's body. If a man can't find one of them, he needs a flashlight and a sex manual."

Holy Cow! Had she really said all those things? This dream trip of hers must have loosened the hinge on her tongue—or her mind. She hoped Selik appreciated her efforts to take his mind off more serious concerns.

Selik choked with laughter. "Only fifty-seven?" he asked dryly. "And do men have as many, or more?"

Rain knew he mocked her. Well, she'd show him. She gave her best Sex Education 101 clinical lecture straight out of medical school. When she finished, Selik's chest shook with laughter.

"Really! What's so funny?"

"You. You know all these details about the mating betwixt a man and woman. Like a bloody book you are, not a woman. Nay, you have ne'er felt as a real woman in a man's arms, I wager. 'Tis certain you do not even know what you want from a man."

"Hah! I'll tell you one thing, Mr. Know-It-All. The best sex I ever had didn't involve . . . didn't involve . . . well, penetration." Realizing the corner she was painting herself into with her loose tongue, Rain practically whispered the last word.

But he heard.

At his muffled chuckle, she added with false bravado, "Was that explicit enough for you?"

"Methinks you deliberately try to shock me. You do not mean the outrageous things you say."

"Yes, I do. I mean, no, I don't."

"Do you back down now, wench?"

"No! And don't think I don't know you're just goading me into saying stupid things."

"Do you say that I cause you to speak your falsehoods?"

Rain bristled. "What falsehoods?"

"The things you said about . . . penetration."

"Oh," Rain squeaked out. Then she yawned hugely with exaggerated loudness. "I'm tired of this conversation. I think I'll go to sleep."

" 'Tis what women do all the time."

"What?"

"Run. Hide. Try to mask their lies when caught in their own traps."

"Really, you're making a big deal out of nothing. I spoke the truth. Many women will tell you that the best sex they ever had was when they were teenagers and would neck for hours and hours with their boyfriends."

"Neck?"

Rain exhaled with self-disgust at the hole she'd dug so cleverly for herself. "Necking is just kissing, but every way possible—innocently, deeply, wetly, tongues—you know, the whole works. As compared to petting, which involves touching, usually with the clothes on, but never any actual sexual intercourse."

"Tongues?" Selik choked out.

"Yes, French kissing."

"French? Hah! Do those bloody Franks dare lay claim to

inventing the deep kiss? Norsemen were tongue-kissing long afore them."

Rain smiled to herself at the conceit of men, of all nationalities, no matter the time in history.

Then Selik snorted distastefully. "And this kissing for hours is more satisfying to you than the mating?"

"It can be. Oh, in an ideal situation, sex would be the end result. But, as I said, ask any woman—would she rather be seduced with hours and hours of kisses, or engage in a session of wham-bam-thank-you-ma'am?"

Selik said nothing, and Rain realized she'd been rambling. She'd probably bored him to death. Or shocked him speechless.

"Are you asleep?"

He remained silent for a long time before answering in a soft voice, "Nay."

"What are you doing?"

He laughed throatily. "Relieving myself."

Rain gasped at his vulgarity and turned to chastise him when she saw through the dim torchlight that he lay on his back with his arms folded behind his head. His lips twitched with a grin, and he winked wickedly at her.

The teasing brute! She turned her back on him huffily.

"Rain?"

"What?"

"What is an orgy-asm?"

Rain felt her face turn hot with embarrassment, and she refused to answer him. Besides, he probably already knew and just wanted to continue baiting her.

Selik stood and put out the torch, then lay back down, pulling the furs over them both.

"Go to sleep, sweetling."

Sweetling! He called me that earlier, too. Rain's heart hummed at the quaint endearment. He probably meant Sleetling. *Oh, well.*

Already half asleep, she said, softly, "Selik?"

"Hmmm?"

"I'm glad God sent me to save you."

She thought she heard him swear and say something like, "Your god must have a strange sense of humor," but she was too tired to ask him to repeat the words.

Her heart broke for the broken man . . .

Rain awakened late the next morning, totally rested—and alone. She stretched lazily under the warm furs, wondering where Selik was.

Suddenly she realized she'd slept soundly through the night. No dreams. No nightmares. She smiled.

Well, what did she expect, she told herself ruefully. She was living inside her nightmare.

Tykir. The memory hit Rain with a jolt, and she jumped up, frantic to check on her patient. Using a small bowl of water, she splashed her face and rinsed her mouth. Without a mirror, she could only smooth the loose tendrils of hair that had escaped her braid.

Her half brother lay where she'd left him the night before, guarded by a young soldier who answered her questions about the patient's progress through the night. Rain breathed a sigh of relief when she found Tykir's skin cool to the touch. No fever, thank God. His pulse was shallow, but regular—to be expected after the traumatic surgery—and his heartbeat was strong.

While she unwrapped his bandages, Tykir awakened groggily. "Am I alive? Or dead? Be you a handmaiden to the gods?"

Rain laughed softly. "You are very much alive, young man, and I hope to keep you that way. And though Selik has referred to me as a guardian angel, I'm a mere mortal, just like you."

Tykir tried to smile through lips white-edged with pain.

"Here," Rain said, pulling out her bottle of Darvon. "I only have six of these left, so we'll have to spread them out. It will help with the pain."

"Nay, I need no magic pellets for pain."

"Take it," Rain ordered sternly and shoved the pill in his mouth. Then she held his head up slightly to drink some water from a wooden goblet.

"Are you a sorceress? I remember you prodding in my wound yestereve and feeling no pain."

"No, I'm a physician. A surgeon," Rain answered as she examined his leg for infection, then replaced the bandages with clean linen.

"Truly? Ne'er have I heard of a woman doing such. And the needles? Surely, they were tools of sorcery."

"No, even in ancient times, acupuncture was a legitimate science practiced by medical men. I must admit, it's not my specialty, but I felt I had no choice in your case."

Tykir frowned. "Didst you claim yestereve to be my sister, or was I dreaming?"

Rain put the final touches on her bandages, then turned to smile at the handsome youth. "I'm your half sister, Thoraine Jordan. They call me Rain for short."

Tykir tilted his head in confusion. "How can that be?"

"We share the same father," she explained, crossing her fingers at the half-lie. "My mother was Ruby Jordan. Do you remember her?"

Rain couldn't believe that, after thirty years of disbelieving her mother's time-travel stories, she now accepted them so readily. Well, what other explanation could there be? It was either time-travel or a damned vivid dream.

"Nay! 'Tis impossible." Tykir grew agitated and tried to sit up, but she and the guard managed to get him to lie back down. " 'Tis cruel of you to missay the truth," Tykir accused her weakly.

"Oh, Tykir, I wouldn't lie about something like that."

Tears misted her half brother's eyes. "I loved Ruby, but she left afore I had a chance to tell her so. I was only eight years old at the time. Why did she desert us?"

"She had no other choice. She was forced to return to her own world after Thork's . . . our father's . . . death. But she knew you loved her, Tykir. She spoke of it often."

"But Ruby and my father married only twelve years ago. How could they have a child your age?"

"I don't understand myself, but time must move faster in the future." Rain had no other explanation for why thirty years in the future would equate with twelve in the past.

"You must tell me more . . . but later . . . not now," Tykir said, slurring his words slightly. "Your pellet truly is magic. I feel wonderful. I feel like . . ." A soft snore escaped his lips, and Rain smiled, brushing wisps of dark blond hair off his face with loving care.

When she left the tent, Rain realized that more men had arrived during the night. About five hundred soldiers crowded the plain, and a meeting of some type was taking place. In the front, a half-dozen leaders addressed the assembly, each dressed so distinctly they had to represent different countries or cultures. Rain was too far away to hear their words, so she edged her way toward the cooking fires, where a group of women worked feverishly to prepare a meal.

She stepped up to one of them, where a huge cauldron of some stew boiled, wafting delicious odors into the cool morning air.

"What's going on?" Rain asked the nearest woman, a middle-aged Viking woman with blond hair plaited and wound in a coronet atop her head. Her pinafore-style tunic worn over a pleated underdress was held together at the shoulders with two brass brooches. It was surprisingly neat and clean, considering her surroundings.

The woman jumped back in surprise at Rain's words. She dropped her ladle and exchanged a quick, guarded look with another, younger woman, dressed similarly but with reddish-blond braids hanging to her waist.

Were they camp followers? Or wives to these fighting men?

"My name is Rain Jordan."

"Sigrid, wife of Cnut," the older woman said hesitantly, putting a palm to her chest, then pointing to the younger woman, "'Tis my daughter, Gunvor."

"I'm starved," Rain said. "Could I have some of that stew?"

The older woman offered her a wooden bowl of the thick broth in which swam chunks of meat along with onions and carrots. Rain took a tentative bite with a crude wooden spoon, then closed her eyes in ecstasy, her stomach rumbling with content. She had eaten practically nothing in more than twenty-four hours, and dishwater probably would have tasted like fine cuisine.

Gunvor stared at her open-mouthed. "Didst thou truly mate with The Outlaw yestereve?" She shuddered visibly with horror at the thought.

"Huh?"

Rain had thought they were staring at her because of her height, although she didn't stand out so much among these taller-than-average women, or because of her strange clothing, or even because of her unusual medical skills. But, no, it was her association with Selik that troubled them. Rain faintly recalled Selik, too, referring to himself as The Outlaw yesterday.

Rain frowned in confusion, returning her empty bowl to Sigrid. Several more women had moved closer to eavesdrop on their conversation.

"Yes, I slept beside Selik last night," Rain admitted, refusing to explain more.

"Oh, how could you bear to have the beast touch you?" Gunvor exclaimed. "'Tis said he is as berserk in the sleeping furs as he is in battle."

"Berserk?"

"Crazed with lust."

Rain raised an eyebrow doubtfully. He certainly hadn't been overcome with passion for her.

"Just the sight of him turns the stomach," another woman added with a shudder. "How could you abide looking at him? He is so ugly."

"Ugly? Selik?" Rain asked in disbelief. "We must be talking about different men. Selik is brutish and much too prone to killing and war, but ugly? Never! In fact, he's probably the most attractive man I've ever met."

The women stepped away from her slightly, as if she might be deranged.

"The scars, the broken nose, the cruelty in his eyes, his hateful ways. Why, 'tis said he cannot even tolerate children in his presence, that he squashes them like vermin under his feet. Truly, do these things not repulse you?" Gunvor asked incredulously.

Rain tried to picture Selik in her mind. Yes, there were scars, lots of them, and an imperfect nose, but they didn't mar the total man with his fine, classic features, his well-developed, muscular body. And the cruelty in his eyes—it was there, but couldn't these women recognize that it masked a deeper pain? Of course, she could never love a man like Selik. He was too vulgar, too stubborn, too war-like, but neither could she deny his innate beauty.

She started to tell the foolish women just that, but Selik approached, muttering vicious curses, and the females scattered like frightened mice.

"Did you have to scare the women off?"

"Spineless half wits," he grumbled. Leaning over the simmering cauldron, he sniffed deeply, then helped himself to a heaping bowl of the stew. He sat down next to her on a large boulder and wolfed the food down ravenously, ignoring her presence.

His hunger touched her oddly. Although he wore the same stained tunic, Rain noticed that he'd bathed and shaved. His pale, platinum hair shone like spun silver down to his shoulder blades. Scrutinizing him more closely in light of the women's harsh appraisal, Rain noticed many scars, old and new. Especially gruesome was an old scar running from his right eye to his chin, a pale jagged line in his deeply tanned face. And the raised white scar tissue on his forearm spelling out the word *rage*—well, Rain shivered at the thought of what horrifying events had prompted Selik to carve the letters in his own skin. At least, she presumed he had.

"Keep your roving eyes off my flesh, Sleetling."

"What?" Rain jerked to attention, embarrassed to be caught examining him closely. "I was admiring all your battle scars."

"Liar." His eyes impaled hers contemptuously, then turned away in disgust. "Have a caution, wench. I am in no mood to humor your airs today. Go off and leave me alone." He used the fingers of both hands to rub his eyes wearily.

Selik's curt dismissal offended Rain, so she persisted foolishly. "How did you get that scar on your face? Was it in the midst of some silly battle where you slaughtered men right and left? Or did the husband of one of those women with whom you *rutted* come after you? No, let me guess. I'll bet you tripped and fell when—"

"Nay, wench, 'twas none of those." Selik's icy gray eyes held hers coldly, speaking of horrors of which Rain suddenly knew she didn't want to hear. She stood to depart, but Selik shoved her rudely back down to the boulder. "You asked, lackwit. Now you shall stay and hear.

"Your father Thork and I were Jomsviking knights together. When Thork was a child, his brother Eric—Eric Bloodaxe, they call him—pursued him bloodly. He even chopped off the smallest finger of Thork's right hand when he was only five. Eventually, Thork ran off to become a Jomsviking, the only way open for him to escape the ambitions of his ruthless brother."

"Selik, stop. I'm sorry. I didn't mean to bring up these painful memories."

But Selik continued with his punishing explanation. "In the final Jomsviking battle afore your father's death, our enemy Ivar—Ivar the Vicious—cut off the remaining fingers on your father's hand and kicked open the fatal sword wound in his side. And that, sweet lover of peace, was after he chopped off the heads of a dozen of our comrades."

Tears streamed down Rain's cheeks. She didn't want to know these horrid details of her father's or Selik's life. She didn't want to feel there was any justification for the violence of their lifestyles. There was no excuse for fighting, or wars. That was what she'd always believed. She still did. She had to.

Selik's lips curled cynically at the changing emotions he must have seen reflected on her face. "I was luckier than most that day. Ivar tried to pluck out my eyes and succeeded only in gracing me with this memento," he said, touching the long scar.

Rain reached out a hand to touch his forearm in comfort, but he shrugged her away defensively. "Save your pity."

"I'm just trying to understand you and the strange time I've landed in, Selik. I know I appear condemning, but—"

"Spare me your explanations, wench. I care naught what you or any other thinks of me. My head was on the chopping block that day, and I have ne'er feared the face of death since. In truth, I welcome it."

"Your head was on the chopping block?" Rain choked out.

"Yea." A cruel smile thinned his lips mirthlessly. "Wouldst like to hear the tale?"

When Rain stared at him in horror, Selik went on ghoulishly, "I *was* godly handsome in those days, just as your mother said, and vain as a rooster. When it came my turn, I taunted Ivar, asking that my fair hair be held back during the beheading so as not to stain the wondrous strands with my life's blood." He ran his fingers sensuously through his long hair in remembrance.

"Selik, I don't want to hear any more. Stop."

He ignored her pleas. "The crowds who came to watch the execution of the famed Jomsviking knights admired my daring and urged Ivar to grant my wish. He called a noble soldier forth, one of his bravest hersirs, to stand in front of me and hold the twisted coil of my hair forward, baring my neck for the executioner's blade. At the last moment, I jerked back deliberately, and the blade sliced off the hands of Ivar's hersir."

Rain gasped and held a hand over her mouth in horror. She heard the echo of her exclamation from the women behind her who had moved closer to listen to Selik's words.

Selik didn't seem to notice any of them, so lost was he in his horrifying reverie.

"Instead of being angry, the crowd cheered my bravery and demanded that Ivar spare my life and the lives of the remaining Jomsviking knights who awaited execution, your father included." Coming back to the present, Selik lifted his chin proudly and taunted, "Now you know the story of my scar. Art thou happy, Sleetling, that your prickly words drew the blood of my memories?"

"No, Selik, I'm not. Sometimes I speak rashly. You seem to bring that out in me," she said wearily, then touched the word *rage* carved on his muscled forearm. "Is that when you mutilated yourself with this scar?"

A deep rumble, like the bellow of an enraged bear, started in Selik's chest, moved up his throat, and emerged from his mouth as a roar of anger. He jerked upright and grabbed Rain by the upper arms, raising her until her feet dangled off the ground and her eyes were level with his, noses practically touching. She could feel his breath against her lips as he jerked out furiously, "Ne'er, *ne'er* ask about that scar. If you value your life, you foolish spawn of Loki, do not even look at it, for I swear I will wring your neck like the scrawny chicken you are." He shook her until her brain practically rattled. "Dost understand, wench?"

Rain could not speak over her chattering teeth but nodded her numb assent.

"Master, master!"

Selik froze as the shrill greeting penetrated his fury.

"Bloody, stinking hell!" he cursed, dropping Rain carelessly to the ground as he turned to face a gnomelike man scurrying crablike toward them on bowed legs. His gnarled hands and stooped shoulders bespoke an arthritic condition. He could be no more than forty years old, despite his aged appearance.

"Thank the gods, I have finally caught up with ye, master," the trollish man said breathlessly when he reached Selik.

"Ubbi, what the hell are you doing here? Did I not order you to stay in Jorvik?"

You-bee. You-bee Rain rolled the strange-sounding name on her tongue silently.

"But, master, I heard of the battle and thought ye might have need of me."

"I am not your master, Ubbi. Endless times have I told you that afore."

"Yea, master. I mean, yea, m'lord. Oh, ye know my meaning, master," he stumbled out.

Selik groaned and raised his eyes wearily to the skies. "Just what I need—a servant I do not want or need *and* a guardian angel."

Ubbi looked at Rain for the first time, and his eyes widened with surprise. "In truth, master, be she a guardian angel?"

Selik's eyes, no longer angry, but twinkling with weary amusement, caught Rain's. "Yea, she claims her Christian god sent her to save me."

Ubbi's rheumy eyes darted from Rain to Selik, then back to Rain. "From what?" he asked dubiously, apparently figuring a mere woman wouldn't do Selik much good in battle.

"From myself," Selik answered flatly.

But Ubbi surprised them both by nodding sagely and saying, "'Tis about time."

Selik threw both hands in the air, as if he gave up on the two of them. Then he turned to Rain. "Show Ubbi to my tent."

"And where should I put Fury?" Ubbi asked sheepishly.

"*Fury!* You brought Fury here?"

"Yea. Methought you might have need of your horse."

"Fury! That figures. Only you would give your horse such a morbid name," Rain commented.

Selik swept her with a contemptuous, dismissing glance. "Go stick a needle in someone's eye—preferably a Saxon's."

"I did *not* stick a needle in Tykir's eye," she asserted defensively, "but I'd like to stick one in yours. And a few other choice places. Have you ever heard of a vasectomy?" she asked innocently. At his dumbfounded look, Rain explained just what a vasectomy entailed. She was pleased to see Selik's face pale at the idea of needles pricking his precious manhood.

"Needles? Eye?" Ubbi sputtered, pivoting his head back and forth from Rain to Selik as they exchanged insults.

"You stuck them everywhere *but* his eye," Selik accused.

"He's alive, isn't he?"

"Humph! You no doubt waved your bloody angel wings over him."

"You just can't admit that a mere woman is a physician."

"Do not be ridiculous."

"Ridiculous! Ridiculous! Hah! I'll tell you what's ridiculous. It's you and all these other Dark Age warriors," she shrieked, sweeping her arm outward to indicate the battered soldiers flooding the vast fields. "You think that war and the taking of human life solve your problems. That's what's ridiculous."

Ubbi, Sigrid, Gunvor, and all the other spectators who'd gathered nearby gaped at her in stunned disbelief that she would dare to yell at the fierce outlaw knight, but there was a suspicious quirk at the edge of Selik's twitching lips. Criminey! She'd fallen right into one of his traps again, Rain chastised herself disgustedly.

"Oh, I give up," she said, throwing out her hands in resignation. She turned to stomp back to Selik's tent and called out to Selik's sidekick, "Well, don't stand there like a turnip, Ubbi. Are you coming?"

"Me?" a slack-jawed Ubbi squeaked out.

Selik grinned infuriatingly.

"Yes, you," she snarled and grabbed his arm so forcefully that she almost lifted his small body off the ground. "Talk about ridiculous names. Who ever heard of a name like Ubbi?"

"What's wrong with me name?" Ubbi asked weakly, scampering to keep up with her long strides.

"Sounds like a stupid Motown song. *You-bee, doo-bee, doo.*"

Ubbi chortled gleefully at Rain's softly sung words. "Oh,

mistress, thank the Lord fer yer comin' to save me master. 'Tis just what m'lord be needin' to lighten his harsh life."

After Ubbi cared for Selik's horse, Fury, a magnificent black destrier with a temperament mean enough to match his owner's, they went to Selik's tent, where Ubbi stowed his pitifully small bundle of belongings.

Ubbi rolled his eyes mischievously toward the sleeping furs. "Didst find the furs soft enuf fer yer fair skin, milady?"

Rain laughed at Ubbi's transparent curiosity about whether she and his master had slept together. "No, Ubbi, I didn't make love with Selik last night."

Ubbi clapped a gnarled hand in exaggerated dismay to his chest. "Oh, mistress, a thousand pardons. I know ye did not mate with the master."

"You know?"

"Yea, 'twould be a far better mood my lord would be in if he had eased himself 'atween yer thighs," Ubbi said impudently, an impish gleam twinkling in his cloudy eyes.

Rain smiled and shook her head. She liked this crafty fellow.

They walked back companionably to the clearing, where large groups of men were hurriedly gathering their weapons, preparing to depart. The Saxons must be getting closer.

"Where are they going?"

Ubbi shrugged. He nodded toward one grizzly-haired giant wearing what looked like a long piece of plaid fabric thrown over his shoulder. "Constantine and his Scots will go back north, no doubt, along with his nephew Eugenius and his Strathclyde Welsh." The two burly warriors in their primitive splendor were ordering their men into ranks. Constantine's eyes looked red rimmed and despairing. Ubbi told her the Scots king had lost his son, Prince Ceallagh, in the battle the day before.

Then Ubbi pointed out Anlaf Guthfrithsson, the Viking king of Dublin, commander of all the Norsemen in the Brunanburh battle. Awestruck, Rain hadn't realized she was in the midst of such historic personages.

She looked back and saw Selik arguing fiercely with Anlaf.
Ubbi followed her gaze and commented, "As to that noble
cur, 'tis hard to say. Mayhap he will go back to Jorvik and
try to regain his Northumbrian empire, but 'tis more likely
he will scoot off to Dublin with his tail 'atween his legs."
Ubbi spat on the ground at his feet to show his distaste, then
went on, "'Tis said Anlaf has hundreds of ships anchored on
the Humber, awaiting his quick departure. One thing is certain, he will not have enough surviving soldiers to man his
longboats."

Rain scrutinized the tall man with the neatly braided blond
hair. Cruelty etched his craggy features, and Rain shivered
with distaste, sharing Ubbi's disdain for King Anlaf.

"Where will we go?"

"We?" Ubbi asked with an arched eyebrow.

"You, me, Selik. And whichever of Selik's men have survived. Are there any, by the way?"

Ubbi shook his head woefully. "Nay, all his hird of faithful retainers were taken in the Great Battle, but there will be
others to follow. There always are—those who know his true
worth, those brave enough to flaunt Athelstan's wrath. But
pitiful few they will be now." The little man sighed wearily.

"Then where will we go? To Scotland? Or Wales?"

Ubbi shot her a look of disbelief. "Nay, Constantine and
Eugenius welcome my master's mighty hand in battle, but
they will not relish him in their lands now. They slither
home to protect their own backs."

"What do you mean?"

"The Scots and Welsh kings will pledge their traitorous
allegiance to the Saxon ruler now that they have lost the
Great Battle, 'til it suits them otherwise. 'Twon't be the first
time. But Selik is a marked man they cannot risk harboring."

"And how about the Viking king?" Rain asked, pointing
to Anlaf, who still argued with Selik. "Will he welcome
him?"

Ubbi's lips curled sardonically. "Welcome, nay. But he
cannot keep him away. 'Tis certain that is why they bicker

now. He prob'ly tries to convince Selik to take his longship and darken Northumbrian shores no more."

Anlaf finally stomped away from Selik, his face purple with rage. He called angrily to his men to follow him.

Selik's eyes scanned the area, his back straight, his stubborn chin lifted defiantly, undoubtedly knowing the crowd saw him as an outcast even among his own people. His steely eyes found Rain's and locked in silent challenge.

Did he expect her to desert him like all the others? She tipped her chin proudly, matching his gesture, hoping he understood that she supported him, no matter what.

Ubbi reached out his misshapen hand and squeezed hers tightly. "Oh, mistress," he said softly.

Never breaking his visual embrace with her, Selik finally nodded solemnly, indicating his acceptance of her silent pledge of loyalty. Several warriors moved then to his side, as well. Rain's misty eyes caressed Selik, and her heart swelled in her chest with an overwhelming yearning to ease the pain of this lonely man.

Rain wished she could erase the bleakness in Selik's eyes and somehow knew she would have to enter his emotional hell to help pull him out. But what would be her fate then? Could she ever return to her own time? And what scars would she carry forevermore?

CHAPTER FOUR

*W*as it adultery if it was only a dream? . . .

Rain watched with dismay as more and more of the soldiers dismantled their tents, gathered their furs and bedding, and left the secluded camp with brisk efficiency. Some departed with military precision under the leadership of Kings Constantine and Anlaf. Others rushed away individually or in small groups, calling out promises to meet later in the northern lands of the Scots, or Dublin where the Norsemen reigned, or Jorvik, the town Rain knew as York, or the Norse lands.

Within hours, the flat-topped plain was almost deserted.

Ubbi tended the cooking fires abandoned by the women who had fled with their husbands. A dozen scruffy soldiers who had chosen to stay with Selik were clearing up the debris and helping Selik to cover the trails of the departing warriors.

"Why aren't we leaving too?" Rain asked Ubbi.

"The master would ne'er leave Tykir, and 'twill be days afore he is well enuf fer travel."

"Is it safe here?"

"Be ye barmy?" Ubbi asked with a mocking snort. " 'Tis

ne'er safe for me lord when Saxons be about. King Athelstan put a bounty on his head long ago, but now he will no doubt want his eyes and tongue, as well."

"Why?"

"You were at the Great Battle. Did ye not see the Saxon he speared near the end, the one he hoisted on his halberd and stuck in the ground soz the noble thane swung from the pike?"

Rain nodded uneasily. "A Saxon thane?"

He shook his craggy head sadly. "King Athelstan's own cousin, Eadric." He wrung his misshaped hands worriedly. "And even worse, Eadric was cousin to that bastard—excuse me language, m'lady—to that wretched Steven of Gravely, who hates Selik with a passion."

"Oh, my God! Then Selik should leave *now*. I'll stay and take care of Tykir while he recuperates. Even if we're discovered here, the Saxons have no reason to harm me."

Ubbi's rheumy eyes shot her a look of disbelief. "And what do ye think they would do to Tykir? Coddle him with chicken broth and sweet wine? Hah! They would just as soon cut off all his limbs and let him bleed to death."

"Don't tell me there's a bounty on Tykir's head as well."

"Nay, leastways, not yet, but he fought on the wrong side in this battle."

"I still say Selik should leave us here and escape while he can."

"Oh, mistress, ye do not unnerstan'. Even if 'twere not fer Tykir, my lord wud not abandon you here alone. Ye belong to him now."

Rain bristled. "Me? Belong to him? Hardly!"

"Now, mistress, do not be fightin' yer fate. The master captured you in battle, and ye be part of the spoils, so to speak. Methinks he even named you hostage, did he not?"

"He *did not* capture me. In fact, *I* saved *him*. And let's get one thing straight—I am no one's prisoner. Nor do I need the protection of some blasted, bloodthirsty Viking."

"If you say so," Ubbi said doubtfully, "but the master

takes his duties seriously. Leastways, he tries his best ter protect those men and wimmen under his shield, 'specially since Astrid . . ." Ubbi's words trailed off and he glanced guiltily toward Selik across the campsite as if he realized belatedly how much he'd disclosed.

"Astrid? Who's Astrid?"

Ubbi groaned. "I beg you, m'lady, do not mention her name to my lord. Please, if ye value yer life."

Rain frowned in confusion. "Tell me who she is, and I promise not to say a word to Selik." When he balked, she added, "On the other hand, if you don't want to tell me, I can always ask Selik."

Ubbi's face blanched with horror.

Rain's curiosity got the best of her then, and she demanded in a steely voice, *"Who* is Astrid?"

"His wife," Ubbi answered grimly, then darted away before she could ask any more questions.

His wife! Rain's heart skipped a beat, and her shoulders slumped. *His wife!* Why had she not considered the possibility that Selik was married? And why should it matter to her? She was just a visitor to this primitive period in history, a time traveler who would surely return to the future once her mission was accomplished, whatever it might be.

No, it didn't matter to her whether Selik was married or not, Rain told herself resolutely, refusing to listen to her aching heart, which told another story. *His wife!*

Selik walked up to her then, but she forgot her hurt and anger when she noticed his full battle regalia. Alarm rippled through her as she pressed a widespread palm to her chest to still her fast-beating heart.

He didn't wear chain mail, as he had the day before, but he did wear thick leather protective gear. The short-sleeved, open-sided, leather garment protected him from neck to midthigh and was worn over a heavy wool knee-length tunic and tight black leggings. A wide, linked silver belt with a huge center clasp accented his deliciously narrow waist, drawing her eyes to his slim hips. The metal belt must weigh at least ten pounds, she realized, and be worth a fortune. Matching silver armlets outlined the muscles of his upper arms.

He had plaited his long hair into a single braid which hung down his back, like her own darker blond one. He held a conical leather helmet in his hands and shifted impatiently from foot to foot as Ubbi led the saddled Fury toward him.

He was everything violent and dark that the logical, pacifist side of her brain hated in a man. And he was everything sinfully seductive and soulfully magnetic that the hormone-humming, completely illogical side of her brain yearned to have, if only for this interlude in time.

Without thinking, she leaned toward him, yearning to touch his sun-warmed skin, until she noticed the edges of his lips turned up in a knowing grin. She jerked back abruptly.

"Have you changed your mind so soon? Do you now want to . . . make sex?"

"No, I do not." *In a New York minute, sweetheart.*

"Really? You were looking at me like a winter-starved cat suddenly given a bowl of cream."

"You overestimate yourself." *Lapping? Now that presents some interesting possibilities.*

"Mayhap we can discuss this later when I—"

His words were cut off as a handful of his men rode up on horseback and waited for his orders.

"Take care of Tykir and the other injured men whilst I am gone." The silky seduction had disappeared from his voice, replaced with cold command.

She agreed, glancing toward the only "hospital" tent remaining. Then Selik's words sank in, and her eyes shot anxiously back to him. "You're leaving us?"

He nodded. "We must needs hide the mountain trail better. And bring back food if we can find a living animal unwise enough to still linger near this camp. Otherwise, we will all shrink to skin and bones from hunger."

His cool eyes swept her body, as if judging *her* skin and bones, weighing her critically from head to toe and back again, with exaggerated emphasis on her size.

She thought she saw a flicker of appreciation in his eyes, and she blushed. *Good Lord! Thirty years old and he has me as flustered as a fifteen-year-old virgin.*

"Be here when I come back," he ordered in a low, husky voice.

"And where would I go?" she snapped testily, as annoyed with herself as with him for rising so quickly to his seductive bait. "You *will* come back, won't you?"

"Are you missing me already, wench?"

Save him, a voice inside her said once again.

Rain couldn't say for sure if it was her own inner voice speaking or some supernatural being. But she didn't like it.

"Why did you jump?" Selik asked softly as he stepped closer, so close she could smell the leather of his armored vest and his own distinctive masculine scent. His warm breath caressed her face as he leaned even closer and whispered, "Could it be I make you nervous?"

"No. I think God just talked to me," she whispered in awe, "and it surprised me."

"I heard naught." His eyes shot upward to the sky before lowering to regard her skeptically. "Does God talk to you often?"

She shook her head. "No, he never did until I came here to . . ."

". . . to save me," he finished for her, shaking his head ruefully. An almost imperceptible flicker of hope sparked in his eyes, then died. "Why do you persist in this foolish story of yours? I no longer believe in God, and He certainly holds me in disfavor."

"You're a Christian?" she asked in surprise.

"Nay. Oh, I was at one time. Leastways, Archbishop Hrothweard baptized me in the Roman church in Jorvik, like many Norsemen who practice Christianity with one hand and the old religions with the other. But I believe in naught anymore, not even myself. In fact, I am a *nithing.*"

"A *nithing?*" Rain shuddered at the utter self-contempt in his flat voice.

Selik shrugged. "A most offensive person. 'Tis the supreme insult for any man, Viking or Saxon. A person beyond redemption."

Rain shook her head forcefully. "Now that is where you are wrong, Selik. I'm not exactly certain why God sent me here, but I do know one thing for sure. God believes you are redeemable."

For just a second, Rain saw hope flash in his silvery eyes, but the light died out almost immediately to its usual dull gray bleakness. And Rain knew she had her work cut out for her.

"I do not believe in eternity," he said, running the knuckles of his right hand along the edge of her jawline in a light caress, "but I do still cherish the odd moment of pleasure. Now that I see your merit as a healer, mayhap I will keep you at my side for a bit longer. And perchance we will share one of those moments. *Or two.* In truth, it has been a long time since I have felt such . . . urges."

A sweet thrill rushed through Rain at Selik's arrogant words. Anticipation. Imagination. Fantasy. All warred with her usual self-control, and logic won out. "No way am I going to be your momentary pleasure, babe." *Especially with a wife in the background.* "Best you curb your urges."

Selik just laughed, then had the effrontery to pat her on the rump in a just-you-wait-and-see fashion.

Indignant at his familiarity, she tried to slap his vulgar hand away, but he was already beyond her reach. Taking the reins Ubbi handed him, Selik put his left foot in the stirrup and leapt into the saddle with the grace of an athlete.

"Here is Wrath," Ubbi said, handing him an awesome sword, the same one Selik had wielded on the battlefield. "I sharpened it for you."

"Wrath! You name your stupid sword? Criminey! That would be like me naming my scalpel. Actually, I kind of like that idea," she rambled on, trying to understand her turbulent emotions. "Healer would be nice, don't you think?"

Selik ignored her completely. "Thank you, Ubbi, for honing the blade. You are my right hand."

Ubbi beamed as if Selik had handed him the world with those few words of praise, and Rain began to think there might still be a softer side to this fierce Viking.

"Keep my bed furs warm for me, wench," he called down to Rain then, jarring her from any complimentary thoughts she had been harboring toward him. Then he caught her eye and winked wickedly.

Rain said a very vulgar word, one she never used in her own time, but which somehow seemed appropriate now. Apparently, it was an Anglo-Saxon term that had descended through the centuries because Selik's eyes widened in surprise and perfect understanding, and Ubbi exclaimed in shock, "My lady!"

Selik chuckled while he donned his leather helmet. "I will remember that sentiment, Sweetling."

Sweetling!

Rain watched sullenly as Selik rode off, laughing, with his men. Despite her annoyance and the fact that the wretched, teasing warrior had a wife, the sound of his touching endearment, "Sweetling," echoed for a long time in her lonely heart.

For the rest of the day, Rain worked closely with Tykir and the dozen other wounded soldiers left behind. Work details had buried dozens of dead men before the armies had left that morning. They'd carried their wounded with them on sledges and crude slings. It soon became obvious why the Scots and Norsemen had failed to take these last of their disabled warriors with them. None had any hope of survival.

Nevertheless, Rain worked desperately to ease their passing, finally turning to her acupuncture needles as a last resort when the Darvon and aspirin ran out. Three of them died before nightfall. A fourth would not make it to morning.

Darkness had already fallen when Rain left the tent, knowing Tykir would sleep through the night. She had placed several acupuncture needles in strategic places on his body to relieve the pain, and as a precaution had ordered one of

Selik's remaining soldiers to tie Tykir securely to the table so he would not jar them accidentally in his sleep.

When she dropped wearily to the ground near the cooking fire, Ubbi handed her a bowl of the stew that remained from the morning and a hunk of flat manchet bread. They tasted wonderful to Rain, and she had to restrain herself from licking the wooden bowl.

"Do you want more?"

She shook her head. "No, save the rest for Selik and his men when they return." She suddenly realized how long they had been gone and looked worriedly around the campsite. Two other small fires burned brightly where men lay about on sleeping furs, and some soldiers stood guard at strategic spots in the distance. But no Selik.

"Shouldn't Selik be back by now?"

Ubbi shrugged.

What would she do if Selik didn't return? Rain wondered, realizing that, despite his vulgar, violent nature, Selik was her anchor in this bungee jump through time. Without him, she would surely plunge to—what? Death? Limbo? Reincarnation? Of all the choices, not once did Rain consider the possibility that she would return to the future. Somehow, she sensed that she had been sent back in time for a purpose.

To save him.

Rain groaned aloud at the inner voice in her head, still unsure whether it was her own subconscious speaking or something else. *Oh, Lord!*

I hear you.

Rain jerked upright and her eyes darted around the fire where Ubbi still worked busily, banking the coals and cleaning up the utensils.

"I don't think you're funny, Ubbi. Not one bit."

"Huh?"

"Oh, don't give me that innocent look. I know you were pretending to be God, speaking in that deep voice."

"God?" Ubbi said with a gasp. "What did I—uh, God—say to you?"

She stood angrily and glared at him as he gawked at her across the fire, open-mouthed and incredulous. Obviously, he hadn't said a blasted word.

"I must have been mistaken," she muttered as she stomped away from the fire, then turned abruptly and came back. "Where am I supposed to sleep tonight?"

He shrugged. "In my lord's tent, of course."

"Humph! He'd better not get any ideas. In fact, if you see him before I do, tell him to spread his sleeping furs out here by the fire. I have no intention of sharing his bed again."

"But why?" Ubbi asked, apparently stunned that any woman would consider it less than an honor to share Selik's bed.

"I *never* sleep with married men."

Ubbi tilted his head to the side as if trying to understand her foreign words. "Married men? But who . . . Mistress, methinks you misunderstood me words afore."

"Oh, I understood all right, but don't you worry about it. This is my problem, and you can be sure I will straighten it out."

"But you want me ter tell me master to sleep out here on the ground?" he asked with utter amazement, then scoffed, "He would flatten me with his shield fer such a suggestion."

"I'll talk to him about it in the morning," she assured him, "but in the meantime, just tell him"—she waved her hand in the air, searching for the right words—"oh, just say he snores too much and I don't want to be disturbed."

She turned once again, smiling, despite herself, at the small choking sound Ubbi made behind her as she walked to the tent.

A soldier told her about a small spring-fed pond at the far end of the clearing, about a quarter-mile away. She rummaged in Selik's chest until she found a clean tunic of worn green wool, some soap, and linen cloths that would do for towels. A half hour later, despite the chilly air and water, she sat soaking ecstatically in the knee-high water, having soaped and rinsed her hair and body several times and washed her underwear, slacks and blouse. After she dried, she put a few dabs of Passion from a small sample bottle in her carrybag behind her ears and at the base of her throat. It was amazing what a good perfume could do for a woman's self-esteem. And it was a link with the future she somehow needed right now.

When she got back to Selik's tent, he still hadn't returned. She bit her bottom lip worriedly as she laid her wet clothes across his wooden chest. She fussed around the small tent, picking up articles, stacking others, hoping her outlaw Viking would return.

Finally, she yawned widely and decided it was foolish to wait any longer. She removed Selik's warm tunic and folded it carefully near the bed furs, donning her wispy bra and briefs, which had already dried. Sliding sensuously between the furs, she fell fast asleep within seconds.

As she had the night before, she slept deeply. No primitive warriors waged violent battles in her dreams, but her sleep soon turned troubled just the same.

Like a Michael Jackson video in which the faces blended creatively from one identity to another, the hero of Rain's dreams alternately had the faces of Brad Pitt, George Clooney, and Selik. Mostly, Selik's image kept recurring, but it was a Selik she had yet to see.

No scars or broken nose marred the purity of his facial features. Gone were the lines that pain and rage had etched mercilessly at the corners of his sensuously full mouth and silver-flecked eyes. This was the godly handsome Viking her mother had described before the tragedies of his life had transformed him.

In her dream, the Brad/George/Selik man knelt on the dirt floor at the side of the fur pallet, wearing nothing more than a primitive loin cloth. He leaned over her, whispering soft words, and she was strangely unable to move, her arms immobilized at her sides. In slow motion, he bent and his long blond hair, like a veil of gossamer cobwebs, brushed across her bare arm. She shivered with the electric shock of just that barest of caresses.

"So beautiful," he whispered as the calloused fingers of his strong hands skimmed over her arms, from the wrists to the shoulders.

All the faces and bodies blended together in that instant and became one—her outlaw Viking.

Rain made a small purring sound, which drew a warm smile of approval from her lover. She did feel beautiful then, probably for the first time in her life. Not too tall or big-boned or unfeminine. Just perfect. She could see appreciation, and so much more, in Selik's smoldering eyes when they locked with hers for one breathless heartbeat. The earth tilted for her then and seemed to stand still.

His fingertips brushed the delicate edge of her collarbone, ever so gently, then moved up to trace the outline of her parted lips. She yearned to lean up and kiss the firm, sensual lips of the ethereal, constantly shifting being above her, but she could not move. Only feel.

He drew his hand away slightly and Rain whimpered, "Please. Don't leave me."

His gray eyes filled with tenderness, and in a voice that seemed to come from far off, he whispered softly, "Never. 'Til the end of time, my love."

The skin of her dream lover shone with pale gold undertones in the shimmering candlelight. Muscles rippled across his powerful shoulders and chest as he moved his hands to explore her taut body. And, oh, dear Lord, blood rushed to every spot he touched with feathery strokes, igniting small fires of longing in their wake.

His hands slid from her face, down her neck, through the valley between her breasts in the lacy, flesh-colored bra, searing a path down to her abdomen. The open palms of his big hand caressed the flat planes of her belly, drawing invisible circular patterns of spiraling pleasure.

Then he backtracked upward, ever so slowly, and lightly touched her hardening nipples, bringing them to crested peaks of such intense pleasure that she cried aloud.

"Shhh, Sweetling. Slowly. Slowly."

But Rain was beyond rational thought, beyond putting a brake on her racing arousal, beyond everything she had ever experienced or thought possible in feminine response. With a few whispery caresses, this man—this dream Viking, this outlaw warrior—had reduced her to a writhing, whimpering mass of flesh desperate for their joining.

She looked down and saw his erection through the loin cloth. And his eagerness for her excited Rain even more. She ached to touch him, but her arms remained locked at her sides in her dream state.

As if sensing that she could not take much more, Selik skimmed the smooth planes from her breasts to the vee between her thighs. Placing the heel of his palm against the silk brief, with his long fingers between her legs, he pressed once, then again, and again, in rhythm, until her body exploded in a million shattering explosions of the purest, most intense climax she had ever experienced.

When her breathing finally calmed, Rain confessed in a whisper of awe to the man whose face no longer shifted but was Selik, only Selik, "I have been waiting for you all my life. Now I know why I was sent here."

Selik's eyes suddenly filled with a fierce longing. "I never expected to see you again, Astrid."

At first, Rain's mind refused to register the significance of Selik's words. But then, through the roaring in her ears, she heard one single word, repeated over and over, echoing through her passion-sluggish brain, "Astrid! Astrid! Astrid!"

His wife.

Selik stood and dropped his loin cloth, supremely confident of his masculinity. He was preparing to join her in the bed furs, to make love to her. No, not her, Rain realized—*his wife.*

The shimmering glaze in his cloudy gray eyes caught her attention, and she recognized the disorientation, almost like yesterday when she had seen him in the battlefield after his berserk bout of violence.

Oh, no! Rain came instantly awake and quickly realized that this was no dream.

Her eyes skimmed the tent area and saw the reason for his strange behavior. His bloody tunic and sword lay where he had dropped them on the ground, still wet with the life fluid of those he had undoubtedly killed that day. It was bloodlust that drove him to her, not lust for her body. And certainly not love. That was apparently reserved for the wife who held his heart.

She had surrendered completely to Selik's masterful seduction, yielding all her defenses as she never had before, but he didn't want her. He had thought she was his wife. Her throat ached with defeat, and she could not speak over her acute sense of loss.

Abruptly, Rain stood and backed away from Selik. Her face flamed hotly with shame over her easy capitulation. Humiliatingly aware of Selik's scrutiny, she knew the instant that violence and rage replaced his smoldering arousal.

"Is this the kind of game you played with those other men you mentioned yestereve—those of the bad ruttings? Do you turn hot, then cold, with all your men? Or just me? Are you one of those women who enjoy teasing men?"

"No," she denied, finally finding her voice. "I was sleeping . . . dreaming. You took advantage of me."

He snorted rudely, pulling on a pair of loose leggings, and raised an eyebrow mockingly. "Lady, your woman heat practically singed the fine hairs all over my body."

Rain raised her chin defiantly, never one to fabricate or hide behind false modesty. "You're right. I did want you. For one moment of insanity. Until I remembered."

"Remembered what?"

"That you're married, you cheating bastard," she snapped, having reached her breaking point. "That you have a wife, Astrid, who's probably sitting at home somewhere surrounded by a bunch of kids. That you didn't want to make love with me. You thought I was your wife."

Rain swiped at the tears that smarted her eyes and turned away, not wanting Selik to witness her further humiliation. "Go away. Just leave me alone."

A long silence followed, during which Rain heard no rustling of cloth which would indicate that Selik had left the tent. Finally, she turned slightly to see what he was doing.

He stood in the same spot as before, just staring at her in horror. "How do you know about Astrid?"

There is passion, and then there is PASSION . . .

Selik was confused and disoriented. He had been gone all day. So much blood. And killing. Captives. Screaming. His brain buzzed with the horror of it all, the violence with which he was still not comfortable, even after all these years.

He tunneled the fingers of both hands through his hair and pulled, hard, to clear his head.

The tall blonde woman stood before him like a majestic goddess, her golden hair in wild disarray, flowing down her back, over her shoulders, caressing the mounds of her flesh-colored undergarment. And the matching wisp of material that barely concealed her womanhood clearly delineated the gentle curve of her narrow waist and hips and drew the eye to legs that were exceedingly long and comely.

This was not Astrid, his petite wife with her fine bones and dainty, shy ways. No, Astrid had died, and this woman, this messenger from the gods, or so she said, was statuesque, hard-muscled, willful—a woman to stand at a man's side, not behind his shield. She was magnificent.

"Nay, you are not Astrid," he said, realizing too late that he had spoken the words aloud.

The hurt which had clouded her beautiful honey eyes turned instantly to outrage. Angrily, she reached down for a tunic of his which lay near her feet, giving him a better view of her enticing breasts as they hung suspended in their lacy cups for a brief moment before she straightened. And he felt his manhood grow harder.

"Don't look at me like that, you horny toad."

His mouth snapped shut, and she jerkily pulled the tunic over her head. Without a belt, the short-sleeved wool garment hung to her elbows and down to midcalf. For some odd reason, he liked the idea of her wearing his tunic. Could she smell his scent in the fabric? Did she like the notion of wearing something which had touched his skin as well?

Thor's Blood! Where do these notions come from? I care naught for this strange wench, or any other.

"I see you've been out raping and pillaging again," she snarled, pointing to his bloody sword and garments on the ground near the tent entrance.

"No raping." He grinned mockingly.

"And you think that excuses your violence? You damned warmonger! You murderer! You—"

"How dare you condemn me? I have just cause to kill. I do naught that has not been done over and over to my people."

"Oh, how I hate war and fighting and men who perpetuate the principle of might makes right!"

Selik could not fail to see the tears misting her luminous eyes, even though she blinked repeatedly, trying to hide them from his scrutiny, as if weeping in a woman was a sign of weakness. What a strange wench!

"Go to sleep. Your shrewish tongue makes my head ache," he said finally. It had been a long day, and his head did, in fact, feel like a hammer pounded inside it. A death knell, no doubt, he thought ruefully. For him, or those he had killed that day? He wiped his hand across his brow. *Thor's hammer! The wench is getting to me with her waspish talk.*

"I'm not sleeping in the same bed with you," she declared vehemently, raising her chin in defiance. "Just forget it, buster, if you think you're going to pick up where you left off."

"What makes you think I want you?" he said in a steely voice. Her willfulness was no longer amusing.

"Go to hell. Better yet, go to your wife, you—you adulterer."

The wench pushed him too far. He did not like talking about his wife. "I asked you afore, who told you about Astrid?"

"You did."

He raised an eyebrow in disbelief.

Her face flushed a becoming pink. "You said her name when—when—oh, you know very well when." The pink of her cheeks now darkened to a deep rose.

"But I never mentioned she was . . . my wife."

"Oh, what difference does it make? Ubbi told me."

Selik stiffened with anger. "He had no right," he said in an icy voice that promised retribution.

Realizing that she might have brought his ire down on Ubbi, she immediately added, "It wasn't his fault. I kind of blackmailed him into telling me. And don't get on your high horse with me—or Ubbi. You're the one cheating on your wife."

"I have never cheated on my wife."

"Hah! You have a weird definition of cheating then. I call what you did with me cheating, and I definitely call what you intended to do cheating. Where do you draw the line, mister?"

"Right now I draw the line with your shrewish tongue," he said, tired of her foolhardy reminders of his beloved wife. "Lie down in the bed furs. Now."

Once again, she foolishly defied him. Even as he moved closer, she backed away, around the edge of the small tent. He grinned ferally, stalking her like the helpless, trapped animal she was. When she was near the tent entrance, about to jump through, he pounced, grabbing her by the waist and lifting her easily into his arms.

For a moment, she did not struggle as her mouth dropped open in amazement. "You picked me up."

"How wise of you to notice."

"But I'm too big. No one has ever picked me up."

"Look again, Sweetling. Your feet are tickling my thighs."

She fought against him then, kicking, scratching, pushing, to no avail. With one arm under her long legs, he pulled her against his body in an iron clasp. The other arm was wrapped around her shoulders, pinning her against his chest with her face firmly tucked in his neck. He inhaled sharply at the seductive floral scent that emanated from her neck, the same odor he had noticed the day before when he had chased her through the forest.

With three long strides, he walked to the bed furs, dropped down lithely without releasing her, then forced her to lie down with her back to him. He covered them both with the bed furs.

With a grunt, he threw one leg over both of hers. Forcing her head to rest in the cradle of his left arm, he wrapped his right arm heavily over her chest.

When she finally stopped struggling after calling him an odd name, "Jerk!", which he suspected was not a compliment!, he began to savor the sweetness of just holding a warm woman in his arms once again.

"What is that scent?" he whispered, nuzzling her neck.

"Probably your body odor," she snapped.

He chuckled. "Nay, 'tis a sweet odor. Like flowers. 'Tis especially strong right here." He ran the tip of his tongue along the sensitive, pulse-beating spot at the base of her neck.

She inhaled sharply, and Selik smiled against her neck, recognizing her involuntary sensual response. How could this woman have said that she had no particular liking for mating with men when she responded so quickly to a man's touch?

"Passion."

"What?"

"It's Passion, you fool."

"Aah, now I understand. Some women exude a musk of passion when their bodies make ready for the mating. 'Tis just that I have never heard of it being a floral scent."

"Oh, you dolt! You really are an egotist. Passion is the name of my perfume."

For a moment, Selik didn't understand. Then he laughed. "Truly, you are amazing. You mock me for naming my sword, and you give a name to your perfume."

Rain elbowed him in the ribs and burrowed into the bed furs, yawning widely. "All perfumes have names in my ti— country. It's not the same thing as naming a gun or a bomb— or a stupid sword," she explained, yawning.

"Stop squirming so much." He smiled, knowing she would be outraged at the wonderful things she was doing to his hardened manhood. "And I will try not to bother you with my snoring. That is what you told Ubbi, is it not?"

"Ubbi talks too much."

"Yea, that he does."

When she was quiet for a long time, Selik said softly, "Rain?"

"Hmmm?"

"Are you awake?"

"Barely."

"Astrid is dead."

At first, her body just lay stiff and silent. He was not sure she had even heard him. In truth, he did not know why he had felt the need to tell her the truth, to redeem himself in her eyes.

Finally, she turned in his arms and looked up at him through the flickering candlelight. She seemed to be searching his face for answers he could not give.

"Oh, Selik," she whispered in a voice so soft he barely heard her. Then she laid her face against his chest and wrapped her arms around him. "Oh, Selik."

For the first time in twelve years, he felt tears mist his eyes, and he drifted off to sleep, oddly comforted.

CHAPTER FIVE

⊛

N *ot only was she an angel, but now she was a rosary*
bead, too . . .

Any soft feelings Rain may have been entertaining toward Selik after his disclosure that his wife was dead van-
ished the second she emerged from his tent the next morning.
Fifteen captives sat shivering on the ground near the large
cooking fire, hands and feet bound, each connected to the
other by one long lead rope, like beads on a necklace.

Several of Selik's retainers stood guard nearby with lethal swords at the ready. Not that any of the captives looked
capable of putting up a fight. They were filthy, underdressed
for the cool autumn morning, bruised, and even wounded.
No wonder blood had stained Selik's sword and clothing last
night. Apparently, food was not the only thing he'd been
hunting.

And—oh, my God—there were three women bound in
the rope chain as well.

I'll kill him. I swear, I have never had a violent thought
in my life, but I will kill that damn Viking for this.

Rain scanned the entire campsite, but there was no sign
of Selik or the soldiers he had taken with him yesterday on

his "hunting" expedition. Rain's lips curled with contempt, and she clenched her fists angrily at her sides.

"Ubbi, where is your master?" Rain demanded to know as she stormed up to the faithful servant, who was stirring the most ungodly smelling concoction over the cooking fire. Whatever it was smelled as if it had burned on the bottom of the cauldron, and a great deal of fat floated on the top. *Great! Roadkill fricasse.*

Ubbi looked up and asked pleasantly, "Did ye sleep well yestereve, my lady?"

Rain growled with impatience at his failure to answer her question.

"He went back to the battlefield," he disclosed reluctantly.

That was not the answer Rain had expected. "Why?"

"To bury his dead."

Rain exhaled loudly with exasperation. "Is he totally, off-the-wall insane? His men are dead. There's nothing he can do for them now."

Ubbi shrugged. "The master blames himself fer takin' men into battle when he saw no ravens aforehand."

Rain forced herself to remain calm. "Ubbi, what are you talking about?"

"Well, 'tis a well-known fact that when ravens be about, it portends a Norse victory. And there was not a raven to be seen the entire day afore or during the Great Battle." He puffed out his chest, as if imparting some great wisdom.

Rain clucked scornfully. "What a bunch of superstitious nonsense!"

"'Tis the truth," he insisted stubbornly.

"Never mind about that. How could you let Selik return to the battlefield? Aren't you worried about him? The Saxons surely still guard that site. He could be killed." Rain wasn't sure why she even cared at this point. After all, she had certainly been looking for him with a killing instinct herself a moment ago.

"'Tis dishonorable fer a Norseman to let the vultures feast on the entrails of his fallen comrades," he asserted.

"And it's honorable to take prisoners? And mistreat them so horribly?" Rain snarled, waving a hand at the nearby captives, who stared dumbly at her across the fire.

Ubbi's cloudy eyes looked up at her in surprise. "'Tis no dishonor to take slaves after a battle. The Saxons, for a certainty, took their fair share of Scots and Norsemen after the Great Battle. You can be sure of that."

"But what will he do with them?"

Ubbi hunched his lumpy shoulders. "Mayhap they might be worth some ransom to the Saxons, 'though I misdoubt that. They be a sorry lot."

Rain threw up her hands in disgust. "Oh, just give me your knife so I can release the captives myself."

Ubbi backed away, holding out of her reach the sharp blade he had been using to cut up what appeared to be several skinned rabbits. "Nay, I cannot."

One red-haired guard—a huge, barrel-chested man wearing a leather tunic and a scruffy fur mantle—started toward her menacingly.

"What is your name?" she demanded to know with more self-confidence than she felt.

"Gorm," he snarled, towering over her ominously, a very sharp sword in one hand. The fetid odor of unwashed flesh and bad breath assailed Rain, but she refused to back down.

"Release those people at once."

The bearish giant smirked. "Not bloody likely."

"I tell you, Worm—"

"Not worm, Gorm," he corrected in an icy voice and moved one step closer, fingering the blade in his hand.

"Yes, well, Gorm, I want those captives released. And I want it done right now."

He chuckled derisively and gave her a rude shove. "Get back to yer master's tent and keep his bed furs warm fer him. Ye be little more than a slave yerself. 'Tis only yer talents in the bed sport that keep you from the same lot as this bunch."

Rain looked to Ubbi for assistance. "Tell this lout that I am not a slave."

To her chagrin, Ubbi ducked his head guiltily and muttered, "Well, ye be more like a hostage than a slave."

"Ubbi! I thought you were my friend."

His eyes widened as if wondering where she ever got that idea. After all, he had only met her yesterday.

"Slave or hostage, it matters not to me," Gorm declared with contempt, giving her another shove, this time harder. "I may just plow yer skinny arse myself."

"You wouldn't dare."

"Would I not? Best ye stay out of me way or ye will find out. Leastways, go to the master's tent, or I will bind ye with the other captives 'til our lord returns."

"That won't be necessary," Rain countered defiantly. "I'll do it myself."

Rain walked proudly over to the line of prisoners and sat down at the end, tying the end of the rope about her ankles in a symbolic knot of captivity. Ubbi gasped and Gorm's mouth dropped open, revealing one missing front tooth. Rain couldn't help herself from feeling noble; this was like the time she and her fellow pacifists had tied themselves to the White House fence to protest increased military spending.

"Gawd! Be ye a bloomin' halfwit?" The heavyset woman next to her moved as far away from her as the rope would allow.

"No, I'm a physician and—" The yellowish tone of the woman's skin caught her attention then, and she asked with concern, "How long have you been feeling ill? I may be able to help you." Rain knew the skin tone could be indicative of something as serious as a tumor or liver disease, or just a Vitamin K deficiency, easily correctable.

The woman's eyes widened in shock. With a shriek, she tried to stand. "Git me away from her. A woman healer! Oh, Lord, she mus' be a witch or a sorceress. Help! She prob'ly has the evil eye."

Gorm stomped over and cuffed the woman across the head, causing her to drop weakly to the ground, where she moaned loudly.

Rain started to protest, but he wagged a filthy finger in her face. "Behave yerself, wench. Ye may pleasure the master 'til his cock falls off, but if ye do not shut yer teeth, I will truss you over the cookfire like the witch this hag accuses you of bein'."

Ubbi was staring at her, wide-eyed with dismay. "Mistress, come back to the tent. The master will not like this."

"No. If I'm a captive, I don't want to be treated any differently than all the rest."

Ubbi rolled his eyes skyward.

For about a half hour, Rain sat stiffly in sullen silence on the cold ground, shivering every time the wind blew. Even with Selik's wool tunic thrown over her slacks and silk blouse, she began to feel a chill.

Finally, bored, her eyes began to roam among her fellow prisoners. She inhaled sharply when they came to one young Saxon man, who was slumped practically unconscious against the woman next to him. Blood oozed from a deep shoulder wound where his leather armor had been torn away.

"Ubbi, come and help this man," she cried out in alarm. "His wound needs to be treated."

Ubbi ignored her pointedly, continuing to saw away at the flesh of the dead rabbits. His red face betrayed the fact that he heard her and chose not to reply.

"Gorm, release that man from the rope and take him to the hospital tent for treatment."

Gorm, the insolent bastard, flashed an ugly smile her way and spat on the ground near her feet.

Rain bit her bottom lip worriedly, unable to ignore a patient who needed her help so desperately. Finally, she stood, jarring the woman next to her, who still cowered in fear, and complained, "Well, if no one else is going to help him, I will." She unbound the ropes at her ankles and went to the tent to retrieve her meager medical supplies.

Ubbi barely stifled a chuckle of amusement at her strange interpretation of captivity. She glared at him until he ducked his head, but not before he shook it in wonder at her antics.

Rain loosened the ropes on the young man, who looked like he was barely out of his teens, and helped him walk to the tent. Despite the protests of the hospital guard, she soon had the sword wound cleaned and stitched. It was not as bad as she had originally thought.

She tried to calm her patient by talking while she stitched the four-inch cut. "What's your name?"

"Edwin."

"Where are you from, Edwin?"

"Winchester," he replied warily.

"Did you fight in the battle for King Athelstan?"

He nodded slowly, as if not sure if he could trust her.

"Why didn't you return to Wessex with the king and his troops?"

" 'Cause I was a bloody halfwit," he grumbled. "I went back to the camp fer my woman, and she did not want ter travel in the dark. The dark! Hah! We got a heap more than dark to fear now."

"I'm sure everything will be all right once Selik returns," she assured him.

"Are ye The Outlaw's wench?" he asked, edging away from her a bit.

"No, I helped him escape from the battlefield and—"

"Ye helped the beast escape?"

Rain stiffened. "Don't call Selik a beast. I don't like it."

The man's upper lip curled contemptuously.

"I mean it, Edwin. He is no more a beast than you or any other man."

Edwin's eyes narrowed speculatively as he studied her while she knotted the thread and covered his stitches with a clean linen bandage. "Have you ever seen a man after he's been scalped by a heathen Viking? Only a beast would scalp a man. And I warrant a man as vicious as The Outlaw would be no different than any other bloody Norseman."

At first, Rain couldn't comprehend Edwin's meaning. Then she gasped and tears welled in her eyes. "You're lying. Selik would never do such a barbaric thing."

"Am I?" Fury turned Edwin's filthy face into an ugly mask. "Know this, my lady, *the beast* had best kill me, and soon, 'cause I would rather die than be a slave to him."

The guard, already pushed past the limits of his tolerance, wouldn't let the prisoner stay in the tent with the other injured men. In a daze, Rain led him back to his place in the rope chain. When she was about to retie him at Gorm's command, Edwin grabbed her and twisted her body so that her arms were pulled behind her back and the fingers of his right hand held her throat in a strangle hold.

"Do not move, wench," he warned, pinching her windpipe until her knees collapsed for lack of air. "I would not hesitate to kill you in a trice, but methinks yer lord holds ye in favor. Mayhap he would release me in exchange fer yer life."

"And what about your woman?" she asked, glancing down at the young woman who was still bound near her feet, gazing up at her and Edwin with horror and fear.

"Blanche kin manage on her own. She be a crafty wench with a talent fer the bed sport. No doubt she will soon have another protector," he said dismissively, ignoring Blanche's cry of protest.

"And you call Selik a beast?"

Edwin squeezed again, and Rain lost consciousness for a second. A moment later, she heard a sharp cry behind her, and Edwin released his hold on her neck. But she had only a moment to wonder why when he fell forward against her back, knocking her onto the ground. When Rain finally shoved him off her and looked down, she saw a battle-ax imbedded in the back of Edwin's head. Blood gushed from the wound, and it was obvious even before she checked his pulse that he had died immediately.

She cried out, "Oh, my God! I've landed in a Dark Age Bedlam."

Looking behind her to see who had thrown the ax, she was surprised to see Ubbi standing with his legs spread in a battle stance and hands on his hips. The gentle little troll had been transformed into a fierce warrior. Fury clouded the little man's face, but he inquired gently, "Mistress, be ye hurt?"

She shook her head, confused and disoriented by all that had happened in just a few short moments. Blood had been shed at her expense, and she needed to come to terms with that horrendous thought.

"'Tis her own damn fault," Gorm told Ubbi angrily. "She never should have released the bastard. All Saxons be the same—deceitful to the core."

"What did you expect him to do, you brute?" Rain lashed out. "He was desperate, and I was his only chance to escape."

Gorm and Ubbi both looked at her as if she was crazy. "He would have killed you," they both said at the same time.

"That's no excuse," Rain countered, the words sounding lame even to her.

"Well, thank the gods, ye be safe," Ubbi said. "Why don't ye go back to the tent now and rest from yer ordeal?"

Rain looked at the prisoners staring at her in awe and shook her head. "No, I can't."

To Ubbi's chagrin, she sat back down and retied her bounds loosely at the ankles. Gorm mumbled, "Bloody bitch," while he dragged Edwin's body off to the trees, ordering some men to bury him "afore the stink of Saxon blood ruins me appetite."

That reminded Rain that she hadn't eaten since the day before. She looked at the motley group sharing her rope and realized that they probably hadn't eaten for a much longer time.

"You have to feed these people," she shouted to Ubbi, who had returned to the cookfire. He stood whistling blithely while he performed his domestic chores as if he hadn't just killed a man.

Without looking up, he called back to her, "The master left no instructions fer feedin' his captives."

"That's ridiculous. What if he doesn't come back?" Rain's heart sank at the reminder of her earlier worries about Selik. She had a lot of complaints for him and many questions that needed answers, but she couldn't imagine living without him. How unbelievable, she thought, tilting her head in wonder, that she would feel so intensely about a man she had just met. Forcing herself to concentrate on the present, she added, "I mean, what if he doesn't come back until tonight?"

Ubbi shrugged disinterestedly.

Rain shook her head in disgust at her predicament, then mumbled an obscenity under her breath as she once again untied her bounds and stomped over to the cookfire.

Ubbi's eyebrows lifted with amusement as he commented dryly. "Is that how they imprison people in yer lands? The captive gits ter tie and untie his own knots whenever the whim hits 'im?"

"Shut up, you fool."

He chuckled and continued sawing away at the bony rabbits, which he then threw into a pile at his feet.

"Is this all you have?" she asked, her nose curling with disgust as she leaned over the cauldron.

"Yea," he answered sheepishly. "I am not too good at cooking, but there be no one else to take on the chore. Perchance could ye—"

"No way! I do not cook."

"Well, that is it then," Ubbi said, pointing to the smelly pot of mush. "It sort of burned on the bottom when the fire got too hot."

"It sort of smells like hell."

He smiled. "Do ye perchance know how hell smells, co-min' as ye do from heaven?"

Rain made a vulgar sound of disgust.

"Just askin'. No need to be rude. Mayhap ye could give this gruel to the prisoners so I kin clean the pot fer the dinner meal." He pointed to the pile of rabbit meat and bones at his feet.

Having no choice, Rain doled the contents of the pot into two wooden bowls and carried them back and forth to the captives who were forced to hold the bowls in their bound hands and drink from them. Not one of them complained about the ungodly mess, being too hungry to care and probably wondering if it might be their last meal.

When she finished, Rain helped Ubbi scour the cauldron near the pond with coarse sand. Then she returned to the captives and approached Blanche, the woman who had been with Edwin.

"Can you cook?" she asked gently, sensitive to the young woman's bereavement. But Blanche didn't seem all that concerned about her dead lover when she sensed the prospect of a reprieve from her imprisonment.

"Yea, I can, mistress," she replied readily. "And rabbit is my specialty. If you let me gather some herbs in those trees, under guard, of course, I can make up a tasty stock pot that would please even a king."

Rain doubted that heartily, but she preferred anything over Ubbi's cooking. It took almost no convincing for Ubbi to agree to give Blanche a chance.

Rain was pleasantly surprised several hours later to find that Blanche hadn't lied. The rabbit stew was thick and savory with wild onions and carrots and mushrooms, not to mention a few spices she did not recognize. Blanche preened, knowing that, at least for the time being, her hide was safe.

Gorm's eyes gleamed with lascivious interest as Blanche bent over the cookfire. Rain shot him a look that said clearly, "Don't you dare." He smirked and countered with a contemptuous leer that challenged silently, "Try and stop me."

War lust and sex lust . . . a powerful combination . . .

Selik returned to camp late that night, weary in body and soul. Dodging the Saxon guards who patrolled the battlefield had taken an alertness that Selik and his exhausted comrades did not have, being still unrested since the battle.

They had buried as many of their friends or acquaintances as they could locate—a horrid enough chore under the best of circumstances; a torment of the mind when they had to fight the flesh-gorged vultures for their prey. The eyes of the dead went first—a particular delicacy for the beastly birds, no doubt—and Selik and his brave men stopped to vomit numerous times in the face of so many eyeless bodies. Not to mention the half-devoured flesh. Or the stench. Oh, gods, the stench! The whole time, wolves and other predators circled the field, waiting for their departure.

So Selik was not in the best of moods when he entered his tent, removed his cross-gartered leather shoes and armor, then dropped to his bed furs without removing his tunic. It took him only a moment to realize that the strange wench who claimed to be his "guardian angel" had flown the coop.

"Ubbi!"

The little man opened the flap of his tent as soon as his little legs could carry him from across the campsite, where he had placed his bed furs.

"You called, master?"

Selik said a very foul word, and Ubbi cringed.

"Where is she?"

"Who?" Ubbi shifted uncomfortably from foot to foot and would not meet his questioning gaze.

"You know damn well who."

"With the prisoners, m'lord. But 'twas not my doin'. Nor Gorm's," he added quickly.

Selik exhaled loudly and forced himself not to shake his faithful servant. Carefully, he spaced each word as he spoke. "Why is she with the prisoners?"

"She sez she be a pacifist—"

"Pacifist?"

"Yea, pacifists are against all fightin', even—"

"Pacifist be damned!"

Ubbi slanted him a condemning look for the interruption and went on. "She sez she be a pacifist, and if me or Gorm would not release the captives, then she would become a captive, too."

"She *is* a captive."

Ubbi raised his chin in challenge. "Nay, she is a hostage. I told her so. And there is a difference, m'lord."

"Yea, and a valuable hostage she is with her medical

skills. I want her back in this tent, where I can guard her so she cannot escape."

Ubbi raised an eyebrow in disbelief at his motives.

"I have not bedded the wench," he said, oddly defensive.

"Have I said ye did?" Ubbi replied quickly, raising both hands in the air defensively.

"Well, I know what you were thinking."

"Hah! Does God speak to you as well? You are becoming as bad as the wench," Ubbi said with a knowing grin, which annoyed Selik even more.

"Bring the wench here," he snarled.

Ubbi backed away from him. "Nay, not me, master. She already threatened to clout me today. Best ye gather her yerself."

Scowling, Selik headed toward the bound captives. "Why did she threaten you with bodily harm if she is such a pacifist?"

" 'Cause I killed one of the prisoners, that surly lad who was making all the threats yestereve."

Selik stopped and looked at his servant, who rarely entered the battle fray. He knew Ubbi must have had good reason to kill a valuable slave. "Why?"

"He was choking the mistress."

"Rain?" Cold terror swept over Selik at Ubbi's casually spoken words. Why would he feel bereft at the prospect of losing a mere wench he had met just the day before?

Ubbi nodded. "And best ye be prepared fer the tongue-lashin' of yer life. She is sore angry with you."

"Well, I am in no mood to hear her shrewish carping on the issue of captives tonight. Mayhap I should just stuff a rag in her waspish mouth and ease myself on her body 'til she is too tired to complain anymore."

Ubbi made a clucking, skeptical sound that questioned the wisdom of such a plan.

A full moon and the campfire provided enough light for Selik to see the prisoners, who lay on the ground, most of them sleeping. A few stared up at him through wide, frightened eyes as he passed. He would have to find some warmer clothing for the mangy lot in the morn or they would never make the arduous trip to Jorvik. And food—his men would have to find more game to fatten their scrawny frames, lest they bring naught from the slave traders.

Selik finally found his troublesome wench at the end of the line, curled into a ball, shivering with the cold even in her sleep. He noticed that she had purloined one of his wool tunics, not that it was any protection against the autumn winds. Instead of being angered by her thievery, he felt an odd satisfaction in knowing his garment caressed her flesh, like a poor substitute for his arms.

"Bloody hell!" he muttered aloud. "The wench is turning me as senseless as an untried boy yearning for his first mating."

Rain's eyes opened slowly as Selik's voice seeped into her consciousness. Still sleep-disoriented, she didn't protest, at first, when he leaned down and untied the loose knots at her ankles.

"God's bones! Some captive you make when you can slip in and out of your bindings so easily."

"It's symbolic," she said sleepily, then yawned widely, forgetting to cover her mouth daintily. But then she noticed his smile and frowned, trying to shove him away.

"Symbolic of what?" he asked, standing up and watching as she sat and rolled the kinks out of her shoulders. No doubt she had developed an ache or two sleeping on the hard ground. A well-deserved punishment for being so stubborn, he decided.

"My protest of your barbaric act." Her face suddenly became hard as she seemed to come fully awake.

He raised an eyebrow in question and folded his arms across his chest. Even his tough flesh was beginning to feel the cold. "What barbaric act?"

"The taking of slaves," she hissed. "How could you? As

much as I hate violence, I understand how some people can justify it as self-defense. But taking captives when the heat of battle is over—well, it's uncivilized."

"I do not have to defend myself to you or any other person. And you do not understand civilization, shrew, if you think Norsemen are the only ones who consider captives part of the spoils of war. 'Tis universal. I know of no country or any people who condemn the practice."

"But what do you know in your heart?"

Her question stunned Selik. There should have been an easy answer, but he could not form the words to defend himself.

A rustling noise drew his attention then, and Selik noticed that their conversation had awakened all the prisoners, who listened intently to what must seem a strange conversation. With a grunt of disgust, he leaned down and picked up the troublesome wench.

Rain exhaled sharply in surprise at his quick movement, but before she could protest, he tucked her face into his neck, wrapped a steely arm around her now flailing legs, pressing them against his hip, and pinned both arms against her body by the enclosure of his right arm.

Selik knew Rain considered herself too big to be picked up by any man, and he delighted in perpetuating her misconception. He pretended to trip and almost fall. She stopped struggling immediately.

"Mayhap, if you would not eat so much, you might stop growing."

"Argh! Put me down."

"Nay, I find the exercise good for me after a long day of riding. Much like carrying my horse."

She stilled suddenly, then asked in a small voice, "Selik, where is your horse?"

Surprised by her question, he answered hesitantly, "'Tis picketed with the other horses near the pond. Why?"

"Would you take me to see Fury? Please. It's important to me."

Selik shrugged. He saw no harm in letting her look at the animal. Besides, he could use a quick bath in the pond. As he recalled, his saddlebag, containing soap and linens, lay on the ground near the horses, where he had left it.

But he did not want to acquiesce too soon. "And why should I? What will you give me for the favor?"

He felt her stiffen immediately. "I have nothing to give."

"Oh? I do not know about that. You could promise to silence your shrewish tongue. Or pledge an oath not to escape." A delicious, heart-stopping thought occurred to him. "Or . . ."

"Or?"

"Or you could kiss me of your own free will," he whispered huskily as he nuzzled her hair. It still smelled of Passion, the perfume she had worn yestereve. And her own sweet, sweet scent.

"Hah! I gave you a lot more than kisses last night."

"Yea, but not really of your own free will, since you were asleep. And, as I recall, there were no kisses." In truth, he recalled a great deal more than that.

How odd, he thought, that he had touched her so intimately and not kissed her! If he had truly thought he was making love with his dead wife in his berserk state, why had he not supped of her lips? Mayhap he had not been as bemused as they both thought. Mayhap he had known exactly who was in his bed furs, but his inner mind wanted to deny the traitorous attraction.

"A kiss? All you want is a kiss?"

He nodded, releasing his hold on her now that they had reached the pond. She slid sensuously down his rigid body until she stood facing him, only a breathing space apart, but not touching.

"And then we will talk?"

He nodded silently once again, unable to move under the spell of her seductive nearness. Truly, she must be a sorceress to entrance him so.

Rain put her hands on his shoulders and leaned up. He felt her sweet breath on his lips before she closed her eyes and brushed her soft lips gently from side to side against his as if savoring that barest of caresses. But the effect was powerful, overwhelming.

She whimpered.

He held himself rigid, fighting against the roaring of blood in his head, the wild beating of his heart. *'Tis just a kiss.*

"Selik," she whispered pleadingly against his mouth.

Moving her hands from his shoulders to the back of his neck, she stroked the tense muscles. And moved closer. Breast to chest. Thigh to thigh. Hip to hip. Manhood to womanhood.

Selik moaned. He could not help himself.

And she moved her lips once again, more firmly this time, shaping, coaxing. She nipped his bottom lip, then suckled at it gently.

He gasped with sheer, utter pleasure, and she took advantage of the opportunity to slip the tip of her tongue between his lips. A brief foray. Over so quickly he might have dreamed it.

And she claims to get no particular joy from the bed mating! What might she do if really aroused?

Selik felt himself harden and elongate against her soft body. Enough of teasing games! He put his arms around her and pulled her tighter against his body. And he took over control of the kiss.

Then, placing a hand on each side of her face, he tilted her face up to the bright moonlight and noted with extreme satisfaction the slumberous, half-lidded eyes, the slightly parted, moist lips. With exquisite care, he traced her lips with the pad of his thumb, then did the same with the tip of his tongue.

She parted her lips even more, and his heart stopped. He rubbed his lips seductively back and forth across hers, making them slick with the juices of their mutual wanting. He pressed hard, wanting all of her, then slackened to a feathery question of a kiss, then hard again. He could not get enough of her. Her taste was an aphrodisiac he could not resist.

When desire pounded in his veins, he could resist no

more and slipped his tongue into the welcome sheath of her mouth. She suckled him, and his hardness spasmed reflexively against her.

A nagging inner voice warned Selik that things were progressing too quickly. This wonderful, intense yearning that he had not felt for so many years, maybe never, would end abruptly with his spilling his seed if he did not slow down this love game.

He pulled away slowly, reluctantly, and said in a raw voice, "Rain, you will devour me with your sweet heat. We must cool down a bit so we can savor the pleasure more." She moved against him in protest, and he held her firm. "Nay, sweetling, I want to love you through the night, and I will not last another moment if you do not stop torturing me."

"I? Torture you? No, I am the one who is on fire," she whispered huskily.

And Selik almost reached his peak.

Putting his hands on her shoulders, he held her firmly away from him. Then he made a raw sound deep in his throat as he noticed the cloudy sensuality of her half-shuttered eyes and the swollen redness of her lips. Lips engorged with his kisses, he thought with inordinate satisfaction. *Holy Thor!*

He forced himself to lean down and grab his saddlebag, which he had dropped by the pond earlier, then pull her bemused, obviously aroused body toward the edge of the pond. Before she could grasp his intent, he dropped the bag, picked her up, and walked into the pond until the icy water reached his midthigh. Then he sat down with her still in his arms.

She shrieked.

He held her firm. "Sit still, dearling. We both need to cool our hot blood for the long night ahead. Besides, I smell like Fury, and no doubt I have spread my smell on you."

"Selik, it's freezing."

"Shh. I know. Just stand."

When she did what he asked without her usual questioning or defiance, he removed her tunic, her *shert* and braies, her shoes, and the sensual undergarments which had a secret fastening between the breasts. She stood naked and shivering before him. Magnificent. Golden hair down to the waist. Long limbs. Slim hips. High, firm breasts. Like all his images of the Norse goddesses.

"Do not move," he ordered raspily, having difficulty catching his breath. It must be the cold, he told himself.

Quickly, he returned to the saddlebag and removed a chunk of soap and some linen cloths, then removed all his clothing. When he returned, she stood in the same spot, scrutinizing his body as intently as he had hers.

"You are so beautiful," she whispered.

"Nay, not anymore. You must be blind." But he could not stop the smile from softening his mouth.

"My mother was right. You look like a Norse god."

Selik shook his head at the coincidence of their thinking. "Mayhap fate has ordained that you be goddess to this god then.

"Come," he encouraged her, then quickly soaped her entire body from shoulders to toes, stopping here and there to show his appreciation for each delectable spot he discovered. When he soaped his hands and massaged the globes of her breasts into hard points, pressing against his palms, she gasped throatily, "I have never, never, wanted a man as much as I want you."

Selik wanted to scoff at her words, but the unexplainable joy they brought blocked his throat. Without words, he handed the soap to her, and she returned the favor, lathering his body. Her delicate surgeon's hands gently eased his muscles and turned his skin hot, even in the cold air and water. When she began to work her wiles on his manhood, he stopped her, reluctantly. "Nay, I cannot take so much pleasure."

The soap dropped between them, and Selik pulled her once more into his embrace. Their soap-slick bodies moved sensuously against each other, and they both smiled.

"Oh," they said in unison, and smiled again.

Selik rubbed his chest against her soapy breasts and delighted as she arched her neck, closed her eyes, and pressed herself tighter against him. "I ache for you," she whispered.

"Enough!" He dropped down into the water, taking her with him and hastily rinsed the soap from both their bodies, then pulled her toward the bank, where he grabbed a fur cloak he had dropped a short time ago and wrapped it about her, but not before nipping and kissing all the sensitive curves of her delicious body.

She stood docilely, staring up at him, aroused to the point of mindlessness. He was in no better condition.

Selik wrung the water from his hair, shook himself like a shaggy dog, then wrapped an arm around Rain's shoulder, pulling her against his side. He began to walk back toward his tent, uncaring of his nudity, taking her with him.

They had almost passed the area where the horses were picketed when Rain stopped short and shook her head as if to clear it. "The horse," she said in a suddenly cold voice. "You promised I could see your horse."

Confused by her sudden change of mood, Selik nodded his head and led her toward Fury, who whinnied softly in welcome when Selik stroked his mane.

"Where's your saddle?" she asked in an oddly shrill voice.

"What troubles you, sweetling?" Selik asked, suddenly alarmed.

"Just show me your saddle."

He pointed to a spot nearby and watched through narrowed eyes as she found his saddle, bent to examine it, then dropped to her knees. He could tell by her heaving shoulders that she was crying. Tilting his head in puzzlement, he drew closer.

"Tell me," he urged, dropping down beside her. Despite his naked flesh, he did not feel the cold.

"These," she said, gagging. "Did you take these?"

He saw the half dozen scalps hanging from the saddle horn and stiffened. Bloody hell! He had intended to destroy the vile things. In truth, he had not even realized he had taken the scalps during his berserk rage that day until they were almost back to the campsite. Though many of his fellow Norsemen took scalps after every battle, he had never done such before. The horror of the carnage he had witnessed that day must have turned his mind. But he refused to explain himself to the sanctimonious wench.

"Yea, 'tis the *behaettie*, a noble Norse practice to prevent our enemies from entering the gates of Valhalla."

She shook her head in denial and rocked back and forth on her heels, weeping silently.

"'Tis not a pretty sight, I know, but 'tis no worse than the Saxon's trophies. They skin Norsemen alive and pin the hides on their church doors."

"Violent men always find excuses for their bestiality," she said wearily, looking him directly in the eye now. The sadness of her condemnation chilled him as the freezing water and cool night air had not.

He shivered and the ever-present ache of his lost soul hung over him like a winter cloud.

CHAPTER SIX

☙

*R*edeeming the beast . . .

Heartsick, Rain staggered to her feet, clutching the length of fur around her naked body. She shivered, but not from the cold. Her mind reeled with shock from the ghastly sight of human scalps hanging from Selik's saddle.

Oh, God! This man—this man who is somehow becoming precious to me—not only takes human lives, but he keeps souvenirs of his depravity.

Selik stood before her, nude and unapologetic, with his head tilted questioningly. The wet strands of his hair blew slightly as they dried in the night breeze. Even in the moonlight, she could see that her horrified reaction to the scalps had transformed his beautiful eyes, which had been luminous with passion moments before, back to their usual blank soullessness.

Briefly, her eyes skimmed his body from wide shoulders, past tightly fisted hands braced on his slim hips, over his flat stomach, even over his well-formed genitals, to long, sinewy thighs and calves and bare feet. She shook her head in awe before his beauty and the fact that it did not matter to her that he was a magnificent animal. Because that was the key word—*animal*. He was, in fact, a wounded beast.

"Yea, I am a beast. I forewarned you of the fact, but you insisted you could save me." Selik's voice rasped thickly with scorn and self-deprecation.

Rain had not realized she'd spoken the words aloud, but perhaps it was best that Selik knew exactly how she felt. Not that it would change anything. A man who could do such a horrible thing was irredeemable.

Who are you to cast stones? the voice in Rain's head asked. She closed her eyes wearily, fearing that she wavered on the brink of some kind of nervous breakdown.

There is good in every man, if you will only look.

Rain's mind reeled with confusion. This whole time-travel experience was probably just a figment of her imagination. She was probably sitting in some Monty Python-type mental institution in a straight jacket. With a Jack Nicholson-type psychiatrist at hand. Yes, it made sense. All this Viking stuff was just a fantasy. No, a nightmare. She put a hand over her mouth to stifle a giggle of hysteria.

Selik snorted with disgust at her oddly timed amusement, and she shot him a glare of what she hoped was an equal dose of disgust. Then she started to walk past him back to the line of captives. She needed to get away from the barbarian to think.

Selik grabbed her by the upper arm as she passed, stopping her. "Where do you think you are going?"

"Don't . . . touch . . . me," she gritted out with evenly spaced words. "Don't . . . ever . . . touch . . . me . . . again."

He released her arm and backed off a bit. Muscles tensed in his jutting jaw, and he said in a steely voice, "Hostages do not give orders."

Rain shrugged dejectedly. "I was a fool to think I was anything more. I was a fool to think I could change you."

Oh, ye of little faith!

"Stop it," she cried out, putting a hand to her aching head

while clutching the ends of the fur together with the other hand.

"Stop what?"

"I wasn't talking to you," she snapped. "It's the damn voice in my head."

Selik almost looked amused, but the smile never reached his cold, cold eyes. "God again?"

"Yes. No. Oh, I don't know. It's probably just my conscience or something."

"Save your conscience for someone who cares," he commented contemptuously. "Or someone who is redeemable. I am not."

"Oh, be quiet. Can't you see I've had enough for one day?" Deliberately ignoring him, she began to walk toward the captives, then stopped suddenly and headed toward Selik's tent. She'd just realized that she needed warmer clothing.

As she picked her way over the cold ground in her bare feet, she muttered, "Criminey! I'll be the only doctor in the world with callouses on the soles of my feet."

A short time later, she was rooting through one of Selik's chests, looking for a tunic and leggings—braies, Selik called them—to wear until her clothing dried, when she looked up and saw him leaning against the tent opening, still eye-bulgingly, heart-stoppingly, gloriously nude.

Rain barely suppressed a groan. *Give me a break, God. You don't play fair.*

"Thievery now?" he asked dryly, looking at his garments in her hands.

"I need some warm clothing. You may be impervious to the cold, but I'm not going to sleep buck-naked out there on the cold ground."

"You are right. You are not going to sleep on the cold ground out there."

When the implication of his words sunk in, Rain twisted her head and looked up at him in disbelief. "You can't possibly think I would sleep with you now. Have you any idea how you repel me? In fact, I repel myself for allowing your hands to touch me so intimately when—when—" She sputtered, unable to come up with words to describe his atrocities. Finally, she explained with a tired shrug, "I feel defiled."

Rain saw his jaw clench tightly, but his eyes betrayed no emotion. "Defiled or not, you share my bed furs."

She stood angrily, holding her fur together with one hand and a tunic and pair of leggings in the other.

He held up a hand to silence her. "Nay, do not think to defy me on this. And, know this, wench, I have no desire to *rut* with you this night. But if the urge ever hits me in a moment of madness, it will be my decision to make, not yours."

"Then it would be rape. But why should that bother you, beast that you are? It's just one more sin to add to your list, and a minor one, I daresay, in light of your other atrocities."

He shrugged dismissively.

"Oh!" she finally said in exasperation, knowing it was useless to argue with the unbending brute. "Just turn around so I can dress."

He did not move a muscle, just stared back at her insolently. "Nay, you will follow the Norse manner. We do not wear clothing in bed. You may wear my garments in the morn, but not in the bed furs."

With a snarl of disbelief, she dropped the fur cloak and slid down into the bed furs on the ground, but not before she noticed Selik's eyes graze the cold-peaked tips of her breasts. A slight twitch at the side of his mouth told her, loud and clear, that her nudity affected him.

Mentally chastising herself for a momentary flush of pleasure at his appreciative scrutiny, Rain burrowed deep under the furs, hiding Selik from view and her flushed face from his too observant stare.

When he blew out the candle and slid in behind her, Rain moved as far away as she could so their bodies would not touch. Still, she felt the heat of his body and imagined that his warm breath tickled her shoulder blades.

She awakened some time before dawn and found that she

had turned and lay willingly in his arms, her cheek pressed against the silken hairs of his chest; one of his legs draped intimately over both of hers. For several long moments, she lay still, feeling his steady heartbeat against her ear, and in her half-sleep she admitted something she could not when fully awake. She didn't hate this man, no matter what he'd done or planned to do. She just couldn't hate him.

She had to help him. But how?

When slivers of light began to creep through the opening in the tent, Rain carefully slipped out of Selik's arms and out of the bed furs. She quickly donned Selik's braies, uncaring of the fact that they were six inches too long and bagged at the ankles. His wool tunic was much too big, but it felt warm and smelled faintly of the not unpleasant masculine skin she had been inhaling all night.

Gorm sat stationed near the captives, sitting with his head leaning back drowsily against a tree trunk. He sat up straighter but didn't stop her when she rummaged through the utensils near Ubbi's cooking fire. When she finally found what she wanted, she turned stoically and headed toward the horses.

I ought to earn two sets of angel wings for this one, Lord.

Making a deal with the devil . . . uh, angel . . .

Selik slept past dawn the next morning, the battering of his body and mind the last few days finally catching up with him. The troublesome wench was gone from his bed furs, but that did not really surprise him. The foolish witch paid no attention to his orders and blithely did just as she pleased.

Selik bristled as he thought about Rain's harsh condemnation yestereve of his taking scalps. A beast, she had called him. Well, mayhap she was right.

But then, the wench was critical of everything he did. She acted as if he were a naughty kitten and she the mistress. Hah! Best she be careful or she would discover she had a tiger in her domain and she was the delectable morsel on which he would dine. Selik smiled at his own mind jest. Mayhap he would repeat it to her later, but he misdoubted she would see the humor. Especially if her mood had not improved overnight.

Selik rose from the warm furs, imagining he could still smell Rain's enticing Passion. He shook his head in wonder at the strange woman who had come into his life—was it only three days ago? It seemed as if he had known her forever. And what a strange creature she was! Imagine, naming a perfume! Did she name her soaps as well? he wondered, smiling. Or her combs?

Selik yawned hugely and scratched his chest as he donned a clean pair of braies and a dark blue tunic. He cinched a wide, silver-linked belt at his waist and put the heavy armlets Astrid had once given him on his upper arms, caressing the fine etchwork lovingly with a forefinger.

He approached the cook fire where the young Saxon girl he had taken captive was stirring a pot. She pulled several loaves of flat bread out of the coals and laid them on a rock to cool. Having ignored the hunger cramps in his empty stomach too long, he grabbed one of the loaves and tossed it back and forth from hand to hand to cool it more quickly.

He never said a word to the quietly working maid. Nor did he comment on her release from the string of captives. He assumed Ubbi had gladly given up his cooking chores.

Breaking off a chunk of the manchet bread, he ate hungrily as he walked toward the horses, where Ubbi was doling out the precious feed he had brought back yestereve.

"Did ye find Sveinn?" Ubbi asked, looking up at him as he worked.

Selik nodded.

"And Ragnor?"

"Yea, and Tostig and Jogeir and Vigi, as well," he answered wearily.

"All buried?"

"All buried. 'Twas the best we could do. The rite of fire would have brought too many Saxons down on our heads. As it was . . ." His words trailed off, but he did not need to finish. Ubbi had been with him long enough to know many Saxons had come and died at his hands once again.

"With all respect, my lord, it has to stop."

"Foolish man, I am nobody's lord. I am a bloody *nithing*."

Ubbi inhaled sharply with shock at this extreme self-insult. And, good Lord, tears glittered in his eyes. Tears! Was everyone losing their senses?

"I care naught what ye say," Ubbi said vehemently, "ye are as noble as the best of 'em. 'Tis jist that ye have stumbled on the bitter stones life has thrown in yer path. The way will git better, though. I jist know it."

"Bitter stones! More like boulders!" He looked around then. "Where didst my guardian angel fly off to now?"

Ubbi darted him a guilty look, then avoided his eyes.

"Oh, Holy Thor! What now?"

"I think you'd best check Fury's right foreleg, master. Seems a mite sore to me."

"Where is she?"

"Who?"

"God's handmaiden! Who the hell do you think?"

"Do you really think the Lord sent her to you?"

"Nay, I think Loki is playing a vast joke by sending Rain to bedevil me."

Ubbi looked wounded, then glanced right and left to make sure they were not overheard before confiding in an awe-filled whisper, "I found a feather in yer bed furs yesterday when I straightened up yer tent."

Selik furrowed his brow in thought. He could not see the connection between Ubbi's discovery and Rain.

"Do you not see, master? It no doubt came from her wings which she hides from us earthy bodies."

"Oh, for the love of Freya!" Selik hooted with laughter, unable to believe Ubbi's gullibility.

As he was wiping the mirth from his eyes a few moments later, Selik noticed Rain kneeling beneath a tree on the other side of the small spring—digging a hole.

Ubbi put a hand on Selik's arm as he prepared to go to

her. "Master, do not be harsh with her. She does not understand our ways."

Selik looked at his loyal servant's worried face and tensed.
Rain had brewed trouble once again, no doubt, and the foolish man tried to protect her from his wrath.

Without another word, Selik spun on his heel and made
his way toward her kneeling body. When he got closer, he
saw that her head was bowed in a prayerful attitude and she
was mumbling some words aloud, something about her Lord
being a shepherd and her lying down in pastures. A fresh
mound of dirt lay in front of her.

Was it some kind of religious ritual? Or had she stolen
some precious object from his tent to hide until her escape?

Exasperated, Selik grabbed her by the forearm and pulled
her to her feet. The small shovel in her hands clattered to the
ground with the abrupt motion.

Rain's mouth dropped open in surprise. "Oh! You scared
me." Then, as if recalling to mind her continuing anger to-
wards him, she struggled to escape his grip.

"What in bloody hell are you doing?"

She raised her chin defiantly and refused to answer.

"I asked you a question," he said coldly, tightening his hold
on her upper arm to the point of pain. "Answer or I swear I
will break your arm."

He saw the tears well in her eyes, a mixture of pain and
wounded pride, but he did not care. She had pushed him beyond his limits of endurance. "Are you planning to escape?"

Her eyes widened with surprise. "What?"

"Was it my gold coins you buried, or a sharp knife, to aid
you in your escape?"

"No, you stupid brute, I was burying your dead."

His breath whooshed out in a loud exhale, and Selik released her. His finger imprints had already bruised her soft
flesh.

"What dead?" he choked out. "Surely my men buried the
captive that Ubbi killed yesterday."

She darted a look of disbelief at him. "You are the most

thickheaded man I have ever met. Do you honestly think I could have dug a hole big enough to bury a man of Edwin's size with this little shovel?"

He looked at the small digging implement and realized that, in truth, he had not been thinking clearly. *Slow down,* he told himself silently. *Stop letting your emotions rule your head. Think.*

"Tell me then," he said more calmly.

She held his gaze, her honey eyes sparkling with challenge. "I was burying the"—she swallowed hard several times before continuing—"the scalps you took yesterday." Her eyes flashed defiantly as she awaited his usual angry outburst.

The scalps. The bloody witch is trying to counter the behaettie. *She never ceases to amaze me.*

"Oh, really, close your mouth, Selik. It's quite unbecoming."

He snapped his slack lips together in chagrin at being caught gawking. "Those words you were chanting—are they a charm?" he asked, still unconvinced.

At first, her brows furrowed in puzzlement. Then she laughed—a clear, surprisingly pleasant sound that carried across the clearing. He saw Ubbi look up hopefully from his work with the horses, as if thankful that he had not yet lopped off her head. *Bloody hell.*

"I was saying some prayers, Selik," she finally explained gently. "Christian prayers for burial."

"You would pray for the salvation of my enemies?" he asked icily.

"I would pray for *anyone,* Selik. Even you. Especially you."

"Save your prayers. You had no right to take what belongs to me. Or bury it without my permission." *By the nines! The woman must have the mettle of a seasoned warrior to have handled the bloody objects. And to face my fearsome fury.*

"I did what I had to do. Will you punish me?"

"Do you want to be punished?"

"Of course not. But I've had plenty of time to think this all through while you snored the night away—"

"I do not snore." *Do I? No one ever remarked on it afore.*

Her beautiful lips twitched at the edges as she tried unsuccessfully to suppress a grin. "Like a bear."

Moving away from the odd grave, Rain motioned Selik to follow her. Amazed that she would order him about, he was equally incredulous that he followed like a meek puppy. Next he would be licking her face. *Aaah! Now that conjures up some interesting possibilities.* He grinned, despite his annoyance. *Next I will be wagging my tail.* He burst out with a chuckle of self-derision at that prospect.

"What's so funny?"

"You. Me. My life."

Rain tilted her head questioningly and dropped down to the ground near the small pond. She pulled up her long legs—seductively outlined in all their glorious length by his braies—so that her chin rested on her knees and her arms were wrapped around her calves.

He had difficulty swallowing past his dry throat.

Sliding down beside her, he rested his back against a tree. Not too close. Her nearness disarmed him mightily and he must remain alert with the wily wench.

"Selik, I seem to have no choice about being here with you, but we have to come to an agreement."

He waited for her to explain.

She licked her lips with the tip of her tongue as if to gather her thoughts, and he remembered how it had felt inside his mouth yestereve. Involuntarily, his traitorous body jolted to immediate awareness.

"I want you to promise to never, never scalp another person again."

He sat straighter. "You have no right to make demands on me."

"I wasn't demanding," she corrected him. "Notice that I asked. Rather nicely, I thought."

"Why should I stop?"

"Well, I wish you would stop just because I asked you to,

but it's obvious that my opinion isn't important enough to you."

She blushed when he failed to correct that impression. In truth, she was becoming much too important.

"Selik, did you practice such barbarism when Astrid was alive?"

He shot immediately to his feet, hovering over her. She did not flinch a speck. "Nay, I did not, but I was a different man then. I had a soul. And a heart. I have neither now. Nor do I want them."

She looked wounded at his words. Bloody hell! Why would she care so much?

"Selik, I would like to make a bargain with you."

"Pray tell. I cannot wait to hear what you have to offer."

"If you will promise never to—to—well, do that awful thing again, I promise I will never try to escape."

He eyed her suspiciously. "So, you were planning to escape?"

"No, that's not what I said," she snapped impatiently, "but I could if I wanted to. After all," she said, fluttering her eyelashes, "I have God on my side."

"I thought you denied being a real angel."

She averted her eyes guiltily. "Yes, well, you never know, do you?"

She was lying through her teeth. And so poorly that she could not look him in the eye or hide the flush of embarrassment from her fair cheeks.

"Ubbi found your feather in the bed furs," he pointed out with dry humor.

"My feather?"

"He thinks 'tis from your wings. You know, the wings you can spread or hide under your skin at will."

He grinned at the surprise on her intrigued face.

Then they both burst out laughing.

"Well, do you agree to my proposal?" she asked finally.

Actually, Selik hated the *behaettie* and always had. But

even worse, he loathed his berserk rage yestermorn when he had seen the half-decayed, eyeless bodies of his good friends lying on the battlefield like refuse. "Mayhap. Exactly what do you promise?"

"I will never try to escape."

"And if you disagree with something I do in the future?" he asked skeptically.

She raised her brow ruefully. "I will whack you on the head or give you a piece of my mind, but I won't leave."

"This is important to you, is it not?"

"Yes. Oh, yes," she said, closing her eyes briefly before speaking. "When I was a young girl, my brother Eddie was a soldier. He was killed in a fight which even the government later admitted was pointless."

"And that is when you became a paci . . . pacifist?"

She nodded. "Later I became a doctor and started working in an inner-city hospital. The murders and mutilations these young gang members inflict on each other is a powerful argument against violence."

"But some fighting cannot be avoided," he argued.

"You may be right about that. I don't know. But back to the scalping thing—if you will do this for me, at least I'll feel I've made one small step toward helping you. It's important to me, Selik."

"Then I agree. As long as you are with me, I will take no more *behaettie*."

Rain pressed her lips together thoughtfully. "About the captives—"

"Do not press your luck."

The outrageous wench just shrugged, as if he should not blame her for trying. "Well, we have a bargain then." She smiled widely, and Selik's heart lurched oddly in his chest, then seemed to expand with lightness. He did not like the feeling.

She stood and held out her hand to him sideways, palm open. He stared at it, confused. Did she want him to hold it?

She seemed to understand his bafflement and explained,

"In my ti . . . my country, we shake hands when we finalize an agreement. Like this." She placed his right palm against hers and closed both their fingers lightly in the clasp, then showed him how to shake briskly up and down. But all Selik could concentrate on was the intense shock of pleasure generated by her skin against his. He never wanted to let go.

He inhaled sharply and could not break contact with her luminous eyes, which showed too clearly that she was equally affected.

Quickly dropping her hand, as if his flesh had suddenly caught fire, he muttered under his breath, "The witch has cast a spell on me."

But Rain heard his softly spoken words. "If there is a spell, then I'm in its thrall too," she replied huskily.

Wonderful! We can both stagger through this nightmare life I lead under the curse of that troublemaker god Loki. Or Rain's own Christian God. Or the devil, for all I know. Bloody hell!

Wars are won battle by battle, even angelic ones . . .

Feeling very pleased with herself the rest of the day, Rain hummed as she worked with the patients in the hospital tent. She wasn't deluding herself that Selik had made any giant leaps toward sudden reformation. It was a small victory, but every journey begins with the first step, she reminded herself.

"Why are you smiling?" Tykir asked from where he lay propped up in his hospital pallet. He had been conscious the entire day and his health improved by the minute, to Rain's delight. She would have so much to tell Dr. Lee on her return.

"I'm smiling because I won a small battle with Selik today. Actually, that's not quite true. It was a compromise. We were both winners in this particular skirmish."

Tykir raised an eyebrow in disbelief. "Selik? I can hardly credit that he would bend to anyone's will." Then he winked lewdly. "The enticement must have been powerfully tempting."

Rain slapped Tykir playfully on the arm. "Behave yourself,

little brother. You are still weak, and I am in a position to make life very uncomfortable for you."

"Ah ha, now the pacifist discloses her true colors."

Rain smiled, knowing Tykir referred to the pacifism lectures she'd been delivering to him all day. "Oh, there are nonviolent means of punishment for an imaginative person. For instance, I could have Ubbi prepare all your meals."

Tykir groaned in an exaggerated fashion. "Oh, please, not that. Better the water torture."

Rain laughed at Tykir's lighthearted attitude. It was so good to see him feeling better, acting much the same as his modern clone, her brother Dave.

"How soon 'til I can travel?" he asked, suddenly serious. "I must get back to Ravenshire afore the Saxons try to confiscate the property."

"One week," Selik said before Rain could answer. He had come up behind her without her noticing and stood watching the easy interchange between her and her brother with a bemused expression on his face.

"Oh, no, he'll never be well enough by then," Rain protested. "At least two weeks more. Maybe even three."

"We will be leaving in seven days, even if we have to carry Tykir on a sledge."

"I will not be dragged about like an old man," Tykir complained indignantly. "Starting on the morrow, I will exercise my leg every day. I will ride in one week if it kills me."

"It just may do that," Rain commented with worry, slanting a look of condemnation at Selik.

"Every day we delay, so close to Brunanburh, brings the danger closer," Selik explained. "Even now, the Saxons could be gathering forces to come after us. Tykir understands why we cannot wait any longer."

"Yea, I do, Selik, and I am grateful that you have stayed with me so long." He cast a gentle look at Rain and squeezed her hand in reassurance. "I come from strong stock. I intend to survive for a good long time. Mayhap I will even dance at your wedding." He jiggled his eyebrows teasingly.

"My wedding!" Rain exclaimed, dumbfounded. "What would make you think I intend to get married—*ever?*"

Tykir rolled his eyes heavenward. "A little angel told me."

Selik looked as if he were going to be sick.

How sweet it is! . . .

That evening Rain sat cross-legged on the floor of Selik's tent, a fur under her bottom and another thrown over her shoulders to protect her from the cold. She worried about the captives sleeping outside on the ground. Even though Selik had somehow found clean clothing and furs for them all— and heaven only knew where he had purloined them, proba- bly off dead bodies somewhere—the autumn night had turned markedly cold.

She wanted to ask him if he could find tents for them as well, but his face went infuriatingly stubborn every time she brought up the subject of the captives. She determined to pick her battles carefully and wear him down with kindness.

Rain dumped the contents of her carryall on the ground in front of her, deciding it was time for a little inventory of all she had brought from the present on her unexpected trip.

Aside from her small emergency medical kit, she carried a meager amount of cosmetics—a mirrored compact, mas- cara, blush, and a tube of strawberry-flavored lip gloss, which would present some interesting possibilities if she ever kissed Selik again. Which, of course, she would not do, she told herself stubbornly, then immediately amended, *Who are you kidding?*

Other than a comb and brush, her wallet and checkbook, a really handy thing to have in the tenth century—ten thou- sand dollars in the bank and not a dime to spend—all Rain had was a Rubik's Cube, which she often used to release tension during breaks between surgery, and two packs of Lifesavers—assorted flavors and Tropical Fruits. She popped a green candy in her mouth and put her belongings back in the bag.

She was fiddling with the Rubik's Cube, the tip of her

tongue pressed between her lips in concentration, when Selik came in a short time later, rubbing his bare arms briskly against the cold.

"Why is your tongue green?"

She stuck her tongue out farther, showing him the tiny circle still lying there. "I'm sucking on a Lifesaver."

"Is it medicinal?"

"No," she said with a laugh. "It's candy. A sweet. Do you want one?"

He looked skeptical but took the yellow one she handed to him. His face lit up with pleasure when he began to chew it, crunching loudly.

"Don't chew it. You just let it sit on your tongue," she admonished. "You're supposed to make it last."

"I am very good at that," he boasted, giving her a quick wink. "Making *pleasures* last, that is."

With a snort of disgust at his inflated ego, she gave him another one, even though it was her favorite color, red. Selik learned quickly and let it rest on his tongue, savoring the sweet flavor. At one point, he stuck his tongue out very far, trying to see if it was red. Satisfied that it was, he insisted on having two more, an orange and a green. She refused to give up another red.

"How many of these lifecircles do you have?"

"Lifesavers," she corrected with a smile, putting the half-empty roll away. "That is all," she lied, crossing her fingers behind her back. Why should she share her Tropical Fruits with the brute? Maybe she would give one to Tykir, though.

"What's that?" he asked, sinking down beside her on the fur.

"A Rubik's Cube. Sort of a puzzle."

He watched with interest as she worked the cube until she finally solved the puzzle. She didn't bother to tell him she had a particular talent for the game and had once won a state competition in solving the puzzle.

"Let me try."

She reset it and handed it to him, smiling inwardly with

anticipation. He didn't even comment an hour later when she crawled into the bed furs, fully clothed. She'd been prepared to argue with him about the Viking custom of sleeping naked, and the unfeeling brute hadn't even noticed. Much later, after she'd been asleep for at least three hours, she opened her eyes to see him still sitting next to the sputtering candle, biting his bottom lip pensively, trying to solve the blasted puzzle.

Toward dawn, she felt him slip in behind her and move closer to her body's warmth. He pulled her hair away from her neck and nuzzled the sensitive curve, then whispered, "Tomorrow you will teach me how to solve the puzzle."

"Uh-huh," she said sleepily.

"Mayhap I will teach you something in return."

Her eyes shot open at that.

CHAPTER SEVEN

&

Temptation, thy name is Viking . . .
    "Ubbi—doobie—doo. Da—da da—da da. Ubbi—doobie—doo. Da—da da—da da."

"Ubbi, stop singing that tiresome drivel over and over and over, or I swear I will cut out your bloody tongue," Tykir growled from atop his horse. "By the Faith! I am beginning to hear your lackwit name-song in my dreams now."

"Now, Tykir, don't unleash your bad moods on Ubbi," Rain chastised teasingly as she drew her horse up alongside her brother.

After two days on horseback, Rain was actually starting to feel comfortable in the saddle of Godsend, the name she'd given to the destrier that saved her and Selik on the battle-field. When Rain had first announced her horse's new name to Selik, he'd protested, "The name is as barmy as you are." Ubbi, on the other hand, had beamed, declaring Godsend's name "jist perfect."

Rain looked over at the little man with concern as he rode another of the horses Selik and his men had brought back from the battlefield during the past week. She was glad Selik had insisted that Ubbi ride, instead of walking with the captives. His arthritis obviously gave him considerable pain.

In the bright moonlight, she could see Ubbi stealing surreptitious glances at her back, a habit the dear soul had developed whenever he thought she wasn't looking.

"Ubbi, is something wrong with my back?"

He jerked to attention. "A thousan' pardons, m'lady. I was jist admirin' the trees yonder."

Rain raised an eyebrow skeptically, knowing they were all damn sick of seeing nothing but trees, especially in the dark. Selik would only let them travel after dusk and before dawn to avoid any encounters with patrolling Saxons.

She rolled her shoulders and said with an exaggerated groan, "Ubbi, my shoulder blades are aching so! I feel like I have a thousand bees under the skin of my back just waiting to burst out."

His mouth formed a perfect O.

Putting a hand over her mouth to hide a smile, she added, "My back is so tense. Do you think you could rub my back when we stop the next time?"

"Me?" he choked out.

"By the way, Ubbi, I seem to have misplaced something that was in my carryall. Have you seen a round thin gold circlet?" She lifted her hands from the reins for a second to demonstrate with her widespread fingers a circle about the size of her head.

He almost swallowed his teeth and whispered in an undertone of awe, not intended for her ears, "A halo! The blessed angel has lost her halo."

It still amazed Rain that she could understand the language of these primitive people and vice-versa. But then, there was a lot about this time-travel experience that astounded her.

Selik rode back then and drew up to her side as the full moon came out from behind a cloud. Clad in leather battle gear, Selik's powerful body moved in the saddle of his massive destrier with easy grace. His long fingers held the reins lightly while he guided the horse with the flexing muscles of his thighs, evident through his tight black leggings.

Rain licked her suddenly dry lips and forced her eyes upward.

With a jerk of his head toward Tykir, Selik asked, "How does he? Need we stop again afore dawn?"

"Nay, we will not stop on *my* account," Tykir asserted, overhearing Selik's question.

Rain knew her brother had to be in excruciating pain, but the stubborn young man refused all offers of a sledge and rode in the saddle with his leg in a soft brace that she and Selik had improvised for him.

"Can you not force my stubborn sister to teach Ubbi another song?" Tykir urged Selik plaintively, changing the subject deliberately to shift attention away from himself. "My teeth are starting to ache with all these *doobie-doobie* words."

Amusement flickered briefly in Selik's shadowy eyes as they met hers in a warm caress. "Hah! What makes you think your sister would be biddable for me of a sudden?"

"Well, leastways, force her to teach him another song. One less jarring on the senses."

Rain's face perked instantly.

"Nay!" Selik and Tykir both snapped out quickly in appalled voices before she had a chance to speak.

"Do not think of starting on that other one—that achy-breaky-heart thing," Selik ordered with a groan. "Good Lord, do they not have any soft melodies in your country?"

"Mayhap 'tis your shrillness," Tykir added. "I tell you kindly, sister, you have a voice that could peel bark off a tree."

"How nice of you to notice that I can't carry a tune, Tykir. I'll remember that when I change your bandages tonight."

Selik threw back his head and laughed, low and throaty, at the bantering between brother and sister. His amusement wiped the lines of rage and pain from his face as it relaxed for the moment, and he looked years younger.

When they finally stopped to camp at daybreak in a thickly wooded glen, Tykir was no longer joking, and Rain removed the dressings on his leg with trepidation. His stitches remained intact and no inflammation marked the wound, but his mouth formed a thin white line of pain. With tightly balled hands, he could barely move from his horse to the pallet they prepared for him.

Rain ordered Ubbi to sterilize her needles over the cooking fire, and within an hour, Tykir slept peacefully, the acupuncture needles stuck in the strategic body points to alleviate pain. A guard sat nearby to make sure that Tykir did not jar the needles in his slumber.

Selik, on the other hand, watched the whole procedure with horror. His golden tan paled and his knuckles whitened as he fisted his fingers tightly.

Rain had no other medical duties to perform, so she went over to the cooking fire and offered to help Blanche prepare the meal.

As Rain turned the large chunks of venison roasting over the low fire, she watched Blanche move with brisk efficiency, preparing dough for the flat manchet bread which would bake in the hot coals. The Saxon girl had cleaned up well. Too well, Rain admitted jealously, as she noticed the men in the camp stop by on one pretext or another to offer their help. One suitor gathered herbs. Another, fresh water. Even Gorm had turned into a rip-roaring Lothario with his clean red hair slicked back wetly into a single braid and his grizzly face newly shaved. If he didn't smile and reveal the missing front tooth, he might almost be handsome, Rain had to admit.

But the disgustingly petite young woman ignored them all. She had her eyes on bigger game. Selik.

Rain tried to ignore the green-eyed monster that slithered just under the surface of her skin every time she saw Blanche cast her sultry eyes his way or swing her hips when she walked by him with assumed casualness on far too many occasions. Rain had to keep reminding herself that the Saxon Lolita was probably no more than sixteen years old, a child really. Hah! she corrected herself immediately—the brunette's knowing glances bespoke ageless feminine wiles, ones Rain had yet to learn. And she was thirty!

Even worse was the fact that Selik—the infuriating Viking—looked pleased. Rain watched with jealousy as Selik's silvery eyes glittered with humor and his sensual lips broke into a dazzling smile when Blanche stood blatantly close to him and displayed in age-old body language what she wanted from him, even as she asked such a simple question as, "Where do you keep the salt, master?"

Not in his bloody breeches, you whore!

Rain glared at Selik with an urge to throttle as his appreciative eyes followed the movement of Blanche's well-curved derrière bending over a basket of greens she had just collected. A Playboy bunny couldn't have posed so seductively.

Criminey! If I did that, I'd probably look like the back end of a horse.

She stole a sideways glance at Selik and noticed with chagrin that his gaze was glued to the same spot—Blanche's posterior. She lost it then and blurted out sarcastically before she could control her jealous tongue, "Looking for a root cellar?"

He turned a wide grin her way and winked. Instantly, she regretted reminding Selik of their first meeting when he'd tried to dump her, saying she could easily find another protector among those soldiers more interested in finding a nesting place for their "manroots."

Selik laughed, unconcerned that he'd been caught ogling the girl. "Are you offering?"

"No, you randy goat."

"Ah, well, I had not really thought I would score with you . . . yet."

"Score? Where did you learn such a modern expression?"

"Your mother. I had much woman-luck in those days, but still Ruby taught me many useful words. Like 'scoring,' 'getting lucky,' and 'striking out.'"

Rain nodded her head in understanding. It was so like her outrageous mother. "Consider yourself struck out."

He flashed her a knowing "this is only the first inning" smile.

Then Selik's other word sunk in. "What do you mean, *yet?* You'd better get one thing through that thick head of yours, Selik—*nothing* is going to happen between us."

"Your body says differently." Selik folded his arms across his chest lazily in challenge.

"That was before I discovered just how brutal you are."

He straightened his back with pride, and his face darkened angrily. "I promised no more *behaettie.*"

"Yes, but you still have captives. And you still plan to kill as many Saxons as you can."

"Yea, I do, sweet pacifist. But that has naught to do with the bedding."

"Oh, yes, it does."

Selik's stormy eyes softened and narrowed craftily as he studied her. She could almost hear the gears grinding in his sly brain. "I heard a voice in my head yestereve as I slept. 'The wench should make sex with you,' it said. Methinks it was your god talking to me."

"Liar," Rain said, unable to stop the smile which sprang to her lips at his blatant attempt at seduction.

Lord, he was a devastatingly handsome man when the grimness left his face. With his head turned slightly to the side, Rain could not see the white scar zigzagging from his right eye to his chin, nor the broken nose. The sharp edges of his strong profile seemed to melt, leaving only the image of a self-confident, ruggedly virile man. Her eyes held his in the charged silence, and she felt a part of herself that had never been touched by any man reach out to him in yearning.

"Ah, well, 'twas worth a try." Then he looked back to Blanche with a gleam in his eyes. "On the other hand, perchance the voice was referring to *that* wench."

Blanche was stretching her arms overhead to break off

some small dead limbs from a nearby tree for her cook fire.
Every red-blooded man within five hundred feet was staring,
practically bug-eyed, at her large nipples clearly outlined
against the taut fabric of her tunic.

Rain saw green. And turned away to hide her jealousy
from the too-perceptive Selik.

"Rain?" Selik asked softly behind her. She looked back at
him over her shoulder, surprised to see that he stood so close.
Gently, he brushed a strand of hair off her face that had come
loose from her braid. She turned to face him and almost staggered under the overwhelming pull of his body heat and
scent. "Do you know how long it has been since I 'made sex'
with a woman?"

Startled by his question, Rain shook her head slowly from
side to side, unable to speak, her eyes trapped in his luminous gray gaze.

"Two years."

"Wh . . . what?"

"And do you know how long it has been since I have even
wanted to 'make love' with a woman?" He made a clear distinction by his intonation between "make sex" and "make
love."

Mesmerized, Rain's eyes traveled hungrily over his face,
still incapable of speech. She longed to trace the chiseled
facets of his sharp cheekbones with a forefinger, to taste the
sweetness of his parted lips, to make his eyes close in slow
surrender to ecstasy. *Oh, Lord!*

When she did not speak, he answered his own question,
"Ten years. Ten bloody, soul-dead years."

Rain gasped.

"Oh, I have rutted with women because I thought it was
what a man should do, because I thought it would make me
forget. But I tired of the meaningless couplings two years ago."

"But you implied that you might go to Blanche," she interrupted.

Selik shook his head wearily. "There have been a hundred
Blanches in my life. But I have not really *wanted* a woman

for such a long time. Until ten days ago. Until I met a maddening, shrewish angel, claiming to hail from the future, who has damn well turned my life upside down and inside out."

"Oh, Selik."

"Do not 'Oh, Selik' me," he warned. "I do not welcome these softer yearnings. I mislike feeling again." He started to say something more, then stopped abruptly, spinning on his heel and walking away from her.

Stunned, Rain just gaped at his departing back. Then she stomped right after him. He was giving directions to Gorm for the scouts when she finally caught up with him.

Without a thought to her rudeness in interrupting a private conversation, Rain put a palm on Selik's chest and shoved. Of course, he didn't budge at all, just stared at her brazen hand in disbelief. Gorm gawked at her as if she had two heads.

"Listen, buster, you can't tell a woman something wonderful like that and then walk away big as you please."

He looked pointedly at her hand still pushing at his rock-hard chest. Raising an eyebrow, he commented dryly, "'Twould seem you have a dark side, after all. For a pacifist."

Glancing down and realizing that she had, indeed, picked up a few violent attributes, Rain dropped her hand as if his chest had suddenly caught on fire. Actually, the insufferable man did throw off a tantalizing heat. *Oh, Lord!*

Selik tilted his head in puzzlement then. "What wonderful thing did I say?"

Rain felt her face flush. "You said . . ." She hesitated when she noticed that Gorm still stood there, listening to her every word with intent concentration and a wide smirk. She glared at him until he snorted with disgust and walked away, muttering.

Turning back to Selik, she continued, "You said you hadn't wanted to make love with any woman for ten years until you met me."

"And?"

"And! There is no 'and,' you dolt. You said it deliberately to tempt me, didn't you? And then—"

"Are you tempted?"

"No!" she exclaimed too quickly and knew by the slow smile that teased his lips that she hadn't fooled him a bit. "Anyhow, is it true?"

"Is what true?" He didn't even try to hide his smile now, and Rain's heart slammed wildly against her chest in reaction. "That I want you? That it's been two years since I have bedded a woman? That I have not really desired a particular woman since my—since—well, for ten years?"

"Yes, all those things," she agreed quickly. Finally, she was getting somewhere with the thickheaded, wonderful fool.

He thought for a while, rubbing his fingertips thoughtfully across his furrowed forehead, then nodded slowly, saying nothing. He just watched her intently.

She waited for him to say more, but he just stood silently like a damned statue. Stomping her foot in exasperation, she finally broke the silence, "Dammit! I know what you're doing here. My mother told me all about you. I should have listened. The ultimate seducer, that's how she described you. Oh, you are slick, I give you that. I'll bet that line has worked on a thousand women."

"A thousand!" Laughter, deep and rich, bubbled up from his throat. "You overestimate my talents, sweetling."

She stepped closer, preparing to shove him again, but Selik put both hands on her shoulders and held her off. A jolt of white-hot fire ignited her skin under his fingertips and shot to all the delicious nerve endings in her body. Instinctively, she leaned closer.

"Nay, keep your distance, wench. My self-control has been pushed to the limits. I want you. Badly. And unless you intend to share my bed furs in the true sense, 'tis best you stay away from me."

Rain couldn't deny that the prospect enticed her. In fact, she would have liked nothing more at the moment than to surrender to all the wild new impulses beating throughout her body. But Rain had never behaved impetuously in the past, and her too-pragmatic brain put forth another message, questioning whether she could compromise her principles by making love with a man who stood for all that she abhorred. She groaned under the weight of all her warring emotions. "Selik, please, will you release the captives and give up fighting?"

"Nay, I cannot." He shook his head sadly, then shot her a challenging look. "But I will teach you things your books never told, bring you pleasures your modern lovers never dreamed. I will make your blood sing and your bones melt. You will never want another man after me."

Rain should have been affronted at his conceit. She wasn't.

She licked her lips nervously, trying to bring her rioting hormones under control. "And how about you?" she asked softly. "Would you want another woman after having me?"

Selik studied her face closely, the passion in his eyes mirroring her own, before answering, "Probably not."

Rain's heart fluttered with hope. "Selik, unless you are willing to stop the bloodshed, I don't think we can have a future," she cried, clutching at his hands, wanting him to understand.

"We have today."

"But that's not enough," she said as her hopes deflated. "Can't you see? Oh, Selik, I'm so frightened."

"Of what?"

"You. Us. There's something powerful connecting us. If we make love, I know it would be incredible. I just know it. You don't have to seduce me with false compliments or enticing sexual challenges. I already want you."

He moved closer, putting her hands on his shoulders.

Rain backed away out of his arms, unnerved by his closeness. She had to make him understand. "I can't get involved with a man in that way, so intimately, knowing he's committed to a life of violence. It's contrary to everything I value, all my beliefs. Can't you even consider giving up your vendetta?"

Selik's face stiffened and his chin jutted proudly as he refused to bend to her wishes or beg for her favors.

"It's hopeless for us then," she whispered softly, widening her eyes to stop the tears pooling in her eyes from overflowing. She failed. "But know this, you stubborn Viking, I don't want to hurt you."

Selik stared helplessly at the tears streaming down her face. After a moment, his face relaxed as his anger melted away. "Do not cry for me," he said, forcing a lighter tone to his voice. "I have survived much worse than the loss of a mere wench. Much, much worse."

Rain's heart almost broke at the lack of emotion in his voice. She wondered who had hurt him so badly, why he was on such a course of bloodshed.

This time, when he turned and walked away, his back rigid and unyielding, Rain did not follow.

"Dear God, how will I ever resist this man?" she asked aloud.

He needs you, child.

"What he needs is a good shot of pacifism."

What he needs is love.

If she didn't stop hearing these voices, she was going to start to accept Ubbi's belief that she really was an angel sent from God. Surreptitiously, checking first to see that no one was looking, she reached behind her back. Yup! Just as she'd thought. Her shoulder blades were flat. She shook her head in disgust then at her own foolishness.

When she returned to the cook fires, Blanche was draining some greens from a pot of boiling water, adding what appeared to be sauteed wild onions and garlic. A dozen loaves of golden-brown manchet bread lay cooling on a flat rock. The perfectly roasted venison sizzled over the fire, throwing off a wonderfully delicious aroma.

The woman was amazing. Rain was beginning to hate her.

"Where did you learn to cook like this?" she asked sweetly.

Blanche's intelligent hazel eyes turned her way, assessing Rain and her question, probably wondering how safe it was to reveal personal information. "My father was a Highland lord and my mother a weaver in his keep. The lord had no particular fondness for me, but he allowed me to work in the kitchens instead of the fields."

"How did you get tied up with Edwin then?"

"My father's lady—the bitch—hated me from the day I was born. As I grew older and more like my father in appearance, her viciousness grew." Blanche shrugged. "I had no choice but to use my other talents, on my back, to escape her wrath."

Rain shook her head sadly, reminded once again what a brutal period of history she had landed in. "In my ti—country, things are different. Illegitimacy is no real stigma, and women have rights. With your obvious intelligence, you could have any job you wanted and support yourself without having to rely on a man—either as a wife or a prostitute."

Blanche laid her cooking ladle aside and stared at Rain incredulously. "Truly?"

Rain nodded.

"How do I get to this country?"

Rain laughed. Oh, if it were only that easy! "It's a long, long way. I'm not sure I could even get back there myself."

Blanche studied her with renewed interest. "Well, then, let me ask you this. Is Selik your man?"

A slow heat spread from Rain's neck up her face, and she shifted uncomfortably. "No. I mean, not in that way. We're not lovers."

"Do you plan to take him as your man?"

Rain cocked her head to the side. "Why do you ask?"

"Because if you do not want him, I do."

Rain's heart froze at the prospect of Selik with Blanche. Of Selik with any woman other than herself. Oh, what a dog in the manger she had become—not accepting him as her lover, but not wanting him to have any other woman, either.

But Blanche's attraction to Selik puzzled her. "The women back at the campsite—they left before you came—they were repulsed by Selik's scarred looks and violent acts. A beast, they called him."

Blanche snorted disbelievingly. "They were blind."

Yes, they were, Rain agreed silently. How perceptive of Blanche to realize that. And how alarming.

When Selik slipped into the bed furs beside her that night, as he insisted on doing every night, Rain saw Blanche watching speculatively. Nothing escaped the discerning woman's eye. She had to know that Selik shared her bed furs—and nothing more—and was just biding her time. But for now, Rain relished Selik's closeness, the heat of his body against her back, his warm breath against her neck.

"Are you ready to open your root cellar, sweetling?" Selik teased. He nuzzled her neck, and she felt sweet shock waves of pleasure shoot to her fingertips and toes.

Rain said a vulgar, modern word.

He laughed, understanding completely. Apparently, some words did not need interpretation.

Rain mentally berated herself for the deterioration in her behavior. Two weeks in another time and already she threatened violence to people around her, usually Selik, and she used language she would never utter in her modern life. It was all Selik's fault, she decided irrationally. Instead of her changing him, he was bringing her down to his level.

Maybe you need to come down off your pedestal.

Oh, go away.

"What did you say?" Selik asked, his hot breath teasing the fine hairs on the nape of the neck.

She groaned. "Nothing."

"God again?"

When she refused to answer, Selik laughed. "Well, then, tell your heavenly being Good Eventide for us both."

Home sweet home, it was not . . .

For another week they traveled clandestinely through the night. Surprisingly, they ran into only a few Saxon soldiers, and they were able to avoid confrontation. Apparently, the Saxons were as weary of battle as the Norsemen and Scots and had returned to their homes. One fleeing soldier told Selik that King Athelstan's men hunted him in Cumbria, thinking he had escaped with King Constantine.

One day when they stopped at a small farmstead to water their horses, Rain got her first glimpse of Selik's obsessive distaste for children, of which the Viking women had told her earlier. Two little boys and one girl, none of them more than five years old, were playing in the mud beside a well while their Saxon mother turned the handle to raise the wooden bucket of water. The minute Selik saw the children, he ordered everyone in his party out of the farmyard, refusing to allow them to alight and quench their thirst. He never once apologized for his thoughtlessness, despite the fact that it took them two more hours to find water again. It was the last time they stopped at a homestead or in the daylight hours.

Despite their relative safety, they traveled slowly because of the slaves, who had to walk, although some of the men who agreed to serve under Selik were released from their captivity and rode with his soldiers. Bertha, the heavyset woman who had declared Rain "barmy" when she voluntarily joined the rope chain, helped Blanche, complaining all the time. She was pleased to see that Bertha's mild case of jaundice had cleared up, thanks to Rain's prescribing a new diet, including large amounts of greens and animal livers, when available. A third woman, Eadifu, a slovenly, thirty-something, coarse-mouthed female, seemed to spend most of her time on her back in the woods, servicing any man with the inclination to taste her dubious charms.

When they finally arrived at Ravenshire, Tykir's ancestral home, Rain looked about with excitement, despite her exhaustion. She had heard so much about this manor from her mother, but this crumbling keep couldn't be the same prosperous estate. Not only did the fields lie fallow and neglected, but the cotters' huts, more like hovels, were deserted and falling down. The primitive stone and wood castle looked more like a fort in the American West, with its wooden palisade high up on a flat-topped hill, called a motte. Rain shook her head in dismay at the neglect and decay.

She turned to Tykir, whose sad face reflected her own sorrow. "What happened?"

He shrugged. "My grandfather Dar and grandmother Aud held out against the Saxon encroachment for as many years as they could without my father or me or Eirik to help. They are both dead now."

"Does it still belong to you?"

"No doubt it does, or leastways to Eirik. Being the eldest, he holds the odal rights, and he is in favor with King Athelstan. The Saxons would not dare steal his heritage. Now me," he added with a grin, "that is another matter. The Saxon king would raze the keep and me with it, if he could."

"Oh, Tykir. All this fighting and animosity! Over what?"

"There does not have to be a reason, sister. You will soon learn that. Saxons hate 'the heathen Norsemen.' Norsemen hate 'the bloody Saxons.' 'Tis the nature of things and always will be 'til one or the other is wiped from the face of the earth."

Rain shook her head sadly. She could have told Tykir that the Vikings would lose this battle to the British, but it wasn't her place to intervene in history.

"Will you be safe here?"

"For a time. Until I heal completely."

"And then?"

"Mayhap I will visit my uncle Haakon. He is king of Norselands now and can always use good soldiers at his back whilst his brother Eric Bloodaxe covets the throne. Or perchance I will become one of the Byzantine emperor's Varangian guards. Nay, better yet, I may join Selik in sending a few more Saxons to their graves."

Rain gasped. "Tykir! Not you, too?"

He dismissed her concern with a wave of his hand, then added with a twinkle in his mischievous brown eyes, "On the other hand, I would not mind visiting your land. If the women there are as intriguing as you and your mother, I could no doubt be convinced to give up fighting for a spell."

Now that was a mind-boggling prospect—Tykir spreading his Norse charms among modern, liberated women. In fact, Rain had a few friends who would gobble up the studly Viking in a flash. Or vice versa.

But she knew from her earlier conversations with Tykir that he did not believe she came from the future, just some distant land. "No, you can't go to my country, Tykir. Unfortunately, I don't have any directions for traveling back."

"Then how did you get here? Nay, do not tell me. I fear you will say that you flew here on angel wings."

Rain smiled and reached over to jab him playfully in the ribs. "Ubbi has been babbling again, I see."

"Like a brook." Tykir returned her smile with brotherly warmth.

They rode into the deserted courtyard, and Selik helped Tykir down from his horse, handing him a makeshift wooden staff to use as a cane. Selik gave orders for the care of the horses and sent some men out to hunt game and scavenge feed for the animals.

When they entered the great hall of the keep, Rain knew that she and the captives had their work cut out for them. Bats hung from the high rafters, sharing quarters with a number of birds' nests. The rushes on the stone floor were so filthy that the straw stuck together in flat clumps. She shuddered under the overwhelming smell of mildew and decay.

While she would have much preferred to eat and sleep outdoors, she had seen the look of anguish on Tykir's face at the sad state of his ancestral home. And actually, it was her heritage as well. Rain had to do what she could to help him.

She decided that the kitchen and sleeping quarters would have to come first. She accompanied Blanche through the closed corridor connecting the hall with the separate cooking facilities after ordering Bertha and Eadifu to bring all the mattresses and sleeping pallets out to the kitchen courtyard for cleaning.

The former inhabitants had stripped the kitchen bone-bare. Not a pot or ladle or chair or scrap of food had been left by the servants when they abandoned the castle. Only a large wooden trestle table remained in the center of the massive kitchen, and a dozen bars of hard soap on the shelf of the scullery. The table had probably been too large for thieves to take or it would be gone, too. And from Rain's experience with these tenth-century people, soap was not a highly prized commodity.

Rain spent a grueling, backbreaking two hours scrubbing the floor and table and dusting the cobwebs from the walls and ceiling, while Blanche brought in the cooking utensils and supplies they'd carried with them from Brunanburh. They soon had the kitchen in reasonably clean condition and the last of their venison roasting over the hearth fire.

She went out to the kitchen courtyard to check on Bertha and Eadifu, who were boiling the few bed linens they'd found, along with everyone's dirty clothing, in large cauldrons of soapy water.

"Yer doin' that all wrong," Bertha complained as Eadifu lifted a sopping garment from the soapy water with a long stick, dumped it carelessly in a cauldron of clean water, creating a six-foot-wide puddle of mud around the pot, then hung it soaking wet from a nearby bush. "Ye must needs wring the bloody tunic, ye stupid lackwit. Do ye think we have a sennight ta dry the buggers?"

"Stick the buggers up yer arse, ye old shrew," Eadifu retorted. "I got better things ta do with me time." She looked over to the edge of the courtyard where a soldier waited, a lewd glint in his eyes and a horrific bulge in his pants.

Bertha noticed Rain's presence and enlisted her aid. "Mistress, tell the bawd ta keep her legs planted on the ground next ta me, 'stead of up in the air. 'Tis too much work fer me ta do here meself."

"Eadifu," Rain warned icily, "if you dare to leave this courtyard before all the laundry is done, I swear I will have you chained in the dungeon." Did they have dungeons here?

she wondered idly before going on. "And you will not eat for a week." This was one slave Rain was beginning to think she wouldn't mind selling herself.

Eadifu muttered something under her breath that sounded like "bloody bitch," but she turned sullenly back to her work.

"And do your work properly, the way Bertha orders."

Bertha beamed like a full moon at being placed in charge.

"Stop twitchin' yer arse every time a man comes within a hide of yer foul scent," she heard Bertha berate Eadifu as she headed for the kitchen.

"Yer jist upset cause ye got no arse worth twitchin'," Eadifu snapped back.

Rain heard a loud splash and hoped Bertha had dumped the slut into the cauldron of cold water. So much for being a pacifist. When push came to shove, it appeared that her principles were open to some flexibility.

Later, after the makeshift dinner, Selik came into the kitchen and told her that he and Tykir and the men were going to a nearby pond to bathe.

"Unless you want me to wait, and we can go together," he offered in a low, husky voice near her ear. The eagle-eyed Blanche watched with interest from across the room.

"No," Rain answered quickly, her skin turning warm at just the memory of their last bathing session.

Selik's gray eyes turned misty with remembered passion as well, and the edges of his full, sensual lips tilted upward in a knowing grin. "Ah, well, may-hap next time."

That night Rain climbed the stairs to a second-floor bed chamber, feeling aches in muscles she hadn't thought of since medical school. Tykir already slept in the room next door, being exhausted from the trip and his still healing injury.

Selik was in the room, removing his clothing when she opened the door. She thought about closing the door immediately and retreating back downstairs at the magnificent sight of his half-clad body. Swallowing hard, she tried not to stare at his clean hair hanging down past his shoulders, his bare, muscular back, and a trim waist exposed by leggings slung low on his slim hips. *Good heavens!*

"Shut the door," he ordered, having already seen her. "'Tis colder than a witch's tit in here."

Having no clean rushes to replace the ones taken from the mattresses, Selik had spread his sleeping furs on the floor before a fire in the hearth. The drafty room was warm only directly in front of the fireplace, and Rain already shivered from her recent bath. But still she stood frozen near the doorway.

"Come closer."

Rain dragged her feet reluctantly toward the fire—and Selik. She had slept next to this man for the past two weeks, knew the smell of his skin, the sound of his light snores, the heat of his flesh. And yet, being here with him in the small bedchamber was different. More intimate. Even the air in the room seemed close, filled with tension.

She wanted to run. And she wanted to stay.

Rain didn't delude herself about Selik's intentions. The consummate lover, Selik knew exactly how she was feeling. She could see it in the smoky depths of his gray eyes which watched her every move with hawk-like intensity, the seductive parting of his lips, and the high-strung stalking movement of his body.

He dropped his pants and stood before her, hands on hips, legs parted slightly—totally naked. Rain could not look away. Sweet Lord! The man did not play fair.

She closed her eyes for just a second to gather strength. The firelight cast flickering shadows on his silver-blond hair, and a golden sheen on the firm planes of his chest and washboard-firm abdomen. He exuded restless energy and tightly coiled power.

"Take off your garments, sweetling," he said in a raw voice.

Rain looked at him in horror.

He glided the tip of his tongue along the seam of his full

lips and laughed. "I will not force myself on you. We will just sleep . . . if that is your desire."

"Hah!" Rain said in a shaky voice, looking pointedly at his huge erection. He grew even longer under her gaze.

"Oh," she moaned softly, feeling her defenses weakening.

And Selik moved closer, reaching for her.

She backed away.

He put the palms of both hands up in the air as if in surrender, repeating, "I will not force you." Then he dropped down to the bed furs to show his good intentions, covering himself. "Come to bed, Rain. It has been a long day, and we are both tired."

Rain didn't believe for one minute that he was *that* tired.

"Selik, our sleeping together all the time is not a good idea."

"So you have said numerous times afore."

"I think I should go downstairs and sleep with Blanche."

"What makes you think Blanche sleeps alone?"

"What?"

Selik shrugged. "She has approached me numerous times. I cannot believe I am the only man she invites to her bed."

You better believe it, Rain thought with a heavy heart, wondering how long it would take Selik to relinquish his celibacy under Blanche's unrelenting temptation. *Oh, hell!*

"There is no choice. You sleep with me," he declared firmly, patting the fur beside him. "You are my hostage."

She groaned. "Selik, I'm not going to make love with you. Why torture yourself?"

"And you as well?" His left eyebrow rose a fraction in question.

"And me too."

He smiled with infuriating satisfaction at her admission.

Giving up, she began to drop down to the furs on the side closest to the fire.

"Nay. Take off your garments first."

Rain stood back up and glared down at him. "I slept in my clothes at the campsites during our trip here."

"That was then. This is now. Whether you come from the future, as you claim, or the bloody moon, you will adopt our ways whilst living amongst us here."

Selik sat up and folded his arms over his bent knees, watching her intently as she began to disrobe.

Rain felt her face flame, but she would not betray her nervousness over undressing in front of the arrogant man. God, she was too tall, too big and gawky. The only times she'd been with men in the past, she'd undressed in the dark to hide her embarrassment over her ungainly body. They hadn't seemed to mind.

The only sounds in the room were the crackling of the fire and Selik's even breathing as she finally stood before him in nothing but her flesh-colored lace bra and panties. His burning eyes seared her skin. When they connected with hers, she jerked back slightly at the jolt of electric heat they transmitted.

"The rest," he urged raspily, waving a hand to indicate her underwear. She could not be sure, but his breathing sounded ragged in the charged silence of the room.

Dazed, Rain didn't even protest, but she lifted her chin defiantly when the wispy garments dropped to the rushes, refusing to cower before his too-close scrutiny. She had enough flaws when fully clothed. Naked, she felt as awkward and unattractive as she had in sixth grade, when she was the tallest student in her class, the brunt of jokes for all the mean, insensitive, teasing boys.

But Selik wasn't mocking her. His eyes caressed every inch of her body. Wherever his eyes touched, Rain felt a tingling heat ignite and warm her skin. For the first time in her life, she felt attractive.

"You are the most beautiful woman I have ever seen," he whispered in awe.

Tears welled in Rain's eyes. "Don't, Selik. Don't make fun of me."

He tilted his head questioningly, then lifted the bed fur next to him, urging her to join him.

When she was lying down, making sure her body did not touch his, Selik said softly, "The men of your time must be halfwits to make you ashamed of your body. Truly, Rain, you *are* beautiful." Ever so gently, he brushed some loose strands of hair off her face.

"I think you are the one who must be halfwitted," she said with a shaky laugh, pleased despite the fact that he was probably just trying to seduce her. Oddly, she wanted to be beautiful for Selik. "Besides, you likened me to a tree and a horse a few times, if you'll recall."

Selik chuckled, tracing a forefinger along the curve of her shoulder. Rain shuddered with the sheer sweetness of pleasure that swept her, so intense it was almost unbearable. "Ah, well, 'tis a well-known fact that I have a fondness for horses and stately trees."

She turned to poke him for his teasing. A big mistake! Her breast grazed his arm, and he inhaled sharply at the electrifying contact. Rain immediately turned over and away from him toward the fire to hide the effect of just that brief touch on her sensitive nipples.

Suddenly, Rain could not help the silent tears that streamed down her face. She wanted Selik so badly, and she wearied of fighting the battle with herself.

"Rain, why do you weep? I will not make love to you if you do not wish it."

You silly man, don't you know that's just what I want you to do?

He ran a hand caressingly along the length of her arm, sending shivers to every erotic part of her body.

"Are you afeard of getting with child? I assure you that you will not carry my seed," he offered softly as he kissed the line of her shoulder over to the nape of her neck. With every rhythmic breath he took, the tip of his penis grazed the cleft between her buttocks.

Rain laughed shakily. "Now that's an original line.

How do you plan on guaranteeing that? Do you have a condom?"

"Nay, I use none of those ridiculous sheaths your mother mentioned." She felt him smile against her neck. "I follow the method of your Biblical Onan—spilling the seed outside the body." When she snorted with disbelief, he laughed. "Are you about to preach me a birth-control lecture, as your mother did to King Sigtrygg's ladies?"

"My mother did what?" Rain exclaimed, turning to look at his grinning face. "Oh, never mind." Really, she had heard more than enough of her mother's outrageous conduct. "But I don't see how you can be sure you have never fathered any children . . . using that method, I mean."

"I assure you, lady, I have no *live* children."

"Well, perhaps that's true, but it's only luck that you haven't if you practice pulling out before climax."

Selik make a choking sound of disbelief. "What kind of woman are you to speak so bluntly?"

"I'm a doctor, for heaven's sake. And I'm telling you, Selik, that a few moments ago you had a bead of semen on the end of your penis—"

Selik made an inarticulate sound deep in his throat, and his eyebrows arched in wonder, probably at her attention to detail.

"Anyhow, if you made love with a woman then, even if you withdrew early and climaxed outside the woman's body, she still could have gotten pregnant."

"I assume that see-man and peen-yes mean what I think they do?" he asked dryly. At her nod, he went on. "But how could conception take place if the seed spills outside the body?"

"Because, you fool, just that tiny drop of semen inserted in a woman's body is enough to make a female pregnant."

"You make these stories up as you go along. 'Tis not true."

"Yes, it is, Selik. As a doctor, I'm telling you, I've seen evidence of it over and over."

Horrified, he stared at her with disbelief, which soon

blossomed into alarm. "I never knew," he whispered, concluding with disgust, "'Tis just luck then that I have bred no more babes."

To Rain's chagrin, Selik turned away from her then.

CHAPTER EIGHT

T *here was nothing sweet about this parting . . .*

"Attend me well, Rain. You will stay here at Raven-shire with Tykir 'til I return," Selik commanded the next morning in his bedchamber as he was packing a leather bag.

Rain rebelled, not in a good mood after a restless night of poor sleep—prompted, no doubt, by sexual frustration, a problem Rain had never experienced before. And it annoyed her to hear Selik speaking so calmly, his demeanor so unaffected as he gathered his belongings.

Wearing only a *brynja,* the padded undertunic which would protect his chest from chafing under metal armor, and a pair of heavy wool braies that clung to his muscled thighs, Selik tried to ignore her.

"Why? Why must I stay here? Where are you going? When will you come back? Hey, you're *not* thinking of dumping me here, are you? No way!"

Selik put both hands to his ears in disgust. "Freya's tit! You have turned shrewish with your endless questions. Just accept my orders and be biddable, for once."

"Me? Shrewish? Hah! And, by the way, I don't appreciate those crude Viking expressions of yours. Not one bit."

Selik's gray eyes widened with exaggerated surprise. "You take exception to my crude words when you told me just a few days ago, in a vulgar fashion even for me, exactly what I could do to myself? As I recall, you very clearly directed me to scr—"

"You don't have to throw my words back in my face like a damn parrot." Rain lifted her chin defiantly and tried to pretend that the warm skin on her face was not a blush, that she was not embarrassed by her increasingly sharp, and sometimes vulgar, tongue. Good Lord! She was turning into a woman she no longer recognized. "Well, you provoked me." Her excuse sounded weak even to her ears.

"You have an answer for everything, wench."

Not everything, Rain thought bleakly. She watched forlornly as Selik folded several of the strips of fabric he wore as loincloths. Suddenly, an image flickered in her head—an enticing image—of Selik in a pair of men's bikini underwear. Hey, Selik in boxer shorts wouldn't be so bad, either, Rain thought.

"Why are you grinning? Do you plot some other mischief to muddle my life?"

"No," Rain said with a smile. "I was just picturing you in modern underwear, the kind men in my country wear." She described all the different kinds to Selik, but he wasn't impressed.

"Why would men care whether they wear silk or linen loincloths? Or whether they had 'designer labels' by that Calvin person?" he scoffed.

"Because they want to impress women."

"'Tis what is inside the loincloth that matters more, wench," Selik asserted, winking at her with supreme arrogance.

"Yeah, well, I still say you'd look better than those cover models in those jockey shorts ads. Hey, better yet," she added, fanning her face dramatically, "in a pair of edible underwear."

Selik stopped his packing completely and turned to stare

at her. She had his full attention. "Now I know you jest with me. People eating underwear?"

"Use your imagination, Selik. You, the supposed sex god of the Dark Ages, should have an idea how they would be used."

Rain knew the moment Selik understood. His neck colored and the flush moved slowly up his face. She loved it! Then his lips tilted in a boyish grin.

"A sex god! I ne'er claimed to be such."

"Anyhow, I've never tried edible underwear myself, but I understand that it comes in different flavors, like strawberry or lemon. I'll bet there's even some that tastes like cherry Lifesavers."

"Really?"

"You'd like that, wouldn't you?" she asked with a laugh.

Selik shook his head from side to side, convinced now that she was fibbing. "Truly, you amaze me, woman. Do you stay up all night inventing these outrageous tales to scandalize me?"

"Are you scandalized?"

"Nay. You disconcert me, and that is, no doubt, your purpose. I will not allow you to divert me, however. Heed me well on this one thing. You swore not to escape, and I hold you to your vow. Stay at Ravenshire with Tykir."

"Will you return?"

Selik scowled at her, refusing to answer.

"But where—"

"Where I go and if I return is my concern. Just follow my orders. And stay near the keep. There are Saxons about, I wager, and the bastards would lop off your winsome head in a trice, never stopping to ask *why* you traveled with The Outlaw. 'Tis enough that they think I favor your company. I have assigned Gorm to watch over you—"

"You wouldn't dare. I don't want that slimebucket within a mile of me."

Selik's face stiffened with menace. "All my men have orders to protect you. Has Gorm done aught to harm you?

On my oath, I will skin the misbegotten cur alive if he has touched even a hair on your fair body."

Fair? Rain honed in irrelevantly on his inadvertent compliment. Selik had called her beautiful last night, but she had doubted his sincerity. Was it possible it hadn't been a line? Could he care for her? Was the emotion he displayed just now a sign of deeper feelings?

But then Rain's heart sunk as his other words sunk in, *I will skin the man alive.* "Selik, please tell me you don't skin people."

He grinned. "It was just an expression, sweetling. Even I draw the line somewhere."

She laughed shakily. "Well, I knew that."

He shot her a look of amused disbelief. "Do you ever admit being wrong?"

Sending a soldier off to war is never easy . . .

A short time later, Rain watched with dismay from the steps leading up to the great hall as Selik mounted Fury. This was the Selik of the battlefield, the warrior of the Brunanburh painting, the man who had haunted her nightmares for years, drawing her back through the tunnel of time.

Wearing a thigh-length tunic of flexible chain mail over a wool hauberk and tight leggings, Selik expertly maneuvered the reins of the horse as it pranced nervously about the bailey awaiting the half-dozen men who would travel with him. He sheathed his lethal sword, Wrath, at his side, and hung his pike and helmet from special saddle hooks.

His eyes, distant and formidable, locked with Rain's. There was no emotional connection now. Rain realized, with foreboding, that his berserk mode had taken over.

"Take care," Rain whispered in a soft, shaky voice.

Selik didn't seem to hear her words as he stared blankly ahead, ignoring her, but then she noticed his Adam's apple move jerkily several times as if he was trying, but unable to speak. He surprised her by nodding. Then, without speaking, he rode off.

Watching his departing back, Rain felt as if he were taking a part of her with him. It was incomprehensible to her how a man she had met so recently could have touched her so deeply. She was beginning to think she would never be able to return to the future if it meant leaving Selik behind.

The moment Selik disappeared from sight, Rain went searching for Tykir, determined to get some questions answered. How could she help Selik if she knew nothing about him?

She found Tykir in his bedchamber with Ubbi exercising his leg. The men had improvised a primitive form of physical therapy by tying a small sack of flour to Tykir's ankle. Lying on the bed, he was raising his leg up and down in slow repetitions.

"Swimming would be a good exercise to strengthen your leg muscles, too, Tykir. And massage. In fact, I can work on the muscles for you when you're done with the leg lifts."

Tykir and Ubbi both looked toward her as she approached the bed, raising their eyebrows skeptically.

"Swimming this time of year? I think not, sister. Methinks the leg would just cramp up."

"It might be just the thing for speeding up the healing process, actually. And you, too, Ubbi," she said, directing her attention toward the little man. "I've been meaning to talk to you about your arthritis. After you're done with Tykir, I want to examine *you*. I think I might be able to help."

Ubbi backed away from her. "Art-rye-tits?" Then he stood and threw his stooped shoulders back in challenge. "Examine me? Nay, ye will not be touchin' me body. 'Tis unseemly fer a maid to even think such."

"Oh, Ubbi, I've seen hundreds of naked men, and your body is no different, believe me."

"Hundreds of naked men!" Ubbi and Tykir both exclaimed.

"Mistress, for shame! Ye should not missay the truth. A woman of virtue such as yerself has ne'er bedded with hundreds of men."

Tykir just grinned as he released the flour weight from his ankle. The idea of such a promiscuous sister amused the fool.

"Don't be silly, Ubbi. I meant that, as a doctor, I have examined many, many men in my hospital."

"Hmmm. There is a hospitium in Jorvik. Is your 'hospital' the same?" Ubbi asked cautiously.

"There's a medical facility in Jorvik?" Rain asked excitedly.

"Yea, at St. Peter's minster. The culdees—priests—care fer the sick an' dying in their own hospitium."

"Oh, that's wonderful When can we go to see it? Is it nearby?"

"'Tis a day's ride from here, but you cannot leave until Selik returns," Tykir explained, his long blond hair falling forward as he leaned on his wooden staff, trying to pull himself up off the bed. "Selik gave orders, and he would have my head, as well as yours, if I disobey."

"No, don't get up," she told Tykir, pressing him back down. She began to massage his thigh through his leggings. At first, her intimate touch embarrassed him. Then he cursed her as she drew out each painful tendon. "Oh, sweet Mother of Thor! Do you save my life just to throw me back in the grave?"

"Don't be such a baby."

Later, he sighed with pleasure at her expert manipulation, his dark lashes closing briefly over big brown eyes so like her brother Dave's. "Truly, you have magical fingers, my sister."

Suddenly, Rain noticed Ubbi inching his way toward the open doorway. "Don't you dare leave. I'm done with Tykir's workout for today, and now it's your turn."

Ubbi rolled his eyes pleadingly toward Tykir, but her brother just laughed. "Let the witch work her wiles on you, Ubbi. Who knows? Mayhap her hands will perform wonders on your flesh as well."

Tykir hobbled out of the room on his makeshift crutch,

chuckling with amusement over Ubbi's apparent discomfort at being left alone with Rain.

Rain had to cajole, threaten, and bribe Ubbi into removing his garments, but even then he would only strip down to his loincloth. She barely stifled a gasp of horror at the misshapen condition of his body.

"Ubbi, how long have you suffered from arthritis?" At his look of confusion, she reworded her question. "How old were you when you first felt a stiffening in your joints? Is it more painful sometimes than others?"

While she asked her questions, Rain checked out every inch of his body with probing fingers, from his bunched shoulders to his knobby feet, except, of course, for his genital area. She knew Ubbi would never allow her to examine him there.

Finally, she forced Ubbi to lie facedown on the bed, despite his protests and obvious humiliation. With alternately firm and gentle pressing and flexing of her fingers, she soon loosened his painfully gnarled muscles.

"Oh, mistress, I have not felt so good since I was a boy," Ubbi said on a sigh, his voice overflowing with adoration.

Rain smiled, happy to help the sweet man. "Starting tomorrow, I'll do the massages twice a day. It would be great if we could find some oil. Also, I'll give you some exercises to do on your own. And we might even be able to gather some herbs to alleviate the pain. Oh, and I just thought of something else—hot mud packs all over your body."

Ubbi groaned, but his rheumy eyes bespoke his heartfelt thanks. "Do you truly think you can make me better?"

"No, I can't cure you, Ubbi," Rain said, patting him gently on the shoulder. "There's no way to correct an arthritic condition, but there are things that can help make a person more mobile and pain-free."

"'Tis a miracle," Ubbi declared, and Rain knew her status as an angel in Ubbi's eyes had just gone up another notch. He practically skipped out of the room.

Suddenly, Rain realized that she'd forgotten the reason

for coming up to Tykir's bedchamber in the first place—to get answers to her questions about Selik. Searching for Tykir once again, she found him in the great hall, directing some of the captives in cleaning out the soiled rushes and scrubbing down the tables.

"Tykir, I meant to ask you something earlier. Where has Selik gone?"

"He did not tell you?"

"No. Is it a secret?"

"Nay," he replied carefully under her intent scrutiny. "He travels back north to the Alban lands of King Constantine."

"Scotland? But Ubbi told me he was unwelcome there."

Tykir shrugged. "'Tis true, the Scots would just as well he go elsewhere, but he has been a good comrade. They cannot in good conscience turn him away from their doors."

"Then why does he go there?"

"To protect me, and Ravenshire."

"What!" That Selik might have a noble cause for doing anything had never occurred to Rain. What did that say about her? And her faith in the man she had been sent to save? Rain did not like herself much at the moment.

Tykir lowered his body to a nearby bench, rubbing his aching leg, and Rain dropped down beside him.

"Tell me," she urged.

"When we returned yestermorn, I found a message from Eirik in a special hiding place we had as children. He warned me that King Athelstan plans a massive manhunt for Selik and that he will raze Ravenshire to the ground if he discovers Selik anywhere in the vicinity."

Rain's blood froze in her veins and her heart went out to her outlaw, who truly had no home—was, in fact, welcome nowhere. "Please go on," she encouraged shakily.

"Selik figured that if he shows his face in the land of the Scots, so far from here, King Athelstan will direct his forces there. The Saxons will have no reason to invade Ravenshire. I am not big enough quarry for him to send a troop of soldiers."

"So he intends to wave his body like a bloody flag in front of his enemies to save you," Rain said, appalled.

"To save *us*," Tykir corrected, his face reddening at her implied insult. "If the Saxons found him here, 'tis not just the keep they would destroy but all who are in it. That includes me, you, Ubbi, everyone."

"But we could have left with him," Rain protested. "Why didn't he give us a choice?"

Tykir shook his head sadly. "I wanted him to stay. I told him so. Do you think I care aught for a piece of crumbling stone and a parcel of land? But Selik is set in his ways."

"And I considered him a beast, brutal and uncaring in all his violence!" Rain was beginning to think she had a lot to learn about right and wrong. Perhaps these primitive people could teach her, with all her advanced education, a few lessons she'd somehow missed in her modern life.

"He is brutal, my sister. Never think otherwise. The truth of his berserk behavior cannot be honey-coated, but he is a good man at heart."

"Why is he like this, Tykir? Please tell me what happened to him to change him from the carefree youth my mother described to this tormented shell of a man?"

Tykir stiffened and his face closed over. "Nay, I will not discuss Selik's past. 'Tis for him to disclose—or hold in his soul, if he so chooses."

"But if I don't stop him—if someone doesn't help him soon, he will surely die."

"Yea, he will. For a long time, Selik has traveled the fast road to Valhalla, uncaring of his own mortality, wishing only to take as many Saxons as he can with him."

"How sad to have violence as a life goal!"

Tykir shrugged and stood, leaning on his staff. "Know this, to the Saxons Selik may be naught more than a berserker. A demon gone mad from the bloodbath that has washed over Northumbria as they try to wipe all Norsemen from their soil. But to many a Norseman, Selik is a brave knight on a quest for noble vengeance. You would do well to remember that."

"But—"

Tykir raised a hand to halt her next words. "Nay, that is all I will say on the subject. Ask Selik when he returns."

But would he return? Rain wondered worriedly as the days, then weeks, went by with no word from her primitive soulmate. More and more, as she and the captives and Selik's remaining soldiers worked to clean up the crumbling keep—a losing battle with their meager resources—Rain relived in her mind their last night together. If he died—*Oh, please, God, don't let that happen!*—Rain knew she would forever regret not having had that one night of love with him.

When a month had passed and there was still no sign of Selik, panic set in. Rain had starting biting her fingernails, a nervous habit she thought she'd long ago conquered. Fighting a queasy stomach, she lost her appetite and at least ten pounds. Tykir and Ubbi, even Blanche and Bertha, avoided her company because they were sick over her endless questions about Selik's safety and return.

"Gawd! I think I will empty me stomach if I hear ye ask one more time when the bloody outlaw will return," Bertha complained in a whining voice as she helped Blanche dress the carcass of a fresh-killed deer. Gorm, one of Blanche's most ardent suitors, had brought the doe back from his daily hunt and laid it at Blanche's feet in the courtyard as if it were a dozen roses. Woman-wise, the wily Blanche had acted duly impressed and batted her eyelashes at Gorm in unspoken promise.

When Rain had shot a disapproving look at Blanche, knowing she preferred to cast her net in Selik's direction, the maid had shrugged, without guilt, and commented, "A woman must cover all her options. Best you think of that, too, my lady, in the event The Outlaw does not return."

Rain studied Bertha then, much pleased with her improving skin color, thanks to the special diet she had prescribed. Thank heavens it was only a Vitamin K deficiency and not a tumor or liver disease that had caused her yellowish skin tone.

"Make sure you save some of the liver for yourself. You still need lots of iron."

Bertha nodded, no longer protesting Rain's every bit of medical advice since she witnessed the daily improvement in her health.

"Do you want me to help you cut that up?" she asked, gulping distastefully at the prospect of handling the bloody carcass. She was not a vegetarian, but as many times as she'd performed surgery on human bodies, she was oddly reluctant to touch raw animal flesh. Probably childhood associations with Bambi, she decided.

"Nay, go off and wear down the planks on the ramparts sum more, pinin' fer yer lover to come back," Bertha snapped with gentle sarcasm. Blanche just smiled at the brash servant.

"Selik is not my lover."

"Not fer lack of tryin', I wager. Nor fer lack of yer wantin' the beddin'," Bertha quipped sagely.

"You are so coarse!"

"Do not be takin' that tone with me, m'lady," the impertinent captive asserted. "I may be jist a lowly servant, but 'tis plain as the wart on a witch's nose, yer like a mare in heat. And The Outlaw—well, he be the stallion circlin' you, waitin' fer the right moment to pounce."

"Bertha!" both Rain and Blanche exclaimed.

Rain couldn't help but laugh then at the image. "Is that really how I appear to people—a mare in heat? Good Lord!"

"Nay," Bertha answered, more gently. "'Tis jist that I be more world-wise in the ways of men and wimmen and their lustful natures. I see the signs better than most, I warrant."

Rain shook her head from side to side in disbelief that she was actually standing there listening to a short, dumpy woman with rotting teeth give her advice on love.

"Leastways, I cannot see why ye do not just flap yer wings and fly off to help yer lover if ye be so worried," Bertha added, guffawing loudly at her own joke.

Blanche smiled mockingly, adding, "Oh, and could you

ask God if he would send a milk cow and laying hens so I can make a pudding for dinner?"

Apparently, Ubbi was spreading his angel stories again, but no one else was buying them.

Rain left the kitchen in a huff, knowing her dubious culinary skills were unwanted. She did, indeed, head for the ramparts, where she scanned the horizon. "Oh, Selik where are you? Dear God, please send him back to me safely. I promise to try harder to help him."

Her prayer was answered immediately with the thunder of distant hooves, followed by the blurry outline of riders on the horizon of a hill about one mile from the keep. Rain rolled her eyes heavenward, saying a silent thank-you as she practically flew down the wooden steps to the bailey.

Love hurts . . .

Selik saw the wench standing on the ramparts, watching for him, then dart away when she recognized his standard. His heart lurched and expanded in his chest, causing him to inhale sharply to catch his breath. *Bloody hell!* He had spent the past four sennights steeling himself to the siren's lure, trying to maintain his single-minded resolve to focus his life on one goal only—death to the Saxons, but, in particular, death to his most hated enemy, Steven of Gravely.

But all his efforts were for naught. Oh, he had killed more than enough Saxons to satisfy his bloodthirsty quest for revenge since he had left Ravenshire, but still Selik could not deny the rush of pleasure as he drew closer on seeing the welcome expression on Rain's face. She awaited him eagerly on the bailey steps leading up to the great hall.

Selik flipped the noseguard down on his helmet to hide any softening in his features. He must sort out these dangerous emotions in private. Mayhap he should just turn Fury around and head back northward.

Did he truly think he could have a life with the wench? Nay, he admitted immediately. 'Twas impossible.

Was it what he wanted, though? Yea, Selik realized with alarm. He had allowed himself to yield to her attraction, and that led down a path he must not, *could not*, travel.

Selik saw Rain's honey eyes search his saddle, then shift away guiltily. Searching for the *behaettie*, she was. Damn her revealing eyes! Despite his promise not to scalp again, the wench did not trust him. For some reason he could not fathom, the injustice of her gesture cut him deeply.

Selik truly hardened his heart then. There was naught here for him in Ravenshire. There was naught anywhere, for that matter, except destruction and death. His death, ultimately. 'Twas his fate. Well, he would rest the night at Ravenshire, then depart in the morn. He would take no one with him, not even Ubbi. 'Twas best that way.

With that resolve, Selik steered Fury past Rain and Tykir and Ubbi and the soldiers he had left behind. Selik alighted from his horse at the other side of the courtyard and led the panting animal toward the outbuilding that housed the horses. Steeling himself to the look of hurt that misted Rain's golden eyes, he ignored her shy wave of welcome.

He had removed the saddle and was providing water and fresh hay for Fury when he heard Rain's soft tread come up behind him.

"Selik, what's wrong?"

"What is right?"

She made a low sound of exasperation. "You know what I mean—why are you avoiding me?"

Selik turned and looked at her then, forcing his face to remain impassive and unmoved by her pleading eyes and softly parted lips. "Avoid? Nay. Mayhap you no longer strike my fancy. I am not interested in you anymore." *Baldr's bones! Do I add lying to my sins now?*

Rain whimpered, her open face clearly showing the pain of his insult, like a slap. "I've been worried about you."

"My lady, I have survived these ten years past without the worrisome fretting of a bothersome female. Do not think I welcome your meddling concern now."

Rain tilted her head questioningly. "And who was the woman who fretted over you then?"

Her question startled Selik, and for a moment he knew his face revealed his pain. "Go away, Rain," he said in a tired voice. "Your concern is misplaced."

"Tykir told me why you left, Selik, and I just want to say that I'm sorry I called you a beast before. I'm trying to understand you, I really am, but—"

"Tykir had no right to interfere in my life, and I will tell him so. And the last thing I want from you is understanding."

"What *do* you want from me then?"

He lifted his chin and stared at her impassively.

"Not a blessed thing."

Rain's face colored, but she persisted. "I've had a lot of time to think while you were gone, and I realize now that there is good in every man."

"And who named you God, to be my judge or any man's?"

Rain cringed under his punishing assessment of her failings, but still she went on doggedly. "I need to remember that whatever evil things you do must be balanced by the crimes against you in your past."

"And did Tykir's blathering tongue reveal those events, as well?" he asked icily.

"No, he told me to ask you."

Selik leaned against a support beam and eyed Rain contemptuously. The witless wench prodded him and did not recognize the danger of his churning anger. "I took no scalps this time. I know you checked."

She nodded reluctantly, no doubt recognizing the silky menace in his voice.

"And didst thou think I had suddenly turned pacifist?"

"Of course not. But it has to be a sign—"

"Sign? Looking for signs, are you? Truly, you are dangerous in your lackwittedness!" He grabbed her by the forearms and shook her, as if that motion could knock some sense into her thick head. "How many men do you think I killed these past sennights? Ten? Twenty? Fifty? A hundred?"

With each increasing number, her eyes widened larger and larger with dismay. Tears welled in her honey eyes and spilled over, some dripping onto his bare hands like liquid fire.

"Selik, I think I love you," she cried out. "God help me, but I love you."

Selik's heart lurched at her totally unexpected declaration. It took all his willpower not to pull her into his arms and relish the moment—and the precious, precious words.

I love you. Nay, it could not be true.

I love you. Why was she teasing him so? Why did the gods torment him thus? His senses reeled with rage. He had not felt so strongly since he had found his wife's body, ravaged and mutilated. Or when he got his first glimpse of his infant son's skull carried on the pike of a Saxon soldier.

I love you. Selik pushed her away roughly and banged his fist against the wood partition separating the horse stalls. The rotting wood crumbled on impact, and he kicked it aside angrily. With a growl of frustration, he spun on his heel.

I love you. Nay, Selik screamed silently. He did not want her love. He could not bear so much pain again.

Holding his hands to his pounding head, Selik rushed through the courtyard, ignoring the calls of concern from Ubbi and Tykir. Without direction, he headed around the keep and off toward the woods and a nearby pond that the Ravenshire inhabitants used for bathing. In a daze, he dropped his garments to the ground and waded into the icy water, continuing past the ledge which led to a steep drop. Seeking the balm of hard exercise, he began to swim back and forth, back and forth across the still waters.

But he could not forget. Not the past. Not the present, with Rain's unintentionally cruel, heart-stopping words. And, most of all, not his empty, hopeless future.

It had been ten years ago, ten long agonizing years, and

yet the images remained frozen in his head as if they had happened only yesterday.

Selik shook his head angrily as he continued his grueling swim, trying to erase the horrendous memories. But the memories of Astrid and his young son haunted him every moment of his life.

Those events ten years ago marked the beginning of Selik's vendetta against all the Saxons, and he had waged it bloodily. The elusive Gravely still escaped his stalking, but Selik had taken hundreds of Saxon lives on the way to his ultimate goal of destroying the demonic Earl of Gravely.

He could not be detracted from his single-minded goal of vengeance by a peace-loving angel from the future. Nay, Selik could not be moved from his chosen path.

But still Rain's words hummed in his head. *I love you. I love you. I love you . . .*

So, now she knows . . .

Still in the stable, Rain stared, stunned, at the doorway through which Selik had departed, his softly muttered words echoing like cymbals in her brain. She doubted that he even knew he had spoken aloud.

His wife's body ravaged and mutilated. His infant son's skull carried on a Saxon pike.

All the pieces of the puzzle that constituted Selik's torment came together with bloodcurdling understanding in Rain's numbed brain. No wonder he had turned vicious, hellbent on revenge.

And she, who had always prided herself on her sensitivity as a doctor and a human being, had dared to judge him and find him wanting. How self-righteous of her! For a blinding moment, she questioned who was the beast in the scenario, and the answer was not Selik.

Ubbi walked into the primitive stable then, leading one of the soldier's horses. He immediately started to turn away when he saw the look on her face.

"Don't you dare leave," she ordered, coming up and

backing the little man against the wall of the building with a finger pressed against his chest. Nervously, Ubbi dropped the reins and the horse ambled back outside.

"M'lady, I have chores—"

"I know, Ubbi. I know about Selik."

"Wha . . . what do ye mean?"

"I know about his wife and his baby. Now you are going to tell me the rest of the details."

"The master told ye how Astrid died, and the babe . . . oh, Asgard, help us . . . he spoke of Thorkel, too?"

Rain nodded grimly.

"Oh, mistress, what did ye do to provoke him into revealing so much?" Ubbi sank down to the dirt floor and put his face in his knobby hands. When he finally looked back to her, his cloudy eyes had an additional misting of tears. He shook his head wearily. "'Tis not good news. Nay, it can only mean trouble if he be talkin' 'bout the horrors in his past."

Rain sank down next to Ubbi and took one of his deformed hands in her own. "Tell me."

Ubbi swallowed visibly. "'Twas more than ten years past. Selik was no longer a Jomsviking knight, and he had been married to Astrid for two years. Ah, a sweet maid she was. Pretty as larkspur in the spring. And young—having seen no more than eighteen winters."

Rain felt macabre jealousy shoot through her veins over the dead woman and her link with Selik.

"The two were inseparable. Always touchin' each other. Wantin' ter go off and be alone. Even when she was big with child, and then after the babe was born. You see, Selik never had a home or family ter speak of. So he cherished Astrid and their child all the more. But Selik finally had ter go on a tradin' voyage to Hedeby. He left Astrid and Thorkel in the fine home he built fer them in Jorvik, thinkin' them safe, but—"

"The Saxons came," Rain finished for him.

Ubbi nodded, his kind face turning ugly with anger over the memories that seemed to hold him in thrall.

"Were you with Selik?" Rain asked softly as she caressed his tensely fisted hand.

"Yea." The one horror-filled word said it all. He swallowed with great difficulty several times, then went on. "The house was burned to the ground, but we found Astrid's body off beyond the orchard. Nekkid, she was, and her legs wuz covered with blood from the top of her thighs to her ankles. Blood and the seed of all the men who had raped her."

Rain jammed a fist against her mouth to stifle her sobs.

"I will ne'er forget, to the day I die, the sight of me master drawing Astrid into his arms, brushing the blood-soaked strands from her face, crooning her name over and over. For a certainty, 'tis the last time I saw him give in to tears."

Ubbi's face darkened with a fierce anger as he seemed to remember something else. "When he laid Astrid's body back down, then I saw—" Ubbi's words trailed off as he tried to get his emotions under control. Finally, he added, "And the head of the Saxon band—Steven, Earl of Gravely—had carved his initials, one on each breast, S and G."

Rain didn't want to hear any more. She couldn't comprehend a human being who would deliberately torture another person in such a manner. Then some of the other things Ubbi had said began to sink in. "Steven of Gravely? Wasn't he the cousin of Eadric, the nobleman Selik killed at Brunanburh?"

Ubbi nodded. "And so the vendetta betwixt the two goes on and on."

"How did it all start in the first place?"

"Steven of Gravely needs no excuse to practice his misdeeds. He truly is an evil man. But he blames Selik for the death of his father, the old lord."

"And did Selik kill his father?"

"Mayhap. There was a battle. Many Saxons and Norsemen died that day. It could have been Selik, or any other, but Steven needed a target for his hatred, and he chose Selik."

"But what he did to Selik's wife—Oh, Ubbi! No wonder Selik is so bitter!"

The little man turned on her then and stabbed her with his

defiant eyes. "Yea, he is bitter and with good reason. For that is not all the bloody demon did that day. He left the crushed, headless body of the babe on the ground near his mother's body. It took Selik weeks to discover where the head was."

Rain remembered Selik's words then. "This Earl of Gravely carried Thorkel's skull on his pike, didn't he?"

"Yea, he hoped ter lure Selik into the open, ter his death. We finally recovered the poor babe's rotting head and buried it with the body, but Selik still tries to capture the elusive Steven—and any other bloody Saxon who crosses his path."

Rain looked down and saw a dark patch on the front of her tunic—Selik's tunic—and realized that she'd been crying and her tears made a steady, hot stream down to her breasts. Like blood, she thought.

Oh, sweet God. Now I understand why you have sent me here.

"So now you know," Ubbi said with finality as he stood and tried to straighten his back in challenge.

"Will you be able to help the lad?"

"I don't know, Ubbi. I just don't know, but I'm going to try."

He smiled then, a smile that didn't reach his sad eyes. "You will, if anyone can, I warrant." He watched as she stood and brushed the dirt off her clothing. "The master has gone to the pond. Find him, lass. Methinks he needs you."

CHAPTER NINE

⚭

S *mile, though your heart is breaking . . .*

 Selik was doing energetic laps from one end of the pond to the other—over and over and over. His face buried in the icy water, he moved his powerful arms expertly in a neat breast stroke, slicing through the calm surface with precision.

Rain sank to the ground near the edge of the pond and drew her legs up, wrapping her arms around them and resting her chin on her knees. She waited patiently for him to vent his rage through the brutal exercise.

Rain's heart went out to Selik, knowing that her words of love had somehow triggered painful memories of his horrid tragedy. She now understood fully the daily torment he suffered and how he'd been caught in a bloody spiral of violence. When the voice in her head referred to saving Selik, this must be what it referred to.

Finally, Selik sprang upward like a beautiful dolphin. He spat out a spray of water, then shook his long hair back off his face. After he swam to lower water, he stood and his legs, weakened by the strenuous swim, almost buckled. Rain wanted to go forward to help him but bided her time, not wanting to startle her outlaw Viking. Her sweet, fierce soul-mate.

He stumbled forward through the shallow depths, not yet seeing Rain. Wide shoulders tapered down to a narrow waist and hips, providing a perfect framework for finely formed genitals and long, sinewy thighs and calves.

Inner torment hazed his eyes, and his lips thinned into a hard line of determination. He was fighting his demons in his usual fashion. Alone.

This is the man I love, Rain thought with a sense of certainty. Awe and pride filled her almost to overflowing as her eyes swept over him caressingly.

Selik stopped suddenly when he saw her, then leaned down to pick up his garments from the ground. Brazen and unashamed of his nudity, he dressed slowly in leggings and tunic. After he cinched his waist with a wide leather belt, he asked in a flat voice, "Why do you follow me?"

Rain just stared up at him, unsure how much to disclose, but sympathy must have shown in her face.

Selik exhaled sharply with disgust. "Who told you?"

"You did."

Selik frowned, then seemed to realize that, in his furor, he'd spoken his thoughts aloud.

"And Ubbi filled in all the spaces."

"I should cut out the man's tongue," Selik commented wearily as he dropped down to the ground next to her and began drying his hair with a shoulder mantle. Then he declared firmly, "I will not discuss my past with you, Rain. So for once, put a lock on your tongue."

Rain started to speak, then decided he was right. Now was not the time. Selik had suffered enough that day. Later. For now, though, she wanted to brighten his life, not add to his misery. To help him forget some of the agony that must pound incessantly in his brain.

She began to tell him about all the mundane happenings at Ravenshire in his absence. When she finally got to Gorm and his pursuit of Blanche, she saw the muscles in his face begin to relax. He actually smiled when she told him of Bertha's lovelorn advice to her and Blanche. He even laughed, his gray eyes glittering with amusement, when she related how Bertha likened him to a stallion and her a mare in heat.

"Are you in heat?" Selik asked finally, seemingly pleased with the blush his teasing words brought to her face.

"Hardly."

"Ah, you persist in these claims of distaste for the bed-sport, for a man's touch? Nay, do not think to lift your haughty chin in defense of that lie. I have witnessed proof of your true lustiness."

"I didn't lie," Rain protested. "And I never said I disliked sex. I just said I could take it or leave it." *At least, I could in my other life.*

"'Twas not the impression I got when . . ." Selik let his words trail off, shrugging.

"It's different with you, Selik."

"Now who is throwing out *lines*?"

Rain smiled at his remembering her modern expression. "It *is* different with you. Oh, don't go preening like a randy rooster," she added, causing him to let out a hoot of laughter. "It's not that you have such marvelous technique. It's just that, well, it's just because it's *you*. There's this sort of celestial rightness to us as a pair."

"Was that a compliment or an insult?" he asked dryly.

Thankfully, Selik's dark mood had passed. Her mother had always said that the way to a man's heart—to a lover's heart, actually—was a woman's ability to make him smile. And Selik didn't smile nearly enough. She thought for a second, then brightened. She knew how to jar this arrogant male's complacent ego and make him laugh in the process. Oh, yes, she did!

"You know, Selik . . ." she said in a voice of exaggerated sweetness, causing his face to tilt with alert suspicion. *Oh, yes, honey, you have every right to be suspicious.*

". . . you know, if we ever made love . . ."

A grin twitched at his thinned lips.

That's right, sweetheart. Smile. Relax your defenses.

". . . *if* we ever made love, I'll bet I would finally find my G-spot." *There! Put that in your macho pipe and smoke it!*

"I know I will regret asking this, but I cannot resist. Pray tell, what in bloody hell is a G-spot?"

I thought you'd never ask. "Well, there is some controversy over this in my time, but many sexual authorities—"

"Sexual authorities? Surely, there are not frauds who claim to be experts on such matters?"

Rain nodded with a smile.

"No doubt they are Franks," he proclaimed with derision. "The men of Frankland have forever believed themselves to be the world's best lovers. I wager they have written some of those books you keep quoting endlessly."

"Hundreds."

"Hah! I know as much as any of those self-proclaimed authorities, I warrant."

No doubt, you do, babe. "In any case, before you interrupted me, I was telling you that many sexual authorities disagree on the subject of whether a woman's G-spot actually exists. Many women claim to have them, though." Rain went on to give Selik a very detailed lesson in female anatomy and a graphic description of a G-spot and what it could do to enhance a woman's pleasure.

At first, he just stared at her, stunned at the explicitness of her words. Then he burst out laughing.

"Truly, I have never met a woman like you afore. You know so many details about the mating betwixt the male and female. Like a damn book, you are. But methinks you know naught. Yea, you are as innocent as a virgin when it comes to the mating, I daresay."

"I am not!"

He burst out laughing once again as he pulled her to her feet and drew her away from the pond, pinching her bottom once when she didn't move quickly enough. As they walked back to the keep, he muttered over and over, between bursts of laughter, "G-spot! Unbelievable! G-spot!"

When Rain saw Ubbi watching anxiously for their return, the faithful servant looked from Selik's laughing face to her annoyed one as she rubbed her sore bottom, and back again to Selik's. Then he smiled widely and tipped his head in congratulations to her.

To Ubbi's mind, Rain had, no doubt, performed another angelic miracle.

And Selik surprised her by turning her face toward him and whispering softly, "Thank you." Apparently, he had understood her motives entirely in trying to lighten his mood.

Beware when God gets you in his crosshairs . . .

Several days later, Selik threw his saddlebag over Fury's back and vaulted into the saddle, preparing to leave Ravenshire.

Rain pulled up beside him on her ill-named horse, Godsend. He groaned inwardly, wondering what misdeed she wished to berate him for now.

"Thank you, Selik, for agreeing to take me with you to Jorvik."

His eyes widened with surprise at her softly spoken words. No doubt she wanted a favor.

"The reason I begged you to take me to Jorvik was so that I might be able to better understand why I was sent here. If I can stand on the same spot where the museum will later be, maybe I will—"

Selik made a loud harrumphing sound of disbelief. "What? Get a message from God?"

"You're impossible!"

He turned and looked at her, shaking his head incredulously. "Is that like the river calling the ocean wet?"

Rain laughed, and his heart seemed to expand in his chest, almost choking.

"Oh, Selik, I lo—"

He raised a hand to halt her next words, knowing that she was once again going to try to tell him that she loved him. And that Selik could not allow. He looked at the enticing wench, having a hard time resisting her tempting words. He had been successful thus far, since that day at the pond, in refusing to allow her to repeat the precious words. As long as he did not hear the words spoken aloud, somehow he could deny the growing bond between them, could pretend that he did not care. He closed his eyes wearily for just a moment.

Oh, God, or Odin, or whatever being is out there, please do not torture me so. I cannot bear to love again. And lose. 'Tis more than any man can bear.

He straightened his shoulders with determination.

Trust in me.

"What did you say?" Selik asked with alarm.

"When?"

"Just now? Something about trust." Even as he spoke, Selik knew it had not been Rain's voice in his head. Oh, bloody hell! She truly was turning him inside out and senseless as a lackwit.

Her wonderful golden eyes widened and seemed to glitter with enchantment. "You heard the voice, too. Didn't you?"

"Nay. I heard naught."

"Liar."

"Men have died for less insult than that."

"I'm not afraid of you."

"You should be."

"Why?"

"Argh!"

"Selik, you really should be careful about losing your temper so much. Every time you get angry with me, a vein pops out on your forehead. You could have a stroke."

He snarled. "The only stroke that is going to occur is that of my blade when I lop off your wagging tongue."

Ubbi guided his horse forward. "M'lord, wouldst ye like me to gag the lady so she does not bother ye anymore?" Ubbi asked Selik with oily consideration. He had been practically dancing with glee ever since Selik had told him yestereve that he could accompany him to Jorvik.

Selik raised a brow at that enticing picture. " 'Twould be

worth a fortune in gold to see you try. And 'twould be worth a double fortune to have *both* your mouths sewed shut and give the world some blessed peace."

Ubbi's shoulders slumped and his lips turned down in dejection at the insult, but Selik could swear he saw the traitor wink conspiratorially at Rain. *Wonderful! The two half-wits are in collusion.*

"Everyone is ready to depart," Ubbi announced then.

Selik looked about with dismay at the motley group of retainers and hangers-on he had managed to accumulate. Even though he had ordered a half dozen hersirs to stay with Tykir, along with Bertha to do his cooking, Selik still had two dozen soldiers and six captives in his traveling party. Seven of the male slaves had opted to join the ranks of his followers. All rode on horseback, even Blanche. Somehow his men had found enough horses in the countryside to steal.

Selik was about to give the signal to move out of the bailey when his eyes froze on the last person in the entourage. *Persons*, rather, he immediately corrected himself. A young woman carrying a babe in her arms rode astride the last horse.

"Get them out of my sight," Selik ordered Gorm through gritted teeth.

"But, master," Ubbi intervened, "her husband was a Ravenshire *churl* fer many a year. He died yestermorn of the fever, and she must get to her family in Jorvik."

"I care not if her husband was a bloody king. I want no ba . . ." His words trailed off for a moment as he sought to control the shakiness of his voice; then he amended, "I want no more blathering, shrewish, troublesome women in my company. I have more than enough with these two," he said, waving a hand toward Rain and Blanche. "Thank the gods I will be done with them both when I reach Jorvik."

"But, master, 'tis cruel ter leave her here without a mate ter protect her and give her sustenance."

"Let her help Bertha in the kitchen. Or let her go to bloody hell. 'Tis not my concern." Selik jerked his head at Gorm, who followed his orders by roughly pulling the woman and the squalling child off the horse. Selik ignored the tears streaming down the young woman's face and turned his horse toward the gatehouse, leading the chain of horses over the bridge. Stiff-backed, he never once turned back to look at the crying babe or its sobbing, forlorn mother.

And Selik refused to look at Rain, knowing the condemnation he would see on her face.

Did your own wife seek escape before the Saxons came? And was she refused aid, like this woman? the voice said.

Selik swallowed hard over the lump in his throat. What was happening to him? A month ago, a year ago, he would not have hesitated to turn the woman and her bloody babe out to fend for themselves. In fact, he would have pulled them from the horse himself.

Without looking at Ubbi, who rode beside him, he reached into his tunic and withdrew a small sack of coins. Tossing it at the startled servant, he ordered in a gruff voice, "Give it to the maid and arrange for her later transport."

Ubbi's cloudy eyes brightened, and he turned his horse back toward Ravenshire, never once questioning which maid Selik referred to, nor his motives. But Selik thought he heard Ubbi mutter, "I knew ye would. I jist knew ye would."

Selik did not like the turn his life had taken of late. It lacked control. Too many people were attaching themselves to him. He determined to rid himself of the whole bloody lot of leeches once he reached Jorvik. Then off he would go again on his quest of vengeance against his Saxon enemies. And Steven of Gravely. *Alone.* That was the path he had chosen long ago. There was no turning back, no fork in this life-road for him. He would not allow it.

Hah! The single word echoed in response to his thoughts.

Selik sneered at the damned voice in his head. If it was God, then he had an ungodly sarcastic tongue. He turned quickly to see if anyone had spoken nearby, but his companions stared straight ahead, concentrating on the rough road. He shrugged, refusing to believe the impossible. No doubt he had spoken aloud. Yea, that was it. He could not accept that it might be that voice in his head again. Never would he believe that it was God—may all the saints preserve his sanity!

You'd better believe it.

He groaned and Ubbi looked his way, raising an eyebrow in question. Selik said a foul word and spurred his horse forward, feeling the need for a good gallop to clear his senses.

It wasn't the Big Apple, but it was a city . . .

Rain could barely contain her excitement when they arrived in Jorvik the next morning. Selik's men surrounded them and kept a wary lookout for Saxon soldiers as they crossed a bridge over the River Ouse, then followed the traffic moving along a thoroughfare Ubbi identified as Micklegate or "Great Street."

Rain's mother had long ago told her that Jorvik, the tenth century name for York, was the gateway between Scandinavia and Anglo-Saxon England. Its trade routes reached out to Ireland, the Shetlands, the Rhineland, the Baltic and even farther.

Her head pivoted on her neck as she tried to absorb all the marvelous sites as they moved through the narrow streets of the market town, shaded by the overhanging thatch eaves of the wattle-and-daub buildings.

The ancient Roman walls, with their eight massive towers that surrounded the city, and some of the buildings lay in ruins in places, thanks to Saxon assaults of recent years. But Ubbi told her no Norse king ruled at the moment, and everywhere an air of rebuilding and prosperity prevailed, the new quickly blending in with the old. Like the people, Rain thought—a vast assortment of Norse, English, Icelanders, Normans, Franks, Germans, Russians, even traders from the Eastern cultures.

The cacophony of their musical, sometimes guttural, tongues provided a discordant background to the sounds of the busy city. Merchants and sailors swore fluently in various tongues as they discharged exotic items from the wide-bellied

cargo ships at the confluence of the Ouse and Foss Rivers—
which Ubbi identified as fine wines from Frisia, amber, furs
and whalebone from the Baltics, soapstone from the Norselands, lava querns from the Rhineland and rainbow-colored
silks from the East.

Craftsmen called out their wares from where they sat
in stalls in front of their primitive homes, selling their
handiwork—ivory combs, bone ice skates, bronze brooches,
belt buckles and armlets, strings of glass and jet beads,
wooden bowls and cooking utensils, jewelry of silver and
gold imbedded with precious stones. Oddly, each of the
streets, or "gates" as the Norse called them, seemed to cater
to tradesmen in a particular product; there was a street of
woodworkers, another of jewelers, still another of glass-
blowers.

"This is like a giant craft festival," Rain said with awe as
she drew up next to Selik. He had been ignoring her since
yesterday, but he didn't turn away now.

"Yea, the artisans impressed your mother, as well," he
recalled, seeming to find amusement in her fascination with
the enchanting city streets. "This is Coppergate, the street
where many of the workshops are located."

Enthralled, Rain stared at the main crosstown artery of
the tenth century city, knowing that some point on this thoroughfare was the site of the later Viking museum.

"Selik, this was the starting point of my journey in time."

He groaned at her mention of time-travel, which he reluctantly accepted but didn't like her to discuss. "No doubt you
expect to stand on Coppergate the minute my back is turned
and just fly through the air with your angel wings to your
own time. Please, my lady, I hope you will invite me to witness that wondrous event."

"Don't be sarcastic. I didn't say that I wanted to return
home." *I might have thought it at once time, but not anymore.
I don't know what I want now.*

Their entourage came to a halt suddenly as an oxen cart

passed in front of them. Selik's soldiers, who rode point guard before and after their traveling party, watched alertly for signs of danger.

"I would love to have a strand of those amber beads," Rain commented casually of the orange-yellow, citrine-like stones being cut and polished by one highly skilled jeweler who sat on a nearby stool. Then she laughed. "Do you think they'd take a check?"

Selik smiled, scrutinizing her with what could only be called fondness, and Rain's heart skipped a beat. She relished the rare moment of companionship and wished she could lean across the small space that separated them and brush his beautiful, flowing hair back from his face. Or trace the outline of his firm lips, curved now in an enchanting smile. But he would probably rebuff her gesture or make some sarcastic remark.

But Selik surprised her with a quick, knowing wink and turned to the artisan. Tossing the wide-eyed young man a coin, he pointed to the amber necklace in his hands. The jeweler tossed it up with a nod of thanks.

Delighted, Rain reached for the necklace, murmuring, "Oh, thank you, Selik. It's beautiful."

But he held it out of reach and demanded teasingly, "I will have one of those Lifesavers in payment."

A piece of candy in exchange for a priceless necklace? Not a bad bargain! "I told you they were all gone."

"But you lied."

Rain laughed. "Okay, but just one." She reached in her bag and pulled out the unopened roll of Tropical Fruits, then handed him a yellow one.

"What is this? I prefer red."

"I gave the last of the cherry ones to Tykir and Ubbi. That one is pineapple, I think."

Selik shot a look of annoyance her way as if she had given away *his* personal belongings. Then he skeptically placed the candy circle on his tongue. A momentary look of surprise crossed his face at what had to be an exotic new taste to him.

"Do you like it?"

"'Tis fine, but I prefer the red," he remarked testily, then reached over and slid the necklace over her head, adjusting it under her single braid. "It goes well with your golden eyes, sweetling."

He likes my eyes. "Have I told you what it does to me when you use those love words?" she said huskily, leaning closer.

But he pulled his horse back. "Love words? What love words?"

"Sweetling. Dearling."

"Hah! Those are not love words. They are just . . ." He stopped himself.

The cart had cleared the street, and Selik moved his horse ahead.

She prodded her horse to follow Selik's lead and soon caught up with him.

"Selik, thank you. I will cherish the necklace. Always." *Because it came from you.*

"'Tis just a trinket. The gifting means naught."

"Oh! It's just like you to give with one hand and take away with the other. Why do you keep pushing me away from you?"

"Why do you keep pushing yourself in my face?"

"Because I was sent—"

"—by God to save me," he finished for her with a disgusted shake of his head. "Please spare me, wench, and be someone else's guardian angel for a while. Better yet, why not fly up and perch on the rooftops of one of these Christian churches," he said, waving his hand to indicate the numerous houses of worship they had passed. "Your squawking wouldst blend in well with all the pigeons."

Rain started to stick out her tongue, but stopped herself in time. Instead, she wrinkled her nose at him mockingly. "Actually, I can't believe how many churches there are here.

I think we've passed at least a dozen. Where is St. Peter's—
the one with the hospitium attached to it?"

Selik pointed to a high spire in the distance.

"Will you take me there?"

"Mayhap . . . yea, I will."

"I might even be able to practice medicine there."

He grinned. "That would be a sight to see—you barging
into the minster and offering your services to the holy culdees. Talk about bulging veins, You may cause a gusher of
bursting blood vessels."

Rain smiled.

"Well, better you attach yourself to them than to me," Selik said gruffly. "Like a shadow you have become to me. You
and that damn Ubbi."

Rain's heart ached at Selik's words. Did this man she was
beginning to love really consider her nothing more than a
pesky nuisance? She hoped not.

"Today? Will you take me today?"

He shook his head, laughing at her pushiness. "I must
discharge all these captives today and rid myself of Ubbi
and the soldiers."

Discharge? Did that mean sell? Rain wanted to ask. *And
me?* But she was afraid of his answer. "Where will you go?"

He shrugged. "Mayhap south, into Wessex."

Rain was about to berate him once again for his continuing quest for vengeance when the most horrendous odor assailed her senses. "Oh, my God, what is that smell?"

"'Tis Pavement—a street one does not soon forget. You
are, no doubt, getting a whiff of the butchers and the tanner-
ies. See, over there." Selik pointed to some buildings where
all types of dead animals hung from giant hooks—the offal
and blood being thrown into the gutters or carried as efflu-
ent to the slow-moving river behind them.

Industrious workers stripped the skin from the carcasses
with bone implements, then covered the skins with what appeared to be a profusion of chicken dung. Still other workers
were curing the skins, which had already rotted for some

time in the earlier piles of chicken droppings, dousing them with what looked like fermented berry juice. Finally, she saw the finished products being stretched on wooden frames and worked into shoes and jerkins and belts.

From the women and children she could see in the back-yards, the buildings must combine homes and workplaces. The smell didn't seem to bother them a bit. Geese and chickens wandered at will in the fenced-in properties, while pigs grunted noisily in small enclosures. Several children sat about playing wooden pan pipes.

In all, the artisans and merchants and families combined to form a picture of peaceable folks. Not at all the image modern people had of Vikings or Dark Age Saxons.

It was not the impression she had carried either, since her exposure to the Battle of Brunanburh, and Selik. Her mind began to work overtime, trying to fit her outlaw Viking into this tranquil domestic scene.

"Selik, what would you do if you weren't a fighter?"

"Huh?"

"I mean, when my mother met you, you weren't set on a lifetime of bloodletting, were you?"

He smiled at her choice of words. "I was a Jomsviking even then."

"Yes, yes, I know, but that wasn't something you intended to do for the rest of your life. In fact, you told me once that you had already quit before . . . well, you said you quit."

"A trader."

"A trader? You mean, like these people who sell their wares along the streets?"

He shook his head. "Nay. I had five trading vessels. I traveled several times each year to Hedeby and even Miklagard, buying and selling."

An awful thought occurred to Rain. *Oh, please God, not that.* "What kind of products did you carry?"

He shrugged. "Everything." He studied her closely and seemed to understand her concern. "Nay, my untrusting wench, I was not a slave trader."

Rain exhaled on a sigh of relief. "Yes, I could see you on a Viking ship, traveling from one trading center to another."

"So happy you approve," he said with a mocking bow of his head. "But actually I was an artisan of sorts at one time. I made . . ." He stopped short, his face reddening as he suddenly seemed to realize that he'd revealed too much.

"What? Don't you dare stop now. What did you make?"

"Animals," he admitted sheepishly. "I carved animals out of wood, but I rarely sold them. Mostly, I just gave them to chil—to family or friends who admired them."

Children. He gave his handiwork to children. Hmmm. Another clue. "I would love to see them sometime. Do you have any with you?"

His face hardened then. "Nay. I have none. I destroyed them all. And I do not bother with frivolous pastimes anymore." He looked her directly in the eye. "My hands are too bloody."

They moved out of the most congested part of the city now and toward the outskirts, where the homes were larger and farther apart, more prosperous. Ubbi drew his horse up next to hers, and Selik pulled back to talk to Gorm. Rain could tell by the strained manner in which Ubbi held his shoulders that the long trip from Ravenshire had taken a painful toll on the little man's arthritis.

"Ubbi, I noticed when we traveled along Pavement that the butchers were slaughtering cattle. Do you think you could take me there tomorrow to talk to them?"

"Why? Are ye hungry?"

Rain laughed. "No, but if I could get some cow adrenal glands, I might be able to make a primitive form of cortisone. It would do absolute wonders for your arthritis."

At first, his face brightened with hope, but then quickly changed to horror when Rain explained adrenals. "Ye want to put cow innards on me body?"

"No, silly man, you would have to take it internally."

He thought for a moment, weighing her words. "By 'internally,' you cannot mean fer me to eat the bloody parts."

"Yes, but—"

"Never! Mistress, I allowed ye to massage me body in a most unseemly way. Ye made a laughingstock of me at Ravenshire by slatherin' hot mud on me, and I did not protest. Well, not too much. I even swam in that icy water of the pond to satisfy yer whims, not to mention the scalding hot baths ye forced me to endure. But I refuse to eat raw cow innards. Even I have me limits."

Rain burst out laughing at Ubbi's long-winded tirade. "Ubbi, I didn't mean for you to eat them raw. At least, I don't think they would work that way. Although . . . hmmm . . . anyhow, I was thinking of mixing the fresh glands with something else, then compressing it into a pill. I'm not sure if it can even be done."

"Hah! But ye would make me be the—what did ye call it when ye were experimentin' with the different exercises?— Jenny Pig!"

"Guinea pig," Rain corrected him with a smile. She reached over to pat Ubbi's twisted hand. Really, he'd been more than cooperative in her various attempts to alleviate his condition. And some of them had helped, too.

"Selik!"

Rain and Ubbi both turned to see a petite, gray-haired woman calling out warmly to Selik from the doorway of a large home. Set apart from its neighbors by a wide expanse of side yard and wooden fences, its rectangular shape followed the Viking style with a thatched roof. Finely carved Nordic symbols decorated the large oak door and window-frames. Several armed men stood guard near the doorway, and Rain saw even more to the side and back of the house.

"Mother!" Selik greeted the woman in a warm voice as he dismounted and handed the reins to Gorm.

"Mother?" Rain asked Ubbi. "I thought Selik said he had no parents."

"'Tis Gyda, Astrid's mother. He is the same as a son to her."

"We have been so worried. Especially when we heard of

the Great Battle. Why didst you not send us word of your safety, you wretch?" the woman chastised Selik before throwing herself into his arms. He lifted her off the ground in a huge bear hug while she clung to him warmly, her pudgy arms wrapped around his neck.

"Selik, my son," she said softly as she drew back slightly and scanned his face lovingly, no doubt looking for new scars. "Put me down now, you big oaf, and let me feed you. You are naught but skin and bones."

Selik laughed lightheartedly, putting her gently to the ground, and threw his right arm over Gyda's shoulder. She barely reached his chest. "I want you to meet someone." He motioned Rain to dismount and come forward.

When Rain stood next to Selik, towering over the diminutive woman, Selik said, "Do you remember Ruby Jordan? Thork's wife?"

"Yea, of course," Gyda said hesitantly, her brow furrowed in puzzlement at his odd question.

"This . . . hostage . . . is their daughter, Thoraine. Her other name is Sleet—I mean Rain."

Rain shot him a look of disgust at his joke which she didn't find a bit funny. "And your other name is jerk," she muttered in an undertone to Selik.

But Gyda overheard, and her face brightened merrily with understanding. "I know that word. Jerk. Your own mother taught it to me." She turned to Selik, wagging a finger in his face. "And it has come in very handy, I must tell you, Selik, on the odd occasion with all these guards you insist on leaving here with me. Gods' blood! I cannot step out to the privy without tripping over one or another of them. But a daughter born to Ruby! After Thork's death? Why, she is too old! 'Tis unbelievable! And such a giant!"

Rain tried to listen to Gyda's long-winded discourse, but the Norse woman spoke too fast. "What is she saying?" Rain asked Ubbi.

"It seems that yer mother taught Gyda the word 'jerk,' that Selik left so many guards that Gyda is tripping over 'em, and that she finds it hard ter believe that yer mother gave birth to Thork's baby after his death."

"And she called me a giant, too, didn't she?" Rain asked, sensing that Ubbi was sparing her feelings.

"Yea, she did," he admitted, "but then anyone taller than a calf is a giant to her."

Gyda stepped closer and put out her hands in welcome to Rain. Speaking more slowly, she said, "Welcome, Rain. Any child of Thork and Ruby is a friend to this house."

Rain squeezed the small woman's hands in return, sensing the genuineness of the greeting.

"Selik says you are a hostage, but you will ne'er be treated as such in my home."

Rain's eyes shot to Selik, who studiously ignored her as he led his horse toward the barn, but any sharp words she wanted to address to him were forestalled by the arrival of the most gorgeous young woman Rain had ever seen in all her life.

"Selik!" the fair-haired beauty, about seventeen years old, shrieked in welcome before throwing herself enthusiastically into Selik's open arms. He swung her around up off the ground in a circle while he hugged her with equal zest.

The jerk!

"Tyra," he exclaimed admiringly when he finally put her back down and scrutinized her boldly from her strawberry-blond head, to voluptuously rounded breasts, to a tiny waist and narrow hips, to her disgustingly dainty little slippers. "You have grown into a woman in my absence. A very beautiful woman."

Tyra put one delicate hand on his chest, slanting a sultry look up at him through sickeningly long lashes, and announced, "Then 'tis past time for our wedding."

CHAPTER TEN

❧

Being cruel to be kind is sometimes just cruel . . .
"You little minx," Selik exclaimed against Tyra's luxuriant hair on hearing her outrageous remark. He laughed and gave her an extra squeeze before putting her back on her feet with a swat on her saucy behind.

He looked up then and stopped short at the look of stunned surprise—and hurt—on Rain's face. Puzzled, he tilted his head, then realized that Rain must have heard Tyra's remark about a wedding and assumed he had pledged troth with the young maid. *Holy Thor!* Tyra was like a sister to him. 'Twas obvious to anyone with eyes in their heads.

But not to Rain, he saw immediately. She bit her trembling bottom lip and widened her eyes to dam the tears welling in their golden depths.

Instinctively, he started forward to tell Rain the truth, to wipe the look of pain from her features, to soothe her with sweet words of explanation. But he stopped himself. Mayhap Rain's mistaken notion of his betrothal could work to his advantage. He had let this attraction between them go too far. He walked around half-hard all the time these days, barely escaping the notice of his men. Could he resist the temptation of her flesh much longer? He must, especially knowing now that he might leave her with child. Better the small pain now than the bigger one which would inevitably come.

He forced himself to turn away from Rain's accusing stare. Leaning down to Tyra, whose head barely tipped his chin, he whispered loud enough for only her to hear, "Have a caution, wench. You have been saying that since you were only five and I a worldly man of eighteen. One of these days, I may take you up on your offer, and then what would you do?"

She flashed him a winsome smile and replied quickly, "Accept, of course."

"Hah! So you say now, but what of all the suitors who beg for your hand?"

Selik knew Rain could hear none of their words from where she stood frozen in rigid pain, but she surely viewed the light banter betwixt them as love play. Even Ubbi scowled at him in silent condemnation.

Tyra played into the role perfectly. Pouting prettily, the spoiled imp put a fingertip to her chin as if pondering in all seriousness the notion of giving up all her suitors for him. "Hmmm. 'Tis something to consider."

"Tyra! For shame!" Gyda intervened finally, shoving her daughter and Selik good-naturedly toward the house and motioning Rain and the others to follow.

Selik forced himself to stare straight ahead and not look back at Rain. He feared he would give in to his softer impulses and confess his charade. Anything to erase the pain he saw racking her at his supposed betrayal.

Betrayal! Now where did that thought come from? Selik wondered. He had no obligations toward the witch from some far-off land.

She saved your life.

"Yea, but I have more than made up for that by listening to her shrewish nagging, have I not?" Selik asked Ubbi.

"Huh?" Ubbi looked askance at him, as if he had suddenly grown two noses.

With forced patience, he explained, "You pointed out that Rain saved my life, and—"

"I did?"

"For certain you did."

"When?"

"Just now."

Ubbi looked skyward and smiled, then slanted a curious look his way. "What else did I say?"

Selik stopped short, hands on hips, and snarled in self-loathing at having allowed himself to be drawn into these hopeless conversations with Ubbi. Finally, he threw up his hands in disgust. "You said you were a horse, and I, the horse's arse."

"I never did!"

Selik slanted him a wry look. "No doubt you thought it, though."

To his surprise, Ubbi nodded vigorously. "Yea, when ye treat m'lady the way ye did back there, well—if I may be so bold as to express me humble opinion—well, ye behaved no better than a horse's arse."

Selik was more amazed than angry. His trusted servant rarely spoke to him in such a manner. "Has she been beaten or starved? Threatened with bodily harm? Nay. I think you forget, Ubbi, that she is a mere captive, like all the others."

"Hah! Believe that, and I will know for certain ye have lost all yer wits. Mayhap they are lodged in that staff ye have been keeping at half mast this past sennight." Ubbi looked meaningfully at the juncture of Selik's braies and snorted rudely, stomping away from him.

Selik felt Rain's presence next to him then, or perhaps he smelled her Passion. But when he glanced sideways, he saw her gaze fixed on Tyra, who was helping Gyda prepare a quick meal for the unexpected guests.

She thinks 'tis Tyra my body yearns for. How can she be so blind? Hmmm. Should I allow her to continue to think so? Yea, I must.

Selik deliberately stepped forward toward the raised

hearth in the center of the great room and put a hand on Tyra's shoulder. He leaned down and whispered a few meaningless words in her ear, and laughter rippled up from the young maid's throat.

He heard Rain gasp behind him. He clenched his fists to keep from turning and reaching out for her.

Please don't go . . . yet . . .

Never, never in Rain's modern life would she have expected that she could feel such pain over a man. A cheating, two-timing, lying slimebucket of a man, at that!

He loves Tyra, she thought.

No, Rain had to be honest. Selik had made her no promises. She'd declared her love for him, and he'd made it more than plain that he didn't welcome her affections. At best, he lusted for her.

He loves Tyra.

Yes, she had to admit it—she was the fool in this picture. Somehow she had painted a scenario of herself as the wonderful savior from the future come to rescue the primitive warrior. Hah! She'd barely saved her own skin thus far.

He loves Tyra.

Oh, Lord, how would she live without him? She hadn't realized until now how enmeshed their lives had become. Even though she'd recognized her blossoming love for him, she'd thought she could control it, like everything else in her modern life—her education, her career, her family, her emotions, her love life. Everything in its neat little compartment, taken out and put away at will.

He loves Tyra.

Rain's shoulders slumped, and she turned away from the happily chattering groups of people who crowded Gyda's great room. Selik and Ubbi stood well inside the room, directing the soldiers on the care of the horses and captives. Gyda stood talking to her servants near the cooking fires, while Tyra prepared the large trestle tables with wooden platters and goblets.

In a mist of tears, Rain spun on her heel, feeling an over-whelming urge to escape the room that contained both Selik and his fiancée. No one even noticed her departure.

Heading back in the direction from which they'd just traveled, Rain walked aimlessly at first. Then, a thought occurred to her.

Coppergate.

If she could get back to Coppergate, the scene of the future Viking museum, perhaps she would discover the key to the time-travel door.

He loves Tyra.

Rain could not think straight, certainly not about her aborted mission to the past. She, who had always been obsessed with perfection, had to admit failure now. It was a bitter pill to swallow.

Nor could she think about Selik and how he would react to her absence. Probably with relief. Even she recognized that she'd turned into a shrewish, self-righteous nag of late.

Most of all, she couldn't allow herself to think of living once again in her sterile, modern world, where she'd once thought herself happy—no, contented—in her niche as a respected physician. But how could that life, which had always seemed so satisfying, suddenly make her skin crawl with dread? What was missing in the picture?

Love, the voice in her head answered.

But Selik doesn't love me, her heart cried out.

And if he did? Would you stay with him?

Yes . . . no . . . I don't know.

Despite the tears clouding Rain's eyes, finding her way through the organized grid system of Jorvik streets proved easy. She soon recognized the craftsmen's shops Selik had pointed out to her earlier. Slowing her fast gait to a slow walk, Rain looked from right to left, trying to recognize the exact spot where the museum would later stand.

Suddenly, she felt all the fine hairs on her body stand up, almost as if electrified. With trepidation, she approached what appeared to be an abandoned building. The closer she got, the stronger the aura. She felt almost as if she teetered on the outer rim of a tornado's spiral. If she stepped forward through the sagging door of the crumbling structure, she somehow knew she would be drawn into the vortex, back through the nothingness of time.

Rain circled the building, tears streaming down her face, alternately stepping closer and jumping back when the magnetic pull increased. Every time she felt the compulsive need to jump over the edge, an even stronger urge held her back. She frowned, not understanding why she hesitated.

"Do not go. Not yet."

Rain jerked with surprise, then turned.

Selik stood a few feet away from her, his usually tanned face pale with what seemed to be fear and concern. *For me?* Rain swallowed hard over the lump in her throat, barely able to make out his features through the gossamer veil of her tears.

Silently, he held out one hand to her, his silver eyes entreating her to come to him. He refused to step forward, as if he sensed the power of the aura that surrounded the scene and how close to the cliff of time she stood.

Rain tried to remind herself that Selik loved another woman, that she had no future in the past. The logical, scientifically trained part of her brain told her of priorities, about right and wrong, and rational choices. The other, softer, womanly part of her brain triumphed, however, as she moved step by slow, inexorable step away from the aura toward her brilliant lodestar in the past.

When she had moved only a few steps, Selik pulled her into his arms, and Rain felt as if she had come home. He hugged her to his chest, his arms wrapped around her back, his long fingers alternately caressing her shoulders and back and waist and hips, even buttocks. Then he pressed her harder against him, as if afraid she would flee again.

Finally, he pulled away a little and held her by both shoulders, his fingers digging painfully into her skin, his face no longer pale with caring, but red with anger. In a harsh voice, he accused her, "You lied, Rain. You promised that if I would do no more *behaettie*, you would not try to escape."

Selik's beautiful eyes flashed angrily, like shards of gray ice. The jagged scar on his cheek stood out whitely against his furiously reddened face. He could barely hiss out his venomous accusation through his gritted teeth.

"I don't break promises lightly, Selik, but I was upset to see you with Tyra."

"Whether I am with Tyra, or Blanche, or a hundred other women is no excuse for breaking your oath. We will discuss this further when we get back to Gyda's home." With those clipped words, he pulled her along behind him toward Fury, who was nibbling contentedly on the grass near the roadway. In one rough movement, he put both hands about her waist and lifted her sideways onto Fury's back. He then swung up into the saddle behind her.

Rain scrutinized him intently, amazed at his vehemence. "Selik, I would think you would be relieved to have me gone. I know I've annoyed you lately. Why? Why do you care if I stay or go? Is it my value as a hostage?"

Selik's narrowed eyes assessed her boldy, as if weighing her merits. Apparently, she came short in his scales, she decided when he looked away, snapping at her, "I owe you no explanations. In truth, you have been treated too softly in the past. That will change now that your word can no longer be trusted."

Rain stared up at him, trying to reconcile this fierce anger with the obvious fear he'd shown moments ago when he'd thought she was about to leave him. When the horse quickened its pace through the narrow streets, she grabbed his waist for balance.

He inhaled sharply.

She decided to test the confusing waters further and slid her hips closer to him.

The edge of Rain's thigh brushed against the rigid hardness between his legs. He jerked as if she'd just short-circuited him. And a sudden, heart-lightening thought occurred to her. Perhaps it was she, and not the beautiful Tyra, who turned him on.

"Move."

Rain looked up and saw Selik's teeth gritted, his lips drawn in against his teeth.

"Wha—"

"Move, *now,* or I swear afore all the Norse gods and Christian saints, that I will turn you in the saddle astride my lap and take you here and now atop my horse in the midst of Coppergate."

Rain considered that enticing possibility for a moment, finding it not at all as appalling as Selik undoubtedly thought she would. But she moved away slightly nonetheless.

"Why did you bring me to Jorvik if you knew Tyra waited here for you?" she asked bleakly.

"I have answered enough of your questions. Know this, wench, there will be a reckoning yet for the trouble you have caused me this day."

"Will you whip me?" she teased, nuzzling her cheek against his warm chest, despite the stiffening of his body.

"Mayhap."

"Perhaps you will resort to the *behaettie* again and scalp me."

He made a small scoffing sound deep in his throat.

"But, no, I don't think you would do that. You told me once that my hair was like spun gold. No one ever said anything so nice to me before, Selik. Did you know that?" She rubbed her cheek, cat-like, against the warm wool of his tunic where it was exposed between the lacings of his leather hauberk. With satisfaction, she noted the rapid jumpstart of his heart's acceleration.

"Do not be so sure of yourself, wench," he growled.

"Well, there are probably some especially excruciating Viking tortures you would employ. Like . . . oh, tickling a person to death. But I'm not ticklish, so that wouldn't work. Although, if you used a feather, and I was naked, and you were naked—"

Selik made a raw sound low in his throat and clapped a hand across her mouth. "Enough, wench! Do not think to sidetrack me with all these suggestive words. What I just might do if you persist is find that bloody G-spot of yours, then dig it out and nail it to your forehead for all the world to see what a wanton tease you are."

Rain waited until he removed his hand from her mouth a short time later and commented in a deliberately innocent voice, "So do you think you know where it is located?"

"What?"

"My G-spot?"

Rain heard a short, strangled sound; then Selik surprised her by cupping the apex of her femininity, through the linen cloth of her slacks, and pressing a thumb against the area just above the pubic bone. "Yea. 'Tis just about here. On the inside, of course."

Rain looked up at him in surprise, astonished that he understood feminine anatomy so well and that, with all her talk of modern sexual manuals and female satisfaction, he had understood only too well every word she'd spoken. Despite his still grim features, he winked at her with supreme masculine conceit.

"Some things a man just knows, without the book-learning."

Rain was the one who made a choking sound then.

If this is punishment, torture me, please . . .

When they got back to Gyda's house, everyone was sitting down at the long tables eating dinner—those of more importance, like Gyda and her family, at the head and, at the other end, Selik's retainers, particularly the captives-turned-soldiers. In an infuriating move, Selik grabbed Rain by the scruff of the neck and pulled her along at a rapid pace toward the head table, as if to show his authority over an errant slave.

Selik sat in the high-backed chair Gyda indicated and forced Rain to sit on a lower stool at his side which he directed a servant to bring forth. Like a dog, she thought, practically gnashing her teeth.

When she opened her mouth to protest, Selik popped a piece of roast venison into it. She tried to stand, but he put a large palm firmly on her head and held her in place.

Through the red haze of her anger and humiliation, Rain barely listened to the friendly conversation around the table.

Gyda flashed a condemning look at Selik for his treatment of her but didn't reprimand him. Instead, she asked, "When will the fighting stop, Selik? All the talk in the streets is of the Great Battle and so many good Norsemen dead or crippled."

"It will never stop, Mother. You know that," Selik said wearily, "not 'til every man of Norse descent is gone from Northumbria." Rain felt the tenseness of Selik's words transmitted through the pressure of his fingers on her scalp.

After making sure that everyone had enough food and ale, Gyda came back to Selik. "Then 'tis not safe for you here in Jorvik. Even today I saw some of Athelstan's royal guard near the harbor."

"They were, no doubt, searching for Anlaf, who is long gone to his Dublin domain. But, yea, I must needs make myself scarce as well."

"What of the Saxon captives you brought with you?" Gyda jerked her head toward the other end of the hall, where Blanche helped her servants over the cooking fire. Eadifu, who was supposed to be scouring pots, talked instead with the three remaining male captives.

Selik shrugged. "You can have any that you want, including the soldiers. All the others will be sold." Rain's blood turned cold at that prospect, not knowing if he meant her as well. Before she had a chance to ask, his hand slipped from her hair to her mouth in silent admonition.

"The young woman, Blanche, would suit to help inside the hall, but the other slut must go," Gyda said. "In truth, you left so many men behind afore to guard me and Tyra that we bump into each other all the time. And no more mouths do I want to feed."

Seeming to notice Rain then, Gyda asked, "And what of Ruby and Thork's daughter? Wouldst you sell her as well?"

He remained silent an infuriatingly long time, and Rain tried to stand up to tell him what she thought of his thinking process. But Selik had furrowed his fingers in her hair and pulled hard to show his mastery in this situation.

"Nay, I will not sell the troublesome wench. Leastways, not yet. I keep her for possible ransom with King Athelstan."

Tyra giggled merrily, as if Selik had said something very funny. "Oh, Selik! You jest, of course. Who would ever want such a giant of a woman?"

"You have a point there, little one," Selik commented in a dry tone of voice, tugging on Rain's hair in emphasis. The brute!

Gyda bit her bottom lip pensively, her eyes darting back and forth between Rain's furious expression and Selik's arrogant flash of a smile. "Surely you would not sell Thork's daughter to the slave traders."

"She is uncommonly shrewish, Gyda."

"I still do not understand how she could be daughter to Thork and Ruby. They were together but twelve years ago, and she is certainly much older than that."

"She claims to come from the future and that time moves faster there, or some such foolishness."

Gyda's mouth dropped open, and she made a clucking sound of disbelief. "But—"

Selik waved her concerns aside. "'Tis of no importance now. As to the slave marts, even did I decide to sell her, who would buy a shrewish woman of such height, especially being so long in the tooth?"

Both Gyda and Tyra stared at him suspiciously now, probably understanding that he deliberately tried to provoke his hostage.

"On the other hand," Selik continued, "Rain is a physician with rare healing skills. In truth, she saved Tykir's leg after Brunanburh." Rain jerked around to look at him in surprise at his rare praise.

"And everyone knows how the Wessex king values good healers," Gyda concluded for him.

"Perhaps you would like a slave to wash your garments and dress your hair, Tyra," Selik offered glibly. Rain put both hands to her head, digging her fingernails into Selik's hand, forcing him to release her hair. Standing proudly, she bent toward Selik, chin to chin, and declared, "I would sooner stick needles in a part of your body you value highly, you bloody barbarian."

"Tsk, tsk, tsk!" Selik clucked. "Spoken like a true pacifist! But not very slave-like language, I am afraid. I will have to devise some method of punishment."

Rain thought then of his earlier comment about G-spots. As hard as she tried to think of something else, she couldn't stop the revealing blush that heated her face.

"Do not be embarrassed, Rain. Gyda and Tyra understand the need for discipline amongst servants and slaves."

"Argh!" Rain choked out, reaching for his throat with an urge to kill. "Do they understand the need for women to murder overbearing, insufferably arrogant men?"

With a laugh, Selik ducked and grabbed her by the waist, throwing her over his shoulders like a sack of potatoes. "Where do you have us sleeping this night, Gyda? I find I must speak to my slave in private about her wagging tongue."

Tyra giggled once again. If Rain could have reached that far from her upside-down position, she would have tried to throttle her as well.

"Above stairs. Your usual room," Gyda said with a laugh. "I will send up bathwater. You both look like you could use a good wash."

"Make sure the tub is large enough, then," Selik said, slapping a large hand over Rain's derrière to hold her squirming body in place, "for two.

"Ouch!" Selik exclaimed when she bit his lower back. He stumbled, almost falling on the wooden steps to the second floor.

When Selik took a nip at her exposed rear end, Rain

gasped out, "Oh! You are an animal." The tip of her shoe barely missed his genitals then, and Selik spread the fingers of one large hand around the inside of her left thigh, high up, with the middle finger pressed against one strategic spot.

"Move one tiny bit," he declared with icy menace, "and I swear you will find a new meaning for the word humiliation."

Rain decided not to struggle anymore.

When they got to the tiny room at the end of the hall, Selik threw her down onto the single pallet against the wall and immediately followed her. Laughing, he pinned her to the thin mattress with his body, his hands holding hers above her head, palm to palm, and his legs twined around both of hers, totally immobilizing her.

"Get up, you big lummox. I can barely breathe," she spat out.

"Good. Mayhap your shrewish tongue will rest now."

"You won't get much ransom for me dead."

"Yea, but I may finally have some blessed peace."

"Hah! You haven't been at peace for years, and you know it. That's why I was sent here, you thickheaded fool."

"So you say. I think that God—if such a being exists, and I doubt it mightily—wants to punish me for all my misdeeds. What better punishment! A true hell on earth—the plague of a shrewish, self-important, self-righteous, loose-tongued woman!"

"Is that all?" Rain snapped sarcastically, trying hard not to be offended by his derogatory comments. She tried to buck him off by thrusting her hips up sharply. It was a mistake. All she accomplished was a reshifting of their bodies so *that* part of him was more perfectly aligned with *that* part of her. And she felt him grow bigger against her.

Selik gritted his teeth, and Rain saw the glint of passion ignite in his silvery eyes before he lowered his long, dark lashes. And when she glanced sideways, she saw the sinewy muscles of his arms, which still held her hands captive, stiffen with tension.

Pleasure and dismay swept over Rain with Selik's instant response. This chemistry had existed between them from the very beginning, requiring only a look or passing glance to ignite the embers of smoldering desire. If she were being perfectly truthful, she would have to admit that her attraction to him had begun long before their first meeting. For years, he'd haunted her dreams, calling to her across time.

"Selik, what do you want from me?"

"Loyalty. But you have shown today that you cannot be trusted. Your word turned to ashes when you betrayed your vow not to escape."

"I told you why I—"

"Nay, do not make excuses. When you gave oath, it was without qualifications. Do not attempt to put conditions on your word now. 'Tis too late."

"Well, then, I'm sorry."

He stared at her a long time, seeming to search for some hidden truth.

"I wonder . . ." He hesitated and did not continue, tilting his head slightly in question.

"What?"

"I wonder who you really are."

"I haven't lied to you, Selik." She held his eyes, finding it extremely important that he believe her, then added, "About anything." She was thinking about her words of love to him. Although she didn't speak her thoughts aloud, Selik seemed to understand, and the tenseness in his jaw softened. His eyes darkened with some emotion, and for the first time, Rain noticed flecks of blue among the gray.

"I can no longer trust your word, and yet I find myself in the odd position of being unable to let you go . . . just yet."

"Because of King Athelstan and my value as a hostage?"

A small smile turned up the edges of his lips, making him so handsome he almost took Rain's breath away. How odd, she thought, that I rarely notice the scar that mars one side of his face. Or the imperfections in his nose. She shook her head slightly from side to side in wonder at her rose-filtered vision of Selik.

"I have survived thus far without you as a talisman, wench. What makes you think I need you to ensure my safety with the bastard king?"

Rain hadn't thought of that before. She frowned. "For the money then. You could use the money I would bring in exchange for the king's having a new healer."

Selik laughed outright then, displaying a beautiful array of perfectly white and even teeth. "Ah, sweetling, I have chests of gold and treasures stored here with Gyda and in the Norselands. The pittance you would bring would not alter the circumstances of my life."

"You have wealth?" Rain asked, utterly surprised.

"I told you I was a successful trader at one time."

"But I thought—you dolt!" she exclaimed, trying once again, to no avail, to shove him off her body, "I thought you had no home because you were so poor. Your clothes are ragged, and other than those armlets, I've seen no evidence of wealth. You must have really enjoyed making me think you were little more than a beggar."

Selik's eyes glittered angrily. "Is that how you define a man in your country—by his wealth?"

"No—well, some people do, but not me. Oh, don't you look down your nose at me so skeptically. Didn't I tell you I loved you, even when I thought you had nothing more than that vicious horse and stupidly named sword?"

"Yea, there is that," Selik responded in a husky voice, "although I do recall ordering you not to speak the ill-advised words of love again. I must devise a suitable punishment for your defiance and for your attempt to escape."

He leaned closer, nuzzling her neck. "Ah. I can smell your passion."

"I'm not wearing Passion today."

"I know." With the tip of his tongue, he traced a path along the curve where her neck met her shoulders and whispered, "'Tis the other passion I speak of, sweetling."

Rain groaned at the sweet, sweet pleasure of that barest of caresses.

"Did you like that, Rain?" Selik arched back, his arms extended straight, intertwining his fingers with hers.

She nodded slowly, running her tongue over her dry lips, then watched, mesmerized, as Selik mimicked her action with his own tongue over his own lips, holding her eyes the entire time.

"I think I have decided on your . . . punishment."

With one deft movement, he moved his legs between hers and spread them wide, exposing her. He slowly pressed himself against her several times until he found her most vulnerable, sensitive bud, then thrust softly against her.

Rain made a low sound of reluctant pleasure.

Selik smiled smugly. "Nay, those mewling little love pleas will not work with me. I am not going to 'rut' with you, sweet witch. Do not get your hopes up in that regard. And do not frown at me so fiercely. Despite all your protestations to the contrary, 'twould not be a punishment at all."

Rain tried to twist out of his grasp, not being foolish enough to buck against him again. But it was just as bad when her breasts, even covered with bra, silk blouse, and wool tunic, grazed against his leather armor, coming immediately erect and aching for his touch.

Selik gasped then, and before she had time to take advantage of the opportunity to escape, he released her hands and shrugged out of his wool tunic and leather hauberk. In the blink of an eye, Selik's hands were back on top of hers, pinning them to the pallet, and he was bare chested, wearing only his tight black braies and short leather boots.

Right to left, back and forth, he rubbed his chest across hers, barely skimming the surface, just enough to tease and tantalize and make her want more.

"Oh."

"You say 'oh' now, but what will you say when I am done with you, foolish wench?"

"What do you mean?"

Selik chuckled. "Do you not want to know what your punishment will be?"

Rain nodded hesitantly.

"Remember that first time we talked, and you prattled on foolishly, as is your usual custom?"

Rain stiffened, not happy with his unflattering description.

"You told me that the best kind of loveplay—the best fantasy for a woman—was to be kissed for hours and hours and hours without any actual—"

Rain groaned. "Do you have to repeat back to me every single word I ever say?"

He smiled and continued. "Mayhap that's what I should do—kiss you in hundreds of different ways 'til you can stand no more, then start all over again and—"

"That's enough," Rain interrupted, feeling a hot blush move up her neck to her cheeks. "You don't have to go any further. I know what you're referring to."

"What, sweetling?" Selik asked, a wicked smile turning up his lips, as he drew out his words sensuously. "Methinks 'twould be a fitting punishment to fulfill your fantasy. And prove you wrong. Because I know for fact 'tis not the best fantasy. Mine is."

Rain gasped.

"Yea, best you take a deep breath, angel. You will need it afore this night is through."

CHAPTER ELEVEN

❦

*H*is kisses were lethal weapons . . .

"You think kissing me will be a punishment?" Rain asked incredulously, then laughed. "You haven't been listening to me very well. I told you I lo—"

Selik clamped a hand over her mouth, his other hand neatly shifting so that it held both her hands in his clasp above her head. He refused to let her finish her declaration. How foolish of him to think that he could deny her love if he never heard the words!

"Yea, that is all I have been doing the last few sennights—listening to your tongue rattle on about this, that, and every other bloody damn thing."

"Mrmpfh! Glumk! Argst!" *You think I talk too much, do you? Let me go a minute, and I'll tell you a thing or two.*

"Holy Thor! Ne'er was there another woman on the face of the earth who thought she knew so much about everything. And did not mind telling one and all what to do, how to do it, when to do it, and where. For the love of all the saints! 'Tis time to put an end to it. You need to be taught a lesson well and good."

Still holding his right hand over her mouth, he leaned

down and brushed his lips across her forehead. "That is the way, sweet shrew. Calm thyself and smooth out those frown lines."

She immediately glowered even harder, and he chuckled appreciatively at her defiance. "Go ahead, then. Wear yourself out in the beginning with these little fights. Every good warrior knows to save his energy for the big battle."

"Damift!" *Dammit. Let me up*.

"What was that, dearling? Didst thou ask for more? Ah, well, ne'er wouldst I be the one to deny a lover her due rights."

His lips swept over her eyelids, across her cheekbones, along the edge of her jaw; Rain's lips parted involuntarily under Selik's palm. How could lips that looked so firm feel so soft? She tried to think of something else to stop herself from arching up for more—ice cubes . . . mammograms . . . trees . . . vasectomies. But she could not get past the delicious sensation of wet, warm lips grazing her cool flesh. Or was it cool lips grazing her warm flesh? She could not distinguish one from the other in the frenzy of tingling sensations he ignited wherever his lips touched.

"If I release my hand from your mouth, do you promise not to speak?" Selik whispered, his breath teasing the wisps of hair on her neck that had come loose from her braid.

"Yecklmqcipekmnfklt!" *Areyououtofyoureverlovinmind!*

"Nay? Ah, well, I will have to direct my kisses elsewhere then."

Selik brushed featherlight kisses along the curve of her neck with little nips and butterfly kisses. When he got to the pulse behind her right ear, he sucked softly on the sweet flesh until he undoubtedly raised a passion mark, then blew softly as if to dry the skin.

When his hot breath inadvertently blew into her extra-sensitive ear, Rain's eyes widened with alarm, her body stiffening with resistance. She couldn't let him know how erotically sensitive her ears were. That chink in her armor could prove her undoing.

But Selik knew. Rain saw the dawning awareness in his hazy gray eyes and in the slow, silky smile that crept across his face.

"So, 'tis the ears for you, sweetling. Mayhap this is one of those fifty-seven erotic points on a woman's body you boasted of once. Just nod your head if I am right."

Rain shook her head vehemently. *Good Lord! Has the man memorized every dumb thing I ever said?*

Selik chuckled with glee, not believing her one bit. "Yea, for some women, the sweet spot is behind the knees, right at the crease. For others, between the thighs. Then there are the tips of the breasts. Even the arches of the feet. But I think I will start my exploration with your ears, dearling. What say you to that?"

She groaned.

"Ah, well, you do not have to say aught. I will kiss each place on your skin until I discover each and every one of your erotic weaknesses."

"Gdmfppppft."

"My thoughts exactly," Selik said as he bit her gently on the earlobe and began a slow—excruciatingly slow—examination of the outer rim of her ear.

"Like a seashell it is, sweetling—all shades of white and pale pink," he whispered huskily as he nipped the edges, taking small, teasing bites. "I wonder, do you taste as good?" Rain groaned and tried to avert her head, to no avail. His tongue traced a sensuous path along the secret whorls whose nerve endings connected to a hot, pulsing region deep in her body.

"Yea, I think I have discovered number one of fifty-seven," Selik said with a soft laugh and began to push the tip of his wet tongue as deeply into her ear as possible. In and out, he thrust with slow, masterful strokes, and Rain's hips arched upward instinctively. Although she pulled back immediately, that one contact with his ever hardening arousal caused that nub of sensation between her legs to swell and ache for his touch. She scrunched her eyes shut tightly, refusing to let him see how little it took for him to turn her mindless with desire.

Then he moved to her other ear, taking endless minutes kissing and nibbling and stroking with his tongue. When he began to repeat the thrusting motion, Rain's arms and legs went rigid with opposition, trying to fight off the spiral of fluttery, swelling spasms she felt growing in intensity between her legs.

Humiliation over her quick arousal heated Rain's flesh. She felt like some love-starved wallflower just yearning for a man's touch.

"Open your eyes," Selik demanded in a whisper near her ear. Even his breath caused little electric shocks of pleasure to shoot through her body.

Rain refused.

Selik pressed his hard maleness lightly against her swollen center.

And she lost the battle.

Rain's eyes shot open, locking with his in carnal embrace, and the spiral spun and spun and exploded between her legs, and shot out with fiery sparks to ignite all the nerve endings in her body.

Selik made a low, hissing sound and removed his hand from her mouth, quickly putting it under her body, cupping her buttocks, and tipping her womanhood slightly against his thrusting hips. Rain couldn't stop her low, keening wail of pleasure.

When her body slumped back in satiation, Selik gently wiped tears from under both her eyes. "Why do you weep?" he asked softly.

"Mortification."

"You jest. I bring you pleasure and you feel humiliated?"

"You did it to degrade me."

"I did? Ah, so now you read minds as well, my guardian angel."

Rain searched his face, just noticing the continuing gleam of desire in his eyes, the beautiful lips slack with passion.

"I climaxed alone. That makes me feel cheap . . . wanton."

"Climaxed? Hmmm. A good word, I think," he said, waggling his eyebrows. Then he grew more serious. "But do not think I did not gain from your climax, as well. A woman's pleasure is a man's greatest gift in the lovemaking. Besides, we have only just begun, and I am saving myself for better things to come."

"Selik, no. I don't want this."

"Neither do I," he said rawly, gazing at her hungrily as the long fingers of his right hand circled the column of her neck, holding it in place for his lowering lips. His other hand still held her arms immobile above her head. Inch by agonizingly slow inch, his lips lowered to hers. Chest to breast, she could feel the wild beating of his heart in their close embrace. " 'Tis a dangerous game I play, and well I know it. But I cannot stop."

"Neither can I," Rain whispered desperately, her breath caressing his lips a hairsbreadth away. "Neither can I."

He traced the outline of her lips with the tip of his tongue and sighed with appreciation as he blew softly against her to dry his own wetness on her flesh. "Your heart is racing fiercely, angel."

"So is yours."

"Are you frightened, sweetling?"

"Yes. Excited and frightened."

He nodded in understanding.

"And you, Selik? Are you as calm as you appear to be?"

He laughed, low and throaty, as he nibbled at her bottom lip, then brushed it roughly with the calloused pad of his thumb. "My lady Rain, I am aroused mightily, and well you know it," he said gruffly. "And I am frightened beyond anything that I ever imagined."

"You? Frightened? Never!"

Selik growled in answer and brushed his lips back and forth across hers, shaping and testing, until he molded her lips to the pliancy he wanted. Then his mouth turned hungry, rapacious in its all-devouring need for her succor.

Rain moaned with supreme satisfaction at the Tightness of his lips on hers and returned his kisses with equal fervor. Selik consumed her, using his lips and teeth and tongue to ravage her helpless mouth. His already firm lips grew turgid with desire.

When he finally tore his lips away from hers, gasping for breath, she cried out, "No, don't stop," then made a low sound of dismay, almost like pain.

He murmured against her lips, "Open your lips for me."

She obliged.

He seared her with his tongue, plunging deep into her mouth, filling her, then leaving her empty and yearning.

"You taste of passion and ageless woman," he whispered rawly between strokes.

She captured his tongue and sucked greedily, then responded huskily, "Your heat is burning me alive."

When his kisses deepened and would not end, when he showed her over and over that she'd never really been kissed before in her entire life, that *he* marked the beginning and the end, she writhed from side to side, but Selik wouldn't let her take any initiative. He held her firmly in place. Rain lost all sense of time and place. But not person. No, she knew exactly who she was, and exactly who her lover was. Selik. Her love. Her soulmate.

Her soft sounds of pleasure and resistance spurred Selik on, and his erection grew huge against her. His silvery eyes blazed forth his passionate need. "Sweet witch, I fear you have enchanted me."

Soft laughter, born of her own pleasure and exultation over her ability to please this man she loved, bubbled forth from her lips. "Then I will haunt you forever, my love."

Desire, hot and molten, erupted through Rain, and the nerve endings in her skin, from her scalp to her toes, were sensitized to the point of explosion. Selik tunneled the fingers of one hand through her hair and angled her face upward for the increasingly frenzied thrusts of his tongue. Rain no longer knew or cared where his lips ended or hers began.

Desire escalated and roiled through her blood. She sucked in her stomach and braced her legs in instinctive resistance to the increasing lack of control her body was exhibiting.

"Rain. Rain, are you listening to me?"

Her eyelids fluttered open, and she was stunned at the utter beauty of Selik's face awash with the pure freedom of his passion for her.

"Rain, sweetling, look at me. Stop fighting your feelings. Relax. Oh . . . like that, yea, just so . . . now, are you listening?"

When she nodded her head, barely able to breathe for the overpowering sensations racking her body, he continued in a low, sensual voice. "This is as close to consummation as we are going to come. Nay, do not moan so. It will be my undoing. A kiss is all I promised here today."

She groaned, then laughed. "If this is your idea of 'just a kiss,' then God spare me from your idea of making love."

"Yea, well, I have been told that my love skills are quite superior," he said with a smug grin. "Now, heed me well, wench, because I want you to do as I order."

"Yes, master."

He grinned in evil satisfaction. "You are learning, wench. Now, when I put my tongue in your mouth this time, I want you to pretend that my manhood is entering your womanhood. Gods' blood! I love the way your lips part when my love words arouse you."

Rain licked her suddenly dry lips.

"When I thrust my tongue inside your mouth, you will pretend—"

"Please, Selik," Rain protested on a groan, "I can use my imagination."

"Can you?" he asked softly, moving closer, then stopped when he noticed the defiant tilt of her chin. "What?"

"I wonder what *you* will be imagining?"

"When?"

"When I return the favor and penetrate your mouth with my tongue. When I thrust in and out of your—"

Selik cut off her words with a hiss of startled pleasure and then with lips that taught her too well that he was a master at this particular art.

When the heat of his kisses drove her almost to the point of insanity once again, when deep within the hot, molten folds of her body a slow rhythm of increasing, thrumming need began, Rain knew that it didn't matter if Selik came from another time. It didn't matter that he was beastly at times. It didn't matter that he often made her angry or hurt her deeply. He was beautiful. And he was hers—her love for all time. Even if this moment was all the time they would have.

"You are driving me mad. Never, never have I felt . . . ah, sweet Freya . . . holy Thor . . ." Selik's hips slammed against her in perfect rhythm with the increasing thrusts of his tongue.

Red lights grew brighter and brighter behind Rain's closed eyelids, then splintered into a kaleidoscope of a million exotic colors as a new pulse point lodged between her legs and convulsed against Selik's hardness.

In a wondrous haze, Rain watched as Selik pulled her hips up off the cot and against him, arched his neck back, and cried out his raw release.

Rain must have lost consciousness for several moments in the aftershocks of the spasms rippling through her body, for when she became aware of her surroundings once again, her arms were free and Selik was slumped against her body. His face nuzzled against her neck, Selik breathed evenly and deeply—fast asleep.

"Well, you could have waited 'til after your bath."

"What did you say?" Selik said thickly, rolling over on his side, taking Rain with him, kissing the curve of her neck.

"I didn't say anything."

"I did."

They both looked up to see Gyda standing in the doorway, a pile of linens in her arms and several of the male servants standing behind her with a large tub and buckets of water, ogling them lasciviously.

Selik sat up immediately. To Rain's regret, Selik's sensuous mood was broken by Gyda's entry. He was probably reminded of his fiancée, Tyra. As he stood and testily directed the servants on where to place the tub, Rain saw that his gray eyes had turned stormy again and the muscles of his arms had roped with tension.

Gyda and the servants left.

As steam wafted up from the huge tub, Selik turned back to her. "Will you bathe first?"

Rain lifted her chin defiantly, her face flaming. "With you standing here watching like a voyeur? Not in a million years!"

"Ah, well! I will go first then," he agreed easily, but pointed a finger at her warningly. "Do you but move one tiny bit off that pallet, you will be in this tub with me. And I swear on the blood of all the gods that you will have soap coming out of every opening in your body."

"Bully," Rain muttered.

"What did you say?" Selik asked, moving toward her menacingly.

"Goody. I said, 'goody.'"

Selik laughed ruefully. "A most horrifying thought just occurred to me. I am beginning to understand your lackwit words."

Selik dropped his braies then, preparing to sink into the tub. Despite her best intentions, Rain's eyes caressed his wide shoulders and bunching muscles. She yearned to trace the letters, R-A-G-E, that he had carved into his forearm. Moving lower, she admired his narrow waist and hips and tightly curved buttocks.

He started to turn, and Rain forgot to breathe. She burst into a fit of choking.

Smirking, Selik sank into the hot water, taking great pleasure in taunting her with his body and with the fact that he was enjoying himself immensely while she sat there wallowing in the dirt of their day-long journey.

Not to be undone, Rain carefully reached over for her

carryall on the floor, making sure she didn't actually move her body, since Selik's narrowed eyes watched her like a hawk. With childish petulance, Rain pulled out a new roll of cherry Lifesavers and popped one into her mouth.

Selik's mouth dropped open with disbelief. "You lied," he accused her. "You said they were gone."

"They were, but I found another package in the back pocket of my slacks."

"Oh, you are a deceitful witch. First you break oath; then you lie."

"Give me a break, Selik. It's just a lousy piece of candy." But Rain sucked loudly, pretending to take special pleasure in the flavor.

"How would you like to have a Lifesaver up your nose?"

"Don't be so ungracious." Rain smiled sweetly and pulled out her Rubik's Cube. While Selik soaped his body and hair, she solved the puzzle, over and over and over and over. She thought she heard him grind his teeth once before he ducked his head under the water and stayed there for an extra long time.

They expected her to kidnap a Viking? . . .

Rain woke early the next morning, realizing as she scanned the little room that Selik hadn't slept with her. Still groggy, she went over to the door. She tried it once, twice, three times, finally accepting with disbelief the fact that she was locked in. "I'll kill the bloody barbarian," she seethed.

Last night, after taking his bath and flaunting his nude body before her in an infuriating manner, Selik had surprisingly left her alone. When she'd completed her private ablutions and the servants removed the tub and wet linens, Selik still hadn't returned. Tired after the long day of traveling and the emotional upheaval over Selik's betrothal—oh, Lord, she had forgotten about *that*—Rain had lain down on the cot, just to rest for a moment, and slept through the night.

But where had Selik slept? More important, with whom? And why had he locked her in?

Despite the early hour—it couldn't be much past daybreak—Rain began to pound on the wooden door, yelling for Selik. After a short time, Gyda answered the door with a clucking sound of disapproval at Rain's behavior.

"Tsk, tsk! All of Jorvik surely hears your caterwauling."

"I'm sorry, Gyda. I didn't mean to awaken you."

"Hah! I have long been about the day's chores."

"Why was I locked in this room?"

"You were confined to your bedchamber because you tried to escape yesterday. You cannot be trusted, and Selik could not spare any more men to stand at your door."

"So, I'm a prisoner now?"

"Were you ever other than that?" Gyda asked, peering up at her through very intelligent, discerning eyes. "Methought Selik referred to you as a hostage from the first."

Rain felt her face flush. "Yes, but I did save his life at Brunanburh and—"

Gyda let out a whooshing sound of dismay and sank down onto the bench opposite her. "You did?"

Rain explained and Gyda listened intently.

"Do you love him?" Gyda asked bluntly when she finished.

Surprised, Rain hesitated, not sure if she could even express her feelings. "I think so. But God help me, there was never a more mismatched, doomed-to-failure relationship in the world. Selik's life is a total contradiction of everything I value. The jerk makes me so mad I could spit. He says the most hateful things to me, tears my heart apart, then puts it back together again with one simple little smile over something as stupid as a piece of cherry candy."

Gyda studied Rain's face intently, seeming to understand her conflicting emotions. "Yea, sounds like love to me," Gyda finally concluded, then rubbed her hands together enthusiastically. "Now, we must needs decide what to do about it."

Rain tilted her head questioningly, curious as to why Tyra's mother would want to help her, but her question was halted by Gyda's next words.

"Didst know that he intends to leave shortly for Saxon

lands? Steven of Gravely has let it be known that he is in Winchester. The demon earl hopes to lure Selik into his death trap. I fear Selik's hatred will blind him to Gravely's devious tactics."

Rain gasped and put a hand to her chest in dismay, recognizing the name of the vicious man responsible for the death of Selik's wife and baby. "No!"

"Yea, and well you should be concerned. Selik may not return alive this time."

Foreboding turned Rain cold with fear. Selik couldn't travel endlessly on this road of revenge and remain unscathed. Someday he would surely die, and she sensed it would be soon.

"I think you may be able to stop him. I have an idea," Gyda offered tentatively.

"Oh, Gyda, anything. I would do anything to help him."

Gyda's face brightened and she leaned forward, grasping Rain's hands. "This is what I think you need to do. . . ."

After hearing Gyda's lengthy plot, Rain stared at her incredulously. "Are you crazy? Kidnap Selik! Restrain him for several weeks until Gravely is gone into hiding once again! Why me? Why not your daughter?"

"Hah! She is too small and fainthearted to handle such a task."

Small! That was all Rain needed—another reminder of her size and deficiencies.

"Were you expecting I could wrestle him to the ground and rope him up? I may be *tall*, but Selik has more than a hundred pounds on me."

"Your sarcasm ill becomes you. Really, you should try to curb such unfeminine traits."

Rain could barely hold back the sneer that wanted to curl her lips. "Bottom line—even if I agreed to your insane plot, I am physically incapable of kidnapping Selik."

"Perchance you know of some herbs that could put him to sleep 'til he could be restrained," Gyda suggested slyly.

Rain shut her eyes wearily for a second, then stared

directly at the elderly woman's questioning face. "Maybe I do, but I must be going mad to even consider such an outrageous thing. Where would he be kept, by the way? Here?"

"Oh, nay!" Gyda exclaimed, putting a hand to her cheek in horror. "'Tis dangerous for Selik to be here even now. I fear that the king's men watch my house."

"I'm sure you have some ideas, though, on where I could imprison him. Oh, Lord, I can't believe I even said that."

"Yea, I was thinking mayhap that Ella would help you."

"Ella?"

"She was a friend of your mother's. She is a prosperous merchant now in the city, due to your mother's help. We shall go see her later today."

"Tell me, Gyda, do you want me to do the dirty work so I can hand Selik over to Tyra on a silver platter?" Rain asked suspiciously, not sure she could trust the woman entirely.

"Mayhap," Gyda said, "but then, if you love him, I think you will do whate'er you can to save him, regardless." She eyed Rain expectantly for several long moments. "Well, what do you think?"

"I think you would have made a wonderful politician."

He was taking her out. Could it be called a date? . . .

For the next few hours, Rain cooled her heels under the close guard of two surly men who shadowed her every move, even when she went to the privy to relieve herself. It was that or go back to her locked bedchamber, Gyda informed her firmly.

With absolutely nothing to do, Rain solved the Rubik's Cube twenty-seven times, walked from one end of the hall to the other sixty-three times, and recited the Hippocratic oath silently sixteen times. Bored stiff, her mood progressively worsened.

So when Selik and Tyra came sashaying merrily through the front door, laughing at some shared joke, Rain forgot all the directives Gyda had given her for the great master plan to save Selik. They looked so blasted beautiful together—Selik in a midnight-blue tunic over black leggings, his narrow waist accented by a gold-linked chain, and Tyra in a green silk, belted, pinafore-type garment worn over a cream-colored chemise that perfectly set off her luscious, wind-blown, strawberry hair.

An unreasonable fury took over, and Rain picked up the nearest object—an apple sitting in a bowl of fruit. Taking careful aim, she threw it directly at Selik's head. But he saw her at the last moment and ducked; the apple splattered against the door directly behind him.

Incredulous, Selik looked first at her, then back to the apple which had barely missed him, then back to her again. His eyes narrowed angrily as he advanced on her.

"I do not believe you are a pacifist at all," he snarled. "What if you had hit Tyra with that apple? She could have been hurt."

"Or you could have ruined my new tunic," Tyra complained, primping prettily before a square of polished metal that hung on the wall.

"Or maybe I could have hit you square in the middle of your cocky Viking face," Rain snapped at Selik while she backed away, on the opposite side of the table from him.

His eyes glittered with anger and his fingers flexed at his sides, probably itching to strangle her. "This 'cocky' has a sound to it I mislike. I take it 'cocky' is not a compliment." Selik continued to walk down the other side of the table in a predatory fashion, keeping exact pace with her, his alert eyes watching her every move, waiting for her first slip. "What bee flew up your arse this morn to turn you shrewish? I thought I had taught you a lesson good and well yestereve. Are you perchance taunting me into another demonstration of my mastery?"

Rain's face flushed at his vulgarity and his reminder of the intimate manner in which he'd chosen to punish her. She didn't think she could withstand another such demonstration of his superior skills in *that* arena. "Save it for your fiancée, Tyra."

"Fiancée?" Tyra interrupted. "What is that?"

"Betrothed, you dumb twit," Rain retorted. "When is the wedding anyway? Maybe I can be the maid-of-honor." Rain couldn't believe her loose tongue. Where was the self-control that helped her survive the awkward adolescence of ridicule, the stringent academic regimen of medical school, failed love relationships, a lifetime of insecurity?

Selik grinned.

She began to retrace her steps in the direction she'd just come.

"Me? Betrothed to Selik?" Tyra laughed.

"What's so funny?" Rain asked, suddenly alert.

"You. Selik is like my brother, *you dumb twit.* 'Tis what you called me, is it not?"

But then Tyra's words sunk in. *Selik and Tyra are not engaged.*

She looked at Selik.

He shrugged with an unapologetic grin.

"Stop teasing her, you lackwit," Tyra retorted quickly. "You have no interest whatsoever in me *that way* and never have. In fact, you have bored me into a stupor these past two hours at the harbor whilst you did naught but talk of the beautiful wench from the future."

Rain's mouth dropped open, and she stared incredulously at the young woman—the wonderful young woman for whom she'd suddenly developed a great fondness—but her lapse in alertness gave Selik the opportunity to leap onto and over the tabletop. He grabbed her and pinned her body painfully against the wall, demanding, "Apologize."

"I'm sorry I threw the apple at you." *Too bad I missed.*

"Now Tyra."

"What?"

"You will apologize to Tyra for your lack of graciousness. Do you forget you are a guest in her home?"

After a long pause, Rain said, "I'm sorry if I offended you, Tyra." *If you believe that, there's a bridge . . .*

"Next time, think afore you react, wench," Selik cautioned as he released her with a swat on the behind. "'Tis a lesson any warrior knows well."

"You shouldn't have locked me in my room."

"Where you are not, incidentally. Who thwarted my orders by releasing you?"

"Gyda, but she assigned these two guards to watch my every move," she said, pointing to the two men who sat at a nearby table watching the entire, ludicrous scene with interest. "I can't even pee without them standing at the privy door counting every drop."

Selik shook his head disbelievingly from side to side. "I am certainly pleased you shared that information with me."

"I begin to see what you mean, Selik," Tyra said. "She does spout some intriguing words. But I can hardly credit that she is a supporter of that nonviolent creed you mentioned— pac . . . pacifism. Why, she is surely more violent than any woman I have ever met."

Rain groaned, beginning to think Tyra might be right.

"Will you still take the shrewish wench to the hospitium, as you had planned?" Tyra asked.

"Nay, methinks she regards herself too highly. 'Twas foolish of me to think a captive would appreciate such consideration."

"You were going to take me to the hospitium?" she asked, totally surprised.

"Yea, 'twas a lackwit idea."

"No, it wasn't."

"Yea, I have decided I do not care to share your shrewish company this morn. My head is aching."

"I'll give you an aspirin."

"Praise the gods! You finally speak a truth."

Rain furrowed her brow. "What truth?"

"You give me an arse burn."

Her lips curling with disgust, Rain tried to control her temper because she really wanted to see the primitive medical facility. Very calmly, she explained. "Aspirin is a modern pill, a painkiller."

"Hah! You name your pills as well as your perfume. See, Tyra, is she not an odd bird? And she criticizes us Norsemen for naming our swords."

Rain was finding it harder and harder to stop herself from clouting him over the head. She clenched her fists so tightly that her fingernails dug into the soft flesh of her palm.

Selik's eyes glittered knowingly.

Tyra glanced back and forth between Rain and Selik as they exchanged insults, seeming confused. "Selik, methought she was a hostage. Why do you allow her to speak so? Should you not cut out her tongue?"

"'Tis an interesting thought."

"I know you think to barter her for your freedom from King Athelstan, if e'er he captures you, Gods forbid, but mayhap you should rid yourself of the crone now. Save yourself the bother. Dost think a slave trader would buy her for one of the Eastern harems? 'Tis said they seek the oddity on occasion, and mayhap her size would not be such a disadvantage."

Rain was beginning to dislike the Norse girl once again.

Selik tilted his head and seemed to seriously consider Tyra's suggestion. "Yea, now that you call it to my attention, I could see her in naught more than a few wispy veils. Mayhap lying on silken pillows beside a marble pool awaiting her master's whim. Perchance she could even—"

"Argh!" Rain growled through gritted teeth, finding it increasingly difficult to curb her tongue, especially when she knew Selik was just goading her. She put her hands to her ears to shut out his teasing words.

"So, Selik, do you return to the harbor to sell her?"

He looked Rain directly in the eye. "Tell me, wench, do you promise to mend your shrewish ways?"

Rain bit her tongue and nodded.

"Will you promise, if I take you to the hospitium, that you will speak only when I allow and obey my every command?"

Rain hesitated but finally agreed with another short nod.

"So be it. But first, come with me. I must bind your breasts."

Rain stared after his departing back. He had grabbed a length of brown fabric from a bench and was already half-way up the stairs before the his words registered.

Bind my breasts?

CHAPTER TWELVE

Just two priests going for a stroll . . .

When Rain caught up with Selik, he was standing in the middle of the bedchamber pulling the brown fabric over his head. Once the cloth had settled into place and he had tied a rope belt about his narrow waist, Rain realized that Selik had donned a monk's robe, complete with hooded cowl.

"Shut your mouth, Rain. 'Tis uncomely to show me your throat—from the inside."

Rain snapped her teeth shut. "What are you up to now?"

Selik turned slowly to demonstrate the full picture of his costume. "I bought this at the harbor this morn when I delivered the captives to the slave trader." Rain winced at his casual mention of selling slaves. "I must needs be more careful in public. A large number of Saxon soldiers patrol the streets and even now may be watching Gyda's house."

"Oh, Selik. How I wish you would leave Britain and go to some land where you could start over and be free!"

His jaw jutting forward stubbornly, Selik declared sharply, "No coward am I to run from my enemies. And freedom ever eludes those who hide in foreign lands."

Rain wanted to argue with him, but she could see by the steely glaze of his eyes that he wouldn't be convinced. At least, not now. She decided to change the subject. "Will you really take me to the hospitium?"

"I promised, did I not?"

"Yes, but . . ." Rain gave up the argument and smiled with exaggerated sweetness, willing to do just about anything to visit the tenth century hospital. She saluted smartly. "Anything you say, master." *You big galoot!*

Selik arched a brow and smiled wryly, his anger fading. "'Tis about time you recognized who is in authority here, wench. And, if you must know, I take you to the hospitium so you may find work to fill your days when I leave Jorvik. I suspect you would make Gyda's life miserable confined to your chamber or helping her clean privies. Or as lady's maid to Tyra."

She started to tell him what she thought of her being lady's maid to the spoiled Viking brat, but Selik put up a hand to halt her words before she had a chance to speak them. "Your prattling annoys me, and we linger overlong. Take off your *shert* so I can bind your breasts and put you in disguise."

Rain made a sort of gurgling sound deep in her throat. "Why do I have to—"

"Nay, no more questions. 'Tis already late. You cannot go into the hospitium claiming to one and all that you are a woman doctor. Never would they grant you admittance."

"Oh."

Selik folded his arms across his chest, tapping his leather shoe impatiently as he waited for her to obey his orders.

Her face heated as she weighed her options—take off her blouse and let him bind her breasts so she could pretend to be a male, or stay imprisoned in Gyda's home and miss seeing the hospitium. Deciding quickly, she began unbuttoning. "What will you use for binding?"

Selik leaned down to a small wooden chest on the floor and rummaged around, finally pulling out a long, scarf-like strip of silk.

She turned her back on him and removed her blouse and bra, waiting. Her amber beads felt cool against her heated flesh.

"Hold out your arms."

Selik took hold of both her hands and demonstrated how he wanted her to raise her arms to shoulder height. Feeling the air on her exposed breasts and the light touch of Selik's fingers under her elbows, Rain almost let her knees buckle with the sudden rush of intense eroticism that rolled over her in waves. She closed her eyes briefly until she regained control of her emotions.

"Do not move," Selik said huskily, then surprised her by stepping in front of her body.

She started to protest, but he seemed to be concentrating on his task, not her traitorous breasts, which had peaked at his first glance. In fact, he barely looked at her body as he deftly placed one end of the strip high up under her left arm, across and above the top of her breasts and around behind, never moving from his spot in front of her.

Twice, he repeated that motion, then proceeded to do the same in the area just below her breasts, which had developed an aching need to be touched. Each time he reached forward under her arms to stretch the cloth behind her, Rain felt his warm breath against her shoulder and choked back a groan of pleasure. Once, his knuckles brushed the underside of her right breast, and Rain felt the shock of the slight caress ricochet all the way to her toes.

When he was ready to bind the breasts themselves, he moved behind her. "I will have to pull hard. It may hurt."

Rain thought the need to be touched was much more hurtful than any pressure from a flimsy cloth could be. When he carefully drew the strip across the middle of her breasts, he asked, softly, "Is that too tight?"

The tickle of Selik's breath against the nape of her neck was Rain's first clue that he was standing so close, peering over her shoulder.

"It must be tighter still, I see. The nipples are still visible."

Rain inhaled sharply. "Is this necessary?"

"Yea, 'tis," he said, jerking the cloth tighter, creating a delicious, quick, abrasive caress across her sensitized breasts. Rain could barely stifle a moan. Then he wrapped the cloth around her several more times, pulling painfully tight. Finally, he tied the ends together and moved around to the front of her, surveying the results. He made a soft clucking sound of dismay. "'Twill have to do, but are your nipples always so large?"

No, you fool, only when you are staring at them and pulling a scrap of silk across them so seductively.

She started to reply, then noticed the edges of his lips twitching with suppressed laughter as he lifted the amber beads in his hand, his knuckles grazing her chest. Apparently, he'd known all along how uncomfortable she was under his scrutiny and near-caresses. And he enjoyed it immensely. "Oh, you are a brute." She reached for her blouse to put it back on, but Selik held her back.

"I have a priest's robe and shoes for you as well."

Somehow, Selik had found a smaller version of the same robe he wore. After she was fully clothed and had skinned back and braided her hair beneath the hood, she looked first at him, then at herself. With a soft giggle, she commented, "We look like Mutt and Jeff."

Selik tilted a brow in question, but Rain just shook her head, knowing it would be impossible to explain the comic strip characters to the Viking. Rain had a sudden, enticing image in her head of Selik lying on her king-sized bed on a lazy Sunday afternoon, coffee in one hand and the comics in the other.

A few moments later, they were making their way through the busy streets of Jorvik. Because of the short distance, they walked. Besides, Selik feared that two priests riding horseback through the city would attract too much attention.

"Must you jiggle your arse so much?" he cautioned once. "Remember, you are supposed to be a monk, not a dockside tart."

"I do not jiggle."

"Hah! And stop touching my sleeve when you want to call my attention to every blessed everyday event happening in the streets. People will think us sodomites."

If he only knew how she restrained herself! Rain wanted to loop her arm with his and rest her head on his shoulder. All her new feelings for him bubbled inside her, threatening to overflow each time she accidentally brushed against him or saw some particularly interesting sight in the fascinating city.

"And I warn you, Rain, do not interfere with aught you see at the hospitium. I care not if they have better healing methods in your country. You are not to tell the culdees how to heal. At the least hint of unnatural talents, the priests could imprison you for practicing black arts."

"Selik, I'm here to learn, but if I can help—"

"One other thing—many of the clergy have a contempt for womanhood. Even if you are the best healer in the world, they would spit in the face of any advice a female would give them. To them, women are the gates leading good men to hell."

Rain couldn't remain silent now. "The gates—oh, that's so unfair! As if women have the power to lead men anywhere! And who's responsible, in the priests' eyes, for a woman's downfall?"

Selik grinned. "No one, I presume, since women—the daughters of Eve—are born with the sin of seduction bred in them."

Rain shoved Selik in the arm with disgust, uncaring if any passersby saw one priest touching another in an intimate fashion. He made her so mad.

"Do not take your ill humors out on me. I merely relate what the priests preach from their pulpits."

"But you love it, don't you?"

"Me?" Selik said with a widespread palm to his chest and exaggerated affront in his voice.

Rain turned away from him in disgust. Once again, she'd

reacted to his baiting just as he'd planned. She decided to ignore him and take in all the amazing sights instead.

But soon Rain's initial wonder over the bustling market city faded as she began to see the wanton destruction caused by the Saxon assaults and the resulting squalor. Part of the city walls had been battered down and homes burnt to the ground. Worse, a large number of people seemed to be homeless, begging for food or coins.

"Selik, why are there so many children on the streets?"

His jaw tensed at her question. "They are orphans, by-products of the Saxon carnage."

"But why aren't they being helped?"

"By whom?" he scoffed.

"Other people who've survived."

"Many of them have trouble enough surviving themselves."

"And the churches—"

"—are too busy feeding their bloated coffers. Bloody hell! There is enough gold in one of their fine chalices to feed the city for a week."

"How about the government?"

"There is none now. The Norse king was exiled, as you know, and Athelstan has not yet appointed a new Saxon ruler." He shrugged. "Even so, the government would not help such worthless curs." He pointed to some nearby children huddled in an alley.

Rain cringed at his unfeeling words. "Because they're *Viking* children?"

"Partly. But any *poor* children—those of the common folk—are of little value. Plenty more where they come from."

"Oh, how cruel!" But really, Rain asked herself, were things any better in her time, when homelessness and child abuse had reached all-time high proportions, when children of third-world countries starved to death, and abortion far exceeded the million mark each year?

"'Tis life. For certain, 'tis one reason why I have vowed to bring no more children into this world."

No more children? Rain's heart melted at Selik's soft-spoken words.

Acting came naturally to the rogue . . .

I will never make love with Rain, Selik vowed as he looked at the city and the pitiful orphans. *Now that I understand the dangers she spelled out to me so clearly, I will never take the gamble of breeding another babe. Especially not on her. Nay, I could not bear the pain of bringing another child into this cruel cesspit of a world. But a babe of my blood, and hers—oh, sweet Lord, the prospect nigh brings me to my knees.*

Selik felt racked with both intense pleasure and torment at the forbidden thought.

"Selik, what's wrong? Why are you looking at me like that?"

He shook his head to clear the bedeviling thoughts.

"Naught is wrong. We are at the hospitium. Pull your cowl farther onto your face."

Selik put a finger to his lips to motion her to silence as they entered the huge, arched double doors that led into the main section of the minster. With a jerk of his head, he indicated for her to follow him.

He went down the main aisle of the central chapel, genuflecting automatically before the crucifix as he had been taught when baptized years before. Rain followed suit, clearly puzzled by his Christian response. Then he veered off to the left, ignoring the monks and other church prelates engaged in prayer and religious duties. A large group of boys from the minster school, sons of area noblemen and merchants, nudged each other and whispered mischievously as they followed a pompously pious, tonsured priest who was lecturing them on church manners.

Finally, after traveling down a number of corridors and through several sets of doors, they arrived at the hospitium, a timber addition to the church structure. A spindly young priest, whose face was still covered with the bothersome pustules of youth, peered up at them from the table where he had been working, rolling strips of linen into bandages.

"Yea? I am Father Bernard. Can I be of help?"

"I am Brother Ethelwolf, and—"

"Ah, Ethelwolf—'the noble wolf'—a fine name for such a large priest as you," the young cleric said enthusiastically, obviously not long removed from his final vows into the Holy Orders.

Rain darted a look of surprise at him.

"And this is my companion, Brother Godwine."

She choked and he slapped her heartily on the back.

"Truly, 'tis unfair. *Godwine*—'friend of God'—'twas the name I chose for my consecration into the priesthood, but another at the abbey had picked it first." The young priest pursed his lips and rambled on with a wistful smile that displayed an ungodly number of rotten teeth for one so young.

Friend of God, indeed! I could not have chosen a more appropriate name for my guardian angel, Selik thought, casting a look of dry amusement at Rain's cheeks, which already reddened with apparent consternation at his priest-name for her.

"Father Bernard, we come from the Friary of St. Christopher in the mountains of Frankland. You have heard of the famous hospitium there, have you not?"

Rain hissed with indignation at his outrageous lie, and he jabbed her with an elbow to remain silent.

"Nay," Father Bernard said apologetically, "but I have been a priest for only a year, and I am training now to be a culdee. Perchance you would like to speak to the head of St. Peter's Hospitium—Father Theodric. He is in the chapel just now, hearing confessions."

"Yea, 'twould be good to meet the esteemed healer, but for now, may we examine your hospitium?" Selik asked. "We visit here in Jorvik, on a mission for our abbey, and would like to learn of all the latest healing methods in the hospitiums we encounter in our travels."

The young cleric raised his brows in question.

"Brother Godwine is an accomplished healer in Frank-land, but since he cannot read or write, I am his scribe, tak-ing notes on our findings for a book Brother Godwine hopes to write. The Holy Father has requested it."

Rain slanted a look of disgust at Selik for portraying her as an illiterate. He just stared back at her innocently.

"You have heard of Bald's *Leechbook*, have you not?" Selik asked Father Bernard, blinking guilelessly.

"Yea, of course."

"Well, Brother Godwine's book will be vastly different. Whereas Bald's book studies the body from head to toe, Brother Godwine's book will go from inside out. And he intends to call it a medical manual."

Father Bernard's mouth dropped open, and a wave of fetid breath almost knocked her over.

"Is that not so, Brother God-friend—I mean, Brother Godwine?" Selik inquired of her.

Rain nodded reluctantly, and Selik knew he would hear more on the subject later.

Yeah, but could she get hospitium privileges? . . .

Selik did annoy her with his continual teasing, and she would tell him about it when they returned to Gyda's house. Unable to read or write, indeed! And writing a medical manual! But she sensed his wisdom in warning her to employ caution. She should not interfere in the culdees' medical prac-tices or let them know she was a woman—and certainly not a woman who came from the future.

"Can you show us around the hospitium until Father Theo-dric returns?" she asked, disguising her voice with huskiness.

Father Bernard scratched his underarm lazily and broke wind loudly, without a hint of embarrassment or apology. Of course he thought she was a man, and Rain supposed men—some men, anyhow—did vulgar things like that. She saw Selik watching her with a blasted smile on his lips, just wait-ing for her usual unbridled reaction. She tapped her foot im-patiently as the young priest bit his bottom lip uncertainly.

"Father Theodric would, no doubt, approve," he said hesitantly.

Rain and Selik moved quickly ahead of him into the hospitium before Father Bernard changed his mind. Rain's eyes devoured every detail of the large hall, which contained more than twenty pallets lined up on both sides of the drafty floor. Culdees in their long, flowing cassocks knelt at the sides of the patients, most often engaged in bloodletting. Rain had seen pictures in medical texts of the procedure involving leeches or bleeding cups placed on the patients, but still she was unprepared for the gruesome sight.

Each of the culdees had two pottery bowls—one for the 'unfed' bloodsucking worms and another for the bloated, blood-engorged parasites. The primitive healers applied the leeches to practically all the patients, regardless of the type of illness or injury, to treat everything from broken bones to stroke.

Rain felt Selik's fingers dig into her upper arm in warning. She tried to shrug him off, but he pretended not to notice.

One by one, the accommodating Father Bernard walked with them by the pallets, explaining the condition of the patients, often introducing them to the culdees who worked tirelessly with the sick. Aside from the bloodletting, Rain could not really criticize the healers, who did the best they could with the primitive materials available to them. After all, the one patient suffering from a stomach tumor could only be kept calm and sedated without the healing effects of modern drugs and medical procedures.

Now the heart attack victim, on the other hand . . . she wondered if they ever used the digitalis plant.

Near the end of the line of pallets, however, Rain couldn't keep her opinions to herself. She sank to her knees next to a culdee who was removing blood-swollen leeches from the wheezing chest of a young girl, about twelve years old, who moaned deliriously from her weakened condition. The rancid smell emanating from the emaciated body was too familiar to Rain to ignore.

"Do you know what's wrong with her?" she whispered to the elderly priest, whom Father Bernard introduced as Father Rupert from the Rhineland. He was wiping the blood off the girl's sunken chest with a damp cloth.

The priest shook his tonsured head. "I have ne'er seen such a malady afore. No matter what I try—herbs, bleeding—naught works."

"The stench, Father—is it always so strong? And are her stools white in color and containing large amounts of fat? Does she continue to lose weight even though you feed her large amounts of food?"

The old man's bleary eyes widened in surprise. "Yea, have you seen other cases such as this?"

"Actually, yes. My niece was recently diagnosed with Celiac disease, and this looks remarkably similar."

"See-lee-ack?"

"Yes, the body develops an allergy—an inability to digest any grains."

"Truly? And what did you do for her?"

"Well, I wasn't her doctor, but I've been told that she can now lead a normal life, as long as she *never* eats or drinks anything made from grains."

He looked at her skeptically, no doubt leery of such a simple cure.

"Try it, Father. What would it hurt? For a few days, don't let her eat any bread or drink any beverage made from grains, like ale. If it is Celiac, you will begin to see a change almost immediately."

The old man tilted his head thoughtfully. "'Tis worth trying, I suppose." He called out his orders to a nearby servant that the patient's diet be changed immediately, then turned back to Rain. "What did you say your name was?"

"Brother Godwine," she answered, then looked up to see Selik watching her intently. His eyes glittered brightly with surprise and what almost seemed like pride in her diagnosis of the young girl.

"Will you be able to help her?" Selik asked as he helped her to her feet.

"I think so, but—" She stopped and addressed Father Bernard. "Could I come back another day and work with the patients? I think I could be of help, and of course, I could learn much from you and the other healers. For my medical manual." She added the last with a rueful glance at Selik.

"'Tis Father Theodric's decision, but he is always complaining about the lack of good healers." Father Bernard looked at her oddly then. "Your voice is very high . . . and melodious."

Rain cringed, realizing that she'd forgotten to lower her voice.

Then his eyes riveted on Selik's hand, which still grasped her arm. As if suddenly understanding the relationship between them, Father Bernard licked his chapped lips; inquiring of Selik, "Wouldst thou be accompanying Brother Godwine if he is permitted to work in the hospitium?"

Selik shook his head slowly from side to side, a decidedly feral look hazing his gray eyes.

Father Bernard giggled nervously and darted a look of appreciative appraisal at Rain's face and form. "Now that I think on it, 'tis certain Father Theodric will welcome your . . . services. We can always use another good . . . culdee, especially if I recommend you to the good father."

Suddenly understanding, Rain's mouth dropped open. *Oh, Good Lord! A gay priest in the Middle Ages. And he's got his radar set on me.*

After that, Father Bernard gave them a quick tour through the garden herbarium, where medicinal plants were grown, and the primitive "apothecary" where another tonsured cleric worked with a pestle and pottery bowls mixing healing potions according to ancient receipts listed in a dusty ledger. Fascinated, Rain decided that she definitely wanted to return to the hospitium and learn all she could about this primitive medical facility.

"When you come back, be certain to identify yourself to the priest on duty. Father Ceowulf often takes my place. We cannot be too cautious. Saxon soldiers have been about all day, searching for some outlaw Viking."

Rain's blood went cold at Father Bernard's words. Could it be Selik they were searching for? Were they nearby?

"Really?" she asked in a shaky voice. "Why would they bother with one Viking?"

Father Bernard shrugged. " 'Tis what I thought as well. Have the soldiers naught better to do than scour the city for one heathen? But of course, I did not say such. King Athelstan has been good to the holy church. In fact, he founded this hospitium just last year. So if the king wants the pitiful Dane, far be it from me to protest. They can hang the outlaw from his toes and skin him alive, for all I care."

Rain cringed, barely aware of thanking the unfeeling Father Bernard for his hospitality and declining his offer of lodging during their stay in Jorvik. As they headed toward the doorway, Rain noticed a commotion. A shrieking man pushed against the large priest whose frame barred his entrance. He begged for a healer to come help his wife, who'd been laboring for three days with the birth of their first child.

"Go home, Uhtred," the priest ordered sternly. "I have told you afore to get a midwife. We do God's work here. 'Tis unseemly for a priest to place his hands on a woman's parts in childbirth."

"But Hilde is dying. The midwife will not come without the coins to pay her, and—"

"Begone!" the priest shouted, pulling the man's grimy hands off his cassock sleeve with distaste. "Guard, come and remove this wretch from the holy church."

"Damn you, damn you to bloody hell," Uhtred cursed as he saw the church guards approaching.

"Wait," Rain intervened. "I'll come with you. Perhaps I can help."

She heard Selik groan at her side.

The man turned eyes of such thanks to her that Rain

knew she would help, no matter what Selik said. But surprisingly, he didn't protest when she started to follow the distraught husband. The priest made a rude sound behind them and remarked, "Foreign priests! Always thinking they know more than anyone else!"

When they opened the front doors of the church, however, they were unable to move. Hundreds of people, many of them children, mobbed the minster steps, screaming and pushing for the loaves of dark bread being handed out by the clerics.

"'Tis alms day," Selik explained. "The poor line up for their pittance of food, and the priests pat themselves on the back for their great beneficence."

"You're very cynical, Selik."

"You are too softhearted," he countered as they progressed slowly through the crowd, following Uhtred.

Rain stopped suddenly as she caught sight of a little boy and girl, about seven and four years old, who stood nearby. That they were brother and sister was obvious, even in the filth that covered them from bare feet to lice-infested heads. The little girl stood with thumb firmly planted in her mouth, listening intently to everything her brother told her.

"Now, ye mus' stand right here, Adela, whilst I try to get us sum bread. Do ye promise not to move?"

"Yea, Adam." She nodded her head up and down, eyes wide with fright as she watched her brother make his way craftily to the front of the mob, pinching a buttock here, darting between legs there, finally pulling a small loaf out of the priest's fingers just as he was about to hand it to an elderly woman in rags.

"Come back, ye bloody toad," the woman screeched, to no avail. Many in the crowd turned to watch Adam's progress, some trying to snatch his precious booty. But there was no way in the world that the imp would give up his hard-won food. He shoved it down the front of his dirty tunic and ran for his life toward his sister.

As Rain moved closer to the children, ignoring Selik's

angry protest as the crowd separated them and Uhtred cried
out in dismay over their delay, Rain saw the boy break the
loaf in half, and the two children gobbled down the meager
loaf of moldy bread ravenously. Obviously, they hadn't eaten
for days.

Rain bent to her haunches before the pair and asked the
little girl, "What's your name, honey?"

Frightened blue eyes turned for help to her brother. "Adam,"
she called, reaching for him with one hand, while the thumb
of the other hand shot immediately into her mouth.

"Why do ye want to know?" the little boy demanded with
narrowed eyes, putting his hands belligerently on his hips.
Rain felt Selik's presence behind her, but he didn't speak.

"You two shouldn't be out on the streets like this. Where
are your parents?"

"Got none."

"Did they . . . die?"

"Yea. What does it matter to such as you? Ye priests care
only fer yer own comforts. Ye would not even come to bury
me mother."

Rain inhaled sharply. "When was that?"

The little boy shrugged dismissively with bravado, hitch-
ing up the loose waistband of his breeches. Rain thought she
saw a brief flash of pain and fear in his eyes. "Last winter."

A year! "And who do you live with now?"

"Huh?"

"Rain, leave off. We have lingered here overlong," Selik
said, taking her arm. "Remember the woman in childbirth."

"Oh, I forgot," she said, shooting a look of apology at
Uhtred. But first she turned back to the little boy. "Who did
you say was taking care of you?"

He raised his head defiantly and snarled, "I take care of
me sister and meself. We do not need any meddlin' priest to
interfere."

"I just wanted to help—"

"Hah! Just like Aslam—"

"The slave trader?" Selik asked with surprise.

"Yea, the slave trader. Keeps tryin' to ketch us, he does. But I be too fast fer the fat old codsucker. Says he knows of a sultan in a faraway land that wants ter have us fer his very own children, to give us a home and good food, but I know what he wants. Yea, I know."

"What?" Rain asked, even as she heard Selik say a foul word behind her.

"He wants to bugger us both, he does, to stick his cock up our arses," the filthy urchin declared with innocent, street-wise explicitness. "Jist like you bloody priests," the little boy declared, spitting at her feet; then he grabbed his sister's hand and disappeared into the crowd.

"Oh, Selik," Rain cried out, when the children were no longer in sight. "We should help them."

"You are out of your bloody mind. I want no children of my own, and for certain I will not care for anyone else's bothersome get. Get that through your thick head."

"But, Selik, did you see that little girl's eyes when she looked back at us over her shoulder? They were pleading for help."

"You see and hear only what you want, wench. Did you hear the coarse-mouthed, filthy pup? He wants no help, and I daresay the tough little whelp could survive on a battle-field, let alone the streets of a market city."

"Please, please," Uhtred begged, pulling on Rain's sleeve. "My wife is dying, and you stand here prattling about worth-less street children."

Rain turned on the distressed man then with anger. "And what makes you think your unborn child is worth more than those two precious children?"

Uhtred blanched, realizing that his hasty words might have jeopardized any chances that the healer would help him. "'Tis sorry I am. But I am so worried about my Hilde . . ."

Rain nodded her head in acceptance of his apology, and she and Selik followed quickly after him. Rain was surprised a short time later when they were about to enter a crude hut. She turned at the last moment and saw that Adam and Adela had followed them. They stood leaning against a nearby tree, watching as Rain bent her head to fit under the low doorway. She waved.

She could have sworn Adam gave her the finger.

CHAPTER THIRTEEN

❧

Desperation breeds idiotic measures . . .

Several hours later, when Rain and Selik emerged from the stifling atmosphere of the little cottage, the children were gone. And Selik's face was drained bloodless of all color.

"What's wrong?" Rain asked, putting a hand on his arm in concern.

"Truly, woman, you amaze me. You just stuck your hand inside a woman's womb, turned a babe, and brought it to life—and you ask me what's wrong?" He shook his head with disbelief. "Do you oft perform such miracles?"

Rain smiled at his backhanded compliment. "A lot of times. Not miracles—births. Obstetrics isn't my specialty, but I've delivered at least fifty babies." She looked at Selik fondly. "It is a wonderful experience, isn't it?"

"Wonderful! There is naught wonderful about all that screaming and blood."

Rain clucked disapprovingly, but she could tell that Selik wasn't being truthful. Witnessing the birth of the tiny baby boy had moved him deeply. She wondered if he'd been with

Astrid when she birthed their child and if this event had reminded him once again of all he'd lost.

And, for the first time in her thirty years, Rain yearned for a baby of her own. What would it feel like to have a life growing inside her, to watch the contractions of her muscles pushing an unborn child forward to life, to touch her own baby for the first time, fresh from the womb?

And what if—oh, God, what if the baby was a living, breathing manifestation of love? How would the child look if it was formed from the blood and genes of both her and Selik? What a wonder that would be!

The yearning grew so strong that Rain had to look away lest Selik read her exposed emotions. *This is dangerous territory you're entering, lady, wishing for something that cannot ever be.*

Ask, and you shall receive.

Rain's eyes shot upward. *Now you say that. How about when I wanted to go back to the future? And are you really saying that if I want Selik, I can have him? And his baby?* Rain closed her eyes momentarily to savor that enticing image.

The answer is in yourself. Search your heart.

"Give me a break," Rain muttered.

"What kind of break?" Selik asked, then added, "Do babies always put such a dreamy expression on your face?"

"Yes." *Especially when I'm thinking of having one with you.* Then she decided to change the subject to a safer topic. "Do you think Uhtred will clean that hut as I advised?"

"Advised? You understate yourself, wench," Selik said with a dry laugh. "You give orders like a seasoned warrior. He would not dare to disobey."

"Well, I was really angry. After going to all that trouble to save his baby's life, it could die in a few weeks living in that filth. How can people live like that?"

Selik was about to speak when he stopped abruptly, pushing Rain behind him. They were about a half-block from

Gyda's house, but she could see the Saxon soldiers surrounding it.

"I will kill the bastards if they harm Gyda or Tyra," he
said in an icy tone of voice.

"Pssst!"

They turned to see a hissing Ubbi hidden between two
houses, motioning for them to come closer. When they
backtracked without attracting the attention of the soldiers,
Selik shoved her and Ubbi farther back between the houses
so they were totally out of sight.

"The soldiers search for you on King Athelstan's orders,"
Ubbi said in a rush. "Sore angry he is over the number of
Saxon warriors lost at Brunanburh to your blade, especially
his cousin Eadric. Dozens of them roam the city and harbor
area. The king offers a hundred gold mancuses for you alive.
Only twenty-five if dead."

Selik's jaw tightened. "Have they harmed Gyda or Tyra?"

"Nay. They ransack the house and outbuildings in their
usual fashion, but do not touch the women. Tostir, one of
Gyda's servants, suffers a broken nose 'cause he did not respond quickly enough to one soldier's orders, and the commander threatens to slit Gyda's tongue if she does not stop
haranguing him. But I think they be safe."

"And my men and horses?"

"All out of sight. Gorm got a warning jist in time."

"Take Rain to Ella's shop. She should be safe there. Then
meet me back here. Do not—*do not*—go to Gyda's house.
They will surely watch it closely from now on."

"No, I don't want to leave you," Rain protested.

Selik's face was steely with determination. "Do not think
to gainsay me on this. Your safety and that of Gyda's family
could be jeopardized by a foolish move on your part. You
will obey me or suffer the consequences."

"But what about *your* safety?"

Eyes flashing angrily, Selik snapped, "My life is my concern, and only mine. Best you understand that now." He

turned to Ubbi. "Take her to Ella's and make sure she stays."

Selik disappeared before she had a chance to tell him to take care, to tell him that she loved him.

With dragging feet, Rain followed Ubbi through the city until they reached the street where the shops displayed lengths of fabric in a rainbow of colors and textures, everything from coarse wool to the finest silk. Some were even fashioned into ready-made garments—tunics and mantles and braies.

Finally, he stopped at one building that seemed more prosperous than the others. Although a young girl worked at the stall in front, Ubbi led Rain around the side to a back door. Knocking loudly, he waited until an elderly male servant answered, then demanded importantly, "We must needs speak with your mistress, Ella. Is she in?" The servant nodded and motioned them into a large hall where a number of workers were cutting and sewing various garments.

"Rhoda!" Rain exclaimed as she recognized the middle-aged woman who approached. "How did you get here?" Without waiting for a reaction, she grabbed her mother's long-time cleaning lady and hugged her warmly. "You have no idea how good it is to see someone from home."

"M'god, not the Rhoda nonsense agin! I thought I was done with that foolishness when Ruby disappeared a decade or so past. Me name is Ella, not Rhoda."

Rain continued to embrace Rhoda, despite her squirming protests.

"Gawd! A bloody priest is caressin' me. I will have to go to confession now, prob'ly get twenty Paternosters fer penance. Be on me bloody knees fer a whole day," Rhoda complained.

Laughing, Rain realized that she still wore the monk's disguise and released the nervous woman from her bear hold. Throwing back the cowl, she exposed her long blond braid and feminine features.

Ella put a widespread palm to her chest. "Lord, me heart

feels like 'tis jumpin' up me throat. Who be you, girl? A barmy comrade of Ruby's, no doubt. She was the only lackwit to ever call me Rhoda."

"Her daughter. Ruby is my mother, and Thork was my father," Rain explained, crossing her fingers behind her back.

"Nay, it could not be so," the woman said, looking to Ubbi who threw out his hands in a "don't ask me" attitude.

"She sez God sent her to save Selik."

The Rhoda person's jaw dropped. "A guardian angel?" she asked Ubbi in a marveling voice.

Good Lord! Rhoda and Ubbi were two of a kind. Rain could imagine Ubbi devouring Rhoda's *National Enquirers* in the future and sharing her insatiable appetite for gossip.

"Yea, and I even found a feather in her bed furs one day," Ubbi disclosed with self-importance.

"Would you two stop talking about me as if I'm not here? I am *not* an angel. I am a human being, just like you two baboons."

"Babe-oons?" they asked simultaneously, and Rain snorted with disgust, refusing to expound.

Ubbi explained the dangerous situation at Gyda's house. Ella agreed readily to have Rain stay with her until the danger passed.

"Please, please come back as soon as possible and tell me what's happening," Rain urged Ubbi as he departed. "I'm so worried about Selik. His hatred of the Saxons may cause him to be careless."

"Do not fear, m'lady. This paltry troop of Saxon whelps pose no real danger to the master. Now, Steven of Gravely, that is another barrel of mead. He follows the devil's own rules of deceit. In the end, Gravely and his loathsome trickery will, no doubt, cause my lord's downfall."

Shivering with apprehension, Rain recalled Gyda's words of warning as Ubbi scurried off. Gyda had said that Selik intended to go into the heart of Saxon territory to Gravely's estate, hoping to finally kill his hated enemy. Now that she heard firsthand from Ubbi how imminent Selik's danger was from Steven, Rain began to seriously consider Gyda's outrageous plan to kidnap Selik until the despicable lord once again went into hiding.

"Rhoda—I mean, Ella, I want to tell you about this plan Gyda has for saving Selik—"

"Plan? Nay, nay, nay!" Ella exclaimed, putting her hands over her ears. "Jist like yer mother, ye are, tryin' to enlist me in her 'master plan' to snare yer father."

"She did?" Rain asked with a smile. Really, she was beginning to see her mother as even more outrageous than she'd ever dreamed.

But Ella ignored her question, rambling on, "Do not be tellin' me of yer barmy plots. Next ye will be tryin' to involve me, I jist know it."

"Well, actually, I do need your advice."

Ella groaned with a resigned sigh and sank down onto a bench against the wall as Rain launched into Gyda's preposterous plan. When she finished, Ella exclaimed, "Blessed Lord, the whole lot of ye have lost yer wits. Unless I disremember, Selik weighs as much as a small horse. How were ye plannin' on overcomin' such a big lout?"

"Herbs."

"And how would ye restrain him?"

"Tied to a bed."

Ella shot her a look of disbelief. "Fer how long?"

Rain flushed and shifted uncomfortably under Ella's too perceptive questioning. "I'm not sure. About two weeks or so, I suppose." Her last words came out in a bare whisper, but Gyda heard her.

"Barmy! I told ye afore, the whole bunch of ye ought to be locked up in a house of halfwits."

"I know it sounds crazy, but what else can we do? I've tried talking to him, but it does no good. He's so stubborn and determined to go after Steven. Even Ubbi believes that if he goes onto the Gravely estate now, he'll be captured and probably—and probably killed." Rain's voice broke, and her eyes filled with tears as she plopped down next to Ella on the bench.

"Love the lackwit, do ye?"

Rain nodded her head with a sob, wiping her nose on her sleeve.

"Well, let me think on it a bit. Where were ye plannin' on keepin' the lad, even if ye were able to kidnap him—not that I think 'tis possible?"

Rain slanted her eyes sheepishly toward Ella, who seemed almost like family to her, even though they had just met. "Is there any chance we could hide him here? The soldiers will be watching Gyda's house."

Ella jumped to her feet indignantly. "I jist knew it. I jist knew it. Ye are pullin' me right into the bloody middle of yer barmy schemes. Fer ten years I have worked me arse off tryin' to establish a biz'ness, and all fer naught if ye have yer way. Oh, Lord! Oh, Lord! I knew things was goin' too well."

When Ella's tirade wound down a bit, Rain asked, "Can you help me?"

Ella rolled her eyes in her head. "Nay, keepin' Selik here would ne'er pass. I have too many workers comin' 'n goin', always stickin' their noses in me affairs."

Rain's shoulders slumped with disappointment.

"How 'bout Selik's homestead outside the city? Much of it was fire-burned by Gravely and his fiendish band, but the foundation and frame fer the barn are still there, as I recollect. 'Twould take only a few hours of labor to put on a new thatch roof."

Rain's spirits suddenly brightened with hope.

"Sum benches and pallets and all the necessaries could be purchased in the city. Mayhap it could work. But people livin' on Selik's land of a sudden when it wuz abandoned fer nigh ten years would draw attention, fer certain. Can ye think of any reason fer yer livin' there?"

A clear, unrelated image flashed into Rain's mind of the two children she'd encountered that day, Adam and Adela, and the vast number of homeless children on the streets.

"An orphanage," Rain answered without hesitation. "I'm going to open an orphanage." Rain grabbed Ella then and hugged her warmly. "Oh, Ella, thank you, thank you. I swear I will repay you for your help some day."

Ella lowered her eyes in an uncharacteristically shy manner and offered hesitantly, "Well, mayhap there is somethin' ye could do fer me."

"Anything. Just name it."

"Could ye perchance put in a good word fer me with Ubbi?"

Rain's mouth dropped open in utter amazement. Then she started to laugh so hard she couldn't stop, finally choking and having to drink a cup of water that a disgusted Ella brought to her.

"'Tis not *that* humorous."

"Oh, Ella," Rain finally gasped out, "it's not you I'm laughing at. It's this whole bizarre comic turn my life has taken. If you had told me a few weeks ago that I would ever play cupid to anyone, let alone to two mismatched Dark Age characters, I would have said, 'No way!'"

"Mismatched!" Ella said, honing in on that one word. "Hah! No more mismatched than you and Selik."

"You're right about that, Ella. You're right about that."

Even pacifists can be pushed to violence . . .

Rain tried unsuccessfully to show an interest in the prosperous mercer's shop Ella proudly displayed for her—the best baudekin silks from Bagdad, Greek Samite, linens of the finest quality known as sindon, similar to a delicate lawn, and of course the famous Yorkshire wool. Even the exquisite embroidery and trims of marten or fox failed to hold Rain's distracted attention.

Finally, Ella gave up trying to entertain or impress her and led Rain up the stairs to her small bedchamber, which she would share with Rain.

Unable to sleep, Rain agonized over the fate of Selik and Gyda's family until Ubbi came for her the following afternoon, assuring her that no one was seriously injured. Even so, her worry increased when she entered Gyda's home and saw the wanton destruction caused by the Saxon soldiers in their pursuit of Selik.

Trestle tables had been overturned and gouged with axes. Barrels and pottery containers of food products—flour, milk, honey, eggs, mead—were strewn everywhere. Tapestries and woven drapes, which had lined the walls to keep out the autumn winds, lay in shredded strips.

Everywhere Rain looked, she saw the inhabitants working diligently to clean up the mess under the stern orders of Gyda and Tyra. Already a large bonfire of damaged goods flamed brightly in the back yard and grew in intensity as more and more of the spoils were added.

"Gyda, I'm so sorry. This is horrible."

Gyda looked up from where she was sweeping up a pile of sticky flour. "We have survived such destruction many a time, and ofttimes worse than this. At least, no one was killed, thank the Lord."

Rain noticed the man with the broken nose that Ubbi had mentioned—Tostir—and went over to examine his injury. There was really nothing she could do for him, other than advise him to hold cold compresses over it to reduce the swelling.

Returning to Gyda's side, she picked up another broom and began to work alongside her. "Where's Selik? I've been so worried about him."

"Gone into hiding, I hope."

"Oh, no! He hasn't gone after Steven of Gravely already, has he?"

"Nay, not yet, but 'twill be soon, I wager. As soon as he is assured of our safety here."

Rain put a hand on Gyda's sleeve. "I've decided you're right, Gyda. We have to do something to stop Selik from killing himself. And that's what he would be doing if he ventured into Saxon lands at this time."

Gyda stopped working and listened intently to Rain's words. "So, a firsthand view of Saxon brutality has convinced you of the danger he faces?"

"Yes, but more than that. Selik goes into a blind rage at the mere mention of Steven of Gravely. Under the best of circumstances, he faces eventual death in his vendetta against the Saxons. But Gravely—any man who could do what he did to your daughter and grandchild—well, I can't begin to think what devious tactics he might use to lure Selik into the open, or what horrendous things he might do to him if he captures him."

Gyda's face stiffened into a hard mask. "I do not begrudge Selik his revenge against Gravely. I would kill the devil myself with my bare hands if I could. But I agree with you that Selik's rage may diminish his abilities to fight off such a fiend." She studied Rain's face carefully. "What will you do?"

"Ella has agreed to help, but I'll need your assistance as well."

Gyda nodded and Rain went on to explain details of the plan. They both agreed that time was of critical importance, since Selik might leave at any moment.

By that evening, not only was Gyda's house back in a reasonably clean and secure condition, but initial preparations had been completed for Selik's "kidnapping." Ella dropped by, offering additional advice, and between the three of them, they made arrangements to have men sent to repair the barn on Selik's property. Gyda sent a servant to purchase the herbs Rain specified, along with some basic household supplies.

And rope. Rain asked for super-heavy-strength rope.

But Selik never returned that day, nor sent any word of his whereabouts. And he didn't return the following day, either. When Rain went to bed the next night, her nerves were strung so tight she couldn't sleep. She walked over to the narrow slit of a window and looked out at the moonlit night.

Where was Selik? What was he doing? Was he even alive? *Oh, God, please keep him safe.*

Oh, the tangled webs we weave! . . .

Selik leaned against the doorjamb, watching Rain as she unconsciously spoke aloud. Her whispery words drifted through the air to him.

Bloody Hell! The wench is praying for me, Selik realized with a start. He was not sure he liked the idea.

He rubbed his fingers across his eyes with weariness. Holy Thor! He wanted nothing more than to lie down and sleep. He had spent the past day and a half trying to elude the Saxon soldiers, leading them on a dangerous chase away from Jorvik, killing one more of Athelstan's loyal followers in the process. And he must leave afore first light if he was going to pursue Steven of Gravely.

A dull sense of foreboding nagged at Selik, unlike anything he had ever felt before. Was it a premonition that he would not return alive from this confrontation with Gravely? Or something else?

"Selik!" Rain had turned and noticed him standing in the doorway. "Where have you been? Why didn't you let us know where you were, you stupid jerk?" Rain's tearful voice of concern contrasted oddly with her insulting name for him.

And, even as she chastised him, Rain launched herself into his arms, almost knocking him over in his exhaustion. She wrapped her arms around his neck and hugged him tightly, as if she would never let him go. Then she kissed his neck and cheek and eyes and brow and chin and lips—all small, frantic kisses. At the same time, her hands touched him everywhere, as if testing that he was really alive and well.

Something new and intense flared deep in his soul, and for a brief moment, Selik hugged her back, relishing the exquisite smell of her clean hair and the warmth of her smooth skin. Finally, he forcefully put her away from him, holding her at arm's length.

"Missed me, did you, wench?"

"Yes, you brute," she said, looping her arm through his and leading him over to the pallet. "Sit down before you fall down, you silly man. Have you slept at all since I saw you last?"

He shook his head, but obeyed her orders, intrigued by the picture of Rain fussing over him.

"Take off your clothes. You smell like a bear."

Her words carried no lascivious intent, but still Selik's lips tilted upward as he removed the filthy garments, except for his loin cloth. In truth, he did not think he could rise to any occasion. Even his bones ached.

His grin grew wider, though, when she lit a candle and returned to the pallet. Kneeling beside him with a bowl of water, she lathered a square of linen cloth with hard soap and began to wash his face and neck and arms with gentle care. Even his malodorous underarms and dust-covered feet.

Selik cocked his head slightly, trying to remember the last time anyone had cared enough to wash his flesh. As a child, abandoned at the court of King Harald in Norway, he was forced to manage on his own. And when he married Astrid, he cared for her, being stronger and unneedful of such ministrations.

But being cared for felt good, Selik realized. So very good.

When she finished and dried him off with a soft linen cloth, she inquired solicitously, "Are you hungry? Shall I go downstairs and get some food?"

He shook his head. "Nay, I just want to rest." He lay down on the small cot, then shifted his weight to the outer edge, away from the wall and motioned to her. "Come, lie with me. Just for a short time. I feel so cold, and I need your body warmth." He still wore only the brief undergarment, and the autumn air chilled the skin.

Surprisingly, Rain did not protest in her usual shrewish manner. Instead, she complied without hesitation, smiling shyly, and squirmed her way into the narrow space he had allotted for her against the wall. He pulled a wool blanket up over them both.

Selik closed his eyes with a sigh as he adjusted their bodies, his chest to her back, his manhood to her buttocks. Her head rested against the inner side of his left upper arm, while his right arm wrapped around her waist. Without thinking, he moved his hand upward and laid it over her left breast and kept it there. Rain accepted his possessive gesture without resistance, seeming to hold her breath. He did not question his good fortune, wondering silently if the wench had suffered a blow to the head. In the past, she would have clouted him by now for such effrontery.

Thank you, God. Or Odin, he whispered in his head with wry humor.

You're welcome.

Selik smiled at the tricks his mind played on him of late and snuggled closer to Rain. In the stillness of the night, as everyone in the household slept, he felt an overwhelming sense of peace, of being right with the world. For now, he could not think of his misspent past, the turmoil of the past few days, and certainly not the lifeless future ahead of him.

Selik relished the sheer pleasure of just holding Rain in his arms. In this moment out of time, he wanted to experience each of the heightened senses expanding and flowering inside him like the petals of a delicate flower.

Pulling her silky braid back over her shoulder, Selik removed the leather thong and combed his fingers sensuously through the long strands down past her shoulder blades. He held the ends up to his face and inhaled deeply, delighting in the combined scent of Gyda's hard household soap and Rain's Passion.

Baring her nape, Selik lightly traced the delicate curve where her neck met her shoulders with his fingertips.

"Selik," Rain moaned.

"Shhh. I just want to hold you. That is all, I swear."

Rain laughed nervously. "Men have been telling women that for centuries."

He chuckled softly. "Well, mayhap I have said the same a few times in hopes of reaping a certain reward, but I mean it now. Truly, I only want to touch you." He hesitated, then admitted, "Nay, that is not quite true. I *need* to touch you."

Rain turned in his arms and put a hand on each side of his face. "It's all right, Selik. I want you to touch me too."

Selik groaned and rolled his eyes upward. *Now you give her to me! Hah! Where were you gods afore I knew the risk of breeding babes? And you, God, how could you put that Onan lackwit in your Bible? Didst thou not realize that men throughout the ages wouldst believe themselves safe from fatherhood in "spilling their seed"? Oh, 'twas a cruel trick you played on mankind!*

Rain had already pushed him to his back and was leaning over him. "Your skin is like stone—hard and rough as pumice in some places," she said huskily, brushing her knuckles across his cheek and jaw. "But smooth and sleek as marble in others." She swept her widespread palms across the planes of his chest and abdomen to demonstrate.

He inhaled sharply at the delicious contact. "You are blind, dearling, if you think such," he whispered, pleased nonetheless by her softly spoken praise. "I am a battered hunk of common stone—granite, no doubt—that is ugly and crumbling with time and the elements."

Leaning on one elbow, Rain reached up and drew her forefinger along the lines of the jagged scar that ran from his right eye to his mouth, then moved down to the rough word, "Rage," which he had carved into his own forearm. "Your scars are like the grains in a piece of seasoned wood. They show your character."

Selik shook his head ruefully from side to side at her disarming words. "I wish you had known me afore. I would have pleased you then, I warrant. And not just in appearance, or in the bedsport. Nay, in all ways. I was whole then. A man."

Rain made a small sound of consternation and sat up with a jerk. Her eyes flashed angrily. "You foolish, foolish *man*. Yes, I said man. Don't you know I have never met anyone, ever, who was more a man than you?"

A vast emptiness in Selik began to fill suddenly. Despite his unwillingness to accept Rain's words, he wanted to believe so badly. For the past ten years, ever since he had failed to protect his wife and child, Selik had felt crippled, less than a man. With her few precious words, Rain was beginning to make him whole again, giving him back a small portion of his pride.

"Thank you," he said in a suddenly raw voice, overcome with this new feeling of completeness. He decided he had to lighten the mood or betray his vulnerability. "Does that mean you no longer consider me a beast?"

"Well, sometimes," she said teasingly, staring at him with such open yearning in her eyes that Selik did not know how he would resist making love to her. And making love was an impossibility now that he knew he could impregnate her with just the tiniest bit of his seed, even if he withdrew early. Especially since he had a foreboding about this upcoming trip to Gravely's estate. In all likelihood, he would not return. And he would not leave another woman and child alone and vulnerable ever again.

But still, a tiny voice of deviltry in his head whispered, *"You could play a bit. You can always stop. What can it hurt?"*

With a groan, he told Rain suddenly, "I'm leaving in the morn. I may . . . I may not be coming back."

Rain surprised him by nodding her head. "I suspected you would be going soon. To Steven of Gravely."

"I have assigned two guards to stay with you and will leave enough coins to pay them for one year."

"A year!" she exclaimed, then seemed to close off all expressions from her face.

"And what will you do when I am gone?" he asked, unable to stop himself from touching the soft flesh of her arm as he nudged up the sleeve of her tunic. He smiled when he felt the fine hairs rise under his light caress.

She touched his wrist, distractedly tracing the pulse beating there with a circling motion of her thumb. Bemused, she answered, "I'll work at the hospitium. I know I could help, and I could learn a lot."

He nodded. "As long as you take the guards with you. And be cautious with the wily priests. They are a sorry lot, some of them."

"Is there any chance you will change your mind about leaving tomorrow?" She stared at him intently, as if his answer was of vast significance.

He shook his head without hesitation. "I have lingered too long already. Gravely may already be gone, eluding me once again."

She bit her bottom lip, as if pondering some momentous decision, then slanted a cautious glance at him under her half-shuttered lids. He narrowed his eyes suspiciously. The wench plotted some mischief, he would warrant. She jumped suddenly and moved away from the pallet, out of his reach.

"I'm going to get us some food and ale."

"I don't want any bloody food or ale. Come back to bed."

"I'll only be a second," she said and was gone before he could stop her.

A short time later, she awakened him, having returned with a huge platter of cold mutton, chunks of hard cheese and manchet bread, and two goblets of Gyda's ale. Although he protested once again that he was not hungry, he ate every bit of food she pushed on him.

"This ale tastes bitter," he complained.

"It's probably just an aftertaste from the spices Gyda put on the meat."

She was, no doubt, right. Gyda did use a heavy hand in the seasoning of her foods. When he finished every drop of the bitter ale, he lunged for Rain and pulled her back to the pallet with him. Nuzzling her neck, he growled, "Now where did I leave off?"

Rain laughed, then pretended to ponder his question with great seriousness. He took advantage of her pause to untie the cord of her tunic and lift the garment up over her head. She wore only the wispy, flesh-colored undergarments, which were no covering at all.

Displaying none of her usual self-consciousness over her

body, she knelt before him, her face suddenly somber. "Se-lik, I love you. No, don't get that bullheaded look on your face. I do, I love you, and—and no matter what happens, I want you to remember that."

Her words touched him in a cold, long-hidden place deep inside him, and the honey of her love flowed over him. His heart expanded almost to the point of bursting, and his whole being filled with a haze of wanting. Not the blood-churning, wall-banging passion he had felt on occasion when deeply aroused, but a gentle, excruciatingly intense heightening of the senses that threatened to splinter his soul.

"Touch me," he whispered. "Please . . . just touch me."

And she did.

With slow, exquisitely slow care, Rain used her fingertips and palms, her lips and teeth, her warm breath and hot toes, her long legs and lace-cupped breasts to worship every inch of his body. Every time he tried to touch her in return or catch her lips in a kiss, she evaded his efforts. "No, let me."

All of Selik's thoughts centered on his arousal as he felt his defenses slipping closer and closer to the edge. When she started to remove her sheer undergarments, he stopped her, finally gaining some semblance of control.

"Nay, dearling, we will not be making love."

Rain lifted her chin in stubborn rebellion. "What do you call what we're doing?"

He smiled at her quick perception. "Playing."

"Don't think you can detract me by flashing one of your devastating smiles."

He smiled even wider. "My smiles are devastating? I had not realized. I will have to practice more, I suppose, now that I know their lethal powers."

Rain jabbed him in the ribs. "Why did you say we wouldn't be making love?"

"I meant that there will be no consummation," he said, suddenly serious.

"Why?"

Oh, Lord! Now what do I say? I cannot tell her the truth.

She would no doubt say she did not care if I gave her my seed. And in a moment of weakness, I might relent.

You could lie.

What? I thought lying was a sin—one of your ten commandments.

Well, sometimes I allow for a little flexibility.

Forcing his face into a bland mask, Selik held Rain's chin in his grasp, demanding her attention. "There is a good reason why I will not penetrate you, Rain. I may engage in battle on the morrow, and I cannot risk weakening my body with consummation. 'Tis the way of many warriors," he lied, almost choking on the words.

Rain nodded hesitantly in understanding.

"But that is not to say a warrior cannot relish a bit of pleasure," he said with a laugh. Before she had a chance to react, he lifted her by the waist and set her astraddle his hips. All that separated her sheath from his sword were the thin fabrics of his loin cloth and her lacy woman's undergarment. Enough, he hoped.

Then he folded his hands behind his head and demanded, "Now, I want you to create some memories for me to take with me on the morrow." *They may have to last me forever.*

Rain's eyes filled with tears, as if she understood. Everything took on a clean brightness then. Like a cleansing summer breeze, her essence surrounded and enveloped him. He was dead inside, and Rain radiated a vitality he craved.

When her lips moved to but a hairsbreadth from his, he urged in a thick whisper, "Say the words again. One more time."

She knew, without questioning, what words he referred to.

"I love you. You damn, sweet, infuriating, loveable Viking, I love you. I love you. I love you. . . ."

Selik heard the words echoing oddly in his head as his body grew suddenly heavy and lethargic. He could not keep his eyelids open. Apparently, he was more tired than he had realized. But the words felt wonderful as they washed over him like a caress.

Before he fell asleep, he thought he heard Rain say something else. "Please, forgive me, Selik. I'm doing this for your own good."

CHAPTER FOURTEEN

*p*artners in crime . . .
   Rain grabbed Ubbi by the hand first thing in the morning and pulled him into Gyda's private solar. She hoped to enlist his aid in getting Selik's dead weight from Gyda's house to Selik's barn outside the city.

"Ubbi, I have a confession to make. I really am a guardian angel sent from God." Rain crossed her fingers behind her back at her blatant deception, then crossed her legs too, just in case.

Ubbi's cloudy eyes grew as wide as saucers. "Well, I jist knew it, mistress. I told the master, over and over, I did, but he would ne'er believe me. Sez ye come from sum lackwit country with lackwit people and lackwit ways, but I knew. I have a sense 'bout such things, I do."

"Well, Ubbi . . . by the way, are you a Christian?"

He appeared hesitant. "I was baptized, jist as the master was, but I still worship the Norse gods, too." He ducked his head sheepishly with the admission.

"That's okay," she said, patting him on the shoulder. "God understands."

"He does?" Ubbi asked hopefully.

"Yes—and, Ubbi, God gave me a message for you." *Am I going to burn in hell for this one, God?*

Nah.

Rain rolled her eyes and looked at Ubbi, whose jaw had dropped practically to his chest.

"God sent me a message?" he asked, gulping with awe.

"Yes, he said you should help me establish an orphanage for all the poor, homeless children in Jorvik."

"Really? Where?"

"At Selik's old homestead."

Ubbi gasped and braced himself against the arm of a nearby chair, as if suspecting he was about to be asked to do something he would not like. "The master will ne'er allow anyone on that land. Besides, the house burned down."

"We're going to use the barn. I had a new roof put on yesterday, and Gyda and Ella are going to send some furniture and supplies there today."

"And my lord Selik agreed to all this?" he asked, blinking incredulously.

"Well, not exactly."

Ubbi craned his neck upwards to get a better look at her face, then groaned and put a widespread palm to his heart. "Oh, Lord, oh, Lord, oh, Lord. The master does not know, does he?"

Rain shook her head. "Will you help me?"

"The master will kill me, fer certain," he cried, pulling desperately at his unruly hair with both hands. "Are ye sure God asked that I help you? Mayhap 'twas some other Ubbi."

Rain smiled. "No, he specifically mentioned you. Unless you refuse, of course."

"How can I refuse one of God's own angels? 'Tis an unfair position ye put me in, mistress."

If you only knew! "There is one other thing, Ubbi, but you have to promise me that even if you decide not to help me, you won't try to destroy my plans."

"Des . . . destroy yer plans," Ubbi sputtered. "How can ye even think I would do such?"

"Well, Ubbi, I have a large—a very large—item I need to have moved out to the farm. Will you help me get it onto a wagon and then up to the loft of the barn?"

"A large . . . What is it?" he asked suspiciously.

"Come with me," she said, motioning him up the stairs. When they reached the bedchamber, she stepped back and let the little man enter first, putting her hands over her ears to shut out Ubbi's shouts of alarm.

"Oh, my God! Oh, holy Thor! The master is dead," Ubbi wailed, throwing himself across Selik's body, which lay perfectly still on the pallet, stone-cold unconscious.

"He's not dead, Ubbi," Rain assured him quickly. "He's just sleeping."

Unbelieving, Ubbi shook Selik's shoulders, to no avail. "The master is dead, the master is dead. What did ye do to him? Did it happen during the coupling?"

"Ubbi! Shame on you," she said, wagging a finger in his face. "And Selik is only sleeping, I tell you. I—well, I gave him some herbs to make him sleep."

"Why?" he asked, squaring his shoulders.

"To save him."

Ubbi plopped down on the edge of the bed next to Selik. "Methinks I do not want to hear this."

"Now, Ubbi, remember when we first met. You were thankful then that God sent me to save Selik."

"Yea, but—"

"And you know how unsafe it is for him to travel into Saxon territory, especially since that despicable Gravely character is there."

"Yea, but—"

"His rage against Steven blinds him to the dangers."

"Yea, but—"

"The bottom line here, Ubbi, is that I truly, truly believe that Selik will be killed if he goes after Steven of Gravely right now. When I talked to Selik last night, I think he had the same foreboding. And that's the God-honest truth."

Ubbi rested his elbows on his knees and put his face in

his hands for a long time. When he finally looked up, he held her eyes and asked, "How long dost thou think he will sleep?"

"A full day. I gave him enough opium—poppy juice—to sedate an elephant."

"Best we get started then," he said, shaking his head with disgust at the part he was going to play in her plan.

How should I torture you? Let me count the ways? ...

Selik awakened groggily to a splitting headache, a dry mouth, and an uncomfortable feeling in his arms and legs. And he had to piss so bad his cock hurt.

As he slowly opened his eyes, he realized that it was daylight already. *God's blood!* He should have been long gone, halfway to Wessex by now. How could he have dawdled so long in bed?

Rain! His eyes shot wide open at his remembrance of the wily wench who had seduced him with her sweet ministrations the night before. No doubt she hoped to delay his departure by allowing him to oversleep.

He started to stretch and arise when he realized that he could not move. He looked down and saw that he was tied to a bed, hand and foot. And worse, a gag across his mouth prevented him from speaking. He sniffed deeply, trying to place the odor that surrounded him. *Hay.* He was in a barn, not Gyda's house, as he had originally thought.

Oh, bloody, bloody hell! Selik gritted his teeth on a silent scream of agony. That bastard Gravely must have entered Gyda's house and captured him during the night. And knowing his inclination to cruelty, he no doubt killed everyone else in the house. Or tortured them.

Rain! Selik suddenly remembered that Rain was in the house with him. *Oh, dear God, if you exist, please do not let her be in Steven's hands. She would be better off dead.*

Desperate, he squirmed and bucked against his restraints, to no avail. He could not break free from the ropes. He closed his eyes then against the agonizing images that crossed his mind, knowing only too well the sadistic pleasure that Gravely would get from torturing a woman like Rain.

"Well, finally you're awake. It's about time. You've been sleeping for two days."

Selik's eyes flew open when he recognized Rain's voice. Was she restrained somewhere nearby? But when he looked sideways, he saw her walking freely toward his bed. What the bloody hell was going on? He struggled once again but could not loosen the ropes. Jerking his chin upward several times, he tried to signal Rain to remove his gag.

She approached his cot warily and untied the cloth across his mouth.

"Hurry and untie me afore Gravely or his hellish cohorts return."

"I can't do that, Selik," Rain said softly, stepping back from his bed.

"Why the hell not?"

"Because it wasn't Steven of Gravely who drugged you and tied you up."

"Drugged . . . ?" Selik's eyes narrowed as his groggy mind began to understand. "Who, pray tell, do I thank for my captivity then?"

"Me," she whispered.

"Argh!" Selik bucked repeatedly up and down on the bed, causing the frame to shake, while straw from the mattress flew about him. But whoever had tied his ropes knew knots well. His eyes knifed Rain's frightened ones then, and he declared in a steely voice, "You realize, of course, that I will have to kill you for this."

"Now, Selik, once you've had a chance to calm down, I'm sure that you'll understand that this was for the best." Her shaky voice betrayed her uncertainty.

"Where are my men?"

"Still in Jorvik."

"Where do they think I am?"

"Gyda told them you went to Ravenshire, that you'll be back in a few weeks."

"And just how long were you planning to hold me here? And, by the way, where are we?"

"About two weeks, I suppose. Until I know for sure that Gravely has left Wessex," she said, sitting on the edge of his small bed, near his feet. "And you're in the loft of the barn at—now, Selik, don't get mad when I tell you this—we're in that barn at your old farmstead."

Selik could feel his eyes bulge with disbelief.

"You just popped a vein in your forehead. I told you before you should be careful about that."

Intense fury clogged his throat so he could not speak, even if he could find the words to voice his raging fury. He squeezed his eyes shut tight and counted over and over and over until he got his temper under control.

"What are those words you're muttering under your breath?" Rain asked casually as she picked pieces of straw off his braies.

"I am counting the ways in which I will torture you once I am free. And I want you to know, wench, that I intend to enjoy the sport immensely."

"You mean, like you punished me by kissing me endlessly?"

He shot her a look that he hoped told her what an utter fool she was to tease him at a time like this. "The only kiss you will feel is that of my knife. First, I think, I will skin you alive—oh, not totally. I would not want you to die afore the other tortures. Perchance, I will pull out your eyelashes next—"

Selik stopped suddenly, cocking his head. "What is that noise?"

A number of shrill, laughing voices rose from below.

Rain looked away guiltily, and Selik wondered what other surprises she had in store for him. "Tell me," he demanded.

"It's the children."

"What . . . bloody . . . children?" he asked, spacing his words evenly, trying to control his splintering patience.

"The orphans," Rain barely squeaked out. When he said nothing, just stared incredulously with his fingernails digging into his palms, she went on. "I decided I would need a cover in case the Saxon soldiers came here looking for you; so, I opened an orphanage."

"Let me see if I understand, Rain. You decided I did not know what was best for my own future, so you drugged me, carted me out to the homestead that I have ordered closed to one and all, tied me up, and welcomed children onto my property when you know full well I detest the sight of the misbegotten, wet-nosed curs."

"That's about it," she admitted with a weak smile.

"And who, pray tell, helped you carry me here, or did you carry me on your back like a horse?"

"There's no need to get nasty. Ubbi helped me—"

"Ubbi! Now, you turn my loyal friend against me, too."

"It wasn't like that, Selik."

"I have to piss," he said with sudden bluntness. "Untie me so that I can relieve myself."

"Oh, I should have thought . . ." Rain rushed quickly to the other side of the loft and brought a pottery urn to his side and was about to untie the cord of his braies.

"Do not even think it," he warned icily.

"Now, Selik, I'm a doctor. I do these things all the time for my patients—"

"I would rather soak my braies like a babe than have you minister to my needs. Truly, you pass the bounds of all that is seemly in a woman. And what were you planning for my other . . . needs?"

"A bed pan," Rain said matter-of-factly. "I fashioned it from one of Gyda's old baking pans."

"A bed . . . a bed pan," Selik sputtered out. "If you ever dare to approach me with such, I swear—do you hear me, you halfwitted bitch—I will make you sorry you were ever born."

She had the good sense, at least, to back away from him then, sensing rightly that she'd pushed him beyond his limits of tolerance for one day.

"Ubbi!" he shouted then and heard the laughter and shrill voices below come to an abrupt halt. "Ubbi! Get your bloody hide up here! Now! I have to piss!"

To Rain he said in a voice thick with loathing, "Best you get out of my sight, wench, for I find the sight of you makes me retch."

She recoiled at his harsh words, and hurt flashed across her face, turning her golden eyes misty and her lips trembling, but she followed his orders and left. He did not care. The woman unmanned him, then expected him to be thankful.

He turned his eyes upward, suddenly suspicious. *Is this your idea of a jest, God? If so, please note, I am not laughing.*

You will.

Heart aches by the dozen . . .

Selik sensed someone standing at the foot of his bed, but he kept his eyes closed. Lord, he was tired of arguing for the past five days with Rain about releasing him. If he heard her say one more time that she did it because she loved him, he thought he would vomit. And Ubbi—the dimwit—believed God had sent him a personal message calling for an orphanage.

The barn was surprisingly quiet, even though it was not yet noon. Rain had, no doubt, gone off to the hospitium in Jorvik, where she performed her good deeds among the culdees. Hah! He would show her a few good deeds when his hands were free—ones he would wager she never read in her bloody medical manuals. And Ubbi, who had been caring for his bodily needs, much to Selik's humiliation, would have a few more kinks in his gnarled muscles when he finished with him.

Finally, still sensing a presence in the room, Selik's curiosity got the best of him and he slitted one eye just enough to see who dared to disturb his peace, meager though it was. *Odin's bones!* It was one of the orphans Rain had welcomed onto his property—the little girl they had seen outside the hospitium days ago.

Although the girl's clothes hung in rags from her scrawny frame, Rain had somehow managed to scrub the urchin clean so he could even see the freckles dotting her ridiculously small nose. And she had braided her blond hair into a long queue down her back.

Selik furrowed his brow, trying to remember what the child's lackwit brother had told them that day. Ah, now he remembered, something about the slave trader, Aslam, wanting the brother and sister for some Eastern sultan. Yea, in his travels he had heard of many men who practiced such perversions. 'Twould be a shame to see this innocent child subjected to such, but it was not his concern. Many horrors filled the world, and he refused to be the crusader Rain would have him be, to right all the world's wrongs.

Inching closer, the barefooted child, who could be no more than four years old, stared at him with wide, sky-blue eyes, her little thumb stuck in her mouth the entire time.

"Go away," he growled, opening both eyes.

The child jerked with surprise at his gruff voice, but instead of running away with fright, she moved even closer. The only sign of her nervousness was that she began to suck rhythmically on her thumb. The girl climbed up onto the bed and sat near his waist, staring at him with a look that could only be called longing.

Selik closed his eyes for a moment, bracing himself against the onslaught of emotions that began to assail him. His skin broke out in a cold sweat, and his heart beat a doleful dirge as it always did in the proximity of young children and the reminder of all that he had lost. He could not allow himself to think of his dead babe and how Thorkel might have looked at the age of every bloody child who passed his way.

He felt a small hand, no bigger than his palm, press gently against his chest, and his eyes shot open with dismay. The bothersome twit still had her thumb stuck between her pouting lips, but she had laid her other hand on his chest.

"Have a caution, lackwit, I bite little whelps like you.

Chomp them up and spit them out for bird feed." He forced
his voice to sound deep and ferocious.

Instead of backing away with fright, she giggled. She actually giggled.

*Lord, my life is turning into a nightmare. I pride myself
on my wordfame as a brave warrior, but I can no longer
even scare a troublesome little mite.*

"Rain! Ubbi!" he shouted. "Get this verminous damned
bloody child away from me!"

Silently, the child moved closer, placing her cheek high up
on his chest, sucking loudly now. He rocked from side to side,
trying to knock her off, but she just clutched his tunic tightly
in one fist and held on for dear life. He thought he heard her
laugh softly. No doubt she thought he played a game with her.

Finally, unable to dislodge the little leech, he peered down
and saw her eyes fluttering sleepily. Once, before they closed
completely, she whispered adoringly, "Da," and snuggled
closer.

Holy bloody hell! The girl thinks I am her father.

The smell of her baby skin enveloped his senses, recalling better days and happier times in his life, and Selik felt
tears well in his eyes. He blinked rapidly to stem their flow,
cursing Rain once again for torturing him so. He lay as stiff
as a board for more than an hour while the child slept
soundly on his chest.

"Adela! Adela! Where are you?"

Selik's eyes popped open. He must have fallen asleep.

Footsteps pounded on the ladder leading to the loft, followed by the grimy face of the boy he had met on the minster steps.

"What are ye doin' with me sister, ye bloody weasel?"

"Adam . . ." the girl said, awakening slowly from her
deep sleep. She sat up and gazed at her brother, reaching out
her arms to him, then immediately plugging her mouth with
the inevitable thumb when he picked her up. *Holy Thor!* The
boy practically staggered under the weight of his sister, who
had wrapped her legs around his waist.

"If ye hurt me sister, ye stinkin' outlaw, I swear—"

"Shut up," Selik snapped, having had enough of children for one day. "Both of you get out of my sight and do not come back."

"Adela, did he touch yer private places?" Adam asked her, and the little girl shook her head vehemently from side to side.

Touched her . . . ? "You had best get your filthy body out of here, you gutter rat," Selik snapped. "And if you ever make such an accusation again, I swear I will—"

"What?" the little bugger challenged, putting Adela to the floor and strutting up close to the bed like an arrogant rooster. His brown hair—Selik assumed it was brown under all the filth—stood out in fifty different directions, being of many lengths due to a bad haircutting. Months' worth of dirt and scabs covered his face and arms, and his tunic and braies were stiff with grease and God only knew what other substances. "What will ye do to me, trussed up so? Ye are not such a fearsome warrior now, are ye, me brave knight?"

Selik would have laughed if he was not so angry. "Move away, you bloody little mole."

"Hah! Mayhap ye would like to try and make me, bein' such a fierce soldier and all," he taunted.

His face flaming with anger, Selik bucked against his ropes. *I will kill Rain for this. I swear I will.* "I will not always be restrained, lackwit, and when I am free, you had best be long gone, for I intend to blister your hide so you cannot sit for a sennight."

Adela tugged on her brother's sleeve, pointing to Selik. "Da," she said, and Adam snorted with disgust. "That scurvy outlaw is not yer father, Adela. Our father was a fiercesome soldier, not a helpless—"

"Ubbi!" Selik shouted, pushed beyond his limits by the coarse-mouthed, filthy excuse for a boy.

His loyal—nay, disloyal—servant scurried up the ladder as quickly as his short legs would carry him. Immediately taking in the situation with the children, he apologized.

"Beggin' yer pardon, master, I had to do sum errands fer the mistress, and what a job it was, too, with a dozen young ones trailing after me, and—"

"A dozen?" Selik choked out. "You have a dozen orphans in my barn, on my property, against my wishes? Rain said there were only six."

"Well, that was two days ago," Ubbi admitted sheepishly. "More and more of the poor wee ones keep comin' every day when they hear of our orphanage."

Selik groaned, then ordered, "Get these two bothersome whelps out of here. Now! And make sure they do not return."

"Yea, master, whate'er ye say," Ubbi agreed solicitously, shooing the youngsters down the ladder. Then he turned back to Selik. "Were ye mayhap needin' the bed pan?"

"Argh-h-h-h!"

"I wuz jist askin'," Ubbi grumbled as he, too, went down the ladder.

Eventually, the piper has to be paid. Unfortunately, she was the piper . . .

Rain deliberately stayed away from Selik for the next two days, unable to cope with his continual demands that she release him, followed by his ghoulish recanting of all the fiendish things he intended to do to her once he was free. Conflicting emotions tore at her—guilt over having betrayed his wishes by kidnapping him and a continuing fear for his safety.

So now she just avoided him and let Ubbi take care of all his physical needs, including bathing and feeding. The children were ordered to stay below.

And the children! Oh, Lord! Their numbers just kept growing and growing. Rain knew she would have to start turning some of them away soon, having already depleted the supply of money Gyda and Ella had given her. She went into the hospitium every day to work, and the monks, in payment, reluctantly handed over cloth bags full of food for her orphans. But they did it in a most uncharitable manner, and many times, when Rain got home, she discovered that the meat was rancid and the bread moldy.

She was sitting in the doorway of the barn, watching the children play, when she spied Adam. Slowly, she stood up and approached the edge of the clearing where the children played a primitive form of Simon-Says. The filthy Adam had eluded her for days, refusing to bathe, and Rain had had enough of his vulgar mouth as well. Once she got hold of him, she intended to scrub him inside and out.

Adam was ordering the other children about in his usual fashion, even those older and bigger than he, when Rain snuck up behind him and grabbed the smelly wretch by the back of the tunic.

"Let me go, ye bloody witch," he shrieked.

Rain shifted her hold and wrapped her arms around his chest in a pincerlike grip. Though he kicked and called her every crude name in his vulgar vocabulary, she would not release him.

"Ubbi, get me some soap and linen cloths and clean clothes for the dirty little snot."

Approaching the horse trough, which had filled with rain the day before, she dropped Adam, then held him underwater for a moment to make sure his greasy hair got wet. He came sputtering up out of the water with more foul names for her than a seasoned sailor. Ubbi handed her a chunk of hard soap, and she told him to help her undress the slippery urchin and hold him still.

After a half hour that seemed like half a day, they finally released the sparkling-clean child from the frigid water. He shook his wet hair off his face, then put his hands on his slim hips and glared up at her, totally unselfconscious about his nudity.

Rain and Ubbi both stared at the little boy in amazement, turning to each other at the same time. "He's beautiful," Rain whispered in surprise.

"Ye are a cod-sucking, arse-licking, no-tit, ugly crone

of a bitch," Adam exclaimed, shoving Rain in the chest, "and I—"

"Saxon soldiers are comin'! Saxon soldiers are comin'!" one of the children cried out, rushing toward them from the road. "Bjorn saw 'em from atop the hill."

Rain and Ubbi exchanged quick looks of dismay, but then immediately told the children to follow the plan they'd practiced over and over for just such an emergency. Adam quickly drew on his dry clothes and herded the children inside the barn like a drill sergeant, spitting out orders right and left. Thank goodness Selik's men and horses were still in Jorvik. They would never have been able to hide them all.

Rain and Ubbi rushed upstairs.

"Selik," Rain shouted as she and Ubbi began to pull bales of hay over near the bed to cover it. "Saxon soldiers are coming," she said breathlessly. "We have to cover you up while they're here."

"Release me," he demanded.

When she just continued to pile the hay over the bed, he bared his teeth and snarled, "Release me, damn you. At least give me the dignity of defending myself if they uncover me."

Rain hesitated only a moment and nodded toward Ubbi, who pulled a knife from the scabbard on his belt and cut Selik free.

"Please lie down and let us cover you, though, Selik," Rain pleaded. "Please."

He shot a look of contempt her way but, surprisingly, complied, telling Ubbi, "Take no chances of antagonizing the bastards. Especially I do not want you taking extra measures to protect me. Do you understand me, Ubbi? I do not care if you get a bloody message from the Pope."

Ubbi nodded.

"Go back downstairs, Adela," Selik said gently with an odd catch in his voice. He was looking behind Rain.

Rain turned to see the little girl staring at Selik with wide, frightened eyes, her thumb stuck in her mouth as usual.

"Get her out of here," Selik ordered Rain, but the child

whimpered and rushed past her, arms outstretched toward Selik.

"Bloody hell!" Selik cursed, then lifted Adela up. She wrapped her arms tightly around his neck, refusing to let go, even when he told her it would be safer to go downstairs with Rain and Ubbi.

The clatter of horses' hooves resounded from the nearby road, almost approaching the yard below, and Selik repeated, "Bloody hell!" Resigned, he lay down on the cot with Adela across his chest, her face burrowed in his neck. Rain and Ubbi quickly raked the rest of the hay over the cot, being careful to lay it loosely over their faces.

When the soldiers stormed into the barn a short time later, all the children were seated at a long trestle table eating bowls of porridge and brown bread. That rascal Adam had done an excellent job getting the youngsters to obey his commands.

The ferocious-looking soldiers, in battle raiment with drawn swords, came to an abrupt halt at the doorway of the barn. Apparently, they hadn't expected such a domestic scene.

The commander, a grizzled, red-haired man, stepped forward. "Where is he?"

"Who?" Rain asked politely.

"Selik. The Outlaw. Who else?" he snapped, coming closer. "This is his property, is it not?"

Rain shrugged. "I know no one by that name. The barn was abandoned, and all these homeless orphans had no place to go, so . . ."

"They are naught but the worthless get of the heathen Danes." He spat on the newly swept floor at Rain's feet, and she bit her bottom lip to stop herself from giving the slob a piece of her mind. "Who are you?" he asked menacingly, stepping closer and grabbing the front of her tunic with a jerk so that she tripped and fell against his barrel chest.

Rain shoved hard against him, pulling out of his grasp. "I'm Rain Jordan, and you have no right to barge into our home like this."

The soldier backhanded her across the face so hard her lip split and her nose started to bleed. Stunned, Rain put a hand to her bruised mouth. No one had ever struck her in her entire life. But she tried to get her temper under control when she saw the children staring up at her with fear. And that silly Adam looked as if he might stab the soldier with his little knife. Luckily, Ubbi saw Adam at the same time and forced him to sit back down.

"Search!" the leader ordered the soldiers, and with wanton disregard for their meager property, they began overturning the chests and barrels in the barn. Flour spilled onto the dirt floor. A pile of clothing was ripped to shreds by one soldier's sword. Two pair of the children's leather shoes were thrown into the hearth fire. While some of the men went outside to search the woods, one young soldier climbed the ladder to the loft.

Rain forced her eyes downward, afraid to look at Ubbi in case her fear would show in her eyes. *Please, God, I beg you. Please don't let the soldiers harm Selik. Please.*

She heard a clattering sound and looked up. The young soldier stepped down off the ladder, scratching his underarms indolently. "Naught up in the loft but a pile of moldy hay."

"Could we use it for our horses?" the leader asked, and prickles of fear turned Rain's skin icy.

"Nay. Smells like it has been here fer years. 'Twould no doubt give the horses stomach cramps." The young soldier yawned widely with boredom, and Rain knew the lazy youth didn't want to have to rake out the loft for his fellow soldiers.

The commander came up to Rain again and grabbed her by both forearms, lifting her to her tiptoes. She barely restrained herself from spitting in his face, but her contempt must have shown on her face because the burly man squeezed hard. Rain felt as if her arms might break, and she couldn't stop tears from filling her eyes at the intense pain.

"Heed me well, wench. Me name is Oswald. I be stationed at the military quarters in Jorvik. If ye hear aught of

The Outlaw, ye are to contact me at once. King Athelstan wants the bastard's head on a plate, and I intend to deliver it." With those words, he shoved her hard and she fell to the ground.

Rain stayed where she was. The children and Ubbi froze in place as well until the noise of the soldiers' horses faded. Finally, Rain stood and looked around at the mess. But she understood how Gyda had felt at the destruction in her home. Everyone was safe, and that was the most important thing.

She looked down then at her bare arms in the short-sleeved tunic. Black-and-blue finger marks marred her white flesh from the elbows practically to the shoulders.

The utter silence began to shatter then as first one child, then another, began to whimper and cry. Rain heard another noise. Footsteps. She looked over to the ladder to see Selik emerging from the loft with the little girl cradled in one arm, wisps of straw covering them from head to toe.

"Adela!" Adam shouted with relief and went over to take his sister from Selik, hugging her warmly and speaking softly to her.

Selik's alert eyes scanned the room. "All safe?" he asked Ubbi, who nodded.

He turned angry eyes to Rain then, and, for the first time, Rain realized the implication of Selik's presence here in the lower level of the barn. In releasing him to defend himself against the Saxons, she'd also released him to wreak his vengeance against her for the kidnapping. She'd thought she would have more time to pacify him, to convince him of her love, to make him realize that what she'd done was for his own good.

"Rain," Selik said in a silky voice oozing with menace. "Come here." He crooked a finger, motioning her toward him, but Rain's gaze riveted on the steely gray contempt in his eyes.

She backed away one step.

Selik stepped forward one step.

"Selik, please understand . . ." Rain felt behind her for the door to the barn and eased her way through the opening.

"Oh, I understand, wench," he sneered, stalking her with a feral intensity.

She wondered at that moment if her greater danger lay with the Saxon soldiers or the enraged Selik. She decided not to take any chances. "Oh, hell!" Rain exclaimed, and turned to run for the woods and safety.

CHAPTER FIFTEEN

⊗

Viking, I'm not afraid of you . . . much . . .

Rain ran as fast as she could toward the woods, but she was hampered by the rising wind, which stung the bruises on her face and arms. And her hip hurt where she had landed when the Saxon commander threw her to the floor.

"This is ridiculous," Rain muttered, thinking that she'd come full circle with her time-travel trip. The first day she'd "arrived" in medieval Britain, she'd run from Selik—the brutal barbarian. Now she was fleeing from Selik—the man she loved.

She stopped suddenly and turned. Selik came to a skidding halt in front of her.

"Make up your mind, wench. Do you run from me, or to me?"

Rain didn't hesitate. "To you."

Suddenly overwhelmed by their near escape from the Saxon soldiers and the anxiety of holding Selik captive for the past week, she reached up and put her arms around his neck, hugging him warmly. "Oh, Selik, thank God you're safe." Standing on tip-toe, she kissed his neck and chin and firm lips.

Almost instantly, she realized that he stood with his hands at his sides, rigidly unresponsive.

"Do not think to sway me with your seductive tricks. I will never forgive you, Rain. Never."

She pulled back slightly, with foreboding, to look at his face. Like shards of gray steel, Selik's eyes stabbed her furiously, and his jaw jutted out with barely controlled rage.

"Selik, let me explain. I know you're upset, but—"

"Upset! Lady, there is no name for the fury I feel toward you. But know this, upset is a sorry understatement." His eyes widened slightly as they scanned her face. "You are bleeding."

Rain raised a fingertip to her cheek and felt the finger welts on her face and the soreness near her nose. "The soldier hit me. It's just a nosebleed, I think."

Selik sucked in his breath slightly, the only indication that he cared one way or another that she had been hurt. His hard gray eyes still regarded her with utter contempt.

He will never forgive me now, Rain concluded bleakly.

"Come," he ordered in an icy voice. "I will deal with you and your traitorous acts inside." He grabbed her arm and started to pull her toward the barn.

"No!" Rain screamed. Arrows of agonizing pain shot from his iron grip on her bruised skin through her arm, up to her neck and down to her fingers.

"What?" he asked, his forehead furrowing in confusion. He dropped his hand when he saw the purpling bruises on both upper arms.

"Oh, hell," he said tonelessly as his shoulders slumped.

Rain couldn't stop the tears from filling her eyes and overflowing at the intense pain she felt, both from her arms and in her heart at Selik's obvious hatred for her.

His long blond hair blew about his shoulders and straw floated up from his tunic and braies, but he just stared at her arms with an unreadable expression on his face. Lifting one arm, he traced the darkening finger marks with a forefinger, light as a feather, as if to erase the pain. Suddenly, the bland expression on his face changed to puzzlement.

"What is that?" he asked, pointing to the small scar near her inner elbow.

"My birth control implant."

"Your *what?*"

"Birth control implant. I had it put in two years ago when I thought I was going to be involved with a man, but then . . . I didn't," she said with a shrug, pulling her arm away from him.

"Exactly what does a birth control implant do?"

"Prevents conception." Really, Selik talked about birth control when all she could think about was her world splintering apart like fine crystal under his shattering contempt.

"I beg your pardon?"

"It's a birth control device. I know it sounds hard to believe . . . Can we talk about this some other time? I don't—"

"And why did you not share this marvelous information with me afore?"

Surprised at the sarcasm that oozed from his voice, Rain answered truthfully, "You never asked."

Selik made a low gurgling sound under his breath. "And how long do these—these implants work?"

"About five years."

Selik smiled widely then.

And Rain shivered because his smile carried none of its usual warmth or affection. It was a dangerous smile—the deadly, sexual smile of a predator.

Confusion washed over Rain. "Selik, is that why you refused to make love with me? You said it was because warriors needed to save their strength before a battle."

He took her arm more gently now. "Come, Rain. We have long-overdue business to attend to, and it cannot wait another moment."

When they entered the barn, Rain saw that Ubbi already had the children working industriously, sweeping up the mess made by the soldiers. The children looked from her to Selik with curiosity, some with fear for her safety in their eyes.

"Ubbi, gather these verminous street rats and take them to Gyda's house in Jorvik."

"Fer how long?" Ubbi asked, not bothering to ask why.

"Until I send word that they may return to *my* home."

"But what if Gyda protests?"

"'Tis no concern to me. I assume Gyda had plenty to do with my lackbrained kidnapping. Let her find a way to deal with the results."

Ubbi shrank back at the anger in Selik's voice.

"Yea, best you back away from me, my traitorous friend. You betrayed me by aiding my enemy," he said, waving a hand toward Rain, "and that we will discuss later."

"Trait . . . traitorous? Oh, ne'er think that of me, master. I did only what God commanded me to do fer yer own good."

Selik stepped closer, wagging a finger menacingly in Ubbi's blanched face. "Well, here is another message for you, Ubbi. Get the hell away from my presence afore I wring your scrawny neck."

Ubbi jumped back and began to shoo the children toward the door, urging them to gather their belongings for a long visit.

Selik's alert eyes scanned the large room and noticed Adam slithering in a clandestine fashion toward the exit. He lunged for him before he could escape, grabbing him by the belt and lifting his small body, kicking and squirming, into the air.

"Were you the witless gnat who taunted me with foul words when I was sorely restrained?"

"Nay," Adam lied boldly, trying to punch Selik's shoulders with his flailing arms. "Ye mistake me fer another. I be jist a helpless, motherless boy tryin' to take care of me poor sister."

"Helpless! Hah! Methinks you were ne'er helpless from the day you came squalling from your mother's womb." He sank down onto a bench then and laid Adam over his lap. Quick as a wink, he smacked his behind, then set him on the floor in front of him, holding him firmly by the shoulders.

Adam spat in his face.

Eyes widening with disbelief, Selik shook his head at the

boy's daring. "Your pride makes a fool of you, boy. Best you learn how to pick your battles more wisely."

His lips thinned grimly, and he flipped Adam back onto his lap and whacked him another five times, this time somewhat harder. When the boy stood before him this time, tears filled his eyes and his stubborn lips quivered. Knowing Adam, his pride hurt more than his behind.

"Do you understand me now?" Selik demanded.

Adam appeared to consider rebelling once again, but finally nodded.

"Go with Ubbi now and take care of the other children," he said, pushing Adam toward the lingering, wide-eyed group. "Ubbi needs someone brave to help him."

At first, Adam just gawked at Selik. When the lopsided compliment had sunk in, he grinned impishly and strutted toward his fellow orphans, calling out orders.

Selik barred the door after them and turned to Rain. "Go up to the loft."

Rain scanned Selik's expressionless face, trying to understand his intentions, hoping for some softening toward her. There was none.

With dull resignation, she climbed the ladder to the loft. She heard Selik moving about below. Unsure what he wanted her to do, she decided to sweep away the hay that she and Ubbi had thrown on the bed to cover Selik and Adela. When she finished, she sat down on the bed furs and waited. What would he do to her? How would he wreak his vengeance for her kidnapping?

Too soon, she got her answer.

"Take off your garments," Selik ordered when he came up the ladder to the loft.

"Why?"

"Do not dare to say me nay, wench. Do as I say. *Now.*"

Rain reluctantly took off her calf-length tunic and the slacks she wore underneath. She hesitated about removing her bra and underpants.

"Everything," he snapped.

When she stood naked before him, her head bent in shame, she began to remove the amber necklace.

"Leave the beads," he said gruffly.

Her head jerked up, but he'd already turned away from her. Over his shoulder, he instructed her, "Lie on the bed."

With dread, Rain did as he instructed. He walked toward the pallet slowly, his eyes taking in every inch of her body from her toes to her long hair, which had come loose from its braid and lay over her shoulders. When he reached for the ropes, still tied to the bedposts, Rain knew what he was going to do.

"No, Selik, please don't do this. I had good reasons for my actions. I only wanted to keep you safe."

He ignored her pleas and spread-eagled her on the bed, tying her securely to the four corners. Sitting on the edge of the bed, he regarded her with contempt, asking with mock consideration, "Would you like to use the bed pan?"

Rain's face flamed and she blinked back the hurtful tears that smarted her eyes. "This is degrading."

"Yea, 'tis," he agreed coldly. "On that, at least, we agree."

He started to walk away from her then, and Rain called after him, realizing that he intended to leave her alone, "Selik, I'm cold." The wind had risen and thunder clapped in the distance, portending a coming storm.

"You won't be for long," he informed her sardonically, but then threw a cloak over her, fur side against her skin. With care, he made sure that it covered her from toes to shoulders. "Rest, angel. You will need it."

It was true what they said about Viking men . . .

Selik stayed away so long that Rain eventually dozed. When she awakened, feeling chilly, the storm was raging loudly outside, rain pelting against the weathered timbers of the barn. Although it was only late afternoon, the interior of the loft was dark and gloomy. Or it would have been except for one thing—dozens of candles burned brightly surrounding her bed.

And she lay naked, her blanket thrown aside.

Her eyes darted wildly, seeking Selik. He sat on a stool near the edge of the circle of candles, his long legs outstretched casually, crossed at the ankles, and his arms folded across his chest. He watched her like a vulture, but the flickering shadows hid his facial expressions.

"Tell me," he said in a flat voice when he realized that she was awake, "what prompted you to betray my trust?"

Rain flinched at the pain of his condemnation but regarded him honestly. "I never betrayed you, Selik. I was trying to protect you." She went on to explain all that Gyda and Ella had told her and why she felt compelled to take such drastic actions. "Will you go after Steven now? Will you leave for the Gravely lands in Wessex?"

He shook his head slowly from side to side. "Nay. Whilst you slept, I got word to my men in Jorvik—those who are still loyal to me. Steven was seen boarding a ship in London."

She exhaled with relief.

"Do not think you have stopped me with your traitorous acts. You only delayed me. I will go after Steven yet."

"Selik, please try to understand. I love you. I was afraid—"

"Nay," he interrupted, "love does not unman the lover. Dost thou really consider me such a poor warrior that I cannot defend myself against such a devilish weakling as Steven of Gravely?"

"That's not the point. Gyda told me—"

"Desist with thy blame throwing. You, and you alone, made a decision to drug and restrain me. You decided to play the man and determine my fate. How dare you? How dare you?"

"I'm sorry," she said weakly.

"And do not think to soften me with tears. I assure you, I will not be moved."

But Rain cried anyway, the tears pooling and overflowing in silent streams down her face, burning when they touched the welts and her bruised nose. She knew she must look a mess. One side of her face was probably red, and her nose swollen. Oh, Lord, that was the least of her problems.

Selik moved quietly toward the bed and sat down. He leaned to the floor and picked up a small pottery container. Dipping his fingers inside, he began to massage the foul-smelling ointment into the bruises on her arms. Almost instantly, Rain felt the pain numbing and then disappearing.

"What is that?"

"Horse liniment."

Rain choked as she inhaled the ungodly odor, rather like that of limburger cheese.

" 'Tis a special concoction of Ubbi's," he said with a grim smile, recognizing her discomfort and, no doubt, taking pleasure in it. "The odor disappears almost instantly."

He used a wet linen cloth to wipe the blood and tears from her face, then applied the same liniment to the welts on her cheek. She thought she might pass out from the obnoxious stench so close to her nostrils.

"Do you know the name of the Saxon soldier who did this to you?" he asked in a tight voice.

"He said his name was Oswald—the leader of a Saxon garrison newly assigned to Jorvik, I think."

"He will not live to celebrate another Christmas," Selik proclaimed with deadly purpose as he put the pottery jar back to the floor and wiped the liniment off his fingers with the linen cloth.

Then he surprised her by untying the ropes that bound her, ordering, "Go wash thyself," he said, pointing to the corner where a pitcher of water lay on a bale of hay. "And relieve thyself, as well," he added with dry humor. "I find the act of holding a bed pan even more degrading than pissing into it."

Rain cringed at the icy loathing in his voice but hurried quickly past the candles into the dark, chilly corner. When she was done, she returned to the bedside. Selik still sat on the bed, his somber expression highlighted by the flickering candles.

"Sit," he said, pointing to his lap.

Rain's heart flip-flopped, but she did not question his command.

"Nay, not that way," he said, turning her to straddle his lap.

Rain felt suddenly exposed and vulnerable, sitting in such a position, naked, while Selik was fully clothed in tunic, braies, and leather boots. She bent her head in shame, then gasped at the air that hit the inner folds of her body when Selik widened his legs.

Selik grinned, almost as if he couldn't help himself. Then he traced the scar at her inner elbow. "You should have told me you could not get pregnant."

"I didn't think it was important."

"Why do you think I refrained from penetrating your body during that ridiculous hour-long kissing bout or the other near-consummation?"

Rain looked up in surprise, searching his eyes. "Because I thought you believed what you said about sex weakening soldiers before a fight. And because . . . because I thought you didn't find me attractive enough."

Selik inhaled sharply and she felt his erection grow and harden against her center. "Are you daft?"

Rain smiled tentatively, for the first time beginning to think Selik might not be going to punish her physically—at least, not in the tortuous ways she'd imagined. "You mean, you *are* attracted to me?"

"You are a witch. Nay, do not think to pretend to be an angel. I see the devilish glint of seduction in your honey eyes. You think to lure me from my anger with your sensual wiles." Abruptly, he pressed her femininity against his raging arousal. "For weeks, I have fantasized about all the things I would like to do to your body, but could not do because of that nonsense you spouted about beads of semen."

Rain smiled, but her smile soon faded as he mentioned a few of his fantasies in sultry whispers as his fingertip still traced erotic circles around the scar on her arm. Rain was *very* impressed with his creative mind. When he raised her arm and put the tip of his moist tongue to the scar, Rain felt a wetness pool, hot and molten, between her legs. She tightened her thighs in resistance.

Selik's eyes glittered. He knew what he was doing to her. Oh, yes, he knew. And loved it.

"Selik," she whispered in a hoarse plea, "take off your clothes, too."

"Nay, this is a journey I intend to begin fully garbed."

"A journey?"

"Yea, we are going a-Viking—on an adventure, an exploration." Although anger and hurt over her betrayal still tensed his face, Rain saw the glint of mischief in his eyes.

"What kind of exploration? What are we looking for?"

"Your G-spot."

"Oh, Selik." She laughed, "That's not necessary."

"Yea, 'tis," he disagreed. "And I might even show you the secret S-spot if I am able to get over my anger toward you."

"S-spot?" Rain asked dubiously, not sure if he was teasing.

"Yea, do not tell me there is something your famous sex exports with their bloody manuals do not know."

Rain choked back her laughter. "Experts," she corrected, "not exports."

He waved a hand dismissively. "'Tis of no import. The truth is, the sultans who first discovered the S-spot guard the secret in their harems. A few Viking invaders learned the secret and perfected the art. No doubt, the information never reached your . . . country."

Selik's lips twitched with amusement. Rain couldn't be sure if he was serious or not. She didn't care. At this moment, all she cared about was Selik and the love she felt for him.

Selik put his hands on the outside of her knees, near his hips, and ran the calloused fingers in a slow sweep up her thighs. "Why are your legs so bristly?"

"Because I haven't shaved in weeks."

"Ah, yes, the leg shaving your mother mentioned."

"You know, I'm getting a little sick of hearing all the outrageous things my mother said and did."

"Well, mayhap you can shave your legs later with my knife.

'Tis very sharp—the one I use to shave my face. Of course, I will watch to see you do it properly."

"Oh, Selik, I lo—"

"Nay," he stopped her gruffly. "You have proven yourself untrustworthy. Do not toss me your lying words. Besides, 'tis not what I want of you."

His open palms moved over her hips then, past the curve of her waist, over her rib cage. When his thumbs reached out and brushed the undersides of her breasts, she sighed.

"Like that, do you?" he asked with a chuckle. "And how about this?"

The heels of his hands lifted the weight of her full breasts and his fingers spread over them, touching everywhere except where she most wanted to be touched. Then, just briefly, his middle fingers flicked the tips back and forth.

Intense, wildly erotic pleasure shot from her breasts to her aching center, and her inner thighs hugged his legs tighter. "More," she pleaded in a hoarse whisper.

But Selik withdrew his hands from her breasts and placed them on the small of her back. Pulling her forward, he adjusted her so that her cleft rode the ridge of his erect penis. Then his hands moved upward, tunneling in her hair, holding her scalp in a firm grip.

She looked into his blazing eyes and begged, "Kiss me. Please."

"I thought you would never ask," he said in a raw voice as he lowered his lips to hers. He angled his open mouth over hers, then, without any soft preliminaries, plunged his tongue into her mouth, searing her. She felt a hot liquid pool at her center, and her center swelled and opened. Reflexively, she rode him with jerky thrusts of her hips until spasms of electrifying pleasure shot through her. She tried to tell Selik that she wanted him, all of him, but she could not speak for his hot tongue, which matched the movements of her hips in the slick sheath of her mouth. His hands were holding her rib cage, moving her from side to side so her nipples brushed abrasively against the wool of his tunic.

She groaned, then exploded in a million wonderful, wonderful sparks of the most intense pleasure she'd ever experienced in all her life.

And she wanted more.

For a moment, she rested her head against Selik's shoulder. She knew he hadn't climaxed. She could still feel his hardness pressing against her and the panting of his breath near her ear told her his iron control was slipping.

Quickly, before he could protest, Rain pushed away from him and slid off his lap, kneeling between his legs. She began to undo the clasp of his belt, then raised the tunic upward, urging him with silent motions to lift himself slightly to accommodate her.

She could not stop herself from touching him then. She brushed her widespread palms over the abrasive dark blond hairs on his chest, along his wide, wide shoulders, across his flat male nipples. She felt the shudders that rippled through his tense body and looked up. His beautiful gray eyes glazed over with passion, and the whiteness of his scar stood out starkly against his flushed skin.

"I love you."

He put a hand to her lips and shook his head. He didn't want her proclamations of love. Well, she would give it to him anyway, but without words—with her body.

This is my beloved. The Biblical words in her head shook Rain. She was not sure they were her own, or God speaking through her, but they seemed to describe her feelings completely. And a sense of wonderful completeness overtook her.

She took off his boots and untied the cord on his braies, pulling them off his legs. When he was fully naked, her gaze swept him lovingly.

"You are so beautiful. You take my breath away."

He smiled, and Rain felt warmed. "I am not, but it pleases me that you think so."

She leaned down then and put her lips to him, lovingly. He gasped, pulling her away quickly. "Nay, sweet witch, you will not end this love play afore it begins."

He stood her upright so her breasts were level with his face and began to pay delicious homage to them, alternately laving and flicking them with his tongue, then taking the tips into his wet lips and tugging.

"Oh . . . oh . . . oh-h-h!"

"Am I too rough? Shall I stop?"

"Don't you dare," she gasped out.

Selik fell back to the bed then, taking her with him, and she couldn't wait. She straddled him and guided his rigid, pulsing length into her body, which welcomed him with soft, clasping spasms.

"Bloody, bloody hell!" he groaned. "'Tis too soon. You are so tight. Nay, do not move. Not yet. I want to savor this feeling for as long as possible . . . forever."

"Selik . . . ?"

He unshuttered his eyes lazily, exposing the depth of his arousal in blazing gray pools that almost seemed to swirl with need, and a mouth swollen with passion. "What?" he whispered thickly.

"I love you," she said, despite his orders to the contrary, and raised her body on his shaft, then slowly sank back down.

"Nay," he protested, but put his hands on her hips to regulate the pace of her rhythm.

"I love you," she repeated against his parted lips and tried to convey with loving kisses the intensity of that love.

"Nay, you love the feel of me inside you."

Rain laughed exultantly. "Yes, that too."

She smiled, barely, between his agonizingly slow strokes.

"What else do you love?" he whispered as he stroked the peaks of her aching breasts with his fingertips.

"I like *that*," she said, gasping, "and *that*," she added as he took one breast into his mouth and grazed the nipple with the edges of his teeth. She arched her back, throwing her head back, and began to keen in a low whimper as the storm between her legs accelerated, turning her mindless and out of control.

Placing his middle finger between her legs, against the throbbing bud, Selik rubbed up and down in the slick groove until she screamed, "I can't . . . I can't . . . oh, God, stop . . . no, don't stop . . . I want . . ."

He flipped her over onto her back, still inside her, and pushed up on her ankles and outward on her knees. Then he tormented her by pulling outside her body, the tip of his rock hardness pressed against her most sensitive fold. She tried to move against him, to pull him back inside her, but he would not allow it.

"Tell me what you want," he demanded in a voice so thick with passion that she could barely understand the words. Rain could see that he was as aroused as she, but still he tormented her by withholding himself.

"I love you, and I want you to love me, too," she said, expressing her fervent wish.

Rain saw the surprise on his face. They were not the words he'd expected. But he closed his eyes, as if in resignation, and slammed into her.

"I love you," she cried, and on each of the hard strokes that drove into her body, she repeated the words over and over and over, "IloveyouIloveyou IloveyouIloveyou . . . ."

The veins stood out in Selik's neck as he imbedded himself into her one last time, almost to the womb, and cried out his own piercing climax, before she joined him in a cataclysmic shattering of her senses, which convulsed and convulsed and convulsed around him, until they finally shattered into little aftershocks.

The weight of Selik's body pressed her to the cot, and she relished its sweet warmth in the afterglow of their lovemaking. At first, he panted, then breathed evenly against her neck.

"Are you asleep?" she asked softly, brushing a hand caressingly over his silky hair.

He made a small strangling sound low in his throat, then lifted his head and smiled. "Nay, I am dead."

She smiled back and felt her heart expand with the love she felt for him. No torment marred his handsome face now.

The lines of pain and bitterness that usually bracketed his eyes and mouth had melted with their lovemaking.

"Why are you gazing at me so?" he asked, chucking her under the chin.

"How?"

"Like a bear suddenly presented with a bowl of honey, when it should be the other way 'round," he said with a growl. He rolled off her to his side, then quickly leaned down and licked her lips. "Hmmm. Yes, I do think I taste honey. Let me check further."

When he finally tore his lips away from hers, breathing unevenly, he nipped at her shoulder and commented, "We have not finished our a-Viking."

"We haven't?" Rain exclaimed, and the note of astonishment in her voice drew a chuckle from Selik.

"Nay, I have yet to show you your G-spot," he said, sitting up, then moving to kneel between her legs. He sat back on his heels, then pushed her knees up to her chest, holding them there with the pressure of his left arm.

Placing his thumb above her pubic bone, he stretched two other long fingers inside her so that they met the thumb from the inside. Then he began a rapid, hard, pumping stroke that continually brought him back to that spot beneath the thumb.

A fiercely intense arousal began at the point of his expert sliding fingers, aided by the wetness of their previous lovemaking. "Selik, I don't know if I like this," she said hesitantly.

"You will."

Unlike her other arousal, which encompassed all her senses, this fiery excitement centered in just one spot. When the first shutters of climax began to shake her, she tried to close her legs, afraid to increase such a powerful cataclysm, not sure where it would lead. But he forced her legs to stay apart with his arm, and, when the first spasms hit her, he did not stop. Over and over and over, his hard fingers rubbed abrasively over that sensitized inner spot until she rolled from side to side, trying to escape. She came and came and came until suddenly she shook and felt a gush of liquid come from her, like an ejaculation.

Selik released her legs then and entered her with his hard, hard length filling her. He soothed her with soft whispers, stroking in and out with slow, agonizingly slow, caresses. "Shh, it will be all right. You were wonderful. Magnificent. Can you do it again, sweetling, with me inside you? Can you? Can you?"

And she did.

CHAPTER SIXTEEN

&

Sometimes today is all we've got . . .

    "I'm hungry," Rain gasped several hours later, and her stomach grumbled redundantly in agreement. She lay in Selik's arms—depleted, wrung out emotionally and physically, and happier than she'd ever been in her entire life.

    "Me too," Selik growled and nipped at her shoulder playfully.

    "Not *that* kind of hunger. Selik, stop it," she squealed as he began nibbling lower and lower. "Keep it up and your precious manhood is going to fall off from overuse."

    His head shot up and his eyes widened in alarm. "Nay, do not tell me. One of your sex manuals claims that a cock can fall off from too much bedsport?"

    Rain laughed. "No, but even if it did, there are surgeons who can sew a penis back on."

    Selik jerked upright and made a snorting sound of disbelief. "For shame, Rain! That statement is so outrageous it does not merit consideration."

    "Listen, Selik, there was this abused woman who cut off her husband's penis . . ."

    When Rain completed her explanation, Selik stared at

THE OUTLAW VIKING 281

her, mouth agape and eyes wide with astonishment. "And it worked as good as afore the cutting?"

"Well, he supposedly performed in some porno films. And, no, I'm not going to explain porno."

"I do not believe you. Methinks you weave these tales for your own twisted amusement," Selik declared with finality, lying back down beside her. "No doubt you will have great fun relating this jest to your friends when you return to your country—how you made the fool of a lackwit Viking."

Rain turned on her side, facing Selik, and laid her right hand on his cheek, tracing his scar lovingly with her fingertips. "Selik, I'm not going back. I'm never going to leave you."

"Do not make promises you cannot keep," he said gruffly and pulled out of her embrace, folding his hands under his head and staring somberly at the roof of the barn. "Besides, I did not ask you to stay."

The storm had ended, but the steady patter of raindrops against the barn boards made their little pallet seem like a tender cocoon of peace and love. But Rain knew this was only a temporary reprieve from danger and hate, and she had to convince Selik of her love while she had the chance.

"I can promise not to go near the Coppergate site in Jorvik," she avowed fervently. "I can promise to stay with you as long as you want me. I can promise to love you forever. I can—"

"Do not do this," Selik protested on a groan of despair, turning to face her again. His sad eyes and tightly pressed lips bespoke his conflicting emotions. Finally, unable to keep his feelings under control any longer, he pulled her roughly into his arms and hugged her tightly. "Ah, Rain," he said on a sigh of utter hopelessness.

When he pulled away, his pain-filled eyes tore at Rain. He told her in a shaky voice, "I cannot protect you. I did not keep my wife and son safe from harm. I cannot promise to do any better for you."

"And who appointed you my protector? Who said you were responsible for the safety of the world? Oh, Selik, can't you see? It wasn't your fault that Astrid and Thorkel died. Stop tormenting yourself with the past and start living. *Living*. Not just existing. Not waiting to die." Rain stopped suddenly, realizing that she'd probably gone too far.

But for once Selik didn't seem angry at her mentioning Astrid and his past. He gazed at her pensively, then said, "Mayhap 'tis true. If I had been able to accept my blamelessness years ago, soon after it happened, perchance I could have lived a normal life. But too much has happened since, too many deaths, on both sides—"

"But if you left Britain, started over somewhere else—"

"Give it up, Rain. I cannot rest until Steven is dead, and Athelstan will never allow me to live with the blood of so many of his soldiers on my hands."

"But—"

"Nay, dearling, we have no future," he said, cradling her against his shoulder, stroking her hair lovingly. "but we have now. Let us make the best now that we can."

Strawberry fields forever . . .

Later, after they had slept for a time, Selik shivered and shook Rain awake. The aftermath of the storm had left the barn drafty with frigid air.

"'Tis colder than a whale hunter's arse on a glacier. Best we move to the pallet downstairs near the hearth or your tits may turn to snowballs."

"And your penis to a popsicle?" Rain asked saucily and moved quickly off the bed to avoid his swatting palm. He had a fair idea of the meaning of popsicle.

They moved downstairs and made sure that the barn doors were barred from the inside and Selik's sword lay nearby, in case the Saxon soldiers returned.

After gorging themselves hungrily on whatever food they could rustle up—manchet bread, cold venison, hard cheese, and watered mead—they pulled a pallet up close to the roaring fire and put several cauldrons of hot water on for bathing. They sat companionably wrapped in one large fur blanket,

feeding the flames with bits of kindling while they waited
for the pot to boil.

"Admit you lied to me afore?"

"About what?" Rain slanted a sideways look at him.

"About your bad ruttings with men."

Rain jabbed him with an elbow in the ribs and he pretended injury.

"I never used those words. I said, as I recall, that I could
take sex or leave it, that I had a poor history of relationships
with men."

"And you still feel the same?"

"Fishing for compliments, are you?" she asked, raising
one brow mockingly.

"Nay, I know how good I am," he boasted. "I merely
wanted you to admit you were wrong, for once."

"I didn't lie, Selik. I know you don't want to hear this, but
I love you. And I think that's what marks the difference in
making love with you."

In truth, he did not mind her saying the words so much
now. Actually, the sentiments warmed his soul and made
him feel more alive than he had in years.

"And if you did not love me, you think you would not have
enjoyed our coupling?" he asked, biting his bottom lip with
concentration.

"I don't know," Rain admitted honestly. "Maybe it would
still have been good. All I know is that from the moment I
first saw you, long before the Battle of Brunanburh, from the
first time you haunted my dreams, there's been a special connection between us. And last night, it was as if two pieces of
a broken whole were finally connected. That sounds really
corny, doesn't it?"

"Corny? I do not know that word, but I like the part about
being coupled," he said with a smile, then caught his breath
at the open look of adoration in Rain's eyes.

"I didn't say coupled, you horny toad. I said connected.
C'mon, let's see if that water is hot enough before you get
distracted—again."

When they had finished bathing, and she helped Selik shave his face and he did *not* help her shave her legs—choosing, instead, to make erotic remarks the entire time—Rain rummaged in her carryall for a comb. While Selik combed his hair and then hers before the roaring fire, pulling the teeth sensuously through the drying strands, Rain looked through her bag to see if she might find a loose Lifesaver she'd overlooked. No such luck.

But she did find something of interest.

"Selik, how do you feel about strawberries?"

"I like them well enough, but the fruit will not be in season 'til next spring."

Rain opened the little metal tube in her hands and applied the strawberry lip gloss. Then she turned and took the comb from Selik's hands. "I've got a little out-of-season treat for you, babe."

Sometime later, Rain whispered, "I sure hope you don't have an allergy—a bad reaction—to strawberries, like some people do."

He retorted with a gasp of pleasure, "Holy Thor! If I do, I will have rashes in some hard-to-explain places."

Exhibitionism isn't all it's cracked up to be . . .

That afternoon, Selik wakened from a deep sleep with Rain's arm across his chest and her knee between his legs. He did not want to open his eyes, burrowing deeper under the warm fur blanket whose silken hairs caressed their naked bodies.

But something had jarred him. A sixth sense, mayhap. Selik came suddenly alert and carefully reached for his sword. Then he slitted his eyes carefully to peer at his surroundings.

A dozen pair of wide eyes stared back at him in open curiosity.

"Ubbi! Where the hell are you, you lackwit?"

Ubbi stepped forward immediately. "Yea, master, did ye call?"

Rain sat up beside him, pulling the furs up to her bare shoulders, exposing his naked body to the cool air.

"Did I not tell you to stay at Gyda's 'til I sent for you?"

"Yea, ye did. Ye surely did, m'lord. But Gyda made us leave. Said to tell ye that she raised eight babes of her own and she be too old to have these noisy, pesky, dirty varmints raining havoc on her home. Oh, and coarse-mouthed, she called them too," Ubbi added, leveling a look of condemnation at Adam who was gawking with interest at Selik's exposed body.

Selik groaned, pulling the furs over his male parts, and glared at Rain, whose lackwit idea it had been to open an orphanage.

"And another thing," Ubbi added, looking with offended eyes at Rain, "that Ella was hangin' over me like a hungry dog on a bone. Didst you promise me to her, as she claims? Am I a side of beef to be bartered?"

"Rain! Oh, nay, do not say you are matchmaking atween Ubbi and Ella?" Selik said with astonishment. "Do you not know that Ubbi has been running from Ella's salivating clutches for years?" But then he remembered how his loyal servant had betrayed him of late and added, "On the other hand, mayhap you need a forceful woman to control you better, Ubbi."

Ubbi inhaled sharply with outrage.

"So, do ye like stickin' it in her?" Adam interrupted them idly, one hand on a jutting hip and his eyes glued with undue interest to Rain's half-exposed breasts where the fur had slipped. She immediately pulled it back up.

All eyes locked on Adam then, unable to believe he would ask such a blunt question.

"What? Why are ye all gawkin' at me? I was only askin'. Bloody hell! How is a boy to learn things if no one will answer an honest question?"

"Someone ought to wash your mouth out with soap," Selik declared ominously.

"The witch already did," Adam snapped, glaring at Rain,

then turned back to Selik. "Did she do the same to you—wash out yer mouth with soap? You use the same foul words as me."

"I have to make pee-pee," Adela said suddenly at Adam's side. He took her hand, leading her to the chamber pot in the far corner.

"Pee-pee?" Selik choked out.

Adam looked at Selik over his shoulder. "The witch sez we cannot say piss anymore. 'Tis too crude." The little boy's voice rang with disgust. He helped his sister adjust her tunic and led her back toward the gaping group, adding disdainfully, "Pee-pee is bad enuf, but ye should hear what she calls *it*."

"It?" Selik asked, then wished he had not.

"A too-too," Adam declared flatly, looking down at the vee of his braies. He folded his arms across his chest, shooting an I-told-you-I-was-gonna-tell look at Rain before nodding in self-satisfaction. "And she sez we have to wash every day, *every bloody day*, and clean our teeth, and say our prayers, and learn to read and write, and do our chores, and so many damn rules me head spins."

Selik looked at Rain's blushing face, then put his head into both of his hands and groaned. His well-ordered life was crumbling around him. A short time ago, all he wanted was to kill Steven of Gravely and mayhap a few Saxons, then die. Now, he was saddled with a guardian angel from the future, a servant who believed he got messages from God, a dozen orphans, and a boy who had to be related to Lucifer himself. How would he ever escape this quicksand of a life?

Looking up, he saw Adam sit down before the hearth, stoke the fire, then proceed to ignore them all and play idly with Rain's Rubik's Cube.

And, worst of all, he solved the puzzle.

All you need is love . . .

The next afternoon, Selik insisted on accompanying Rain to the hospitium for her usual rounds. They both wore the monks' habits, as before.

Selik was not in a good mood. The weather had turned frigid last night, even for early November—too cold for him and Rain to sleep in the loft. Which meant twelve squirmy, squealing, curious bodies had slept beside them, not to mention a loudly snoring Ubbi on a nearby cot. And Selik did not even want to think about Adela, who had crept into the pallet between him and Rain during the night and snuggled up against his chest like a frightened kitten.

"I still say, it's unsafe for you to be prowling the city streets with so many Saxon soldiers about," Rain complained for what had to be the hundredth time.

"I would much rather face a troop of bloody Saxons than stay one more minute in that madhouse back there."

"You've seemed restless all day, Selik. I'm afraid to ask this, but are you leaving soon?" She looked up at him from the shadow of her monk's cowl with eyes so hopeful that Selik had to restrain himself from taking her in his arms and promising anything that she desired. But that he could not do, and not just because the sight of two monks embracing near the minster steps would horrify the passersby.

"I expect word today from Gorm on Steven's whereabouts. He will meet me at Ella's shop."

He saw the fear in Rain's eyes, but she bit her bottom lip, restraining her usual protests. He was oddly touched that she tried to curb her shrewish tongue for his benefit.

"Well, I'm not going to fight with you over this anymore. Oh, don't look so pleased with yourself. I still don't agree with you. I just don't want to waste any more of the little time we have together."

"What will you do after I'm gone? Return to your home?"

Despair flashed briefly across her face before she masked it and lifted her chin bravely. "No, as long as I know you're alive somewhere, I'll stay. Probably continue going to the hospitium every day and run the orphanage, if you'll let us stay on your property."

"And if I never return?"

Rain's bleak eyes locked with his and she seemed to

swallow hard before speaking. "I don't know." Then she seemed to force her mood to lighten and poked a finger in his chest. "But know this, you stubborn Viking, if you are alive somewhere, hiding from me, I'll find you. Maybe even kidnap you again."

"Nay, you would not dare do such again. I forbid it."

"Not even if I captured you so I could have my way with your body?" she asked, slanting a look of exaggerated sultriness at him.

"Well, mayhap," he conceded with a grin.

Just before they entered the side door of the hospitium, Rain put a hand on his sleeve to halt his progress, and said nervously, "Before we go inside, there's a little something I need to tell you."

He narrowed his eyes suspiciously. Whenever Rain used that tone of voice and mentioned "a little something," it usually meant she wanted a favor, or he was not going to like what she said.

"Bernie has the hots for me," she said, blushing.

At first, his mouth dropped open. He snapped it shut with a grunt of disgust. Truly, the wench had a knack for surprising him. "I think I can guess what 'the hots' are," he remarked when he finally got his amazement under control, "but who in the name of Thor is Bernie?"

"Oh, you remember Father Bernard—the young priest we met that first day, the one with acne—zits—all over his face."

"And you have become so familiar you call him Bernie?"

"Not familiar, really. He's so young. I just humor his crush, but I don't want you to get upset if you notice him putting the make on me."

"Rain, I have no idea in the world what you just said. But if he dares to lay one finger on you, I will knock his rotten teeth down to his toes."

She started to protest, but Selik pushed her through the doorway and gave her waist a proprietary squeeze. Unfortunately, Father Bernard was standing there, ready to greet the target of his "hots," with wounded eyes riveted on Selik's intimately placed hand. With deliberate deviltry, Selik looked the monk straight in the eye and spread his palm, moving lower to Rain's right buttock, which he grasped suggestively.

Rain jumped and turned on him.

He told her baldly, "Begging your pardon, Brother Godwine. I was reaching for the door handle."

Rain was not fooled one bit by his fake innocence, although Father Bernard accepted Selik's explanation. The first chance she got, she hissed at Selik, "Door handle? Hah! How would you like it if I grabbed *your* handle?"

"I would like it fine," he said with a wink. "In fact, you may pump my handle any time you like."

"Tsk! Behave yourself, Selik, or I'll never get anything done here today." In her assumed husky voice, she said, "Father Bernard, you remember Brother Ethelwolf, don't you?"

Unaware of their whispered exchange, the young priest ignored Selik and turned to Rain. "You have not been here for days," he complained. "Father Theodric has been asking for you. Did you not promise to discuss brain fevers with him?"

"Yes, but I've been busy at the orphanage and couldn't come 'til now." Rain tried hard to keep her voice low and husky to hide her sex.

"That orphanage! Why do you waste your talents with the filthy Danes? They are naught but little heathens," he whined, and Rain felt Selik stiffen behind her. She pinched his arm in warning.

"They are God's children, Father," she chastised the young priest, "no matter their origins."

"Well, I still say ye should reside at the minster. We could always find a place for you to sleep."

"I wager he could," Selik whispered near her ear. "Under his scrawny body."

She flashed Selik an admonishing look, afraid he would betray their disguises.

"Brother Godwine! Brother Godwine!" Father Rupert

called out to Rain. When they approached the pallet where he knelt, she saw that the deathly ill girl was now sitting up.

Father Rupert beamed at Rain. "You were right. A change in diet was all Alise needed. Her father will be coming to take her home today."

Rain knelt beside Father Rupert and examined the girl she'd diagnosed with Celiac disease her first day at the hospitium. Alise was still far too thin, but with care, she would recover with no ill effects. "Now you do understand, Alise, that you cannot ever, for the rest of your life, eat grains again? Even one bite of bread could set your disease off again."

"Will I ne'er get better?" the little girl asked tearfully.

Rain shook her head. "But isn't it a small price to pay for feeling well again?"

Alise nodded, and Rain told Father Rupert to make sure the girl's father understood the disease and the importance of a strict diet.

For hours, she worked side by side with the culdees, examining the patients, listening carefully to their diagnoses and remedies, many of which came from the revered *Bald's Leechbook* prepared about twenty-five years earlier. Surprisingly, many of the recipes they followed proved effective, even by modern standards, especially the herbal ones. Rue was used as a capillary anti-hemorrhage agent. Henbane, known to modern doctors for its properties in blocking nerve fibers and as a hypnotic, induced sleep. Pennyroyal settled the stomach. Woodruff and brooklime, both rich in tannin, relieved burns when applied in butter with the root of a lily.

Her biggest complaint was against the widespread practice of bleeding for almost every ailment. But she followed Selik's advice on observing, offering minor advice, but doing nothing to call attention to herself as a modern physician.

Occasionally, she even forgot that Selik accompanied her and would look up suddenly to see him leaning lazily against the wall, his finely honed Viking body a spectacular picture, even in a monk's garb. How could anyone miss his beautifully sculpted face, his gracefully long fingers, his beautiful smile?

"What is that wonderful scent?" Father Bernard asked suddenly, sniffing near her cowl.

"'Tis Brother Godwine's Passion," Selik answered devilishly as he took her arm and moved her down the aisle.

Father Bernard just gaped after them, stuttering, "His . . . his . . . did you say passion?" He practically drooled.

Finally, disgusted with Selik's snide remarks, Father Bernard commented testily under his breath, "Why does the big lump not get down on his knees and help, instead of standing around idly?"

But Selik overheard him and commented boldly, "I am observing, *Bernie*, for our book."

Father Bernard's face colored, highlighting the pus-filled pimples that dotted his face. "Methinks Father Ethelwolf's arrogance is unseemly for a priest," he complained to Rain. "And frankly, it appears to me he is observing more than he should."

Rain looked up then and noticed, just as Father Bernard had, that Selik's appreciative eyes were fastened on her posterior as she bent over to pick up a wad of linen.

She hissed to get Selik's attention, but instead of being embarrassed at being caught in the act, he winked. *He winked.* She heard Father Bernard make a low, strangling sound, and Rain realized she had to get Selik out of there before he gave them both away.

"We've got to go, Father Ethelwolf," Rain announced suddenly, pulling on Selik's sleeve. "I just remembered that we must stop at the mercer's to purchase more cloth for the children's tunics."

"Oh, but you cannot leave yet," Father Bernard protested. "Father Theodric will be here shortly."

That was just what Rain was afraid of, especially with Selik being so blatant in his attraction toward her. The highly intelligent Father Theodric saw too much. Already he raised questions she couldn't answer about healers in Frankland whose names she didn't recognize, about how she'd gained her vast medical knowledge, and even about her feminine characteristics.

"You must pray that God will help you control your baser instincts," he'd told her once after she shrieked girlishly when a mouse darted over her foot in the minster herbarium. He referred to what he must consider her effeminate nature. If he saw her with Selik, the sexual chemistry that sizzled between them whenever they moved within looking distance would undoubtedly cement the idea in his head.

"Tell Father Theodric that I will see him tomorrow, and we can discuss brain fevers and the vaccinations I mentioned to him. I will have plenty of time, since Father Ethelwolf will be unable to accompany me."

"Huh?" Selik asked, looking up from the bag of food he was examining near the door. "Why will I be unable to come with you?"

"You will be transcribing all your mental notes onto parchment. For our book. Remember?"

He waved a hand in the air dismissively. "Ah, I can do that anytime. We will discuss that later." He turned then to Father Bernard. "But now I want to know who is responsible for the pig swill you have been giving Brother Godwine as his *laece-feoh*—the physician's fee?"

Rain turned to Selik with surprise. She hadn't realized that he knew about the rotting food the priests sent for the orphans.

Father Bernard's face turned bright red. "'Tis not a physician's fee, just a gift, a favor from the minister to the orphans."

"Are you saying, *Bernie*, that Brother Godwine's healing skills have no value?"

"Nay, I ne'er said such. But well, 'tis good enough for the scurvy lot," he mumbled defensively, pointing to the food. "Leastways, 'tis the same food we priests eat each day."

"Ah, then that is different," Selik said with a resignation Rain knew was false. "You will not mind then having a bite of this." He reached in the cloth bag and pulled out a hunk of pork that smelled to high heaven.

Father Bernard backed away but Selik followed, pushing the putrid meat in his face, against his lips.

"Selik," Rain protested, pleased that he defended her, but afraid he would attract undue attention.

Selik ignored her pulling hands and told Father Bernard icily, "Do not ever dare to give Brother Godwine such spoiled food again. Dump this in the cess pit. 'Tis not good enough for the dogs in the street."

He shoved away from the shaking priest angrily and grabbed Rain's arm, pulling her through the door.

"Selik, we have to bring food back for the children. I'm sure I would have been able to salvage some good things from that bag."

"Nay, you will not. You need not beggar yourself by accepting charity from such tight-fisted clerics. I will buy all that you need."

And, much to the delight of the Jorvik merchants, he did. In the end, he hired a wagon to cart all their goods back to the farmstead—fresh beef, ten live laying chickens, a milk cow, raw vegetables, crisp apples, mead, honey and flour.

"Selik, people are going to wonder where a monk got so much money," she whispered worriedly as he once again pulled out his pouch of coins at a merchant's stand.

He responded by telling her, loud enough for the merchant to overhear, "Brother Godwine, are you truly sorry that I stole the bishop's hoard he was saving for a new jeweled chalice?" When she eyed him warily, he went on. "Even you must admit, the orphans cannot eat gold and garnets."

The merchant muttered under his breath in agreement, "Bloody priests! Care more fer jewels than the poor." To show his support, he threw in a couple of extra loaves of bread.

"See. I have some uses," Selik boasted as they headed toward Ella's shop.

Rain couldn't help but smile then, and Selik smiled back

at her in all his glorious beauty. Her heart filled with all the love she felt for him. She wanted to say so many things to him, but didn't know how. So many feelings blossomed within her. She wanted to shout to the world her wondrous love for this man, and to hug it to herself in secret savoring. This was the love of a lifetime—a thousand lifetimes!

Was this why she had been sent back in time? She had thought she was sent to save Selik, but maybe this love was just a gift from God. If so, how was she to help Selik?

Love.

Rain cringed at the return of the voice in her head. *Love? That's all? How can love save Selik?*

Love begets love, child. Love begets love.

Rain groaned aloud.

"You have that look on your face again, sweetling, and you are muttering. Talking to God, are you?"

Rain shot a look of disgust at Selik and his too perceptive observation. "Yeah, and he sent a message for you."

"Oh, really!" Selik laughed. "Do not tell me that Ubbi and I are both blessed with these miraculous messages of yours."

"Don't be so sarcastic."

They had almost reached Ella's shop, and Selik was about to open the side door when he asked, "So, what was the message? Does he want me to do penance for plowing the virgin fields of one of his angels?"

Rain shook her head as if he was beyond hope.

"What God said, honey, was, 'Tell that bad boy, Selik, to hold on to the seat of his pants because I'm sending the love boat his way.' "

Selik burst out laughing and put an arm around her shoulders, hugging her warmly against his side. Rain couldn't resist wrapping her arms around his waist and joining in his laughter.

When they both turned forward, Ella and all the workers in her shop were staring at them with wide eyes and gaping mouths.

"The priests are huggin' each other. Oh, holy Lord!" one

freckle-faced young woman exclaimed, making the sign of the cross.

"Gawd! No doubt, the Almighty will send a pestilence down on this shop fer harborin' such doin's," another woman exclaimed. "Frogs, I warrant. The Lord has a partiality to frogs fer punishment, I hear tell."

"I will have no such perversions in me shop," Ella declared vehemently, advancing on them with a broom in hand. It was only as she got closer that Rain saw the recognition in her eyes. She was putting on a show for her workers. "Come into me side room and tell me yer bizness. Then begone with ye—ye sodomites."

When she closed the door behind them in her primitive "office," she turned on them angrily. "Are ye daft? Do ye want to put me out of bizness? If the townsfolk hear I condone such depravities, they will shun me like maggots on a Yule pudding."

Selik pushed the hood down off his head and sat on a high stool, grinning at Ella.

"Do not think ye can turn me with one of yer winsome smiles," Ella grumbled. "I am well past the age fer carin' whether a man be bow-legged or ungodly handsome."

"Ungodly handsome, am I?" Selik asked, fluttering his long eyelashes at her.

"Nay, I was referrin' to yer being' bowlegged, you fool."

"Ella, did you tell Ubbi that I would give him to you if you helped me?" Rain asked.

Ella's face grew pink. "Well, and what if I did? I got tired of waitin' fer you to fulfill yer promises."

"I said I would put in a good word for you, not deliver him on a silver platter."

"I will take him without the silver platter, thank you very much!"

"When you two wenches are done bickering, could we get our business completed so we can get back to that madhouse afore dark?"

They spent an hour picking out lengths of warm wool

fabric for the children's tunics and mantles, linen for tiny chemises and loincloths, yarn to be knitted into hose, and even some fine silk from Damascus that Selik insisted be made into garments for Rain. Ella also agreed to have a nearby leather worker make up a dozen pairs of children's shoes. They would all be delivered in a few days.

"And who is goin' to be payin' fer all these goods?" Ella asked craftily.

"I will," Selik said, without question, and pulled out his almost depleted sack of coins. "By the by," he said, stopping in his counting out of the money, "did you ever pay Rain the money you were holding for her mother when she left unexpectedly?"

Ella's face turned bright red and she shifted nervously from foot to foot.

"You see, Ruby invested money in a business Ella started years ago," Selik explained to her, his eyes twinkling with mischief. "No doubt Ella forgot to give it to you."

Rain turned to Ella. "Is that so?"

"Yea, well, 'twas a small amount. About—"

"One hundred mancuses, at least," Selik finished.

Ella sputtered with indignation. "Nay, 'twas more like fifty."

"Well, I'm sure you will give it to Rain as soon as possible," he added, patting her hand indulgently.

Ella shrugged his hand away with chagrin, telling him not to rush back. She could do without his kind of business, the coins he had handed her being far less than the fifty mancuses she would have to give Rain now.

Rain and Selik were both laughing as they left the shop. Rain wished time could stand still just then, that they could stay as happy and carefree as they were at that moment.

But their peace was shattered immediately with the emergence of Gorm from a nearby alley. He motioned them off the city street, and they followed him into the doorway of an abandoned building.

"Eirik sent word from Athelstan's court at Winchester.

Steven is in Frankland, visiting his Uncle Geoffrey in Rheams."

Selik nodded grimly.

"Oswald and his soldiers patrol Jorvik like bloody scavengers, killing and maiming any who even resemble Danish men of fighting age. We should leave Northumbria with haste. 'Tis only a matter of time afore they discover yer whereabouts."

"Yea," Selik agreed, and Rain's heart dropped to her toes. "Meet me tomorrow night with as many of my men as are willing to risk their fortunes with me. Come to the farmstead, and we will leave from there."

"On horseback?"

"Yea, bring Fury with you."

When Gorm left, Selik turned to Rain and put a fingertip to her face, wiping the tears that seeped from her eyes. "Shh, dearling," he said softly, taking her into his arms, "you knew 'twas only a matter of time."

"But it's too soon," she cried. "It's too soon."

CHAPTER SEVENTEEN

&

*S*ometimes God needs to give clueless men a nudge . . .
    The sun dropped below the hills and the autumn wind picked up as they walked back to his homestead, a dreary backdrop to the silence that formed a rigid barrier between Selik and Rain. Ever since they left Jorvik, Rain had avoided his eyes. As if he could not see her tears!

A frigid blast of air stirred the dry leaves under their feet, and Rain shivered. Despite their wool mantles, the coming winter seeped beneath their monkish garments, reminding them of the pending change of seasons.

Where will I be come Christmas? In truth, where will I be next sennight? And how will I survive now that I have known Rain?

The chattering of her teeth jarred him from his deep thoughts, and he pulled her under his mantle, despite her rigid shoulders. He should have bought her a fur-lined cloak in Jorvik. Now there would be no time. He should have done many things, now that he thought on it, but as had happened so often in his life, opportunities slipped through his fingertips like sand, sealing his fate.

Tell her you love her.

Selik closed his eyes momentarily on that painful advice from his inner voice. *I cannot. There is no love left in me. Besides, she should go home—to her own country, her own time. 'Tis safer there. I saw what a good physician she was today. Her healing skills would be better served in another world.*

Tell her. Trust me, you should tell her.

"Are you putting these voices in my head?" he asked suddenly.

"No," she snapped, looking at him through red-rimmed eyes, swiping at the tears on her blotched cheeks. "Are you putting them in my head?"

"You look awful."

"Thank you for sharing that information," she retorted, raising her chin proudly and stomping off in front of him.

He smiled and stepped on the hem of her monk's cassock, pulling her to a jarring halt. Before she had a chance to spit out the venomous words that obviously hovered on her sharp tongue, he steered her toward a nearby cow byre on the outer edges of his land, little more than a three-sided shelter. "Come. Let us warm up a bit afore continuing."

She complied stoically, then walked to the far corner, away from the wind. And from him.

"Rain, do not turn from me," he pleaded softly, feeling a painful constriction in his chest. "There is so little time left."

Tell her. What do you need to convince you, a clap of thunder? Tell her.

She kept her back turned to him, but he saw her shoulders shaking with silent sobs. Despite his best intentions, his feet had a mind of their own. They moved one step closer to Rain and the danger she represented to his bleeding heart.

Tell her.

Something deep inside, long hidden, melted and exposed a part of him so vulnerable, so open to pain, he could not bear to think on it. And he moved another step closer.

Tell her.

"I love you," he whispered, so softly she could not possibly have heard. Still, the words burned his lips and made his hands tremble.

And she turned. "What did you say?"

He closed his eyes and clenched his fists. And moved another step closer.

"Tell me, dammit," she cried out, a sob catching her unsteady voice. Then she whimpered in a low plea, "Tell me."

"I love you," he groaned out. "God help me . . .'twas He, no doubt, who brought you into my life . . . but I love you. I do."

He thought he heard a clap of thunder in the distance and rolled his eyes upward. *That was not necessary.*

Rain lurched into his arms, jolting him backward and almost knocking over the ancient walls of the byre with their combined weight. Wrapping her arms around his neck, she alternately hugged him tightly and held his face between her two hands, kissing every bit of skin above the neckline of his monk's robe, the whole time saying, "I love you, too. Oh, God, how I love you! IloveyouIloveyouIloveyou. . . ."

Selik smiled against her neck, feeling the wetness of her tears even down near her throat, and he wondered why he had not told her afore. It felt so good.

"Say it again," she begged, pulling away slightly so she could see his face.

He turned her so her back was to the wall, both his arms extended on either side of her head, hands against the wall. Leaning closer so he could smell the sweet scent of her breath and her Passion on the pulse point of her neck, he whispered fervently, "I love you."

"Again."

"I love you."

"Again."

He laughed, a joyous spirit of well-being surging through him, and lowered his lips to hers. "Imlufayahu."

At the first taste of her lips, open-mouthed and clinging, a ravaging hunger swept him. Trembling, he kissed Rain with all the pent-up need of a starving man. Her fingers dug into his shoulders and she cried out, shuddering, her senses apparently as inflamed as his.

Desire roared in his ears like a mighty dragon, and he ground his hips against her womanhood. The dragon's breath ignited a fire in his vitals, and he surrendered with a low growl to the inferno.

In a frenzy of savage need, he raised the hem of Rain's robe and untied the waist cord of the braies she wore underneath for warmth. At the first touch of his hand on her bare skin, Rain cried out as if in climax. How could her skin feel so hot when the air around them was so cold? And, sweet Freya, how could she be so wet with woman-dew when he had barely touched her?

Quickly reaching between them, he raised his own robe and untied his braies, letting them drop to the ground. He put his hands on her waist and raised her off the ground. "Wrap you legs around my hips, dearling," he said huskily, then braced her shoulders against the wall with his chest and plunged into her with one long, hard, impaling stroke. Her hot inner folds seared him as they adjusted around him with small spasms of welcome, and she screamed, "Selik!"

He arched his shoulders and reared his neck, trying to hold on to his control. Still imbedded in her sweet, moist depths, he groaned out, "Do . . . not . . . dare . . . move."

But she defied him with an exultant cry as old as Eve and rolled her hips.

He could not wait. He withdrew, then slammed into her tight sheath. Over and over. In and out. Shorter and shorter strokes. Harder. Harder. Harder.

The walls shook.

He gasped.

She moaned incoherently.

He cried out her name.

She screamed.

His hardness became so huge that he felt close to bursting.

Rain tried to writhe from side to side in the confines of his embrace, her hips bucking wildly, mindlessly.

"Let it come, sweetling," he pleaded in a raw voice. "Let it happen." He cupped her bottom and tipped her womanhood slightly, then lunged into her one last time.

Her thighs went rigid and her ankles locked tighter around his waist as her body convulsed in deep, milking clasps on his manhood. His man-seed exploded into her womb, and Selik saw all the colors of the most beauteous rainbow behind his eyelids.

His knees gave way then and he dropped to the ground, taking Rain with him. Panting for breath, he felt her heartbeat thundering beneath his, and Selik felt so alive he wanted to scream his ecstasy to the heavens.

A simple thank-you will do.

Selik laughed and pulled away slightly from Rain, whose passion-bemused eyes gazed up at him with such adoration that he felt blessed by the gods.

Uh, I beg your pardon. I think you mean one God. Me. Let's give credit where credit is due.

Selik gave a short salute heavenward.

"Now I know what it feels like to 'make love,'" he said softly as he brushed Rain's beautiful golden hair back off her face where it had come loose from her braid. "I have experienced naught like this in my entire life."

"I love you, Selik. I don't know what the future holds for us, but at this moment, I love you so much."

A short time later, after they had helped each other dress, laughing at the condition of their garments and the pieces of straw found in the oddest places, Rain remarked teasingly, "I wouldn't be surprised if I have splinters on my behind from your rough treatment."

"Oh, you poor wee thing," he soothed, tucking her under his shoulder as they resumed their walk home. "If you have splinters, I will pluck them out for you. With my teeth."

"Is that a promise?" she asked saucily.

"'Tis a holy vow," he proclaimed, pounding a palm against his chest for emphasis. "And then I will soothe the broken skin with my tongue, and I will—"

Rain slapped a hand over his mouth. "Enough! Keep it up and we'll have to stop at another cow byre."

Much to their embarrassment, they had dawdled so long that by the time they arrived at the barn, the wagon driver had already delivered the food goods and was turning around to return to Jorvik. The driver waved a greeting but did not stop.

"Gawd!" Ubbi spat out with disgust after taking one look at them when they entered the barn. "You two look like you been rollin' in the hay."

"Must have been the wind," Selik mumbled.

After they'd removed their monks robes and moved closer to the fire for warmth, Ubbi added, staring pointedly at Rain, "The wind did a good job chafin' yer lady's neck and lips, I see." Then he peered closer at Selik, chortling, "And is that a bite mark on yer earlobe? Yea, I think 'tis. 'Twas a biting wind, no doubt."

"Put a hold on your tongue, little man," Selik warned. "I have yet to determine your punishment for helping to plot my kidnapping."

"Nay, I did no plottin'," Ubbi declared, raising his chin indignantly. "I merely carted yer body out here. And ye must weigh as much as a bloody horse, if I must say so meself."

Selik glared at Ubbi, then remarked in an innocent voice, "By the by, Ella sends you her fond regards."

Ubbi's face turned almost purple with consternation and he sputtered for words, "Ye . . . ye . . . ye are not to be meddlin' in me personal affairs."

They all laughed then, even Ubbi.

This time he was really *leaving . . .*

Rain relished this brief moment of shared laughter before turning to help the children, who were storing all the items that had been delivered and busily performing the duties she had assigned to them days ago. Because the number of children had increased so, she and Ubbi had decided that each child must share in chores, even the youngest, three-year-old

Maud, who was setting the long trestle table with wooden trenchers and spoons.

The oldest ones, Humphrey, Jogeir, and Kugge—about ten years old—went outside to chop firewood, while the younger children carried armloads of logs and kindling inside, and still others stacked it near the roaring hearth. Several of the girls swept up soiled rushes from near the kitchen area and put down fresh ones. Others tended the cow and chickens in the lean-to shed.

Blanche was stirring a bubbling cauldron over the fire.

Blanche! "What are you doing here?" Rain asked, walking up and putting a hand on the maid's arm.

"Gyda sent me to help with the children," she explained, shooting a longing look toward Selik. And Rain knew she had ulterior motives for coming to the farmstead.

Frowning, Rain walked back to Selik, where Adela was tugging on his pant leg hopefully, her thumb, as ever, stuck in her mouth. Rolling his eyes with exasperation, he picked her up in his arms, trying not to appear pleased by her appreciative giggle.

"Where's that little bugger, Adam?" he asked her, and she pointed with her free hand to the corner.

Oh, boy! Rain thought. *Now the you-know-what is going to hit the fan.* While all the other children worked industriously, seven-year-old Adam reclined on one of the pallets, his head and shoulders propped against the wall, one leg crossed over a bent knee, playing with the Rubik's Cube.

Selik set Adela gently to her feet, then stormed over toward Adam. He ignored Rain as she cautioned softly, "Now, Selik, he's only a little boy."

Standing next to the cot, legs braced apart and hands on hips, Selik asked icily, "What the hell are you doing, lying about like a lazy slug?"

Without moving his body an inch, Adam scanned the room and the busily working children, then peered up the awesome length of Selik's body until he met his eyes. Fearlessly, he answered, "Overseein'."

"Overseeing?" Selik sputtered out. Then Rain saw laughter flash briefly in Selik's eyes at the boy's audacity before he hid his mirth. "Your overseeing days are over. Get your arse off that bed and help carry some firewood in."

Adam seemed to consider all his options, then decided wisely that he'd best follow Selik's orders. But he made sure he got the last word in. "Is arse a word the witch allows ye to use? Seems ta me it be on her 'no-no' list."

Selik reached out to smack his butt as he passed, but Adam swerved agilely out of his way. She thought she saw him stick out his tongue.

Selik's eyes locked with Rain's then, glittering with silvery amusement. He shook his head despairingly. "Do you realize what a job you have taken on here? That wet-nosed little whelp will cause more deviltry than all the rest combined."

Rain put a hand comfortingly on his arm. "Honey, I think if your son, Thorkel, had lived, he would have been just like Adam."

At first, anger flashed across his face at her mention of his dead son, turning his jaw rigid. He clenched his fists whitely at his side. But then he seemed to ponder her words, and his hands relaxed, reaching out for her. He put his arm around her shoulders, drawing her against his side, and chuckled. "I think you are right."

"And, Selik . . ."

"What?"

"I think he deliberately sets out to antagonize you, just to get your attention."

"Hmph! He has more than succeeded."

"He's been taking care of his sister for so long. I think he just wants someone bigger and stronger to lean on. Someone he admires, who—"

"Stop while you are ahead, Rain. Even I am not so thick-headed as to believe that."

Blanche prepared a veritable feast, making good use of the plentiful assortment of foods Selik had provided—beef stew with vegetables and thick gravy, manchet bread, freshly churned butter, crisp apples and pears, and honey still in the comb. The children ate a tremendous amount of food, and Rain knew she would have to find some way of providing for them, especially through the harsh winter months. Perhaps she could come to a better system of payment for her services at the hospitium. She would think this through after Selik left. His departure tomorrow night hammered continually in her mind.

After the meal, some of the children helped Blanche clean up. Others assisted Ubbi in dismantling the long trestle table. The one-piece wooden top was leaned against a far wall, and the benches arranged near the fireplace wall with straw-filled mattresses for sleeping. Other mattresses lay on the floor in front of the fire.

The children yawned sleepily with full stomachs and the heat of the blaze, but still they listened attentively to the bedtime stories Rain was telling them while she ran a comb through one after another of the little girls' hair. Head lice had been a severe problem in the beginning, but better hygiene had already eradicated most of the pesky varmints. She intended to keep it that way with careful supervision.

"Once upon a time there was a little girl named Red Riding Hood," Rain started, and as she related the cherished stories of her own childhood for her mesmerized audience, she had trouble keeping her eyes off Selik, who sat on a pile of bed furs with Adela nestled snugly on his lap like a contented cat. The darling little girl even rubbed her cheek against his wide chest every so often in a kittenish fashion.

Selik was peeling apples for the children. His long fingers—his wonderfully slender hands which could perform magic on her body—removed the skins in long, curly spirals and carefully cut the fruit into slices in a manner she must be crazy to find erotic. But she did. With a joyful chuckle, he offered pieces to each of the children, who opened their mouths for him like newborn birds. She imagined those same fingers peeling off her clothing, skimming her body, separating her secret folds. When his tongue flicked out and licked the juices from his fingertips, she imagined . . . Oh, Lord.

"Finish the tale," one of the children whined, and Rain realized with embarrassment that she'd stopped midway through her story. Selik smiled at her and held out an apple slice. She reached for it but he held it out of reach, forcing her to open her mouth for him. When he placed it in her mouth, his fingers lingered for a second on her lips, and her tongue licked the sweet nectar from his fingertips. Her eyes locked with his, and Rain saw the deep want in their silvery depths, matching her own.

This is your beloved, the voice said.

Rain quivered inside with deep agreement.

She noticed the children staring at her in question. And Blanche rattling her pots jealously. Trying hard not to stammer, Rain continued with her story. "And then Red Riding Hood said, 'Grandma, what big eyes you have. . . .'"

While she continued with other bedtime stories she thought might interest them—*Robin Hood, Aladdin and His Magic Lamp, Peter Pan*—she saw Selik reach for a small block of wood and a paring knife. She even told her own version of *Little Orphan Annie*, thinking it would have particular significance to these homeless children.

She brightened suddenly on thinking of one particularly relevant tale, *Beauty and the Beast*. When she finished with, "And they lived happily ever after," Selik raised an eyebrow and asked, "Hah! Now I know where you get your halfwit notions. Were you thinking to turn my beastly self into a prince with one of your kisses?"

Rain just smiled.

Then Selik related sagas of legendary Norse heroes— Ragnar Hairy-Breeches, Harald Fairhair, and others. As he talked, Selik's fingers drew magic from the lifeless piece of oak with his sharp knife. First the ears of the wolf emerged, then the eyes and muzzle, even the fine details of the animal's fur.

The figure that emerged was a crude, quickly executed rendering, the edges rough and unfinished, but his artistic talent shone through. He handed the wood sculpture to Rain as if it were a priceless object of art, which it was to her.

"For remembrance," he whispered.

Tears welled in her eyes at the reminder that he wouldn't be with her much longer. And she choked back a plea for him to change his mind. Her time for resistance and fighting to mold Selik into something he was not had ended. Now she just wanted to cherish every minute of the remaining time they had together.

Selik stood and laid the sleeping Adela on a nearby cot, pulling a woolen cloak up tenderly to her tiny shoulders. Then he picked up three of the bed furs and held his hand out to Rain, leading her toward the ladder.

"Yer goin' to sleep up in the loft?" Ubbi asked incredulously. "'Tis colder than a glacier up there."

"Rain will keep me warm," Selik answered huskily, pushing her ahead of him up the ladder.

And she vowed that she would.

He could teach modern men a thing or two about love-making . . .

Selik wanted this night to last forever. With bed furs piled under and over them, and a dozen candles illuminating their bed place, he paid slow, soul-searing homage to Rain's body. Meticulously, his fingers explored every part of her form, memorizing, storing pleasures in his mind for future retrieval. With each whimper and mewling cry of pleasure he drew from her, his heart soared. Truly, a woman's pleasure was man's aphrodisiac.

No dark shadows of the past haunted Selik tonight. He thought only of *now*, and the memories he must make and cherish with Rain, his beloved Rain.

"Will I ever see you again?" she asked, her soft voice breaking as she bravely tried to stifle her sobs.

"Mayhap."

"But, Selik, if you die, then I've failed. If I was sent back in time to save you, and I—and I can't, then what was the point?"

He smiled gently and pulled her into the crook of his shoulder, caressing her gently. He fingered the edges of her hair, tenderly traced the line of her jaw, brushed her collarbone with a whispery caress. "I think your God accomplished all that He wanted—if 'twas He who sent you. Can you not see that you have healed me of my shame? You have melted my heart, taught me to love again. Even if we never meet again, I cannot regret that."

"If that's true, then why do you have to leave?"

"Steven," he said flatly. "I could stop blaming the entire Saxon race for Astrid's and Thorkel's deaths, perchance even give up my vendetta, but not against Gravely. I love you, Rain, but honor demands I remove his demon presence from this earth."

She resigned herself then and gave herself up to their mutual enjoyment.

When he knelt between her legs and lay upon her body, his thundering heart pounded against her breasts. She looked up at him in wonder, murmuring, "Our hearts seem to beat with the same rhythm."

"Yea," he answered softly, putting a hand over her breast, between their two hearts. "They seem to be repeating one word—love, love, love, love. . . ."

He saw the unquenchable pain in Rain's honey eyes flecked with rings of gold, but he soon turned it to molten desire. He felt the rigid tension of cold regret in her arms and legs, and he loosened them into clinging, writhing vines of mindless heat. When her lips opened to challenge his decisions once again, he silenced her with his consuming mouth.

When he imbedded himself in her sweet flesh, she cried out her ecstasy. He thrust in and out, slowly, slowly, until her body began to ripple with tiny convulsions of mind-shattering pleasure. "Oh . . . oh . . . oh . . . God . . . please!"

Selik held himself rigid inside her until her arousal

peaked and shattered, then began the rhythm again. He controlled her, set the pace. Slow, fast, slow, fast.

"Tell me," he demanded in a low, raw voice.

"I love you."

"Again."

"I love you."

"Again."

"I . . . a-a-ah . . . sweet Jesus . . . I love you!"

Still he held himself in almost painful control, filling her with his rock hardness, surely as far as her womb, refusing to let go of his own tightly coiled, mind-boiling need.

"Now, again," he said with an exultant cry of masculine pride as she screamed his name, and he stroked her almost continually spasming woman-folds with long, long, agonizingly slow, intensely sensitized caresses of his manhood.

"Tell me again."

"I love you, dammit. Please . . . oh, please . . ."

Selik laughed aloud, a low, masculine roar of pleasure, then arched his back and threw his head back, his veins feeling as if they were about to burst in his neck. Rain wrapped her legs around his waist, tossing her head from side to side, and he slammed into her. His sorely challenged self-control broke loose then, and he poured his man-seed into her with a roar of pleasure so intense that his soul was surely marked forever.

"I love you, dearling. Forever," he cried out as she vibrated hotly around him in one last shattering expression of her continually peaking pleasure.

"I love you, too." Then, in the aftershocks of her progressively smaller spasms, she choked out, "You're killing me."

He smiled against her neck, panting to regain his breath. "Yea, but what a way to die!"

They fell asleep in each other's arms then, sated and intensely relaxed. When dawn light crept through the loft window, Selik sat up with distress.

"Wha-what?" Rain asked groggily, sitting up beside him.

"Ah, sweetling, I wanted to make love to you through the night, but I fell asleep."

Rain laughed and wrapped her arms around his waist, her breasts rubbing enticingly against his chest hairs. "Oh, yeah! Big talk!"

He lowered her to the bed and growled against one hardened nipple, pressing his burgeoning manhood against her. "Big? You want big?" he said, laughing, and he gave it to her.

Gone, gone, gone! . . .

Hours sped by like minutes the rest of the day. Selik made all the boys come outside to the woods with him, where they pulled one dead tree after another to the barn clearing and cut them into logs. By early afternoon, they had stacked enough wood beside the barn to last for months.

Then he sat down with Rain and Ubbi at the table. While they ate bread and hard cheese, washed down with mead, he told Ubbi, "Go into Jorvik on the morrow. Gyda will tell you where I have coins stashed.

"Rain, you are not to depend on the culdees and their tightfisted charity for your daily bread. Use my funds, and if you need more, go to Gyda."

Rain nodded, unable to speak over the lump in her throat.

He handed her a piece of parchment, telling her, "I have deeded over the farmstead to you."

Rain gasped. "No, I don't want it," she cried, shoving it back into his hands in a panic. Selik behaved like a man about to die, getting his affairs in order.

"Take it," he said firmly, shoving it back in her hands. "The Saxon soldiers may return, and you will need proof of ownership. I have dated it back to last spring so they will not think I have been here."

For hours, he kept adding details for Rain to remember—the name of a Viking man in Jorvik who might be willing to till the fields for them come spring, a reminder to get the money Ella owed her, a warning to be careful of the roaming Saxon soldiers, advice on how to handle the wily culdees at the minster. On and on he went, when all Rain wanted was to cling to his shoulders and beg him not to go.

Once, when he stood to replenish his goblet of mead, Adam walked up and kicked him in the shin. "What was that for, you bloody imp?" he snarled, grabbing him by the scruff of the neck and lifting him high in the air.

"Fer leavin', ya damn heathen bloody cod," he said on a sob, flailing out at him. "Yer jist like all the rest. Me father. Me mother. Nobody ever stays," he blubbered, kicking wildly with his arms and legs.

Stunned, Selik just stared at the angry boy for a moment, then groaned, almost painfully, and drew Adam into his arms, hugging him tightly to his chest. At first, Adam fought him mightily with scratching hands and vulgar obscenities. Finally, he calmed down and buried his face in Selik's neck.

Selik said nothing, just stared at Rain through his slate eyes, and walked with Adam to a far corner of the barn, where he sat down with him on his lap and talked soothingly for a long time.

Rain's heart felt like fine crystal shattering into a million tiny pieces. She didn't know if she could survive without this man—the other side of her soul, the beat in her heart . . . her forever love.

Dinner was a solemn, silent affair that night, even though Blanche went out of her way to make a spectacular farewell meal—golden crisp chicken, roasted venison, boiled vegetables, egg-and-honey custard, fresh fruit. Even the children sat still, uncommonly quiet, darting frightened eyes from one somber adult to the other, questioning, not understanding all the undercurrents.

Gorm and the soldiers rode up at nightfall, leading the saddled Fury behind them. Selik strode forward and spoke with them, and Rain cringed before the fierce warrior into which her lover had transformed himself. He wore leather braies under his calf-length flexible chain mail. A wool tunic of deep blue covered the armor, and a heavy fur mantle covered all. He attached his sword, Wrath, and his helmet and pike to his saddle, then turned back to Rain.

She walked up to him, daunted by this stranger in fighting garb, but there was not the usual berserkness in his eyes now, only a deep, abiding love. She hoped she hadn't weakened him with her love.

"Come back to me, Selik."

"If I can," he promised in a soft voice, raising his gauntleted hand hesitantly. Then, as if unable to help himself, he caressed her lips with his cold fingertips. "If I can."

"I'll come after you if you don't," she cried out as he dropped his hand and swung up into his saddle. "Do you hear me? I'll come after you."

He smiled grimly, then raised the helmet to his head. He looked down at her and mouthed the words, "I love you. Forever."

He turned his horse then, without another word, and Rain sank to the ground, her knees giving way. Only then did she weep out all her pain and misgivings over Selik's departure.

"Keep him safe, God," she prayed with racking sobs. "Do you hear me, dammit? You gave him to me. Don't you dare take him away. Please, God, oh please, I beg You, keep him safe."

Unfortunately, the voice in her head was deathly quiet.

CHAPTER EIGHTEEN

⟨☖⟩

P *ox on you, too! . . .*

A cloud hung over the small farmstead during the following weeks as the weather turned bitter and gray. All the inhabitants of the crowded barn worked somberly at their assigned tasks, as if sensing some impending doom. Uncommonly quiet, the children continued to chop and stack firewood, wash clothing, milk the cow, gather eggs, and clean the barn. Rain almost wished for their previous shrieks and childish mischief.

Even Adam had turned into a model child. Well, that was an exaggeration, she immediately amended. His filthy mouth spat out the usual vulgar words, but now he often apologized afterward. He played tyrant with the other children, taking naturally to a leadership role, but he tried hard to mellow his orders with compliments these days. It touched her heart deeply, and frightened her, to see the concern for Selik in his big brown eyes.

After two weeks of fretting and endless pacing, Rain decided to follow up on an earlier idea she'd had concerning the smallpox that often plagued these medieval people. She didn't want to do anything to change the course of medical history, but she saw no harm in vaccinating her small brood. She asked Ubbi for his help.

"Well, now I know ye are truly addlewitted," Ubbi exclaimed, throwing down the small quern stone he was using to sharpen his knives and sword. He'd been in a bad mood since Selik left because his master had ordered him to stay and protect Rain and the orphans. And his arthritis had been acting up. Her request now didn't help. " 'Tis one thing fer God to send me a message to kidnap the master. But to go and collect the ooze from pox sores on cows? Nay, I will not do it."

"Ubbi, honey—"

"Do not be honey-ing me," he warned, folding his arms across his chest adamantly.

"I can go," Adam volunteered.

"You will not," Rain and Ubbi both exclaimed in horror.

"Well, if Ubbi fears the bloody cows—"

"Best ye go help yer sister empty that chamber pot she be swingin' from side to side," Ubbi sputtered out, "lest I be wipin' up the soiled rushes with yer face. And stay away from cows—*any cow*." He turned back to Rain with a shake of his head. "Gawd!"

Did you call?

"Did ye hear that?" Ubbi cried out. "Did ye? Oh, now ye done it. Turned God on me, ye have!"

Rain smiled. Sometimes God came in handy.

This kid could survive in the hood, anyday . . .

Ubbi returned at nightfall, grumbling that he had traveled through twenty hectares of farmland before he could find a stead with a diseased cow.

"Did you wear gloves? And make sure your mouth was covered when you drained the sores? Was the cow already dead?"

"Yea, yea, yea," Ubbi said wearily.

"Don't sit down," she ordered with a screech, "and don't touch anything."

Ubbi jumped from where he was about to plop wearily onto a bench before the fire. "Now what?"

"Take off all your clothes so that I can burn them. I don't want to take any chances of contagion."

He was too tired at that point to argue with her.

The next day, she vaccinated all the children, along with a horrified Ubbi and Blanche, who'd become downright hostile toward her since coming to the barn. Using a sharply pointed knife, Rain made a small scratch on each of their arms and inserted only a tiny amount of the pox substance—enough to fit on the head of a needle. Over the next few days, other than slight fevers and some nausea, everyone seemed to survive the ordeal without any lasting harm.

Satisfied with the results of that project, she decided to return to the hospitium. Besides, she needed to buy more supplies in the city—thick fabric and heavy thread to make additional mattress covers for the pallets, special seasonings that Blanche requested, more wooden trenchers and spoons, and yarn for knitting hose for the children. Gyda had promised to come out one day to instruct the girls in that fine craft, which Rain had never mastered.

Ubbi, sick of her constant queries about Selik and his fate, encouraged her. "Please go. Give us some rest from yer constant blatherin' about the master. He kin take care of hisself, I tell ye."

Adam insisted on coming along to protect her. She started to protest but decided it wouldn't hurt him to see the hospitium. Maybe he could even be of help. But first she had to warn him not to give away her male disguise as a monk. He thought that a grand jest on the minster priests, many of whom were less than generous with the city orphans.

Adam's street urchin skills proved invaluable. He maneuvered her through all the shortcuts of the city, bargained mercilessly with the vendors, and showed her an out-of-the-way shop that specialized in imports from the East, including exotic spices.

Later, he sat on a high stool in Ella's shop, waiting for the shop workers to bundle up the fabric and thread that Rain had ordered, munching on honey cakes and watered mead like the lord of the castle.

"Someone ought to knock the little bugger down a peg or two," Ella grumbled as Adam chastised one of her workers for being too stingy in measuring the fabric lengths, but her voice held a tone of admiration as well. "Lord, if the pup lives to manhood, he should be somethin' to see."

Rain agreed, especially when they went to the hospitium. Adam followed her around, not like a puppy, but a colleague. He was like a dwarf physician as he soaked in all he saw around him with fascination, asked intelligent question after question, and seemed to glow with wonder.

Rain saw a doctor in the making. Too bad Adam would never have the chance to realize that dream in this primitive society.

Father Bernard was not so pleased with Adam's presence. "Really, Brother Godwine, must ye bring all your companions onto the holy church grounds. First that brutish giant, Brother Ethelwolf. Now, this heathen gutter rat."

"Who sez I be a heathen?" Adam snarled pugnaciously. "I say me prayers ev'ry night. And besides, I be part Saxon jist like you, *Bernie*. Was yer mother a whore, too?" He asked the last with the wide-eyed innocence of a well-fed cat.

Father Bernard sputtered and almost choked on his outraged tongue. "Why, you, little—" He grabbed for Adam's arm, intending to teach him a lesson.

"Did Brother Godwine tell ye he jist spread cow pox over the skin of us poor orphans?"

"What?" Father Bernard dropped Adam's arm like a hot ember and rushed to the washbowl, where he began to scrub his hands over and over, muttering, "God is punishing me for my sins. Oh, I must go to confession at once."

Rain had a feeling she wouldn't be welcome at the hospitium for some time. She flashed a look of chagrin at Adam, not really angry. Truthfully, she was beginning to think she might be of more help opening her own clinic in the spring.

And she had enough to do over the winter months worrying about her orphans. And Selik.

Too bad Lifesavers couldn't really save lives . . .

More than a month passed, and still Selik hadn't returned. Rain carried on her "normal" life—caring for the children's needs in the cavernous barn which had become more a home to her than her plush city apartment in the future, going into the hospitium on the occasions when the blustery winter weather permitted, and visiting with Ella and Gyda.

Rain tried to remain hopeful as Christmas approached, telling the children all the Yuletide stories she remembered from her youth. *A Christmas Carol. The Night Before Christmas. Frosty the Snow Man. Rudolph the Red-Nosed Reindeer.* And to their delight, she talked a grumbling Ubbi into helping her bring a huge evergreen tree inside the barn, where they decorated it with pine cones and strings of holly berries.

On her last trip to Jorvik, she'd come across a merchant selling sugar—a very expensive commodity in this primitive society which relied on honey for its sweetening. Suddenly inspired, she poured out the precious coins and took the sugar home with her, hugging it to her chest, along with a small crock of Gyda's preserved cherries and another of molasses. If Selik came for Christmas, as she hoped, she would have a special present for him.

"Are ye barmy?" Ubbi asked later that day as she poured all her ingredients in a pot with water over the open fire. "Wastin' all that sugar! On what?"

"Lifesavers," Rain said, raising her chin defensively. "I'm going to make cherry Lifesavers for Selik for Christmas."

Her first batch was a disaster. Not only did the shapes, which she poured on a greased piece of marble, resemble anything but circles, but they didn't harden properly, and they tasted horrible.

She heard Adela whisper to Adam, "Tastes like chicken droppings," before surreptitiously slipping hers into a chamber pot.

Rain and her mother had made lollipops once when she was a little girl. They'd turned out wonderfully, and she'd figured Lifesavers had to be somewhat the same. Her mother's recipe had called for corn syrup, though. Maybe it was the molasses she'd substituted. Or perhaps she hadn't used the correct amounts. And maybe an open fire wasn't the best cooking method.

So she tried again. This time the candies hardened, but they tasted more like molasses than cherry, and they weren't sweet enough.

Over and over she experimented, squandering much-needed money as she bought more and more sugar until Ubbi finally put his foot down. "Enough! If he doesn't like these, I know a part of his body I kin stick 'em in. Besides, yer turnin' the wee ones sick with all this tastin'."

Rain smiled sheepishly. He was right, and she knew as well as he did that most times the children pretended to like her candies just to avoid hurting her feelings. Actually, the last batch wasn't too terrible, and she wrapped several dozen of the squiggly shapes in thick parchment, tied it with a bright ribbon, and put it under the tree.

By the time Christmas arrived and they all sat before the fire—the candle-lit tree a beautiful sight in the corner, a wonderful feast cooking on the fire—her hopes began to falter. Selik still hadn't come for her.

Days went by, then weeks. The winter winds howled outside, and the Christmas tree, which she'd doggedly refused to dismantle, shed more and more of its needles, a stark reminder of her dying hopes.

Ubbi and the children shifted their eyes in pity when she passed, and Rain began to accept what they already knew. Selik was not coming back. Ever.

Who says women can't be knights in shining armor? . . .

Two weeks after Christmas, when they arrived back at the farmstead after a trip to Jorvik to visit with Gyda, her worst fears came true. A wounded and distraught Gorm lay before the fire, being tended by Blanche and Ubbi. All the children cowered in the background, huddled together in fright.

"What happened?" she cried out, running to his side. She threw off her mantle and began to examine his injuries. None of them was serious, except for some cracked ribs, which she bound tightly with strips of linen, but bruises and cuts covered his entire body from head to foot.

"'Tis bad, m'lady," he told her, turning grim eyes up to hers as she worked over him. "What happened . . .'tis very bad."

Rain didn't ask about Selik. She feared the answer.

"King Athelstan's men were waiting near the Humber where the master's longship was hidden."

Rain inhaled sharply. *Please, God. Please!*

"They killed three of our men outright. Two others they tortured to death." Gorm swallowed repeatedly as if to hold down a vomitous bile, and his eyes widened and glazed over with the gruesome images in his mind.

Rain clenched her fists tightly, tears streaming down her face—afraid to know Selik's fate, but at the same time, needing to know.

"They left me fer dead, thinkin' all the blood on my chest was mine, but 'twas Snorr's. Oh, God, 'twas Snorr's. I bin delirious with fever in a cotter's hut these past sennights."

His eyes held Rain's then, almost in pity, and she braced herself for what would come next.

"They took the master captive. They did terrible things to him afore they took him off. Oh, holy Thor, they did. If only I could have killed him afore they left, I would have and gladly. For he is truly better off dead than in the hands of such villains."

Rain honed in on only one thing. Selik was alive. *Thank You, God!*

"Where did they take him?" she asked, her mind already cataloging all that she would need to do in preparation for her journey.

"Winchester. To King Athelstan."

Rain nodded, having expected as much. "I need to get to Winchester. Perhaps I can convince King Athelstan to release Selik. He always said the king has great admiration for healers."

"But he has even more hatred for Selik," Ubbi noted regretfully. "Ye must know that."

"Yes, but I've heard he's a compassionate king, willing to listen to both sides."

He shook his head doubtfully.

"Ubbi, you go into Jorvik and tell Gyda I need two horses so Gorm and I can go to Winchester."

"Three horses," Blanche interrupted. "I go, too."

They all looked at her in surprise. "I know my way around Winchester. I lived nearby most of my years."

Rain thought for a second, then agreed, "Three horses. Also, Ubbi, tell Gyda to send more of Selik's money, and ask her if she or Ella can send someone out to help you with the children."

"I will not be stayin' this time," Ubbi declared vehemently.

"You have to, Ubbi," Rain pleaded. "Who else will take care of all the children?"

"I will," Adam spoke up. "And do not be thinkin' I cannot do it, either. If ye leave me with a bit of coin, I kin manage a few measly orphans."

He probably could, but no way would she leave a seven-year-old boy to supervise a dozen children, some of them a lot older than he.

"Ubbi, you have to stay. Be realistic. Your arthritis is so bad these days, with the damp weather, that some mornings you can barely get out of bed. How could you ride a horse for that length of time?"

Reluctantly, he finally agreed. "I would hold ye back. I must think of what be best fer the master."

She hugged him in thanks and went up to the loft to pack her few belongings. Fashioning a sort of fanny pack around her waist, she put in her amber necklace, the dragon brooch she hadn't worn since her arrival, and the rest of the coins Selik had left with her. Over that, she wore two pair of Selik's wool braies and two long tunics, a fur mantle, gloves, and the monk's robe.

Didn't they ever hear of the Geneva Convention rules of conduct? . . .

Three days later, just outside Winchester, Rain and Blanche and Gorm were apprehended trying to enter the walled city after nightfall. The Saxon soldiers came up out of nowhere, surprising them. When Gorm raised his pike to fight them off, one soldier killed him in one fell swoop of his sword. It happened so quickly that it took a moment for Rain to realize that Gorm lay on the ground with a sword stuck through his chest, his eyes staring up at them in deathly horror. Blanche sobbed loudly on the horse next to hers.

Rain made the mistake then of turning angrily on the vicious soldiers. "I demand to see King Athelstan immediately. We have come to plead the case of the captive, Selik."

"The Outlaw!" they all exclaimed at once, and at just that mention of an association with Selik, the Saxon guards forced them from their horses, which they immediately confiscated, bound their arms behind their backs, and marched them with pikes jabbing into their backs to their leader.

"Master Herbert, these two came skulking about the castle gates seeking The Outlaw. Another be dead outside the walls," one of the guards explained.

"We were not skulking," Rain corrected, and the guard shoved her and Blanche into the barracks-style room where a mean-looking man sat leaning against the wall in a bored fashion drinking mead from a wooden goblet. He was better dressed than the other soldiers who sat about the trestle tables drinking and playing dice. Several women sat on the laps of some men, who fondled them openly.

"Shall we inform the king?" their guard asked Herbert,

whom Rain assumed was the castellan, the head of the king's
troops at Winchester.

Suddenly alert, Herbert ignored the guard's question as
he insolently studied their dirty attire, their hands still tied
behind their backs. They'd been riding for two days, rarely
stopping, and personal hygiene hadn't been a top priority.
The haughty Herbert leaned back casually and took another
long swig of his mead. He'd probably assessed and labeled
them as of no importance, based on their appearance.

"Yes, tell the king. I need to talk to King Athelstan immediately," Rain said with an urgency that turned her voice
higher than usual.

Herbert's brow shot upward and he stood abruptly, knocking over the bench, then walked toward her. She heard several soldiers snicker.

"A priest speaking on behalf of the heathen Dane? Now
that is an oddity," he said silkily as he walked toward Rain.
She could barely stop herself from backing away. When he
stood in front of Rain, his head coming only to her nose, his
hand darted out and flipped back the cowl on her head, revealing her long blond braid. Reaching out, he tugged hard
on the end of her hair, then used the small knife in his waist
scabbard to cut the leather thong. Her hair billowed out
around her in a wispy cloud of static.

Herbert gave a low whistle, and some of the soldiers inhaled sharply, then made vulgar remarks. "I think I could
even bugger a monk if he had hair like that," one young man
exclaimed, then immediately ducked his head when his
comrades began teasing him about his sexual preferences.

With a quick flash of his knife once again, Herbert slashed
her monk's robe from neck to hem and shoulder to wrist. As
the drab brown fabric fell to the rush-covered floor, Herbert
looked over her double layers of tunics and braies, which
made her look heavy, then up and down what he must have
considered a massive height for a woman. His upper lip curled
with distaste.

Herbert eyed Blanche then, and she slanted her eyes at him seductively and jutted her breasts out in blatant invitation. With disgust, Rain saw Herbert's mouth go slack and spittle pool at the edges.

She was beginning to think she'd better act quickly. For sure, she was not going to seduce this soldier into leading her to the king with her good looks. "Listen," she interrupted his lascivious perusal of Blanche's charms, "I'm a physician—a surgeon in my country. Your king will want to speak with me."

Herbert said a vulgar word, and his fellow soldiers laughed snidely. "A woman physician? I think not. The only wits a woman has are betwixt her legs." The soldiers guffawed in agreement.

Rain stiffened her shoulders angrily. "And the only intelligence you have is—"

Before Rain had a chance to finish, Herbert's fist shot out and hit her chin. With a snap, her neck went back and she fell to the ground, her head striking the timber wall with a loud thud.

I am woman, hear me roar! . . .

Rain didn't awaken until the next morning, when she found herself lying on a hard dirt floor that smelled strongly of stale urine, dampness, and other horrid odors. Her arms had been untied and she sat up with a wince, putting a hand first to the goose egg on the back of her head and then to her aching chin. Moving her jaw from side to side, she decided the brute hadn't broken it, but not for lack of trying.

Hearing a squeaking sound behind her, she sat up sharply, causing her jaw to throb even more painfully. *Rats,* she realized immediately. They had put her in a damp underground room, and there were rats in the vicinity.

Rain stood to get her bearings. The cell was no more than eight-by-eight feet and bare, except for a bench under the lone narrow window slit, a slop bucket in the corner, and, on the floor near the thick wooden door, a pottery jug of water and a trencher with a piece of moldy flat bread and a hunk of meat. A rat nibbled on the meat.

Rain's survival instincts kicked in. She was alive. Selik was alive. That was all that was important now. She still had hope.

With determination, she braced herself and walked over to kick the rat away, picking up the bread. The squealing rodent could come back later for the grayish meat, but she might need the stale bread for sustenance. And the water, of course.

By late afternoon, Rain's hopeful spirits flagged. The screams and moans coming from nearby cubicles told her of other prisoners being held in the underground dungeon. No one had come to her cell in the many hours she'd been there, and she faced the frightening prospect of sleeping in this rat-infested hole.

She stood on the bench for what must have been the hundredth time and peered out the small window, which was on a level with the outer bailey. She had screamed for help endless times to the soldiers and servants who passed by, but to no avail. This time she just leaned her aching chin on the window ledge and stared out hopelessly.

Two well-dressed men were approaching from off to the left. One of them, a tall, dark-haired man in his early twenties, walked briskly, arguing loudly with his companion. His fur-lined mantle swished open to reveal a beautiful blue tunic with a silver linked belt, worn over dark braies and fine leather boots. As he turned his face, Rain gasped. Oh, my God! He looked just like her brother Eddie, who had died in Lebanon.

The fine hairs stood up all over Rain's body as her eyes riveted on the dragon brooch holding his shoulder mantle in place. Quickly, Rain lifted her two tunics and burrowed beneath the waistband of her braies. Thank God, the soldiers hadn't yet discovered her waist pack. She pulled out the brooch, then looked back at the man, who drew closer. The two brooches matched exactly.

He must be Eirik, Rain realized immediately. Her half brother from the past. Tykir's brother.

"Eirik," she called out hopefully, but he didn't hear her. "Eirik!"

Still he ignored her. In a moment, he would have passed and all Rain's prospects for release with him.

Okay, God, how about a little help here? Rain prayed frantically.

She shouted, "Eirik!" at the top of her lungs. Just then a slight wind came up, carrying her scream, and Eirik turned toward the window, his dark brows furrowing in confusion.

"Eirik, over here!" she yelled.

He came closer, ignoring the complaints of his companion, who wanted to return to the castle hall. Hunkering down, he peered into the little window.

"Eirik, thank God you finally heard me. Hurry. You've got to get me out of here. I'm your sister—Oh, I know you've never heard of me, but I'll explain everything later. Just have the guards release me. We have to help Selik—hurry!"

"I have no sister," Eirik snapped and was about to stand.

"Yes, you do. I'm Rain—Thoraine Jordan. Ruby's daughter. See," she said, holding the brooch up for him to see.

"Let me see that," he snarled, trying to grab the pin, but she pulled it out of his reach. Once she gave up the brooch, she might not have any proof of her identity. Funny, she'd never thought of the priceless heirloom as evidence before. She almost giggled hysterically.

Eirik squinted, trying to peer at her features through the window. "Bloody hell!" he said finally, then stood and walked away.

Stunned, she just stared after his departing back. He hadn't believed her after all. She sank down to the bench and let the tears run down her cheeks in endless streams. She didn't care so much about herself. It was Selik. She feared desperately for his life and what the damn Saxons had been doing to torture him the past week.

A grating of the door hinge jarred Rain to attention, and the huge door swung outward, allowing Eirik to enter.

Eirik ducked his head and entered the tiny room, dwarfing it by his size and magnificent clothing. He scrutinized her coldly. "Talk," he finally ordered.

"Have a seat," Rain offered, wiping at the wetness on her cheeks and waving to the bench on which she still sat. "Would you like some refreshments?" she asked with mock politeness.

"Your sarcasm is misplaced, wench," Eirik snapped. "I know not who you are, but one thing is certain—you are not my sister."

Rain stood and walked up to him, pushed beyond her endurance. She glared at him, hands on hips.

Eirik looked her over disdainfully, then had the nerve to say, "You are big . . . for a woman, that is."

"Tall."

"What?"

"Tall. I'm tall, not big, you Dark Age jerk."

His lips twitched with a smile. "Jerk—that is a word I know. I learned it once from—" He stopped abruptly, his eyes widening with understanding. Then he took her by the arm and pulled her toward the door. "Come. We will talk in my room."

With little protest, the guard allowed Eirik to lead her from the prison. Apparently, Eirik held a position of some importance in King Athelstan's court. In fact, she remembered Tykir saying something to that effect. Maybe he would be able to help Selik.

Eirik's small but opulent room was in a far corridor of Winchester Castle, a favorite residence of the king. Now that they were alone, Rain couldn't help herself. She launched herself against Eirik's chest, hugging him tightly. "Oh, God, you have no idea how much you resemble my brother Eddie. I didn't know how much I missed Eddie until I saw you. You could be his twin."

"And where is this Eddie now?" Eirik asked hesitantly, putting Rain away from him.

"Dead," Rain said, sniffing loudly. "Killed in Lebanon more than ten years ago. He served in the Marines and . . ." Her words trailed off as she realized that Eirik didn't understand most of what she'd said and that he was staring at her with suspicion.

Rain bent her head, trying to gather strength, and noticed her fisted hand. She opened it and saw the dragon brooch—the precious pin her mother claimed was given to her by her husband Thork. Unable to think of anything to say that would convince Eirik, she merely handed him the brooch.

He motioned Rain to sit in the only chair while he sank down onto the bed, stretching out his long legs. He undid the brooch on his shoulder, letting the fur-lined mantle fall behind him on the mattress. For a long time, he just stared at the two pins in his large palms. Rain thought she saw flickers of pain and tightly held emotion in his pale blue eyes.

Finally, his eyes lifted and locked with hers. "Tell me," he demanded hoarsely.

When she finished her unbelievable story, he said, "I ne'er believed Ruby's story of coming from the future; nor do I accept it from you."

Rain waved a hand in the air dismissively. "Ruby is my mother. Whether you think we came from another time or another country isn't important now. The most important thing is getting Selik free. Can you help me? Have you seen him?"

"I just came from his prison," he said, rubbing the nape of his neck wearily. "And, nay, I cannot help him. I have already tried. Selik has pushed Athelstan too far. The king will not bend this time."

Rain couldn't stop the low, mewling sound of distress deep in her throat. She shivered with the cold fear that swept over her and wished she could crawl under the furs on Eirik's bed and sleep and sleep. And when she awakened, this whole nightmare would have ended, and she would be back in Selik's arms.

"Perhaps if I talked to the king, I could convince him."

Eirik slanted her a look of disbelief. "Not bloody likely."

"But I've heard that Athelstan has a need for good healers. I'm a surgeon—a good one, Eirik. There are medical marvels he's never dreamed of that I could tell him about, services I can provide—"

"You are a physician? Truly?" Eirik's mouth slackened with amazement.

Rain nodded. "I graduated from college when I was twenty and went through medical school in a record four years. I have a rather high I.Q.," she said with an embarrassed shrug of her shoulders. "Then I served a two-year internship in an army hospital to pay off some college loans before becoming a surgeon. I've been helping at the hospitium in Jorvik, but believe me, I know much more than those primitive healers."

"Boastful, are you?" Eirik said, grinning.

"No, desperate."

"In your desperation, wouldst you, perchance, lie?"

"I'm not lying," she said with a groan. "What can I say to prove what I tell you? Let me think. In my time, we can artificially inseminate a woman who had previously been unable to conceive. We can reattach a limb that has been severed totally, and even regain some of the bodily functions. There are heart and kidney transplants. All children are vaccinated against smallpox, and—"

"Enough!" he said, holding up two hands as if in surrender. "The king may be interested in your tales of such a strange world, even if they are not true. Whether he will consider a reprieve is a totally different story, however. Do not get your hopes up needlessly."

"Just get me in to see the king," she said. "I'll take care of the rest."

Eirik nodded, then shook his head in wonder. "A sister? That will take some getting used to." He stood, seemed to hesitate, then held out his arms for her, enclosing her in a huge bear hug. "Later you will have to tell me about this Eddie person, my twin. No doubt he was fiercely handsome and very brave." He deliberately puffed his chest out.

Rain sniffled and looked up at him. "Yes, and extremely arrogant." Suddenly, she thought of something else. In a soft shaky voice, she asked, "Can I see Selik?"

Eirik shrugged uncertainly. "I will see what I can do, but Rain . . . I am not sure Selik would want you to come."

"Why not?"

He grimaced and tried to joke. "He is no longer as comely as he once was."

She put a hand to her chest and closed her eyes for a moment to fortify her courage. Then she looked directly at him. "For God's Sake, Eirik, I'm a doctor. How badly hurt is he?"

"No mortal wounds, as far as I could tell. But—well, there is not a part of his body that has not been battered or broken."

"Broken?" she gasped out.

He nodded. "A broken arm, cracked ribs—oh, Rain, I do not know. I just got back today from Norsemandy and only saw him for a short time."

Rain lifted her chin defiantly. Someone would have to pay for Selik's torture. She began to think there was nothing more deadly than a former pacifist. But for now, she had to get Selik free.

"Go and arrange for my audience with the king. There's no time to waste. And see if you can find some medical supplies—linen strips, ointment, anything."

"First you had best bathe and change your garments. The king will not see you in such attire, stinking up his noble air." He grinned as she jabbed him in the arm with mock annoyance.

A short time later, Rain had bathed and washed her hair and donned the clothing Eirik had provided for her—a beautiful belted tunic of deep amber silk over a soft, cream-colored wool chemise. She sat anxiously wringing her hands

as she listened to Eirik speak of his meeting with King Athelstan.

"The king will grant you an audience on the morrow, but
a short one only. Know this—Athelstan can barely speak
over his fury at the deaths Selik has caused and his glee at
finally having caught The Outlaw. 'Twill be nigh impossible
to convince him to soften his attitude."

Rain swallowed hard. *I'll be talking to You about this
later, God. Depend on it.* "And can I see Selik?"

He nodded.

"When?"

He held out a hand to her. "Best we get it over with now."

There is always hope if God has your back . . .

They walked outside the castle, across the bailey, and
then entered an underground room under the soldiers' bar-
racks that held the prison. Rain assumed it was the same
dank dungeon she'd been held in earlier. It didn't look any
better at night in the morbid shadows of their torchlight. Nor
did it smell any better. And the screams and moans seemed
to have increased.

Despite Eirik's warnings, despite Rain's medical experience in a city hospital, nothing could have prepared her for
the horror of Selik's tortured body.

He lay on a hard bench with his arm thrown over his face.
His clothing lay in shreds, and he shivered in the cool dampness. Rain eyed Eirik's fur-lined mantle, vowing that it
would cover Selik when they left.

"Selik," she said softly and saw his body stiffen. Slowly,
he lowered his arm and turned, as if afraid of what he might
see.

"Rain!" He sat up and groaned with pain. Then he shot
an angry glare at Eirik. "How could you have brought her
here to such a hellhole?"

"I was in the same prison, just down the hall, until a few
hours ago," she remarked and heard Selik curse under his
breath, something about stubborn wenches.

She moved the torchlight closer and cried out at her first look at his face. Both eyes were black-and-blue and swollen almost completely shut. His nose appeared to have been broken again. And his hair—oh, sweet Jesus—his beautiful blond hair had been cut off completely, chopped so close to the scalp that bloody gouges showed through in some places.

"Your hair," she moaned. "Oh, Selik, they cut your beautiful hair."

Selik tried to laugh, but it sounded more like a grunt. "By the nines, my body feels like a chopping block, and the wench worries about such vanities as hair."

Rain knelt in the rushes beside the pallet and put her arms around his waist, tears rolling down her cheeks.

Absently, he ran a palm over her hair, crooning, "Hush, sweetling, hush. You should not have come."

Rain knew she didn't have unlimited time with Selik and quickly regained her composure. She made him lie down so she could examine his wounds. Clucking, she cleansed and bandaged the numerous cuts and bruises on his totally battered body. She sent Eirik for a straight stick which she used to set and bandage his broken arm. She stitched gashes on his thigh, forearm, and abdomen, much to Selik's dismay at the first sight of her needle. With the linen strips, she tightly wrapped his cracked ribs, as well as a swollen knee. She had to repeatedly send Eirik to dump the pail of bloody water and get fresh water to clean his wounds.

Finally, Selik looked much better, dressed in a clean tunic and braies Eirik had brought for him. They set food, some coins, and other items in a basket at his feet.

Selik sat on the bench and pulled her into the crook of his good arm, kissing the top of her hair gently. He touched the swelling at her jaw and shook his head sadly. Then he forced himself to brighten. "So, Eirik, what do you think of my angel?"

Eirik arched a brow. "Angel? I do not know about that. Methinks she has the gentleness of a battering ram." Rain reached out a foot to give Eirik a playful kick, but he jumped out of the way. Then Eirik added, more seriously, "But after the way she just cared for you, I must believe her claim of being a physician."

Selik smiled at her as best he could with his cracked and swollen lips. "You should have seen her deliver a babe in Jorvik. She outshines all the culdees at the hospitium. Truly, your sister is a fine healer. And she saved Tykir's leg from the healer's knife."

Rain looked at Selik with surprise. She hadn't realized that he was so proud of her medical skills. He winked at her, and her heart did flip-flops of sweet love for him.

Eirik questioned Rain about his brother's injuries and thanked her for her help.

"Where is Ubbi?" Selik asked then.

"Back at the farmstead, caring for the children. He wanted to come, but his arthritis is paining him terribly."

"Rain, I want you to go back to Northumbria. You should not be here," Selik said urgently.

"I told you I would come after you," she teased, nuzzling his neck, clucking over his butchered hair.

"I find no humor in your words, wench. And stop fretting over my bloody hair. It will grow back," he said, rubbing his chin against the top of her head. "The important thing is that you *must* go back to Jorvik."

"I can't, Selik. I have to meet with the king tomorrow."

He removed his arm from her shoulders and turned her so he could study her face. "Why?" he asked in a suddenly cold voice.

Rain felt her face flush. "I just want to meet him," she said lamely.

"You would not dare try to ransom yourself for me," he said evenly. "Would you?"

"No, of course not—I mean, I never thought of that. Now, Selik, don't go getting stubborn on me. What I was thinking is that maybe if I offered the king some phenomenal medical remedy, he might be willing to release you."

"It would have to be mighty phenomenal," Eirik commented dryly.

"And what remedy, pray tell, did you plan to offer?" Selik asked cynically.

"I don't know," Rain said on a groan. "I haven't thought that far, but there are many, many medical wonders that I could pick from." She smiled then. "I remember my mother telling me that King Athelstan was a celibate, that he deliberately abstained from—you know, so that he wouldn't have children. He wants the throne to pass to the true blood heirs, his young nephews."

"And?" Selik and Eirik both asked dubiously.

"I could give the king a vasectomy."

Selik choked and burst out laughing, obviously remembering the time Rain had explained the procedure to him and Ubbi. "Lord, I would love to be a fly on the wall if you performed such an operation on him. Sticking a needle in that bastard's cock would give me a lifetime of pleasure."

"Needle? Cock? Are you two going to share the jest?" Eirik finally asked with exasperation.

Rain explained, and Eirik grimaced painfully. "We are all laughing, but he just might be interested. Being celibate has been sore hard on him." He grinned at his pun.

Selik gave Eirik a look of disgust and turned back to Rain. "I am serious, Rain. I want you to leave Winchester."

Fortunately, she had no chance to respond because a guard knocked on the door and told her and Eirik they had to leave.

Selik stood painfully and took her face between both his palms. With the tenderest care, he placed his lips gently against hers and whispered, "I love you."

"I love you, too, Selik. More than I ever dreamed possible."

Then Selik pushed her toward the door, adding, "Next time you are talking to that God of yours, tell Him to stay out of my bloody head."

Rain swiveled around. "God has been talking to you?"

"Like a blathering lackwit. Day and night. He offers more advice than a shrewish woman."

Thank You, God, Rain whispered silently. Somehow, she knew that God would not be speaking in Selik's head without a reason.

There was hope, after all.

CHAPTER NINETEEN

✣

Sex: a favorite subject, even a thousand years ago . . .

Rain didn't speak to King Athelstan the next day. Nor the next. Each time her appointed interview came due, he suddenly had other, more pressing engagements—a portrait sitting, an audience with a representative of the Frankish king, a chess match.

Rain should have been pleased that Eirik had gained her release, but each wasted minute that fled by left Rain in nerve-racking despair about Selik's condition and whether he was being tortured further. The Winchester castellan refused permission for her or Eirik to see Selik again. Rumors flew of a public flogging and execution sometime in the near future.

She was sitting in the ladies' solar on the third afternoon, fidgeting nervously, fighting to control her temper among the insipid chitchat of the court ladies who gossiped over their needlework. *Needlework!* Hah! The only needlework that interested Rain right now was sewing a few mouths shut.

The Lady Elgiva, a stunning, raven-haired widow from Mercia, approached her, a fine lavender samite robe swirling about her exquisite figure as she walked. She was one of the few females who bothered to treat Rain with any consideration, probably because her place in the Saxon court was just as shaky as hers. Some said Elgiva was hopelessly in love with the celibate king.

Elgiva asked politely, "May I join you?"

Rain nodded toward the windowseat at her side.

"You have not had your audience with the king yet?" she inquired.

"No," Rain said with a sigh. "If I could only talk with King Athelstan, I think I might be able to convince him to release Selik." *Are you listening to me, God?* "I've heard he's a fair man."

Elgiva raised a perfect eyebrow. "Fair is one thing, but the king is no fool. He would not trust Selik. The Outlaw is just as likely to turn and stab him in the back—or kill a hundred more Saxon soldiers."

Rain felt her face flush with anger. "Selik's word is gold. If he made an oath, even to a Saxon king, he would keep it."

Elgiva tapped a graceful forefinger against her cheek thoughtfully. Rain had never seen such a beautiful, creamy complexion in her entire life, and she wondered how the king could resist this woman's beauty.

"Do you love Athelstan?" she asked suddenly, unable to control her curiosity.

Elgiva leveled an assessing look at Rain, seeming to weigh her words carefully. Finally, she raised her chin haughtily and admitted in a soft voice, "Yea, I do."

"And is it true that he took a vow of celibacy to protect the royal bloodlines for his young nephews?"

Tears pooled in Elgiva's hazel eyes, and she nodded.

"Does he love you?"

"Yea, he does. We have known each other since he fostered at the court of his aunt, Queen Aethelflaed, in Mercia. But there is no hope for us," she said, her voice cracking with emotion.

Rain put a hand gently over Elgiva's. "I understand perfectly what it's like to love a man and know there is no future."

They both sat silently for several moments. Rain laughed lightly then. "Too bad I couldn't have brought some birth control pills for you from the fut—from my country."

Elgiva's posture went suddenly alert. "Birth control pills?"

Rain explained and told her about all the methods available for women. Elgiva was *very* interested.

"And you say that patch under your skin protects you from conceiving a child?"

"Yes. Implants are still somewhat experimental, but supposedly they last for about five years."

Elgiva's lush lips formed a perfect O of amazement. "Could I have one?" she whispered hopefully.

Rain smiled. "No, unfortunately I wouldn't have any idea where to get another."

"I will have yours then," she said imperiously.

"No, that wouldn't be safe."

Elgiva's shoulders slumped. "The future holds naught for me then. I may as well return to my home in Mercia. 'Tis torture to be near Athelstan and not be with him."

"It's funny, but when I was talking to Selik and Eirik the other day, I laughingly mentioned giving the king a vasectomy."

"A vas . . . vasectomy?"

Although her face paled when Rain explained the intricacies of the operation, Elgiva asked, "And the man can still . . . you know . . . perform?"

Rain nodded.

"And the pleasure is the same?" she asked incredulously.

Rain nodded again.

"Could you do it for Athelstan?"

"Oh, no! I was just teasing. It would be impossible without anesthetics and painkillers." Rain suddenly thought of Tykir and the operation she'd performed on him with acupuncture.

"It can be done! I see it on your face. I had heard you were a healer, but this—oh, 'twould make you world-renowned."

"Oh, no, no," Rain quickly interjected. What she didn't

want was fame, or to change the course of history. "I couldn't do it."

"Have you ever performed a vas—vasectomy?"

"Well, yes, but . . ." Rain found it impossible to explain modern medical facilities to this Dark Age lady, and Eirik had warned her about discussing the future or time-travel in a land suspicious of sorcery. "Besides, do you honestly think the king—any man here, for that matter—would let me tamper with his manhood? Men are really touchy about such things, even in my country."

"Athelstan would if I asked him to," Elgiva asserted, her slight laugh betraying her uncertainty.

"There's pain and discomfort for a few days after the operation. The king would think I'd maimed him."

"You could explain."

"Elgiva, it's out of the question."

"If you say so," Elgiva agreed much too quickly.

"We'd have a better chance of Selik telling the king how to find your G-spot," Rain commented dryly, then slapped a hand over her mouth, wishing she'd kept her mouth shut.

"What is a G-spot?" Elgiva demanded to know.

Rain groaned, then explained, despite Elgiva's constant interruptions to ask, "And what didst thou say the meaning of ejaculation is?", or "orgasm?", or "You say women in your country demand the same pleasures as men?" When she stopped talking, Rain turned around, horrified to see that several of the other gentle ladies had sidled closer, eavesdropping with avid interest in their conversation.

"Humph! 'Tis just like men to keep such information from women," Elgiva complained. "I had a husband onct who considered himself quite the lover, but he ne'er mentioned any G-spot. No doubt he saved those pleasures for his mistress."

Then Elgiva smiled mysteriously, and foreboding rippled over Rain in waves.

One clever woman is formidable, two together is spectacular . . .

"I'm sick to death of King Athelstan's court," Rain complained to Eirik later that day. "And I'm even sicker of all the useless people who stand around posturing and begging for his favors."

Eirik just smiled patronizingly at her, having heard her complaints enough the past two days to know them by heart.

They were seated along with a hundred or so other people at one of the numerous trestle tables in Athelstan's great hall, where yet another feast was taking place. They'd been placed so far down the salt that she could barely see the king or his closest advisors. The abundance of smoke from the poorly ventilated hearths at either end didn't help much, either.

Even by modern standards, the fare surpassed sumptuous—baked lamprey, veal and beef custard pies, swan neck pudding, lentils and lamb, pigeons in grape sauce, poached mustard-glazed pike, quail stuffed with dates, whole sides of beef and venison. And that was just the main course. Servants also carried in huge platters of cabbage with marrow, herbed beets, creamed parsnips, pickled mushrooms, a vegetable gruel, artichokes with blueberry rice, even a medieval salad consisting of turnips, shredded cabbage, dried fruits, mustard, brown sugar, and honey. For dessert, there was gilly-flower pudding, almond creme, elaborate subtleties, custards, stewed fruits, and honey cakes. And barrels and barrels of wine and mead.

Rain would have given her eyeteeth for a pepperoni-and-mushroom pizza. And a diet Coke.

The king and his closest friends stood, about to leave the dais for their evening's entertainment—music, storytelling, dice and board games. Rain accepted that another day had gone by and Selik still lay in that damned dungeon. And she'd accomplished nothing. There would be no other opportunities tonight to approach the king.

"Pssst!"

Rain twisted around, looking for the source of the noise.

"Pssst!" she heard again and looked the other way, noticing a flash of lavender material in the shadows of a hallway.

She stood, telling Eirik she had to visit the garderobe, and walked toward Elgiva, who put a finger to her lips to indicate silence, then crooked her finger for Rain to follow. Once they'd gone down several winding corridors, she stopped and whispered, "You have several minutes to present your case to the king."

Rain grabbed both of Elgiva's hands in hers and squeezed. "Oh, thank you, thank you. How did you manage to convince him to see me?"

"Well, 'tis not exactly an audience I have managed," Elgiva said, shifting her eyes slyly.

"Exactly what have you managed?" Rain asked suspiciously.

"I talked to him today about the vasectomy, and he was not yet convinced. In truth, he said, 'The day I let The Outlaw's wench within two hides of my cock is the day I declare myself lackwit and give up my throne,' or some such foolishness. Methinks I will need more time to persuade him."

Rain groaned, feeling her case for Selik slowly slipping away. "Elgiva, get to the point. You said I would have an opportunity to speak to the king."

"Yea. Athelstan intends to visit his scriptorium to view the manuscripts completed today by his scribes. If we just happen to be passing by at the same time—well, he cannot turn us away. Can he?"

Rain closed her eyes and gritted her teeth, fighting for courage and the right words to use in what might be her only opportunity to speak to King Athelstan.

Are you there, God? I could use a little help here.

The blasted inner voice remained stone silent.

Sometimes eloquence isn't enough . . .

King Athelstan stood examining an illuminated manuscript while a tall monk pointed out its finer details. Dozens of candles lit the airy room, which had a number of high stools placed before tall, lectern-style desks containing parchment and colored inks.

"Elgiva!" the king exclaimed with delight, just noticing her in the doorway. "I thought you had retired for the night."

"Nay, I was restless and decided to walk for a bit." She placed both her dainty hands in the king's, and Rain saw the love they shared in just that little gesture.

Athelstan was a good-looking man of medium height, about forty years old. His flaxen hair, with golden highlights, gleamed in the flickering candlelight, and Rain couldn't help but admire the magnificent couple these two beautiful people made.

Emotion filled the king's eyes, and he leaned toward Elgiva, brushing his lips against hers lightly. He seemed oblivious to the priest who hovered in the background. Rain stood in the shadows near the doorway.

Rain turned away from the intimate scene and walked from desk to desk, admiring the exquisitely detailed illuminations—some copies from other books, others original compositions. Unfortunately, most of these priceless books would never survive the wear-and-tear of the centuries.

"Dearling, I would have you meet my new friend, Rain," Elgiva said, drawing the king over to where she stood. "She is the one I spoke of earlier this day."

The king raised an eyebrow and stepped closer, with Elgiva on his arm. "Ah, the self-proclaimed physician." His lips twitched slightly with a smile, and Rain somehow knew he was thinking about vasectomies.

"Not self-proclaimed," she asserted. "I have many years' education and experience in some of the best hospitals in my country."

"Do you mean hospitiums?"

Rain shrugged. "They're about the same thing."

"And these hospitiums in your country allow females to study?"

"Yes, we're quite . . . enlightened."

"Hmmm." He studied her through eyes that Rain could see were very intelligent. "I have a medical manuscript here

that one of my scribes is working on," he said, walking over
to a huge tome. "'Tis in Latin."

Rain looked at some of the pages. "It's beautiful, but I
can't read Latin."

"Ahh," he said, shooting an "I told you so" look at Elgiva.
Apparently, all healers were supposed to know Latin.

His condescension irritated Rain, and she blurted out,
"Some of the drawings are wrong." She immediately regretted her outburst.

Rain heard the priest gasp with outrage behind them, and
the king's shoulders stiffened at her boldness.

"Show me," the king demanded.

Rain looked to Elgiva for advice on how to proceed with
the king, but the Saxon woman's silent face spoke volumes.
Rain was on her own.

"I don't want to alter these beautiful illuminations. Give
me a blank piece of parchment and a pen, and I'll show you."
With a few quick strokes of the quill, which she dipped in
thick black ink, Rain sketched the interior of the body, showing the location of the lungs, heart, liver, stomach, pancreas,
large and small intestines. "See," she pointed out to him. "Your
illustration has the liver and stomach in the wrong places.
Also," she added, doing another sketch, this time of the heart,
"this is how the heart really looks when it's dissected. There
are four sections—the two above we call the atria, and the
two below the ventricles—and the blood is pumped into and
out of the heart through these veins and arteries."

She stopped, suddenly aware of the ominous silence in
the room. The priest was peering over the king's shoulder,
and both men were staring at her as if she'd just sprung a
halo. She wished she had. A pair of wings, as well, would
come in handy right now. Lord, when would she learn to
keep her mouth shut?

"Father Egbert, is it possible that what the wench says is
true?" the king asked.

"Nay, of course not."

But they could all hear the hesitation in the cleric's voice.

"Mayhap you would come back on the morrow and discuss this further with me?" Father Egbert asked Rain tentatively. "Your sketch is, of course, incorrect, but I would be interested in hearing more of your theories. Where didst thou study?"

But the king interrupted, his eyes narrowing, as he asked, "You mentioned dissection. Surely, you did not cut a man's body open for your inspection."

Uh-oh! Rain sensed she was treading on hallowed ground.

"Did I say dissection?" she said, hoping the heat of her face didn't betray her. "I must have meant inspection."

The king eyed her speculatively. "Exactly who are you?"

"Rain—Thoraine Jordan. I believe you met my mother once—Ruby Jordan."

Athelstan's brow furrowed in concentration, then brightened. "The lady who claimed to come from the future? The one with the outrageous undergarments?"

"Don't tell me my mother showed you her lingerie, too?"

The king grinned. "Nay, but her word-fame spread far and wide." He motioned for the cleric to leave them alone, telling him that he would discuss the manuscripts with him further the next afternoon. Then he turned back to Rain, obviously fascinated. "And who was your father?"

"Thork—Thork Haraldsson." Rain crossed her fingers behind her back, but only halfheartedly. She was actually beginning to believe her mother's preposterous claims of her being conceived in the past and born in the future.

"Aaah, then Eirik would truly be your half brother, as he claims."

"Yes."

"Now I understand his concern for you. And The Outlaw? What relationship do you share with that heathen beast?"

Rain dug her fingernails into her tightly clenched fists, trying to control her temper diplomatically. Finally, she held his eyes honestly and announced proudly, "I love him."

The king's upper lip curled with contempt. "Then you are a fool, for he is a dead man."

Rain licked her dry lips and sought for the right words. "King Athelstan, in my ti—in my country, people regard you as a fair king. You carry many titles. The Warrior King. The Scholar King. The King of All Britain. But you are most remembered as a just king, a ruler who would give even the most hardened criminal a second chance if he repented."

"You waste your breath, my lady, if you think to gain a second chance for The Outlaw. Do you have any idea what he did to my cousin Eadric at Brunanburh?"

"Actually, I do. I was there." She ignored his gasp of surprise and went on. "But as horrible as it was, do you have any idea what Eadric's family has done to Selik?"

The king's eyes widened with interest. "Explain yourself."

Quickly, Rain recapped all that she knew of Eadric's cousin, Steven of Gravely, and what he'd done to Selik's wife and baby. She saw tears in Elgiva's eyes at mention of the baby's head being carried on a pike. But the king's eyes flashed angrily.

"That is Selik's view of the event. He no doubt provoked Steven."

Rain wanted to ask what possible provocation there could be for such brutality, but curbed her tongue.

"And 'tis no excuse for the ten years of war he has waged against me and my soldiers, who had naught to do with the alleged event."

"I agree. There's no excuse for violence. But there have been outrages on both sides, and Selik's only excuse is that he went berserk after finding his wife and baby. It was the only way he could survive without going insane."

Rain didn't know what else to say. *Please, God, help me to find the right words. Let the king understand.*

She inhaled deeply and went on. "Let me say just one more thing. If you were not a king, and you had married a woman—like Elgiva, for instance," Rain speculated, and saw the quick look of longing Athelstan and Elgiva exchanged, "how would you feel if you came home one day to find her body raped and mutilated and your son's headless body lying in the dirt. And consider even more the fury that would overcome you to hear that your baby's head was being carried on a pike by your enemy. What would you have done?" Rain had to swallow hard over the lump in her throat. In a choked whisper, she repeated, "What would you have done?"

Tears streamed down Elgiva's face, but the king's lips thinned angrily, and he raised his chin defensively, almost as if she were holding him personally responsible for the outrages.

"I will not release The Outlaw," he vowed, "no matter how eloquently you plead his case. Now, begone." He waved her dismissively toward the door. "I wish to speak to Elgiva in private."

She was in the hands of the devil . . .

The next day Eirik left for Ravenshire, having heard reports of villains marauding on his property. Assigning a guard to accompany her and a maid to sleep on the pallet in her chamber, he promised Rain he would be back as soon as possible.

Rain saw Blanche occasionally with the castellan, Herbert, apparently having landed on her feet—or her back, to be more accurate. She ignored Rain disdainfully whenever she approached.

Elgiva warned Rain not to push her case with the king. He had heard her pleas, and being a fair man, would act accordingly.

So, Rain spent her days pleading with the castle guards to let her see Selik and talking for hours with Father Egbert about his medical manuscript. Father Egbert had, in turn, introduced her to King Athelstan's personal healer, who was affronted and, at the same time, fascinated by her "outrageous" medical theories.

She was heading once again toward the outbuilding that housed the prison when a magnificently garbed man approached her. The man, well over six feet tall, wore a long cape of black wool of the softest, finest quality, lined with golden fox fur. His midnight-black hair lay in silky splendor down to his shoulders. His pale blue eyes gazed out at her in amusement, clearly aware of her appreciation of his beauty. In fact, the man looked a lot like her brother Eirik, except that his features were more finely honed, almost too perfect.

He bowed slightly and took her hand in his. "Are you the Lady Rain?"

"Yes."

"I have heard so much of you. Perchance I can be of some help in your endeavors."

"Really?" Rain asked hopefully, not even caring that he held her hand too long, or that the softness of his fingers caressed her palm.

"Would you like to see the prisoner, Selik?"

"Yes—oh, yes. Can you get me in?"

"Mayhap. I wonder . . . ." he said, eying her oddly. "I wonder if you will pay the price."

"The pr . . . price? Oh, yes, of course. I have money with me. How much?"

The gorgeous man waved her concern aside. "We can discuss that later. This is the question—though: Are you willing to pay any price to gain The Outlaw's release?"

"Yes," she asserted vehemently. "Any price."

He smiled then, but Rain shivered. It was not a nice smile.

"Come," he said, folding her arm in his. "For now, we will visit your lover. He is your lover, is he not?"

Rain nodded, flushing at his intense perusal.

"Good. Yea, 'tis very good."

The splendidly dressed man led her blithely past the ingratiatingly smiling Herbert and the guards who had previously refused her admittance. They didn't even question the nobleman.

"What did you say your name was?"

He patted her hand. "Later. We will discuss all that later."

They arrived at Selik's cell door. As they stepped inside, she tried to pull her arm from out of the crook of the man's arm, but he held her fast. Rain started to question his action, but stopped dead when she saw Selik. She was thankful then for the support of the man's arm.

Selik's nude body half-lay, half-sat upon the bench. He seemed immune to the cold air. New cuts and bruises marred his beautiful body. His short hair stood out in filthy spikes with the scalp showing through. Ropes bound his hands behind his back, tied to a hook in the wall. And a filthy rag across his mouth prevented any speech.

But his eyes screamed his fury.

He stood abruptly, shaking with rage, and tried to rush toward them, but the short length of rope connecting him to the wall held him back.

Rain was hardly aware that the man had put an arm around her shoulder and pulled her tightly to his chest until she tried to move closer to Selik. She wanted to hug Selik close and assure him that she was trying her best to gain his release.

Selik's eyes flashed angrily as they darted back and forth between her and the man, and unintelligible grunting noises emanated from behind his gag. Of course, Selik was furious with her. He'd told her to leave Winchester, fearing for her safety.

She pulled against the man's grasp now and realized suddenly that he prevented her from going to Selik. She raised questioning eyes to him, but before she could speak he lowered his mouth to hers and kissed her open mouth passionately.

In a quicksilver movement, with his mouth still covering hers, he whisked her through the door and pinned her against the corridor wall out of Selik's line of vision, clamping a hand over her mouth. Then, loud enough for Selik to hear through the open doorway, he said, "See, my love, The Outlaw is just a beast. I told you that you need not waste your concern over such filth. Come, let us go back to my chamber, and I will show you *once again* how a true man cares for his woman's needs."

Rain heard a loud, strangled growl of outrage inside the cell. And the man beside her laughed with devilish glee as he pulled her back out to the prison entrance with his hand still clamped over her mouth.

And Rain knew she was in the clutches of the demonic Steven of Gravely.

CHAPTER TWENTY

❦

S *he would do anything to save Selik. Anything! . . .*
    In the corridor near the outside entry to the prison,
Steven stopped abruptly and pinned Rain against the stone
wall, still holding a palm over her mouth. Although he was
about the same height as Selik, he carried none of the muscle
and bulk that honed Selik's wonderful body.

His leanness was deceptive, however. Steven's narrow
hips slammed against Rain's stomach and held her against
the wall like a battering ram. His wiry left forearm lay
across her chest, near her neck, no less impenetrable than a
steel bar.

"I am going to release my hand from your mouth, and
when I do you will remain silent," Steven said. "Do you understand?"

She glared up at him. *Go ahead, you damn fool. They'll
hear my screams in America.*

He laughed low in his throat, an evil sound, and Rain
understood why people likened him to Satan. His fingers
dug into her left shoulder, so painfully she thought the skin
might break.

"Listen well, bitch, I care naught for you—whether you

live or die, prosper or perish. But The Outlaw—ah, 'tis another matter. If you do not heed my words—*exactly*—he
will not only die; he will suffer indignities and pains you
could never imagine."

Rain's heart crashed against her chest wall, and her blood
raced with anxiety. She didn't wonder how he would be able
to torture the king's prisoner. He'd just gained easy access
when she'd been unable to get past the guards for days. The
sadistic gleam in his pale eyes bespoke his evil intent, and
she knew he would take pleasure in enforcing his threats.

"Now, will you remain silent when I take my hand from
your mouth?"

She nodded.

He removed his hand, and she breathed deeply, trying to
get her galloping heartbeat under control.

"Rain—'tis your name, I believe," he said with a sneer.
"We are going to walk back to the castle together. You will
act as if we are friendly acquaintances. Not by a look or a
word will you betray your less than fond affections for me."

She said nothing, and he punched her in the stomach.

Rain bent over, moaning, "Oh—oh, God!"

"Do I make myself clear?"

She tried to nod as she straightened, but apparently she
hadn't responded quickly enough. He slammed her shoulders back with two palms against her chest. Her head hit the
stone wall with a dull thwack.

"Speak, bitch."

"I understand," she said dully, her ears ringing from the
head blow.

He put his arm around her shoulders in what any passerby
might consider gentleness and led her out through the bailey,
into the great hall of the castle, up stairways, through corridor after twisted corridor, until they reached his bedchamber. Along the way, Steven nodded but did not stop to speak
to those they passed. She saw no one she recognized, except
for Blanche, who smirked, then laughed derisively, probably
thinking she'd dumped Selik for this handsome nobleman.

When they got to his remote chamber, Steven opened the door and shoved her inside roughly. A young man and a young woman, both well-dressed and exceptionally attractive, looked up in a bored fashion from the far side of the room, where they were playing chess.

The man, about sixteen years old, raised one brow lazily and commented, "It did not take you long to nab The Outlaw's wench."

"Did you think it would, Efric?" Steven asked dryly, throwing his fur-lined cape over a chest and dropping down to a low chair. He extended his long legs, and Efric came over and knelt before him, smiling in an oddly sweet manner, then proceeded to remove his soft leather boots.

"Did she come willingly?" the slim, blond-haired woman said, coming toward them in a pronounced mincing fashion, her hips swinging. The deepness of the woman's voice confused Rain until she realized, with a gasp, that the woman was really a man. A cross-dresser, for heaven's sake.

"Not quite willing, Caedmon. It took a little convincing."

Caedmon's pouty lips parted expectantly, and Rain suspected that the idea of her pain turned the loathsome man on.

"You can be sure that she will be more than willing afore long, though." Steven grinned conspiratorially at his two cohorts.

Both Caedmon and Efric looked at Rain, licking their lips as if she were a tasty morsel being offered to them.

"I will never be willing where you are concerned, you filthy pervert," Rain snapped, moving away from Steven and his slimy friends. "I will scream this castle down. King Athelstan will never allow you to keep me captive here."

"Oh, you will not be captive," Steven said. "You can walk out that door right now if you choose." He poured a goblet of wine and sipped as if he could not care less what she did. "'Tis your choice, but . . ."

Rain began to edge toward the door.

". . . but then Selik would be dead afore morn."

Rain stopped, gulping. She turned on him, spitting out, "You are evil."

"Thank you." Steven shrugged, gazing at her with amusement. "Goodness is an overrated commodity, in my opinion. Whereas evil—'tis amazing how quickly so-called good people accept evil when 'tis to their benefit. You, for example."

Rain was afraid to ask what he meant.

"Now, I wonder . . . I wonder just what evil you are willing to accept in order to gain your lover's release."

Rain shivered deep inside.

"Of course, I will have to kill Selik eventually. 'Tis a shame. He is a pleasure to torment. Honorable men always are."

How ironic, Rain thought. Honor was the one thing Selik thought he had lost long ago. "Why do you hate Selik so?"

"He killed my father, that is why. I was only ten when my father died and my brother Elwinus barely out of the swaddling cloths. We had no family to care for us, only the castellan, Gerard." He said the man's name with utter loathing, and closed his eyes as if in pain. When his eyes opened again, he snarled, "I did not know what evil truly was until I *knew* Gerard."

"But that wasn't Selik's fault. If he did actually kill your father, it would have been in battle and—"

"Not The Outlaw's fault!" Steven shrieked in a rage, grabbing her by the shoulders and shaking her fiercely. "Because of him—just know this, you stupid bitch—Selik will die for the havoc he has caused in my life, but not afore he suffers mightily."

"He has already suffered."

"But not enough," Steven said, shoving her away with distaste. "Not nearly enough."

"What do you want from me?"

"I am not certain yet. You could start by removing your garments—all of them—so I can assess what you have to offer."

Rain forced herself to remain calm, not to say anything

that would provoke him into harming her or Selik. She darted a look at the two other men in the room.

Steven waved a hand in the air. "Pretend that Efric and Caedmon are not here. Leastways, they are not like me. They disdain the female form totally."

Steven, a bisexual! "I can't do this," Rain protested.

"Efric, go to the guard at the prison—you know which one, the big brutish man with the lisp. Tell him to start by pulling out all The Outlaw's fingernails and toenails. Stay and watch that it is done; then bring them back to me."

"No!" Rain cried out.

"You object? Why? You have only to do as you are told to stay his tortures."

Rain removed her clothing. Everything. And stood before the three men in shame while they made rude remarks.

"Her breasts are like udders," Efric whined and pinched her repeatedly.

"And she is so tall, not womanly at all," Caedmon twittered, prodding her with his pointed shoes, then kicking her hips, her buttocks, her thighs and calves. "I am more a woman than she is."

But Rain didn't care what the two jerks said about her; she was more alarmed by Steven, who was removing his clothing. She backed away, fearing she was about to be raped. When he stood before her, totally naked, his erection standing out before him like a weapon, he smiled at Efric and Caedmon, then turned to her with a sneer. "In truth, you are not to my taste, either. I like my women more delicate and much younger."

But they made her watch while they performed their perversities. If she closed her eyes or turned her head, one of them would pinch her or kick her until she complied. Hours later, Rain began to understand their twisted minds. Sex with her would give them no pleasure—thank God she was spared that—but pain and degradation would. And all of it was directed in some odd way toward Selik.

Finally, Steven pushed her into a nearby windowless

room—more like a large closet. Sinking to the floor, she heard the lock slip into place.

Oh, the evil in some men! . . .

For days, Rain suffered indignities and violence she never imagined possible. When her body was not being assaulted with kicks or slaps or punches, they left her for long periods alone in her closet room. Rain had landed in hell, and she did not know how she would ever climb out.

Why didn't Eirik return? The problems at Ravenshire must have been greater than he'd anticipated.

She hoped no one had told Selik she was missing. As if he would care after the scene Steven had orchestrated with her in his cell! But still, she couldn't bear to have him hear of her degradation and blame himself for once again failing to protect someone he loved. And he would never be able to accept the fact that Steven punished her in his place.

Sometimes she wished she could just die. But not for long. She was a survivor. Mostly, she boiled inside with anger and knew she was no longer a pacifist. A pacifist could never contemplate the violence she intended to inflict on Steven if ever Selik were freed.

On the afternoon of the fifth day, a large tub was brought in, and she bathed and washed her body. When she emerged from the tub, Efric and Caedmon dressed her hair and posed her before a sheet of polished metal. It was amazing, after all she had endured, that her face exhibited none of the bruises and cuts that marred the rest of her body. Thank God, they had not raped her . . . yet. Other than her swollen lips and her red eyes, caused by so much crying, she looked the same as always.

Steven forced her to don a silk tunic with lacings from the neckline to the belted waist. He wouldn't allow her to wear anything underneath; but he threw his fur-lined cloak over her shoulders, saying, "We are going for a walk. I think you need some fresh air."

She gazed at him suspiciously. Steven did nothing without an ulterior motive.

He laughed, pleased at the contempt in her eyes. He had told her over and over that her resistance pleased him. She wished she could stop fighting.

"We are going to visit your lover."

Rain began to shake, afraid of what Steven would do next, unable to understand his devious mind.

"You will say naught whilst we are there. Do you understand me, Rain?" He took her chin in a pincer-like grip.

She nodded.

"If you do aught by look or word to show you are with me unwillingly, Selik will be dead by nightfall. Do you believe me?"

She nodded again, and he released her chin. Before they left the room, he pinched the nipples of both breasts so they stood out painfully against the thin silk of her tunic.

How quickly love turns to hate! . . .

Selik paced back and forth along the short distance the rope would allow. His hands were still tied behind his back. For days he had heard nothing and seen no one.

He tried to forget the image of Rain with Steven when they had visited his cell five days ago—five agonizing days, during which he had imagined the implications of the two of them together.

Trust in her.

One part of him wanted to believe Rain had been with Steven against her wishes, to listen to the voice in his head, but she had appeared willing. Women had always found Steven godly handsome when he plied his insidious charms, and he remembered clearly that Rain had permitted Steven to put his arm around her shoulders. Even worse, he recalled in perfect detail Steven's words to her outside the cell, referring to him as a filthy beast, encouraging Rain to go with him back to his bedchamber. As hard as he had strained to listen, he had heard no struggle, no pleading words from Rain on his behalf.

Trust in her.

Selik tried to block out the inner voice. He wished he could die. None of the torments visited on him by Athelstan's vicious soldiers could compare with the pain of Rain's betrayal.

But then, at other times, he hoped he would live to enact his revenge. On them both.

He heard a rattle near his cell door, followed by the squeak of rusty hinges. He gasped when he saw Steven enter, followed hand-in-hand by Rain.

Her hair was beautifully dressed, and she wore a magnificent fur-lined cloak. She stared at him through wide golden eyes, expressionless pools filled with an emotion he could not understand. Her lips were rosy and swollen, as if they had been kissed endlessly.

A sweet, recently awakened part of him died inside.

"Argh!" he raged and lurched forward against his ropes. He would kill her, as well as Steven, if he could reach them.

Rain's eyes widened and pooled with tears. He noticed the dark circles under her eyes then. No doubt due to sleepless nights spent under Gravely's panting body. Did she moan for her new lover the way she had for him?

His heart felt as if it were splintering inside his body, and he feared there were tears in his eyes.

How could she? How could she?

Steven smiled at him then, a twisted sick curve of the lips, and pulled his cloak off Rain's shoulder. With a flick of his fingers, he pulled the laces from her tunic. Standing behind Rain, Steven parted her tunic, baring her breasts with their aroused nipples for his view. Then he put his hands under her breasts and raised them high. Bruises marred the white flesh of her breasts from their love play. All the time, Steven was smiling at him.

Rain dropped her head in shame. Even a woman in love, as she must be with the handsome Steven to allow such intimacies, would not want her body bared before another man, a former lover. But she said nothing, not a word, to stop

Steven. Not even when he put one hand on her womanhood, rubbing sensuously, and another hand under her chin, forcing her to look up.

"I hate you," Selik said to Rain with all the venom that boiled in his blood. "I hate you more than Steven, and that is an ungodly amount. You took my love and spat on it, and for that I will never forgive you."

He turned away from her then and felt the wetness on his cheeks. He heard a low choking sound behind him, quickly stifled, but he did not turn again until they were long gone and the door closed behind them.

Pacificism be damned! . . .

After that, Rain didn't care anymore. Her lack of resistance angered Steven, and his brutality increased. Rain wondered if she would be alive in another week—if, in one of his rages, Steven would go too far and kill her. Or if he might change his mind and assault her sexually. That she would not be able to accept.

Through it all, she didn't scream for help because she still needed to protect Selik.

A week after her ill-fated meeting with Selik, Caedmon came running into Steven's bedchamber, yelling, "That bitch Elgiva is looking for Rain. She went to the king, and he agreed to a search of the castle."

Rain barely raised her head from where she sat on the floor of her little room, able to hear everything they said through the open doorway.

"Hurry, Caedmon, pack all our belongings," Steven said anxiously. "Efric, get the horses. We will leave immediately."

Rain dozed off, or perhaps she passed out. She did that a lot lately. Steven had struck her on the head several days ago, and she feared she had suffered a concussion. She heard the door open some time later and Efric exclaim in a rush, "Bloody hell, Steven, the king and the bitch are headed this way. Someone told Athelstan they saw The Outlaw's wench with you at the prison."

Suddenly, Rain realized that Steven was about to escape. Once again, he would elude punishment for his evil deeds. He would not pay for raping and killing Selik's wife, for decapitating the baby Thorkel, for his mistreatment of her, for all his horrendous acts. Rain couldn't allow that to happen.

While the three men picked up their chests and leather bags, Rain stood, unnoticed, staggering painfully. She saw a knife on the table beside the bed, picked it up as if in a trance, then ran toward Steven's back screaming, "You bastard! You bastard!"

Steven turned at the last moment and flung out an arm. The knife was deflected and, in her weakness, she tripped. Instead of the knife going into Steven's back as she'd intended, it grazed his forearm. Still, blood flowed freely down his sleeve.

At first, his eyes just widened in amazement that she would dare to attack him. His angry eyes turned with horror to the blood soaking his tunic. Then she saw his booted foot swing out. She couldn't move fast enough to escape the blow that hit her in the stomach.

In a blurry haze of pain and nausea, Rain saw King Athelstan's face bending over her. "Blood of Christ! Who did this to her?"

Someone else answered, "Steven of Gravely."

"Where is he?" Athelstan's voice, icy with rage, asked.

"Gone."

Gonegonegonegonegonegone . . . The word kept echoing in Rain's benumbed brain as she felt her body being lifted in someone's arms.

She heard a sobbing voice behind her then and recognized Elgiva's voice saying, "Oh, Athelstan, look how that beast beat her!"

"El . . . Elgiva," Rain gasped, stretching an arm in her direction.

"I am here," Elgiva said, stepping into her line of vision, brushing matted hair off her face with a gentle hand.

"Promise . . ." Rain choked out. "Promise me . . ."

"What? What do you want me to promise, my dear friend?"

"Do not . . . do not tell Selik. He must not know."

"But why?"

Rain saw the tears running down Elgiva's cheeks. And the pity. She must look really bad to arouse the horror she saw reflected on Elgiva's face.

"He would blame himself for not protecting me," she said in a raw voice, licking her cracked lips. "He couldn't live with that pain again. He just couldn't."

"But—"

"Promise," Rain demanded, clutching at her arm with more strength than she realized she still had. "Promise."

Elgiva nodded.

And Rain fainted into blessed oblivion.

The first steps are the hardest . . .

Several days later, Rain sat up in Elgiva's bed. Other than the bruises that marred every inch of her body and the emotional scars that would never go away, Rain felt almost normal. Apparently she had not had a concussion after all.

And, for the first time in days, Rain realized that she wanted to live.

"Did he rape you?" Elgiva asked as she adjusted the bed linens around her. The Saxon lady had been nursing her the past few days. If anyone was an angel, it was she.

Rain shook her head.

"Well, that is a blessing. You have undergone a horrible experience, but the worst is over."

"I know. I should be thankful for that, but I can barely control the mind-boiling, blood-churning, violent anger that rages inside me against Steven of Gravely."

"The worst thing is that Gravely escapes with no punishment for his vile acts."

"Oh, I don't think so. I believe he'll get his just deserts sometime, either in this life or another. But I can't let my hatred for him consume me now. I have to put my rage aside or it will eat away at me like a cancer. I need to heal now, Elgiva. And, oh God, I need Selik."

Elgiva shifted her eyes and sat next to Rain on the edge of the bed. "That is what I wanted to discuss."

"Selik?" Rain asked, her voice rising with alarm.

Elgiva patted her hand reassuringly. "Do not fret. He is safe. In fact"—Elgiva inhaled as if for strength—"in fact, he was released yestereve."

"He . . . was?" Rain asked slowly, her brow furrowing with confusion.

"Yea, after seeing what Steven had done to you, Athelstan finally believed that Selik had provocation for his vengeful acts. He levied a huge wergild on The Outlaw and exiled him for life from all of Britain. An armed guard will take him to Southampton on the morrow, where he will be put on a ship, never to return to this land again."

Rain smiled and started to get up from the bed. "I must go to him at once.

"Nay, you are too weak yet."

"Then send him to me. At once. I've got to see that he's all right. And we've got to pack my belongings so I can go with him tomorrow." Excited at the wonderful news, Rain began to list in her mind all the things she needed to do to prepare for a trip. Where would they go? she wondered. Could they send for Ubbi and Adam and Adela and the other orphans?

Elgiva shook her head sadly. "Rain, he refuses to see you."

"But why?" Rain sank back down to the bed, frightened by the concern in Elgiva's teary voice.

"You would not allow me or Athelstan to tell him why you were with Steven. So, he believes—"

"—that I was with Steven willingly. That I was his lover," Rain finished for her.

"He says he hates you, Rain. I am sure, in time, when he is more in control of his senses, he will recognize his mis-thinking. But he has been in a rage since his release, drinking and cursing and—"

"Help me dress," Rain said firmly, forcing herself to endure the pain of her battered body. "Whether you help me or not, I'm going to find Selik and talk to him."

After many futile arguments, Elgiva helped her don one of her own garments—a soft white wool tunic over a blue chemise. She put the amber beads lovingly around her neck and the dragon brooch at her shoulder. Standing before the polished metal on Elgiva's wall, Rain saw dark circles under her eyes, and the weight she'd lost showed in her hollowed cheeks, but otherwise, no one would suspect the massive bruising hidden under all her garments.

"Will you tell him the truth?" Elgiva asked as she helped her walk down the hall, carefully, like an aged cripple.

Rain shook her head. "No—at least, not now. Maybe someday, when we've both had a chance to heal, but Selik couldn't handle it now. He's suffered so much already. I just know he would revert to his former life of bloody vengeance."

When they arrived at the door of Selik's chamber, Rain heard some movement inside.

"Shall I come inside with you?" Elgiva asked with concern.

Rain shook her head. "No—but, Elgiva, thank you for all your help." She hugged her friend warmly, then smiled expectantly.

Finally, she and Selik would have a life together.

Who says big boys don't cry? . . .

Selik heard a knocking sound, but at first, he thought it was in his mead-sodden head. He tried to sit up several times, with no success.

He looked to his side and jolted. A nude woman lay beside him in the rumpled linens. He groaned. 'Twas Blanche.

He frowned, trying to remember. He had been drinking heavily the night before, but he knew for a fact that he had gone to his bed alone. What was the wench up to?

He rubbed his eyes wearily, suddenly remembering why he had drunk so much yestereve. The bastard king had released him yestermorn, with no explanation. He'd been ordered to pay an enormous fine, turn over his property in Northumbria, and leave Britain forever.

He did not care.

He had lost much, much more.

Rain! his tormented mind cried out, as it had for days. *Rain . . . Rain . . . Rain . . . Rain . . .*

How could she? he kept asking himself over and over. There were no answers, just the inexorable facts. She had been with his most hated enemy, Steven of Gravely.

Gravely was filth in his eyes, and now Rain was too. He would never, *never*, forgive her for her betrayal.

The pounding at the door continued. Selik forced himself up off the bed and staggered toward the door, uncaring of his nudity. No doubt Athelstan had sent another messenger to remind him of his departure on the morrow. It could not be too soon for him.

Ill-prepared for the sight of Rain standing before him in the doorway, he leaned against the door for support. Bloody hell! She looked like an angel standing there dressed in white, gazing at him through tear-filled golden eyes. Wearing his amber beads like a bloody badge of love. Damn her. He forced himself not to reach out for her, reminding himself that she was far from an angel. A dark angel, mayhap, for any goodness in her was surely wiped out by association with Satan's own helper, Steven of Gravely.

"Selik!" she exclaimed on a hoarse whisper and held out both arms for his embrace.

Was she halfwitted? Did she truly expect him to welcome her back into his loving arms as if naught had transpired?

He stepped aside as she reached for him, moving back into the room. She followed and saw Blanche's naked form in his bed for the first time.

She gasped and clamped a hand over her mouth in horror, staring up at him through wounded, accusing eyes.

How dare she accuse him? Even if he had not actually touched a hair on Blanche's winsome flesh, how bloody dare she reproach him?

Blanche sat up and shot a contemptuous, triumphant look at Rain. She let the bed linens fall down to her waist, exposing her full breasts proudly. "Send the bitch away," the slut cajoled. "Come back to bed, sweetling."

"Shut up."

Blanche whimpered at his harsh words, and Rain looked up at him hopefully.

"What do you want?" he demanded of Rain, pulling on a pair of braies.

"You," she said in a low voice, darting a look at Blanche, then back to him in question. "You."

"Never."

"Why?"

"How can you ask? I would never take Steven's leavings, and I understand that is just what you are. The servants say he left several days ago, no doubt anticipating my release. Did your lover refuse to take you with him?"

"He was never my lover. Never," Rain said vehemently.

For the first time in days, Selik felt hope rise like water within his parched soul. He put his hands on both her arms, noting how she winced. Did his touch repulse her now? "What do you mean? Are you saying you were not with Gravely willingly?"

Rain hesitated and her eyes pleaded with him oddly. Selik felt all his hopes die.

"Get out," he demanded, turning away from her.

"Selik, it wasn't the way you think," she pleaded, moaning as if he had kicked her in the stomach.

"How was it?" he snapped, turning on her with barely controlled rage. At that moment, he could have strangled her with no regrets for all the soul-searing pain she had caused him.

Her shoulders slumped and tears slipped from her eyes. She would not answer, and that was all the answer he needed.

"I love you, Selik," she finally said.

"I hate you. I never want to see you again," he declared icily, digging his fingernails into his palms. "Never."

"Can't you just trust me, Selik?" she begged. "Can't you remember our love, and just trust?"

Her soft sobs tore at his breaking heart, but he could not surrender to her traitorous kind of love. With determination, he walked to the bed and slipped under the linens with Blanche, turning his face away from Rain. For a very long time, he heard Rain standing near the door, crying raggedly.

When the door finally opened and closed with a dull thud, he shoved Blanche away from him with distaste and ordered her to leave his chamber. Whining and then cursing, she left the room with a slam of the door. Selik sat up in bed then, putting both hands to his face.

And he cried for all he had lost.

CHAPTER TWENTY-ONE

❧

*A*pparently, cluelessness is not terminal . . .

Two days later, Selik awakened from a drunken stupor and knew he could not go on without Rain. It did not matter if she had been with Steven of Gravely, or Lucifer himself. He loved her and could not live without her by his side.

Trust in her.

"God, if love of Rain does not kill me, You will with this bloody, infernal, never-ending badgering," Selik muttered as he walked carefully, liked an aged cripple, to the doorway and yelled to a passing servant for bathwater. His own voice seemed to rattle inside his head, and he put both hands to his ears to hold in his loose brains.

Loose brains is right, my boy. Did I not tell you to trust in love, and what did you do? Reject the best thing in life I ever gave you, that's what. And by the way, I do not care for your mentioning Lucifer in My presence.

"Oh, Lord," Selik groaned. "Isn't there some miracle you have to perform somewhere—like Iceland?"

Selik knew Rain had returned to Northumbria the day after his rejection of her. Athelstan had delighted in telling him that he had sent his own armed guard to accompany her.

Selik was sure he would be able to come to some agreement with King Athelstan allowing him to stay in Britain, especially if he bartered his soul to the bloody Saxon, but—

Not your soul, the voice interrupted, *that precious commodity belongs to me.*

Selik looked skyward and crossed his eyes in frustration. "I meant that if I pledged my loyalty to him and paid a *wergild* equal to a king's ransom, he might allow me to live on my own land." He immediately chastised himself for carrying on a conversation with an invisible being. Perhaps he was finally going totally insane.

Go to her.

"Rain must hate me now."

She has good reason. If she does, convince her to love you again. You were e'er the master of seduction.

Selik grinned ruefully. Suddenly, another thought occurred to him. What about Steven of Gravely? He could not allow him to escape again without punishment for his crimes. Yea, he should first go after Steven of Gravely and wreak his final vengeance.

Vengeance is mine.

"Says who?" Selik snapped back, hands on hips, addressing the ceiling of his bedchamber.

Sayeth the Lord, you lackwit.

"What did ye say, master?" asked one of the servants who was bringing in two buckets full of hot water. The scruffy lad was looking curiously at the rafters to see whom Selik addressed.

"Never mind."

Selik shook his head at his growing conversations with himself. He no longer knew where his conscience left off and the spirit voice began. But then he began to think about the voice's advice. Mayhap it was indeed time to set aside his vendetta against Steven, to establish some greater priorities in his life. *Like Rain.* He could seek Steven later—next month, next year, whenever. But the most important thing now was to find Rain and tell her that he still loved her.

He thought he heard a great sigh of relief from above.

For the first time in days, Selik smiled, and it was like a great weight had been lifted from his shoulders.

She came full circle . . .

A devastated Rain arrived back at the farmstead finally. Not only was she crushed by the loss of Selik's love, but she suspected he would go after Steven with deadly force now in his quest for vengeance. She felt that she had come full circle. All that time spent trying to heal Selik's bitterness and persuade him to abandon his quest for revenge seemed fruitless if Selik was just going to pick up the self-destructive gauntlet again.

"The thickheaded bastard! How could he have thought you would consort with Steven willingly?" Ubbi exclaimed as he fussed over her many still-unhealed bruises.

"Steven is a handsome man, on the outside. And he can be very charming when he wants to be. He's a consummate actor."

"Well, still, Selik should have trusted in you."

"Yes, he should have," Rain said, her voice faltering. "He didn't love me enough, apparently. If he did, he would have known I could never betray him. But my being with Steven blindsided him, placing one more brick in the wall of his hatred for Steven."

Rain gathered Ubbi and the children to her. She needed to feel loved by someone.

King Athelstan had invited Rain to return to his court at a later date so he could talk to her more about the medical marvels of her country. Rain had promised she would, but she doubted she would ever see the "Scholar King" again. In parting, she had hugged Elgiva, who laughingly thanked her for specific details on the rhythm method of birth control. Not surprisingly, the king had refused her halfhearted offer of a vasectomy, especially when she'd mentioned the acupuncture needles she would need to use for a local anesthetic.

"The master will come back, my lady, once he comes to his senses," Ubbi said, reaching over to pat her hand.

Rain wasn't so sure, but a little part of her soul that hadn't yet died hoped he was right. Inside, she prayed, *Please, God, send him back to me.*

Trust in Me.

Rain wasn't sure she trusted anyone anymore.

Only Adam drew back from the excitement of her homecoming, silently wounded by Selik's absence. She had explained to the children that the king had pardoned Selik on the condition that he leave the country, that he couldn't come back to see them first.

Adam came up and put his hand in hers, sensing her pain, and whispered, "I will not leave you." Then he went off to whittle on a piece of wood, staring ahead angrily. The wonderful little boy was like a grown man in a child's body, far too perceptive for his age. Adela sat beside him on a bench near the hearth fire. Silently, with her thumb in her mouth, she laid her head against her brother's arm in comfort.

The first few days, Rain remained hopeful that Selik would return for her. Her body grew stronger, and she tried not to think about the evil Steven and his friends.

Then days went by. And weeks.

Rain walked the lonely fields of the farmstead. She tried desperately to forget the precious love she'd held in her hands for a brief moment in time. And lost.

Then Adam disappeared, and Adela lay listless and moaning in her pallet with a stomach pain. Rain suspected the malady was psychosomatic, that Adela missed her brother so much that her emotional pain had become a physical one.

The late winter snows and blustery winds came, rattling the timbers of the ancient barn, exaggerating Rain's growing feelings of loneliness and inadequacy and despair. She wanted to return to Jorvik and the Coppergate site so that she could travel back to the future. At least there, in the familiarity of her old life, she might be able to put back together the shattered pieces of her heart. She wanted to cry on her mother's shoulder, knowing Ruby would under-stand.

But she could not leave until Adela was better. And Adam returned. Where had the foolish imp gone? Adela said he had an errand to do in Jorvik. That had been almost a week ago.

The cold weather aggravated Ubbi's arthritis, and he remained in his pallet, apologizing profusely for his weakness. Rain tended lovingly to the dear man who had become like a father to her. She would miss him terribly.

Ella, who came to visit her occasionally, but more likely to cozy up to Ubbi, offered Rain more advice than she cared to hear. "Best ye git yer chin off the ground and look about. There be other fish in the sea besides that Selik. Find yerself another man, I say."

"Easier said than done," Rain retorted.

The next week, Rain received a letter from Elgiva. The chatty note gave her news of the court and Elgiva's growing relationship with the king, then mentioned casually that Selik was still at Winchester. Apparently, he and Athelstan had come to a truce of sorts.

Rain gasped and tears smarted her eyes. Despite all her protestations to the contrary, deep inside, she'd been hoping that Selik would come to his senses. If he still loved her, even if he believed she'd been with Steven willingly, he would have come back to her. He must not love her anymore.

And, if he no longer loved her, she had no future here in the past. Stoically, Rain began to make plans. No matter what Ubbi said, or Gyda, or Ella, Rain would not be dissuaded. She was going home. To the future.

Two days later, on Good Friday, Rain kissed all the children and Ubbi good-bye, hugging them tearfully. She gathered together the dragon brooch she had brought with her, the amber beads Selik had bought for her, and his precious wood carving of a wolf. When he'd given it to her, his words had been, "for remembrance." She hadn't realized then how appropriate the sentiment would be.

She walked alone to Jorvik and the Coppergate site where her whole time-travel experience had started.

Almost seven months had passed since the day she'd stood under the scaffolding in the Viking museum in York. She wondered if any time would have passed in the future. Maybe not. Maybe her mother would still be asleep back at the hotel. Maybe she would emerge from the plaster on the floor, dust herself off, and resume her old life as if nothing had ever happened.

Then again, maybe not.

Do not kill the messenger . . .

Selik walked toward the Southampton harbor, having finally escaped the Easter revelry in the crowded Winchester castle the day before. He could now make his way back to Northumbria and Rain, at last. After weeks of negotiating, Athelstan had agreed to allow him to stay in Britain on the condition that he pledge his loyalty to the king—not against his fellow Norsemen, but in any other military endeavors. And, of course, the Saxon treasury was now significantly larger. His ship should be ready to sail in a day or two, having sustained some winter damage.

He hoped Rain had received his missive telling her of the king's insistence that he stay at court until they arrived at this tentative truce, but he was uneasy about the crafty Saxon merchant who had accepted his coin with oily promises of a quick delivery.

As he neared the harbor landing, Selik noticed the longship of Hastein, a Jorvik merchant. Mayhap, if Hastein was returning to Northumbria before Selik's ship was ready, he would travel with him.

"Selik, just the man I have been looking for," Hastein called out in a blustery voice. "I have a gift for you."

His interest jarred, Selik helped Hastein onto the wharf, no easy task since the ship owner was carrying a roll of heavy tapestry which seemed to be moving oddly. And emitting grunting noises.

Noises Selik regretfully recognized.

He stood stone-still. Nay, it could not be so, he told him-self with a shake of the head, even as Hastein unrolled the tapestry with a grin and a flourish.

And a cursing Adam came jumping to his feet.

"You bloody cod-sucking cur!" Adam snarled, going for Hastein's thick belly with hands clawed.

Selik grabbed him by the back of his filthy tunic, which stank of fish, and lifted him off the ground. Cursing and flailing, Adam called Selik and Hastein names even Selik had never heard before.

Hastein explained briefly that the scurvy whelp had stowed away on his ship in a barrel of salted fish. He gladly turned him over to Selik, claiming the boy had nigh turned his sailors to murder with his filthy mouth and arrogant manners. Finally, Selik carried Adam over his shoulder to a nearby clearing, where he dumped him on the ground.

"What are you doing here, Adam?"

Selik sat down and propped his back against a tree, wait-ing for Adam's response. True to form, Adam refused to sit and stood over him, hands on hips, glaring furiously.

"I came to see you, you bloody bugger."

"Watch your language."

"Me language is not the problem."

"What is?"

"The mistress. Rain."

Selik sat up straighter. "What is wrong with Rain?"

"She be goin' away."

Selik felt a tight, squeezing sensation near his heart, and for a moment he could not breathe. "Where?"

He shrugged doubtfully. "Back where she came from, I think."

Selik inhaled sharply. "Did she get my missive telling her of my delay?"

Adam glared at him suspiciously. "She got no messages from you."

Selik groaned. "How long since you have seen her?"

Adam shrugged. "Two sennights, mayhap." He scowled at Selik. "Are ye goin' back to her?"

"What makes you think she would want me?"

"Are ye such a bloody lackwit ye do not know when a woman loves you?"

Selik felt a grin twitching at his lips. "And you know of such things?"

"I may have seen only seven winters, but I know when a wench spends a mancus of gold on sugar and nigh poisons a dozen poor orphans jist to make a present for a man. Humph! If 'tis not love, then I do not know aught." He handed a filthy sheaf of folded parchment to him, tied with an equally filthy ribbon that might once have been blue.

Viewing Adam suspiciously, Selik opened the package carefully. At first, he just stared at the items before him. Several dozen red objects stared back at him, like bloodshot eyes—some circles, some egg-shaped, others looking like squashed radishes. "What are they?" he asked, raising his eyes to Adam's.

Adam made a snorting sound of disgust. "Do ye know nothin'? They are Lifesavers. Cherry Lifesavers. The mistress made 'em herself fer yer Christmas present, but ye ne'er came. And ye made her cry, too."

Selik picked up one of the candies, about to pop it in his mouth, when Adam put a hand on his arm. "I would not be doin' that if I were you," he cautioned.

"Why not?"

"They taste like horse shit."

Two days later, Selik said his farewells to King Athelstan. He would be leaving on the morrow. For Northumbria.

"And who is the churlish boy standing next to you?" Athelstan asked.

Selik looked down at Adam, who was so grateful that he was going back to Jorvik with Selik that he stared at him like a lovesick puppy. He swallowed hard before he was able to speak. Then, putting a hand on Adam's shoulder, he told Athelstan, "This is my son, Adam. My adopted son."

Better late than never doesn't always hold true . . .

Five days later, Selik's longship turned into the Humber. Selik begrudgingly credited Adam's persistent prodding of his seamen for their rapid progress. More than one fierce Viking had been heard to remark, "Throw the little bugger over the side."

No sooner did his ship hit the confluence of the Ouse and Foss Rivers at Jorvik than Selik rushed ashore and headed for his farmstead. And Rain.

Adam followed close behind, giving him instructions on how to behave with Rain. "Make sure ye do not yell. Ye have a tendency to roar on occasion."

"Be quiet."

"And mayhap ye ought to pretend ye liked her Lifesavers. Women like sweet words."

"Be quiet."

"Perchance ye could remark that she does not look quite so ungodly tall as last time ye saw her. She worries about bein' big, ye know."

"Be quiet."

"And whatever ye do, do not be throwin' her on a bed and plowin' her first thing."

Selik inhaled sharply and stopped dead in his tracks. Hands on hips, he turned to glare at the impudent scamp.

"I know, be quiet."

Adam was the first to see the children playing in the fallow fields of the farmstead. Noticing Adela, Adam ran ahead and hugged his sister warmly. Then he threw his shoulders back and puffed his chest out with self-importance as the other children questioned him about his great adventure.

Hearing the noise, Ubbi came out of the barn and exclaimed, "Well, 'tis about time. We had given up on you."

"Where is Rain?" Selik asked immediately, his eyes darting about the farmyard. Ignoring Ubbi, he rushed inside the barn, but it was empty, the early spring weather having drawn everyone outside—except for Ella, who was stirring a pot over the fire.

Ella! Bloody hell! She must finally have trapped Ubbi.

Seeing him for the first time, Ella scowled condemningly and muttered, "Bloody bastard," before turning her back on him rudely.

"Where is she?" he asked Ubbi once again when he went back outside.

Adela came rushing at him, wrapping her little arms around his legs. He whisked her up into his arms, and she wrapped her thin arms around his neck, kissing his face wetly. "Missed me, did you, Adela?" he asked, twirling her high above his head, to her delighted squeals.

She nodded her head up and down vigorously. He noticed that her thumb was no longer planted in her mouth. She seemed happy and unfearful, unlike the shivering child he had first seen on the street in Jorvik.

"He is me father now," Adam boasted to the other children, jerking a thumb toward Selik.

"Fer shame, Adam, tellin' such tales," Ubbi chastised the little boy. He darted a look of apprehension toward Selik, knowing how he misliked reminders of his lost son.

"He is, too. Yea, he is," Adam protested indignantly to Ubbi. "He ado . . . adopted me."

Ubbi looked up at Selik in question.

He shrugged. "I had no choice. He came for me at Athelstan's court and threatened me with Lifesavers if I would not do his bidding."

Adam grinned at him, happy as a pup.

Selik put Adela down gently and looked directly at Ubbi. Ubbi's eyes shifted nervously.

"Where is she?" he asked in a low voice, almost afraid of the answer.

"Gone."

He closed his eyes for a moment and put a hand to his heart. *Please, God, please!*

Trust in me.

Hah! Look where it got me so far.

Perhaps you haven't trusted enough.

He inhaled deeply and asked, "When? When did she leave?"

"This morn."

Selik's eyes shot open. "This morn? How could that be? The very day I return to Northumbria, she chooses to go back to her own country?"

"She goes every day," Ubbi said with disgust.

"Every day?"

"Ye sound like a bloody parrot."

Selik growled menacingly at Ubbi, and he backed away. "Tell me afore I pull out your tongue."

"She goes to Coppergate every day. Packs that bloody bag of hers, says good-bye to all of us, cries a bit—Lord, the woman can cry a goodly amount—and—"

"Argh! Spit it out afore I pull out your tongue and tie it in a knot."

"Testy, are ye?" Ubbi said. "What I bin tryin' to tell ye is that she lost the aura."

"Aura! What aura?"

Ubbi threw his hands up in the air. "I jist knew ye would ask me that, master. Truly, I do not understand these things. The aura—'tis what God sends down to bring His angels back to heaven, I s'pose. I do not know, really."

Selik began to understand. He had felt the strange pulling sensation that day on Coppergate, months ago, when Rain had tried to go back to the future. She claimed her time-travel had begun there. 'Twas the site where she believed she would have to go to return to her own time.

A chill spread over Selik's flesh, and he braced his hands at his sides for strength. "When did she leave?"

"Afore midday. She is usually back by now," Ubbi said, biting his bottom lip worriedly. "Mayhap it finally worked fer her today."

Selik looked at the lowering sun in the sky. It was late

afternoon. Had the "aura" finally worked for Rain on the very day he returned? Surely, God could not be so cruel. He looked upward then. *Could You?*

You wound Me with your lack of trust.

Selik turned on his heel then, without saying another word, and headed back toward Jorvik.

CHAPTER TWENTY-TWO

❦

Vikings never give up the fight, especially for a woman . . .

He did not meet Rain coming back to the farmstead. Nor did he find her at the Coppergate site.

And, most frightening of all, the aura had disappeared. Selik tramped all through the abandoned building and its yard. Nothing.

Rain must have come, found the aura, and gone.

Tears filled his eyes, and he rocked from side to side. Was this to be his punishment for the past ten years of bloody fighting? How could he bear the pain of her loss for the second time? For a long time, he stood staring about him, unable to move. He felt as if a huge weight lay over him, crushing out all his life forces, his will to go on living.

Finally, with a groan of despair, he turned and headed back toward the farmstead. He walked woodenly through the city streets, unseeing, racked with the pain of his lost love.

Recriminations hammered away at him. He should have loved her more. He should have trusted her and cherished her love while he had it. He should never have rejected her at Winchester.

He was nearing the minster steps when he saw Bernie—Father Bernard—enter the huge oak doors. A sudden thought occurred to him. He had much wealth. Mayhap he would make a donation to the hospitium in Rain's memory. That would please her. He could even ask the church to mark his donation in the church records in her name. Perchance Rain would read of it many years hence and know that he had come back to her. That he had, indeed, loved her.

"Father Bernard," he called out as he rushed through the church aisles and caught up with him near the entry to the hospitium.

The priest turned abruptly, then gasped. "Father Ethelwolf! Where is your priestly garb?"

"I am not a priest, Father Bernard," he confessed.

"Tsk! Just like Rain, you chose to play your foolery in God's house. For shame!"

"So you know Rain—Brother Godwine—was a woman?" he asked with a slight smile.

Father Bernard's upper lip curled with disgust. "Yea, and most angry Father Theodric was at her deception. At first, he would not allow her to work in the hospitium."

"Rain was still working here?" he asked in surprise. "Until when?"

"'Til now," he answered irritably, obviously confused by the question.

It took only a moment for the cleric's words to sink in. *Now.*

Suddenly hopeful, Selik brushed past Father Bernard, and his eyes scanned the hospitium, finally locking on the tall, tunic-clad figure bent over a patient.

Thank You, God.

Oh, ye of little faith. When will you learn?

Selik gave a small salute upward and smiled. Then, frozen in place, he gazed at Rain longingly, wanting to savor the wonderful gift God—or whoever—had just given him.

Rain finally stood. With her back to him, she put a hand to the small of her back, as if to stretch tired muscles. Her body went rigidly still then, as if sensing danger, and she turned abruptly. She inhaled sharply and her eyes widened.

"Selik?" she whispered.

For one brief moment, her golden eyes lit with happiness at seeing him, but they immediately hardened, turning both wounded and angry at the same time.

He stepped closer and reached out for her, but she backed away. "Don't touch me," she ordered.

He halted and tilted his head in question.

"So you finally came back," she sneered.

"I came as soon as I could. Athelstan insisted I stay and—"

"For two months?" she asked incredulously.

Selik felt his face grow warm. "I sent a letter."

"I never got it," she retorted disbelievingly, glaring at him haughtily. "Aren't you supposed to be in exile or something? Won't King Athelstan set his men on you?"

"Athelstan has given me permission to live in Northumbria again."

Her brow creased in confusion. "Why would he do that?"

"I pledged my loyalty to the Saxon king. And my services, if ever needed."

"You gave your oath to the Saxon enemy?" she asked, clearly amazed.

"I have no real hatred for the Saxons themselves, just Steven. I know, I know, 'tis not what I always proclaimed. You taught me that, dearling."

He saw the pulse in her neck jump at his endearment, and with a barely suppressed grin, he stored the information away for future use. "Leastways, Athelstan is not so *very* bad."

"Why have you come back, Selik?"

"Because I love you, Rain. I forgive you for all you did with Steven. In time, I will forget. Just come back."

Rain did not soften and jump into his arms, as he desperately wanted. Instead, she stiffened and her eyes flashed.

"And where is Steven?"

"He fled to Frankland."

"And will you go after him?" she asked in a cold voice.

He stared at her levelly, unable to comprehend the anger in her voice. "Not yet."

She launched herself at him then, pummeling his chest, scratching at his face. "You bastard! You stupid bastard!"

"What? What?" He could not understand her anger. Finally, he was able to hold her forearms immobile at her sides, his body a distance from hers to avoid her kicking feet.

To his dismay, quite an audience of intrigued clerics had gathered nearby, listening to their every word.

"Why are you so angry, my love?" he asked softly, trying to ignore his audience.

"Because you're as blind as a bat and can't see the facts in front of your face. Because you're still continuing this bloody vendetta against Steven. I hate the evil man. I wish he were dead, but I'm not going to ruin my life going after him. Nothing's changed at all, has it, you jerk? And I'm not your love. I'm not your anything. Not anymore. By the way, where's Blanche?"

"I do not know where Blanche is. Perchance in Winchester. I think I saw her with one of Athelstan's guards."

"Did you just pass her off to another man, like a possession?" she asked venomously.

He was beginning to understand. "Rain, I was never with Blanche—not in *that* way. I just pretended for your benefit. I saw you with Steven, and I wanted to hurt you back."

Rain stared at him, disbelieving, for a moment before she swung an arm wildly and punched him in the stomach.

"Oomph!" He bent over from the waist, then wheezed out, "Why did you do that?"

"To hurt you, you bastard. Just like you hurt me."

Selik stared at her as he rubbed his stomach, wanting more than anything in the world to touch her face, to kiss her lips, to show her how much she meant to him. How sorry he was for all the pain he had inflicted on her. "I love you, Rain."

"That's not what you said before I left you in Winchester."

"I am truly, truly sorry. For all the hurts I caused."

Tears streamed, unheeded, down her face, and he placed

a gentle hand on her shoulder. "Ah, sweetling, do not weep. Please. I am here now."

She shrugged his hand away angrily. "Too late. Too damn late." Her head bowed in dejection before she whispered brokenly, "I waited and waited for you. And the only way I could survive was to stop loving you. It's too late."

"Nay! 'Tis never too late," he cried. "I love you." He grabbed her arms and shook her gently. "Do you hear me? I love you. I love you."

When she did not respond, he finally stopped and said wearily, "Come back to the farmstead with me. In time, we will be able to settle our differences."

"No. Now that you're back, I'm staying here in Jorvik with Gyda. I won't live in the same house as you again."

His heart skipped a beat, sensing some message she did not speak aloud. He narrowed his eyes. "Do you fear weakening in my presence?"

"Hah! Still the supreme egotist!"

"You love me. I know you do. You have just buried it for a time, as I did my feelings afore you came into my life."

She refused to respond, but he saw her lips tremble and knew he was making some headway. He just needed time. "If you prefer, stay with Gyda for now. We will start over again from the beginning. I will woo you like no other woman has been courted in the world."

She almost smiled, but then she shook her head as if to clear it. "I'm going back, Selik," she told him gently.

"Nay, I will not allow it."

"You can't stop me," she snapped with exasperation. "I'll continue to go back to the Coppergate site every day until it finally works. And eventually it will send me back. I know it will." Her voice was not quite as certain as her strong words.

Well, God, what do we do now?

What's this "we" business? It's up to you now.

Selik poked a finger in her chest and grinned, having a sudden inspiration. "Nay, you will not leave. Wouldst like to place a wager on it, *my love*?"

With that, he pulled her into his arms and kissed her ravenously, slanting his lips over hers, savoring the sweet taste of her breath, the heat of her skin. At first she struggled; then she too succumbed to the all-consuming passion they both shared. With a soft moan, she opened her mouth to his.

When he finally pulled away, staring hungrily at her parted lips and misty eyes, he urged rawly, "Come home with me, Rain."

She seemed to waver, then pushed at his chest. "No. It's too late."

He gave her one more quick kiss, then released her.

"I will be back on the morrow. Be here."

"I will probably be gone by then," she stated stubbornly.

"Do you think so? I do not. By the by, what kind of fabric would you like for your wedding dress?"

"Wedding dress?" she sputtered. "Are you listening to me? Get this into your thick head. I . . . am . . . leaving."

"Did I tell you I adopted Adam?"

Her eyes widened with shock. Good. Best to keep the wench guessing. He used to know that about women. He had forgotten over the years. Well, he would have to hone his skills now.

He continued. "Didst know that the little scamp stowed away on a ship and came all the way to Southampton to find me? To bring me back to you?"

Her mouth hung open now. Another good sign, he decided, and went for the kill. "Adam will, no doubt, insist on being my—what did you tell me that time about modern wedding rituals? Oh, I remember—my best man."

Rain made a strange gurgling sound.

"And Adela can be your wench-of-honor."

He turned then and left, without another word. He had much work to do before dark.

How many times can a heart break? . . .

Rain stared at Selik's departing body. She could barely keep herself from running after him. He looked so damned wonderful.

He no longer had the magnificent long blond hair that she had loved, but he looked just as good in the short style which barely came to his neck. Somehow it drew more attention to the sharp edges of his cheekbones and jaw, made him more handsome, less beautiful. A deep blue, short-sleeved tunic stretched across his wide shoulders, going only to his knees. The well-defined cords in his muscled calves and thighs stood out under his tight braies as he walked away. A thick, silver-linked belt accented his narrow waist.

Would this be the picture Rain would take back with her to the future?

Just before he opened the doorway to the church, Selik turned and his eyes, a startling gray against his tanned face, held hers for a long moment. As if in promise.

She'd told him that she didn't love him anymore, but that wasn't true. She loved him more than life itself.

She had to go home. And it wasn't just stubbornness that made her stick to that decision. Even though she could never forget Selik's lack of trust and ugly words at Winchester, she had already forgiven him for that. And his still harboring that mistaken notion of her infidelity—well, she could even accept that, hurtful as it was.

But Selik intended to continue his blood feud with Steven of Gravely. What kind of future would they have if she stayed? The next time someone hurt him, whether it was Steven or some other enemy, which would inevitably happen in these violent times, he would be off on another round of vengeance. The cycle was never ending. And she refused to be part of it by staying in his life. She just couldn't bear such continuing pain.

Trust in love, the voice said.

But Rain was afraid to trust anymore.

Oooh, he didn't fight fair . . .

"Well, what did ye expect?" an exasperated Ubbi exclaimed back at the farmstead when Selik told him of his failure with Rain. "Ye are blind as a bat, just as she said.

And I thought ye had more sense than to go blundering after her so clumsily."

"If I am willing to forgive Rain for her—for her betrayal with Steven, why can't she forgive my harsh words?"

"Betrayal! Betrayal! Is that what ye said to her? Well, no wonder she rejected ye!"

"Explain yourself," Selik demanded.

"Do ye have any idea what condition my lady was in when she returned from Winchester? Her body was one big bruise from her shoulders to her toes. And all because of you!"

Stunned, Selik demanded that Ubbi tell him everything.

When he finished, Selik raked his hands through his hair distractedly. "But I saw them together."

"Ye saw what ye wanted to see."

"Why did Athelstan not tell me?"

"Because the mistress begged him not to tell you."

Selik felt a huge lump forming in his throat, and his heart beat so fast he could barely breathe. "Why? Why did she convince the king to keep this information from me?" he asked, still disbelieving.

"Because she said ye would blame yerself fer not protectin' her, just as ye wasted so many years blamin' yerself fer Astrid's and Thorkel's deaths."

Selik exhaled loudly, as if he had been kicked in the stomach. *Not protecting her.* Selik repeated Ubbi's words silently. A loud buzzing roared in his ears and he braced himself. He feared what he would hear next, but he had to know. "Tell me all of it."

For an hour, Ubbi talked, sparing him no details, not of the degradations Steven had subjected Rain to, nor the condition of her body once Athelstan and Elgiva found her finally.

"Why did she not scream for help?" Selik asked finally. "The castle is not that large."

Ubbi just stared at him.

"To protect me?" he asked in horror.

Ubbi shook his head in disgust, no doubt thinking Selik's

self-recriminations would be punishment enough for his lack of faith in the woman he loved.

Ubbi was right.

Selik banged his bruised fists, then his head, against the timber walls of the barn. How could he have been so blind? How could he have been so cruel?

Because you're human.

Selik stormed out of the barn and turned his horse for Jorvik. He had to talk to Rain immediately.

Gyda's house was dark and silent when he arrived, everyone already having retired for the evening. He waved aside a guard who recognized him and entered without knocking. Weaving his way through the dark in the familiar household, he made his way toward the upper guest room.

Rain lay on the small pallet, awake and staring at the ceiling. Candlelight flickered over her golden features, and Selik stopped momentarily in the doorway, frozen by his rapidly beating heart and his love for this woman from the future.

Rain jerked upright when she noticed his presence. "What are you doing here, Selik?" she asked coldly.

"Forgive me," he said softly, stepping into the room.

"Forgive *you*? I thought you were going to forgive me," she remarked coldly, standing and moving to the other side of the room, away from him.

"I kn-know," he choked out. "I know what Steven did to you, and I will never forgive myself for the things I said, for my lack of trust."

"Oh, great! One more thing to add to your load of guilt! Do me a favor, Selik, just forget the whole thing. I'm the one who was harmed by Steven. Let it go." Her shoulders slumped in defeat, and she looked up at him bleakly. In a choked voice, she added, "Let *me* go."

"That I can never do, heartling. *Never!* Now that I have found you, I will never let you go."

On those words, he turned and left Rain to her sleep. But sleep eluded her the rest of the night as she pondered all he'd told her, just now and earlier that day. Imagine, little Adam stowing away on a ship. And Selik adopting him. And what about Selik pledging himself to King Athelstan?

At least, she could go home knowing she'd accomplished some good in this mission back in time.

With a troubled mind, Rain doggedly headed toward Coppergate the next afternoon, having finally fallen into a troubled sleep and not awakening until late morning. She knew that if she put off her decision to go back to the future, she might never summon the courage again.

But an odd thing happened. She couldn't find the Coppergate site. Day after day, for the past few weeks, she'd gone to the site, finding it with no trouble. But suddenly it had disappeared. Well, not exactly disappeared. Where the abandoned building had once stood was now an eight-foot-high timber fence patrolled by two armed guards.

No! He wouldn't have. Would he?

Rain walked up to one man and said, "I need to go inside that fence."

"Nay. 'Tis forbidden for anyone to enter."

"Who says so?"

"The new owner."

Rain folded her arms across her chest and glared up at the burly guard. "And who might that be?"

"Master Selik of Godwineshire."

"Godwine . . . Godwineshire?" Rain stammered out.

"Yea, 'tis the new name for my master's lands outside Jorvik—the Land of God's Friend. If ye want to enter this property, ye will have to discuss it with him."

"Oh, you can be sure I will."

Rain rode Godsend the two miles beyond the city to Selik's farmstead, rehearsing the entire time the tongue-lashing she would give the arrogant Viking. Plagued with painful memories, she refused to look as she passed the cow byre where Selik had told her he loved her for the first time. He had made sweet love to her on that very spot. It seemed so long ago.

As she got closer to his holdings, she noticed a lot of unusual activity. Some workers were plowing the long-dormant fields. Others were rebuilding the house and doing repairs on the barn.

Two more cows and several horses grazed in a temporarily fenced area. She even thought she heard the grunting of pigs and the quacking of ducks.

She dismounted from her horse and was immediately surrounded by children, even Adam who waved to her from the background. He was leaning lazily against the barn with a piece of straw in his mouth—probably "supervising" again.

"Where's Selik?" she asked him.

He motioned toward the rectangular Viking-style house—a very large house—which was quickly taking shape, its sides already half erected.

She found Selik cutting timbers on the other side of the structure, wearing only low-slung braies and leather shoes.

Oh, Lord.

He stopped working when he saw her approaching and wiped the sweat from his brow with a forearm—a beautifully muscled forearm, it was, too.

Oh, Lord.

He smiled.

Oh, Lord.

She forced herself to look at some point over his shoulder. "What the hell do you think you're doing?"

"Building you a house."

"What?" She looked quickly back at the building with surprise. That wasn't what she'd meant. "The Coppergate site. I'm talking about that."

"Oh, I decided to buy the land. Methinks it will be a good property to hold for future gain," he said with bald-faced innocence. "What think you?"

"I think you're crazy. I think your brains have turned to mush. I think you have some nerve. I think—"

"So, what day do you want to get married?"

"Argh!" she screamed, pulling at her hair.

"Do you think Bernie would perform the ceremony for us?"

"You are brain-dead. Do you hear me?"

"Methinks your screeching can be heard all the way to Jorvik, sweetling."

"And don't call me that name anymore."

He grinned. "Oh, did I tell you that King Athelstan asked me an odd question afore I left Winchester? He wanted to know how to find a G-spot. Seems someone was talking to Elgiva and—"

She walked away, face flushing hotly, and didn't hear the rest of his sentence, but it sounded very explicit.

The next day, Selik showed up at the hospitium, looking absolutely gorgeous in a gray wool tunic with black braies and mantle. His eyes sparkled almost as much as the twelve children who stood beside him in brand-new clothes and shoes, their faces spit-clean from recent baths—even Adam's hair was slicked back wetly. She wondered how Selik had managed that. Even she had trouble luring the children to bathe.

"I threw them all in the horse trough," he remarked dryly in answer to her unvoiced question.

"What do you want, Selik?" she asked, looking over to Bernie and Father Theodric, who were frowning in her direction, not liking all the company in the hospitium.

"You," he said somberly, his eyes no longer glittering with mischief. "Just you."

The following day Ubbi came, shifting uncomfortably. "Please, mistress, will ye not come home? He is driving everyone mad with all his demands."

Rain didn't need to ask who the "he" was.

"He finished the house, fixed up the leaks in the barn, plowed two hectares of land, took in five more orphans, is fixin' to—"

"He took in five more orphans?" Rain asked.

"Yea. Saw 'em in the streets and said he could not resist. Next, he plans to build a house jist fer the orphans."

"He does?"

"Yea. Plans to call it Rain's House. Now me, I be thinkin' of goin' to Norway."

"Ubbi! You would never leave Selik." *Rain's House?*

"Yea, I would. Like a bear, he is, when he is not workin'. Cannot stand to be still. No doubt, he starts thinkin' 'bout you and—"

"Ubbi, did Selik send you here?"

He glanced from side to side, everywhere but at her intent eyes.

"Tell the jerk I'm not coming back."

He groaned and turned back for home with slumped shoulders.

The fourth day, Adam came alone and followed her around, grumbling, "Yer poisoning him, ye know?"

"Who?"

"Me father. Who else?"

Rain frowned, then realized that Adam was referring to Selik.

"He keeps eatin' all them god-awful Lifesavers ye made, even when they make 'im gag. They be crampin' his stomach somethin' terrible, but he sez if a man loves a woman he should be willin' to eat her cookin'."

Rain couldn't help but burst out laughing. "Adam, you are making that up."

"Are ye accusin' me of lyin'?"

"Like a rug."

The fifth day, Gyda came, complaining about Tyra and all the time she spent at the farmstead helping Selik with the children. "I fear the neighbors will begin talking of her unseemly conduct. How will she find a husband if she spends so much time alone with Selik? Can you talk to her, Rain?"

Not in a million years!

Rain shouldn't have been jealous of Tyra. But she was.

She should have wanted Selik to find another woman to love after she was gone. But she didn't.

The sixth day, Ella arrived with a beautiful green silk tunic with gold embroidery along the edges and sleeves.

"What's that for?" Rain asked.

"Me weddin' to Ubbi. I want ye to wear it fer me weddin'. Will ye be me witness?"

"Ella! How wonderful! Ubbi never told me. The stinker!"

"We are goin' to have it outdoors at the farmstead. Will ye come?"

"Of course."

That sound you hear is sweet surrender . . .

Rain rode out to the farmstead with Gyda and Tyra the day of the wedding. Tyra looked like a combination of Jessica Alba and Reese Witherspoon, sitting on her white palfrey in a stunning bluesilk tunic. Rain felt more like a tall Bette Midler.

A festival atmosphere reigned at the farm. Long trestle tables set up with tons of food were being arranged by servants whom Selik must have hired; a harpist was playing in the background, and the farm was crowded with guests whom Rain recognized from Gyda's neighborhood in the city. Even Father Bernard was there, probably to perform the ceremony.

A trellis-type apparatus had been erected before a makeshift altar decorated with hundreds of spring flowers. Gyda sat on a bench nearby weaving some of the flowers into a circlet for the bride's head.

"What do you think?"

Rain turned to see Selik standing behind her, very close behind her. She stepped away. "Very nice, Selik. I don't know how you managed this in such a short time."

"Gyda and Ella helped."

She nodded, uncomfortable under his intense gaze. He wore a black tunic over black braies and boots, the stark

color set off only by his pale hair and a silver belt and armlets.

She licked her lips, desperately wanting to reach out and
touch the jagged scar on his face and the word *Rage* on his
arm. His eyes riveted on her mouth, intense with yearning,
and Rain's knees almost buckled under the onslaught of
warmth that washed over her.

"I love you, Rain."

"No," she whimpered and forced herself to break eye
contact. Her eyes scanned the farmyard, taking in all the
improvements—the completed house, new outbuildings and
fences. He must have had a great deal more money than
she'd thought to do so much so quickly.

"Would you like to see your house?"

She groaned. "It's not *my* house, Selik."

"Athelstan gave you this property, I understand. So truly,
the house is yours, even if you do not want me."

Don't want you? Don't want you? Rain felt as if she were
sinking fast and sought some anchor, any anchor. Her eyes
darted around the farmyard, then stopped dead. Could that
be Eirik and Tykir standing there talking to Ubbi? Why
hadn't anyone told her they were coming?

She heard horses approaching the farm and turned.
Guards wearing the golden dragon emblem of the House of
Wessex accompanied a well-dressed woman. Elgiva! Rain's
head began to ring with confusion.

Something was not right in this picture.

Tykir and Eirik might come for Ubbi's wedding, but not
Elgiva. And the floral head circlet that Gyda was weaving—
well, somehow Rain couldn't picture Ella wearing such a
frivolous hair adornment. Her eyes caught a swath of green
cloth draped around the altar, and she looked down at her
dress. The same fabric.

She turned on Selik angrily.

"Now, Rain, be reasonable," he cautioned, seeing the
dawning understanding on her face.

"You *didn't*, Selik. Surely you didn't plan all this without my consent."

"Come, I want to show you that building over there," he said, taking her arm firmly and pulling her along beside him before she had a chance to create a scene.

The rectangular building, much smaller than the house and barn, sat by itself near the edge of the clearing. He shoved her inside and barred the door.

Her eyes quickly scanned the large room. Benches lined one side, several pallets covered the floors, and at the end a high table and built-in shelves lined the walls. The pungent smell of new wood filled the air.

"Selik, you can't lock me in here forever. Let me go."

"I will, but first I want to show you this new . . . building."

"Is this the orphanage Ubbi spoke of?"

Selik looked surprised. He leaned against the doorjamb, watching her every reaction like a hawk. "Nay, 'tis much too small for that, if you would look closer."

"Then what?" she asked, puzzled.

"A clinic. For you." He looked at her with such hope in his eyes, almost childlike in open yearning for approval. "You said once you would like to open your own small hospitium—clinic, I mean—and, well, I did not know exactly what an examination table looked like, but I figured waist-high would be sufficient. And the shelves could hold your healing herbs and receipts. And—"

"You planned my wedding *and* my clinic? Without asking me first?" She couldn't help herself. She started to cry.

"You do not like it," he said, clearly hurt. "Ah, well, 'tis not worth weeping over. Hush now, I only wanted to please you."

"The clinic is wonderful. It's you. You're impossible."

"I know," he said with absolutely no guilt.

"Selik, you can't do underhanded things like this."

"You did."

"What do you mean?"

"You kidnapped me when you thought 'twas for my own good. You came after me in Winchester when you thought 'twas for my own good. You even bartered your pain when you thought 'twas for my own good." Selik said the last words bleakly, his voice full of self-recrimination.

"And you think that excuses your planning my wedding without my knowledge? Because you think it's for my own good?"

"Yea," he said and smiled broadly, folding his arms across his chest.

Rain shook her head in wonder. "That's the most convoluted, twisted logic I've ever heard in all my life," she said, laughing.

"I love you," he said softly.

She closed her eyes, trying to wipe out Selik's image saying those wonderful words. She couldn't. She clenched her fists and scrunched her eyes tighter.

"I love you," he repeated.

Her pulse raced, and she felt an odd humming in her ears, rather like a wedding march. She opened her eyes and pleaded, "Selik, even if I could forget everything you've done, it doesn't erase the fact that, at the first major injustice that arises, you are going to go off seeking revenge. It's the kind of man you are."

He smiled and breathed a deep sigh of relief, as if he'd just won a major battle. "'Tis odd you should mention that." He pushed her onto a stool by the examining table and laid a heavy parchment in front of her. "There."

She looked down at the thick paper with the indecipherable scratchings. "Selik, I can't read medieval English. What is it?"

"A wedding contract." He ignored her gasp and went on blithely, "I will read it for you."

She looked up at him in amazement, and the humming in her head grew louder.

"I promise to love you forever, of course."

"Of course."

The humming intensified.

"And I will give you a dozen children."

"A dozen? There are already a dozen children running around out there."

"Nay, I mean a dozen more of your own."

She slanted a cynical look up at him.

"Do you doubt my ability?"

"Never," she laughed. "It's my ability to care for so many children that I doubt."

He waved a hand airily. "I will help you."

Rain made a scoffing sound.

"And I promise that every morning you will awaken with a smile on your face."

"You are outrageous."

"I know. 'Tis one of the wonderful things about me."

"Selik, you have a way of making me smile even when I'm so mad at you that I could spit."

He beamed. "'Tis another wonderful asset of mine.

"Would you like me to read the rest for you?" he asked, smiling at her with such open adoration that Rain felt blessed. "I think you will like this part. It says you may stick needles in me if you want . . ."

She laughed.

". . . and I promise to never embark on any act of deliberate revenge or violence without my wife's consent. Even when it involves my own beloved wife and children."

Rain put a palm to her chest in dismay. She was sinking fast, and Selik was her only anchor.

His face turned suddenly somber then, and he knelt on one knee to bring himself eye-level with her. "Will you marry me, Rain?"

The music in her head turned into a full-blown orchestra.

"Yes," she said softly, taking his face between her hands and kissing him gently.

At first, Selik was not sure he had heard Rain right. He stared at her, stunned. But then her single word sank in, and he let out a whoop of delight, "Thank God!"

You're welcome.

"Oh, dearling, I have been trying so hard to please you. I truly am trying to change. But still I was fearful you would never give in. 'Tis about time."

You can say that again.

Happily-ever-afters sometimes take a thousand years . . .

Later that night, after the most wonderful wedding in history, Rain lay in bed in her new home with her new husband. She didn't think she could be any happier.

"Are you sure you can be content staying in the past, sweetling? Will you not miss your mother?" Selik asked, leaning up on an elbow to gaze down at her.

"Believe me, my mother will understand."

"And your hospital? Someday you may regret the lack of more advanced medicines and tools."

Rain shook her head. Her heart filled almost to overflowing at the mere thought that this wonderful, handsome, outrageous man was her husband. How could he think she'd want anything more? "I can do a great deal of good here in the clinic you built for me. We both can."

"I worry that you will be sorry someday."

"Selik, I love you. As long as I have you, I'll never be sorry."

"I love you, too, dearling," he whispered, nuzzling her neck and then lower, and still lower. He chuckled and raised his head suddenly. "I forgot to show you your bride gift."

"Selik, you have already built me a house and a clinic. I think that's more than enough."

"Yea, but this is more . . . personal. Since you were so gracious to mention the G-spot to me when we first met, I am going to introduce you to the famous Viking S-spot." He tickled her in a very sensitive spot for emphasis.

"I don't believe there is such a thing."

"Hah! Woe to the unbelievers!" he said, quoting the infernal voice, which had disappeared once Rain agreed to be his wife. He ducked his head, laughing. "The tricky thing about the S-spot is that it can only be found with the tongue."

Rain gasped. "Oh . . . oh, I think you've found it."

And she soon became a believer.

And the god-spirit looked down and was pleased.

READER LETTER

Dear Reader:

A wise editor once told me that in the best novels, the writer makes the reader laugh, as well as cry. That's what I hope you experienced in reading *The Outlaw Viking*. If I tugged at your heartstrings over my tormented hero, Selik, and laughed at the cluelessness of men throughout the ages, I will have succeeded.

A funny thing occurred to me when reviewing this book after fifteen years since it was first published. Some things in life age well. Wine. Scotch. Men and women with good bones and healthy physiques. Well-crafted furniture. Master paintings. And books. Yes, I said books.

As I've been updating seventeen of my backlist titles for reissue in the coming year, I must say with a shameless lack of humility that my books do age well, especially *The Outlaw Viking*. There is, of course, the need to update . . . Dolly Parton would not be considered the epitome of the sexy lady today; nor would Kevin Costner, nor, God forbid! Mel Gibson, appeal to the younger reader. Even so, in the process of these new readings, I have been remarkably surprised at how enjoyable they are, even after all these years.

And that doesn't just apply to *my* books. Think about the books on your keeper shelves. Aren't there some that withstand the tests of time, that merit repeat readings? Can you tell how much I love books?

The Outlaw Viking is the second in a loosely linked series (the books stand alone and can be read out of order), the first of which is *The Reluctant Viking*. After that comes *The Tarnished Lady*, *The Bewitched Viking*, *The Blue Viking*, *My Fair Viking* (retitled *The Viking's Captive*), and *A Tale of Two Vikings*. Two new books in that series have also been published recently, *Viking in Love* and *The Viking Takes a Knight*, with more books yet to come.

I love hearing from readers, and, as always, I wish you smiles in your reading.

Sandra Hill
PO Box 604
State College, PA 16804
Shill733@aol.com
www.sandrahill.net

GLOSSARY

Alban lands—Celtic Scotland.
Behaettie—scalping, to prevent the enemy from entering Valhalla.
Battle of Brunanburh—937 A.D., Anglo-Saxon victory over the combined Norse and Scottish forces.
Baudekin—silk brocade interwoven with gold and silver threads.
Berserker—an ancient Norse warrior who fought in a frenzied rage during battle.
Braies—slim pants worn by men, breeches.
Brynja—mail armor.
Castellan—one who oversees a castle in the absence of the castle's lord.
Churl—a peasant.
Coppergate—a busy, prosperous section of tenth-century York, where merchants and craftsmen set up their stalls for trading.
Culdee—an ascetic monk.
Cumbria—a section of southwestern Britain.
Eoforwic—Roman (and later Saxon) name for York.

Ell—a measure, usually of cloth, equal to 45 inches.

Halberd—a weapon consisting of a long shaft with a doubled-edged axe blade on one end and a spearhead on the other.

Hauberk—a long, knee-length defensive shirt, often made of chain links or leather.

Hectare—a unit of measure equal to approximately two-and-a-half acres of land.

Hedeby—a market town located in present-day Germany.

Hide—a primitive measure of land, equaling the normal holding that would support a peasant and his family, roughly 120 arable acres.

Hird—permanent troops, war band.

Hospitium—a hospital, often attached to a minster.

Jerkin—a sleeveless, collarless, short jacket.

Jomsviking—an elite group of Viking mercenaries.

Jorvik—Viking-Age York, known by the Saxons as Eoforwic.

Mancus/es—a weight of gold of about seventy grains or equal to six shillings or thirty pennies/pence (one shilling=five pennies).

Mercer—a dealer in textile fabrics.

Mercia—an early English kingdom located in central and southern Britain.

Miklagard—Viking name for Constantinople.

Minster—a church, often connected with a monastic establishment.

Motte—a flat-topped hill in which a castle was built.

Nithing—one of the greatest Norse insults, indicating a man is less than nothing.

Norsemandy—tenth-century name for Normandy.

Samite—heavy silk fabric, sometimes interwoven with gold.

Sennight—one week.

Strathclhyde—a region of southern Scotland.

Thegn—a member of the aristocratic class of men ranking between earls and ordinary freemen, and granted lands by the king or by lords for military service.

Thrall—a slave.
Wattle and daub—an early method of building.
Wergild (or wergeld)—a man's worth.
Witan (or Witenagemot)—the king's council of advisors, precursor to the English parliament.

Can't get enough of *USA Today* and
New York Times bestselling
author Sandra Hill?
Turn the page for glimpses of her amazing
books. From cowboys to Vikings, Navy
SEALs to Southern bad boys, every one
of Sandra's books has her unique blend of
passion, creativity, and unparalled wit.

Welcome to the World of Sandra Hill!

The Viking Takes a Knight

⊘

*F*or John of Hawk's Lair, the unexpected appearance of a beautiful woman at his door is always welcome. Yet the arrival of this alluring Viking woman, Ingrith Sigrundottir—with her enchanting smile and inviting curves—is different . . . for she comes accompanied by a herd of unruly orphans. And Ingrith needs more than the legendary knight's hospitality; she needs protection. For among her charges is a small boy with a claim to the throne—a dangerous distinction when murderous King Edgar is out hunting for Viking blood.

A man of passion, John will keep them safe—but in exchange, he wants something very dear indeed: Ingrith's heart, to be taken with the very first meeting of their lips . . .

Viking in Love

⟐

*C*aedmon of Larkspur *was the most loathsome lout* Breanne had ever encountered. When she arrived at his castle with her sisters, they were greeted by an estate gone wild, while Caedmon laid abed after a night of ale. But Breanne must endure, as they are desperately in need of protection . . . and he is quite handsome.

After nine long months in the king's service, all Caedmon wanted was peace, not five Viking princesses running about his keep. And the fiery redhead who burst into his chamber was the worst of them all. He should kick her out, but he has a far better plan for Breanne of Stoneheim—one that will leave her a Viking in lust.

The Reluctant Viking

✧

The self-motivation tape was supposed to help Ruby Jordan solve her problems, not create new ones. Instead, she was lulled into an era of hard-bodied warriors and fair maidens. But the world ten centuries in the past didn't prove to be all mead and mirth. Even as Ruby tried to update medieval times, she had to deal with a Norseman whose view of women was stuck in the Dark Ages. And what was worse, brawny Thork had her husband's face, habits, and desire to avoid Ruby. Determined not to lose the same man twice, Ruby planned a bold seduction that would conquer the reluctant Viking—and make him an eager captive of her love.

The Outlaw Viking

🔸

As tall and striking as the Valkyries of legend, Dr. Rain Jordan was proud of her Norse ancestors despite their warlike ways. But she can't believe it when she finds herself on a nightmarish battle-field, forced to save the barbarian of her dreams.

He was a wild-eyed warrior whose deadly sword could slay a dozen Saxons with a single swing, yet Selik couldn't control the saucy wench from the future. If Selik wasn't careful, the stunning siren was sure to capture his heart and make a warrior of love out of **The Outlaw Viking**.

The Tarnished Lady

Banished from polite society, Lady Eadyth of Hawk's Lair spent her days hidden under a voluminous veil, tending her bees. But when her lands are threatened, Lady Eadyth sought a husband to offer her the protection of his name.

Notorious for loving—and leaving—the most beautiful damsels in the land, Eirik of Ravenshire was England's most virile bachelor. Yet when the mysterious lady offered him a vow of chaste matrimony in exchange for revenge against his most hated enemy, Eirik couldn't refuse. But the lusty knight's plans went awry when he succumbed to the sweet sting of the tarnished lady's love.

The Bewitched Viking

✧

Even fierce Norse warriors have bad days. 'Twas enough to drive a sane Viking mad, the things Tykir Thorksson was forced to do—capturing a red-headed virago, putting up with the flock of sheep that follows her everywhere, chasing off her bumbling brothers. But what could a man expect from the sorceress who had put a kink in the King of Norway's most precious body part? If that wasn't bad enough, Tykir was beginning to realize he wasn't at all immune to the enchantment of brash red hair and freckles. Perhaps he could reverse the spell and hold her captive, not with his mighty sword, but with a Viking man's greatest magic: a wink and smile.

The Blue Viking

❧

*For Rurik the Viking, life has not been worth living since he left Maire of the Moors. Oh, it's not that he misses her fiery red tresses or kissable lips. Nay, it's the embarrassing blue zigzag tattoo she put on his face after their one wild night of loving. For a fierce warrior who prides himself on his immense height, his expertise in bedsport, and his well-toned muscles, this blue streak is the last straw. In the end, he'll bring the witch to heel, or die trying. Mayhap he'll even beg her to wed . . . so long as she can promise he'll no longer be . . . **The Blue Viking**.*

The Viking's Captive

(originally titled MY FAIR VIKING)

⊛

*T*yra, Warrior Princess. *She is too tall, too loud, too fierce* to be a good catch. But her ailing father has decreed that her four younger sisters—delicate, mild-mannered, and beautiful—cannot be wed 'til Tyra consents to take a husband. And then a journey to save her father's life brings Tyra face to face with Adam the Healer. A god in human form, he's tall, muscled, perfectly proportioned. Too bad Adam refuses to fall in with her plans—so what's a lady to do but truss him up, toss him over her shoulder, and sail off into the sunset to live happily ever after.

A Tale of Two Vikings

⌘

*T*oste and Vagn Ivarsson are identical Viking twins, about to face Valhalla together, following a tragic battle, or maybe something even more tragic: being separated for the first time in their thirty and one years. Alas, even the bravest Viking must eventually leave his best buddy behind and do battle with that most fearsome of all opponents—the love of his life. And what if that love was Helga the Homely, or Lady Esme, the world's oldest novice nun?

A Tale of Two Vikings will give you twice the tears, twice the sizzle, and twice the laughter . . . and make you wish for your very own Viking.

The Last Viking

⚬

*H*e was six feet, four inches of pure, unadulterated
male. He wore nothing but a leather tunic,
and he was standing in Professor Meredith Fos-
ter's living room. The medieval historian told
herself he was part of a practical joke, but with
his wide gold belt, ancient language, and callused
hands, the brawny stranger seemed so . . . authen-
tic. And as he helped her fulfill her grandfather's
dream of re-creating a Viking ship, he awakened
her to dreams of her own. Until she wondered
if the hand of fate had thrust her into the loving
arms of . . . **The Last Viking**.

Truly, Madly Viking

&

A Viking named Joe? Jorund Ericsson is a tenth-century Viking warrior who lands in a modern mental hospital. Maggie McBride is the lucky psychologist who gets to "treat" the gorgeous Norseman, whom she mistakenly calls Joe.

You've heard of *One Flew Over the Cuckoo's Nest.* But how about *A Viking Flew Over the Cuckoo's Nest?* The question is: Who's the cuckoo in this nest? And why is everyone laughing?

The Very Virile Viking

❦

*M*agnus Ericsson *is a simple man. He loves the* smell of fresh-turned dirt after springtime plowing. He loves the feel of a soft woman under him in the bed furs. He loves the heft of a good sword in his fighting arm.

But, Holy Thor, what he does not relish is the bothersome brood of children he's been saddled with. Or the mysterious happenstance that strands him in a strange new land—the kingdom of *Holly Wood.* Here is a place where the folks think he is an *act-whore* (whatever that is), and the woman of his dreams—a winemaker of all things—fails to accept that he is her soul mate . . . a man of exceptional talents, not to mention . . . **A Very Virile Viking.**

Wet & Wild

∝

What do you get when you cross a Viking with a Navy SEAL? A warrior with the fierce instincts of the past and the rigorous training of America's most elite fighting corps? A totally buff hero-in-the-making who hasn't had a woman in roughly a thousand years? A dyed-in-the-wool romantic with a hopeless crush? Whatever you get, women everywhere can't wait to meet him, and his story is guaranteed to be . . . **Wet & Wild**.

Hot & Heavy

❧

*I*n and out, that's the goal as Lt. Ian MacLean prepares for his special ops mission. He leads a team of highly trained Navy SEALs, the toughest, buffest fighting men in the world and he has nothing to lose. Madrene comes from a time a thousand years before he was born, and she has no idea she's landed in the future. After tying him up, the beautiful shrew gives him a tongue-lashing that makes a drill sergeant sound like a kindergarten teacher. Then she lets him know she has her own special way of dealing with over-confident males, and things get . . . **Hot & Heavy**.

Frankly, My Dear . . .

&

*L*ost in the Bayou . . . *Selene had three great passions:* men, food, and *Gone with the Wind*. But the glamorous model always found herself starving— for both nourishment and affection. Weary of the petty world of high fashion, she headed to New Orleans for one last job before she began a new life. Little did she know that her new life would include a brand-new time—about 150 years ago! Selene can't get her fill of the food—or an alarmingly handsome man. Dark and brooding, James Baptiste was the only lover she gave a damn about. And with God as her witness, she vowed never to go without the man she loved again.

Sweeter Savage Love

⊛

*T*he stroke of surprisingly gentle hands, the flash of fathomless blue eyes, the scorch of white-hot kisses . . . Once again, Dr. Harriet Ginoza was swept away into rapturous fantasy. The modern psychologist knew the object of her desire was all she should despise, yet time after time, she lost herself in visions of a dangerously handsome rogue straight out of a historical romance. Harriet never believed that her dream lover would cause her any trouble, but then a twist of fate cast her back to the Old South and she met him in the flesh. To her disappointment, Etienne Baptiste refused to fulfill any of her secret wishes. If Harriet had any hope of making her amorous dreams become passionate reality, she'd have to seduce this charmer with a sweeter savage love than she'd imagined possible . . . and savor every minute of it.

The Love Potion

&

*F*ame and fortune are surely only a swallow away when Dr. Sylvie Fontaine discovers a chemical formula guaranteed to attract the opposite sex. Though her own love life is purely hypothetical, the shy chemist's professional future is assured . . . as soon as she can find a human guinea pig. But bad boy Lucien LeDeux—best known as the Swamp Lawyer—is more than she can handle even before he accidentally swallowed a love potion disguised in a jelly bean. When the dust settles, Luc and Sylvie have the answers to some burning questions—can a man die of testosterone overload? Can a straightlaced female lose every single one of her inhibitions?—and they learn that old-fashioned romance is still the best catalyst for love.

Love Me Tender

☙

O*nce upon a time, in a magic kingdom, there* lived a handsome prince. Prince Charming, he was called by one and all. And to this land came a gentle princess. You could say she was Cinderella . . . Wall Street Cinderella. Okay, if you're going to be a stickler for accuracy, in this fairy tale the kingdom is Manhattan. But there's magic in the Big Apple, isn't there? And maybe he can be Prince Not-So-Charming at times, and "gentle" isn't the first word that comes to mind when thinking of this princess. But they're looking for happily ever after just the same—and they're going to get it.

Desperado

☙

*M*istaken *for a notorious bandit and his infamously* scandalous mistress, L.A. lawyer Rafe Santiago and Major Helen Prescott found themselves on the wrong side of the law. In a time and place where rules had no meaning, Helen found Rafe's hard, bronzed body strangely comforting, and his piercing blue eyes left her all too willing to share his bedroll. His teasing remarks made her feel all woman, and she was ready to throw caution to the wind if she could spend every night in the arms of her very own . . . **Desperado**.